Struggling, Finnlay forced his legs to move. He wanted to turn around and see the face of this Angel of Darkness, but he was held completely, his life draining away with every breath.

Again the voice spoke, a whisper now, close and terrifying. 'Just when I thought everything was falling apart, you come to me. Easily and foolishly. Take a final look at the sky, Enemy. It will be the last time you see it.'

With that, Finnlay gasped as pain seared his whole body. He stiffened, then darkness folded in on him and he lost sight of everything

Also by Kate Jacoby in Victor Golancz/Millennium
EXILE'S RETURN
First Book of Elita
BLACK EAGLE RISING
Third Book of Elita

Acknowledgements

My thanks to my family and friends for their love and patience. Thank you also to Leslie Gardner, Jo Fletcher and Kerri Valkova. Much love to Karen Pender-Gunn. Thanks also to Karen Mitchell, whose patience, I'm sure, must run out one day. And a big thank you to Peter Oliphant for the beautiful *Battle of Shanogh Anar*.

In 1341, Lusara was a strong, independent nation whose wealth was both admired and envied by her neighbours. But she was also a country devastated by civil unrest as the major Houses battled with each other. All of this came to an end when Selar of Mayenne used his brother's armies to conquer Lusara and make himself King.

Selar swept the old order aside and married Lady Rosalind MacKenna. Daughter of the Duke MacKenna, she was descended from the old royal family and Selar used this to found his own royal line. With ruthlessness and fierce determination, Selar crushed any opposition to his rule and punished the whole country for daring to stand against him.

Of the old Houses, only a few survived with any power. One of these was led by the young Earl of Dunlorn, Robert Douglas. His father had died a hero fighting Selar. Scion of the oldest House and heir to a long tradition of serving Lusara, Robert was forced to hide the secret part of his nature: he was a sorcerer – in a land where such a thing was both feared and reviled – and most certainly outlawed. Robert carried the hopes of his conquered people, but, seeing no other way to help them, he agreed to work alongside Selar. In return for his oath of allegiance, Selar gave Robert the power to help his people. The two men became friends, and for some years a quiet peace flooded a relieved land.

However, this peace was not to last. Jealous of Robert's influence, the powerful Guilde moved against him. Robert found no support with the King for his defiance and, shattered, he left the court for his home. When his young wife died of a fever days later, Robert left Lusara, planning never to return. Now the people of Lusara had lost their one chance of freedom.

But three years later, Robert broke his self-imposed exile,

returning with his most trusted friend, Micah Maclean, at his side. Determined merely to husband his lands, Robert's plans were abruptly interrupted when he discovered his brother Finnlay had come looking for him. Finnlay demanded Robert act: he should take up the leadership of the secret sorcerers' Enclave – or failing that, Robert must make a stand against Selar and free their people from tyranny.

For many reasons, Robert had to refuse, but before he could go much further, he was forced to rescue a young girl from Guilde soldiers. Robert discovered that she was one of the children abducted during the House feuds before Selar's conquest. Her name was Jennifer Ross, daughter of the Earl of Ross – and she was a sorcerer whose powers were far different to any within the Enclave. Robert took Jennifer back to her father's lands at Elita and continued home.

When Selar discovered Robert had returned to Lusara, he grew fearful and imprisoned the newly elected Bishop Aiden McCauly in order to plant his own man and gain a firm hold on the wavering support of the Church. And the King had a new friend, the Guildesman Samdon Nash, who remained constantly at his side. Then tragedy struck. Robert's uncle, the Duke of Haddon, was embroiled in a futile rebellion and killed by Selar's ruthless forces.

Stunned, Robert was tortured by guilt – but he had sworn an oath to Selar and even now could not break that vow. He had to remain constant to his promise never to take arms against the King. He believed that no matter how he tried to help the people, he would fail. This was the only way . . .

But when he and Finnlay were caught in an accident in the hills above Nanmoor, Robert was injured and lost his memory. Finnlay, using his own powers to try finding his brother, was captured, charged with the heinous crime of sorcery – and word flew across the land. A real sorcerer had been caught, the truth was no longer a secret.

With Jennifer's help, Robert mounted a rescue and returned Finnlay to the safety of the Enclave, but there were questions to be answered, loyalties to be proved. The Enclave demanded Robert go before their powerful talisman, the Key – the very thing Robert had avoided for most of his life.

The Key took possession of Robert and told all who were witness part of a prophecy which sent a wave of shock through the Enclave. Robert was Bonded to Jennifer. They shared the rare gift of mindspeech. They were called the Enemy and the Ally – and against them was a creature of evil known as the Angel of Darkness.

On the precipice of ignorance, only this Angel of Darkness truly understood the choices before them all and the devastating consequences for Lusara. Linked by a tradition handed down over five centuries, this man harboured a secret ambition. He knew and wanted the Ally, but he was ignorant of the Enemy's true identity. And unlike the others, he knew exactly what the Bonding meant and the grave danger it was to him. Too late they would come to know him by another name: Samdon Nash.

For Robert Douglas, however, the choices were all too limited. Banished from the Enclave and forbidden by his oath to Selar to help his country, his honour cried out for action. His feelings for Jenn were a sharp confusion that demanded attention, but he was held back, paralysed by something he'd kept concealed all his life. This one factor alone, which he'd fought to deny, to avoid, to conquer, dominated his actions in a way nobody could have foreseen – nor even have understood – for it was at the heart of the prophecy the Key had given him as a child, the part of the prophecy the Key had kept secret from the Enclave. It was destiny, fate, something he had no choice but to obey.

In the silence of his own mind, Robert gave this curse another name. He called it the demon.

Excerpt from *The Secret History of Lusara*
Ruel

Part One

Where once the glorious pennant flew
and brilliant trumpet hailed the dawn,
the dread usurper defiled our spirit
and left no place for peace to hide.
Where graceful spire and buttress arched
o'er the tranquil holy place
rapaciously and brutally the cursed serpent
       cut down Lusara's pride.

from *Battle of Shanogh Anar*
by Thomas McKinnley

Part One

1

'I need not tell you how the divisions among us hurt not only our mother Church, but also the welfare of our state. It is at times like this that we must show our unity to the country. These debates and whisperings must stop. Dissent is our greatest enemy, my brothers. We must be of one mind. With all of us working together we can overcome these small difficulties and once again take our place among the leaders of our country.'

As Bishop Brome paused to take a sip of wine, Deacon Godfrey drew in a deep breath and held it, trying to stifle another yawn. The Bishop's Palace was one of the oldest parts of Marsay and even though it afforded a magnificent view of the Basilica, most of it – and this room in particular – also drew the afternoon heat. Beads of sweat gathered in a minor conspiracy and trickled down Godfrey's back. He didn't dare shift, not even to move a hand to fan himself. He had to stand as still as his brethren, all gathered before Brome as he ate dinner.

Over the last year Brome had displayed an enormous appetite for the finer aspects of his position. In summer he almost always ate here, in the small hall where tall windows faced west to catch the evening light. Ancient oak beams stretched high between walls of grey stone from which hung a collection of six silk tapestries, a gift from King William over a century before. It was said the *gift* had been more a bribe to gain the support of a Church set against William's marriage to the widowed Lady Jardine.

Godfrey's attention was drawn back to Brome as the Bishop resumed his discourse in between mouthfuls of roast beef steeped in a sauce so full of peppercorns Godfrey could smell them from where he stood. Beside him were others of his rank, while in front, Archdeacons Hilderic, Francis and

Ohler waited patiently. Or rather, Francis and Ohler appeared patient. Hilderic gave the impression of something quite different.

'We have had a difficult year,' the Bishop continued, 'with that foolish rebellion from Blair and his cohorts. Thankfully we no longer have to deal with the financing and administration of the hospices. Our brothers in the Guilde have assured me that the work we began in that area over a thousand years ago will continue under their beneficence.'

Godfrey swallowed against a sudden dryness in his mouth. Hilderic, no more than three feet in front of him, had abruptly stiffened. His shoulders appeared hard as rock and his head had come up. Godfrey could just imagine the expression on his face.

'Which brings me to the reason I called you here this afternoon.' Brome put down his knife, pressed his fingers against a stiff linen cloth and picked up a jewelled goblet. He leaned back in his seat, his watery eyes scanning his captive audience but meeting no gazes. He had never been an attractive figure, but now, approaching his fiftieth year of soft living, fat had begun to obscure the lines of his face, almost swallowing up his small mouth and round nose.

'I am aware that the Guilde's investigation at Kilphedir is still to be completed and there is, at this time, no absolute evidence that sorcery is once again alive in Lusara. I'm sure that, given time, Governor Osbert and his assistants will divine truth from lie. However, I also feel it is fitting for us to communicate to the Guilde our full support both for the investigation itself and for whatever actions they deem necessary as a result of their findings.'

'Forgive me, Your Grace.' Hilderic almost pounced and Godfrey's stomach clenched in horror. 'But surely that's a little presumptive. Until Governor Osbert returns with some conclusions, we don't know what action the Proctor will take. How can we condone something we know nothing about?'

Brome's eyelids flickered rapidly, but his voice was steady. 'We don't need to know, Archdeacon. Guilde business is Guilde business – and it's exactly that kind of dissent I was referring to. My sainted predecessor, Domnhall, though gifted in many ways, did to some extent damage our relations with our traditional allies. Surely you can see that my desire to support them on this matter is a small attempt to heal the rift which has developed between us. I know not whether the rumours of sorcery hold any truth any more than I know for certain whether Finnlay Douglas is at the heart of them. What I do know is that the eradication of sorcery has always been the responsibility of the Guilde. It's up to us as spiritual caretakers to support them in such a difficult and dangerous task. They're well suited to it – much better than we. Our support will be much appreciated by the Proctor.'

'I wonder if he'll appreciate it as much as the handover of the hospices together with so much Church land,' Hilderic growled. Godfrey tried to edge forward, but couldn't do so without drawing attention.

Brome, however, got to his feet. His attendant pulled the grand chair back from the table, but Brome didn't go far. 'That is not a matter up for discussion. Hilderic, you will draft a letter pledging our support for the Guilde.'

'I, Your Grace?'

'Of course. You performed such duties for Domnhall – or would you rather I placed the task in the hands of someone else – along with other duties you feel you're no longer able to perform?' Brome drew himself up and clasped his hands together, affecting piety. 'I did not bring you all here in order that you might question my authority. We will send a letter pledging our support for the Guilde and we will send it today. I will see it on my desk by sundown, Hilderic. That is all.'

Father John crossed the busy street and headed down the old alleyway to the Almsgate. Waving a greeting to the brother on duty, John continued on past the refectory and into the cloister. Here in the vaulted shade it was not so hot, but the cooler air did little to stifle John's agitation. The conversation with Murdoch and the rumours flying around the capital for the last week had spoiled his sleep, his appetite and his work. If John didn't find some calm from somewhere, Hilderic would begin to notice his distraction – and begin asking questions.

Was it possible that Finnlay had been caught? Murdoch seemed sure. But the damage of such a revelation on a country so encompassed by a hatred of sorcerers would bring doom upon them all. Both he and Murdoch would have to be very careful – at least until Osbert came back with his report – and until they were sure no suspicion was directed at either of them. As John turned into a corridor towards Hilderic's study, he sent up a silent prayer that the Governor would find nothing at all.

The corridor wasn't silent. John was alone, but he could clearly hear voices from behind the study door. Hilderic was there and ... Deacon Godfrey – and Deacon Godfrey was very angry.

John approached the door with caution, checking over his shoulder to make sure no one was behind him.

'You have no idea of the problems you cause us all! By the gods,' Godfrey's voice seemed to smack against the door, 'do you want to end up in a cell beside McCauly? At least he's committed no real treason – but you? If you don't learn to keep your own counsel they'll find some excuse to execute you! Damn it, Hilderic! Are you even listening to me?'

'You've turned, haven't you?' Hilderic snapped back. 'Too many years as Chaplain to the Guilde. You side with them – and that worthless snake, Brome. Well, I won't! Somebody has to stand against them and if I have to do it alone, I will!'

'But you'll achieve nothing but your own demise! There are other ways to help McCauly, Archdeacon. Quiet ways. I beg you, please refrain from this open resistance.'

John swallowed and strained to hear Hilderic's response, but there was nothing more than a muffled echo through the door. After a moment, John reached up and knocked confidently, as though he had just arrived. A single word from Hilderic bade him open the door.

The two priests stood at either end of the room, the working table a wall between them. John swallowed and tried to look like he'd heard nothing of the argument.

'Ah, Father John,' Hilderic grunted. 'Good. Take a seat. I

have a letter to draft for the Bishop. Thank you, Deacon. I'll consider your advice.'

Godfrey's jaw moved a fraction, then his mouth came together in a thin line. With a short sketch of a bow, he turned and left the study, closing the door behind him.

John took his usual seat at the table and laid out his paper, ink and pen. When he was ready he glanced up at Hilderic, who was watching him with thundercloud eyes.

'To be addressed to the Proctor,' he began with precision. 'From our beloved Bishop. All the usual titles.'

John nodded and bent his head to his work. Hilderic continued dictating, pausing every few words for John to catch up. His tone was thick with irony, clipped and hard.

'Suffice to say, my dear Proctor, we will of course do our utmost to aid whatever slaughter you see fit in the wake of your investigations. I hold no fear that you will act precipitously, and that all hands and heads cut off as a result of your greed and fear will have at least a token crime manufactured for them. By all means, shed blood with our blessing and know that in all matters, we grovel at your feet for any little trifle you care to. toss in our unworthy direction.' Hilderic took a deep breath and turned back to his desk.

John finished scratching down the last few words and managed to hide his shock. Was the Archdeacon serious? Did he really want this letter written out for the signature of the Bishop?

'There's no rush, Father,' Hilderic murmured without turning around. 'Brome merely wants to read it over his supper. You may deliver it yourself. I trust you to give him a faithful copy.'

'Of course, Archdeacon.' John rose to his feet, gathering his things with trembling hands. Hilderic had as much as signed his own death warrant.

He was outside in the corridor again before he dared glance at the words he'd scrawled. He couldn't give Brome a letter like this! But John didn't have the authority to change it.

Taking a deep breath, John turned and walked down the passage until he reached the tiny chapel of Saint Catherine.

The door was open and inside, seated on a chair before the altar, his head in his hands, was Godfrey.

John should have moved on. It wasn't polite to disturb a brother's prayer – but he couldn't. There was something of desperation in Godfrey's demeanour, worn frustration and weariness. For someone so competent and brilliant, Godfrey looked to be facing the end of his world.

After a moment, John moved and Godfrey glanced up. Their gaze met for a long minute, then, straightening up, Godfrey waved John into the chapel.

'How bad is it?'

Without hesitating, John held the page out and watched Godfrey read. The Deacon reached the end of the page, then came to his feet. He crossed to the votive candle suspended above the altar and touched the paper to the flame. As it took light, Godfrey glanced back at John. 'The first draft is never the best, is it, Father?'

'No, Deacon.' John sighed with relief. 'Never.'

The Guilde Hall echoed with the clamour of a hundred voices. The noise rose to the vaulted roof and rattled around, gaining strength, before descending again. Vaughn raised his hands and came to his feet. Slowly the noise diminished as all attention focused on the dais. Vaughn clasped his hands together and gazed across the vast room at all the faithful faces turned towards him. They were afraid and shocked and completely unready for what faced them – but face it they would.

'It should come as no surprise to you that we might find sorcery again within our shores.' Vaughn lifted his voice above their heads, clear and full. 'Five hundred years ago we stood alongside the old empire and battled against the evil that had worked its way into our lives. We won that war, defeating our enemy. We chased them across two continents and dedicated our sacred duty to the complete eradication of all those who dabbled in the arcane. Why do you find the prospect of a similar battle horrifying? Have we grown weak over the centuries? Is our sacred duty less than that of our ancestors?'

Vaughn put his hands on the table before him and leaned forward. 'The Guilde never made the assumption that we were successful in our bid to destroy every single sorcerer. Certainly the people believed it, but we've all heard the stories of reputed sightings a century and more ago. Hope would have us believe that there are no more sorcerers – but simple sense insists we must expect some survivors, perhaps even a whole community of them!'

The Hall erupted. Guildesmen rose to their feet and cried out, but Vaughn didn't hear the words, just the sentiment. This time he raised only one hand and allowed them to see a smile. And why shouldn't he smile? In weeks, perhaps even days, he would have the evidence he'd been waiting years for. Evidence so he could prove to everyone that sorcery was real – and that Robert Douglas was guilty of the most awful of crimes. How delicious, too, that young Finnlay should be the one to be discovered, that he should be the instrument of his own brother's downfall. Years before, when Robert had been on Selar's council – already an enemy – Vaughn had paid particular note of young Finnlay as he visited his brother in Marsay. It hadn't taken Vaughn long to work out that he was a sorcerer, but Robert had stopped him before he could do anything about it and cast some evil spell on him. Vaughn had found himself unable to speak of the incident since, which only fuelled his hatred for Robert Douglas. But this was something different entirely and Vaughn had no trouble speaking it aloud.

'We will be facing evil in its darkest form, but we are not unprepared. We will find a way to identify those sorcerers amongst us and how to fight them. When the time comes, we will make our stand once more – and this time we will triumph completely!'

Applause burst across the Hall. Vaughn smiled, nodded, and sank back into his seat. He steepled his fingers together and glanced to his left and right, collecting the gazes of his board of Governors. Only Osbert was missing. Osbert – and Nash. Samdon Nash, Alderman and favourite of the King. Perhaps already the most influential man in the country.

Yes, Vaughn nodded as the applause died down. It was definitely time to do something about that.

Godfrey felt quite naked without his clerical robes. The old shirt and worn tunic felt ridiculous and uncomfortable – and one of his boots had a stone in it. How had he ever worn secular clothes happily? Had so many years as a priest spoiled him this much?

He felt like such a thief, sneaking into the old tavern deep in the bowels of Marsay like this, a hood pulled up around his face. It was more to hide his tonsure, but still he cringed beneath the smelly hessian. It was no act, shrinking down inside it. It made his flesh crawl.

But at least Payne was there, waiting for him, dressed casually in nondescript clothes. Payne was a good man, like Duke Donal McGlashen: Lusaran born and true. Between them they were the only two such left on Selar's council. His face might be known, but nobody would expect a high ranking Earl – a member of the King's council at that – to frequent a place like this. A place where no questions were asked, where even the innkeeper didn't look up when the door opened.

'I thought you'd changed your mind,' Payne murmured as Godfrey sat down. Their booth was well back from the pathetic fire and, despite the warmth of the summer evening, Godfrey shivered.

'I was detained.' A jug of ale landed on the table, making Godfrey jump.

'Relax; you'll make yourself noticed with all this twitching and shaking. Try to look as if you were born in those clothes.'

'One would hope by now that I had done something to get out of them.' To hide his discomfort, Godfrey pulled the jug closer and peered over the lip. Even in the dim rushlight he could see grease marks and breadcrumbs floating on the surface. With a sneer of distaste, he began to push the thing away.

'Take a drink,' Payne grunted. 'You're supposed to be used to this.'

'Well, I'm not,' Godfrey hissed, but took a mouthful anyway.

'If we're going to meet like this again you'll have to learn to be more flexible about small details like a clean cup. You should remember that most of the people in this country live like this all the time – many more now than ever before. You'd be surprised how quickly the finer things in life disappear under such circumstances.'

Godfrey forgot his ale and gazed steadily at the handsome young man. It was amazing how, even in these blighted surroundings, Everard Payne still managed to look at ease. Had he done this kind of thing before?

'Tell me,' Godfrey left his hands around the jug of ale, 'when you took my letter to Robert last year, did you see any possibility then that he might decide to do something?'

'About what?'

Godfrey dropped his voice. 'McCauly.'

'Would you have him storm the dungeons and wrest the man from Selar's hands?' Payne leaned closer. 'Why this sudden interest in Robert? Is it because of the rumours?'

'No, my interest is in McCauly.' Godfrey frowned. 'I fear I may have a problem developing and I just don't know what to do about it.'

Payne sat back again, once more relaxed. 'Hilderic?'

'What have you heard?'

'Oh, this and that. He's becoming noted for his outspoken opinions – none of which do his reputation any good.'

'He won't stay quiet. He blames himself for McCauly's arrest. If he'd not told Selar about Robert's return, Selar wouldn't have felt so threatened.'

'Selar would have found out sooner or later.'

'But that's just it – the timing. Hilderic believed that passing on the news would distract Selar from McCauly, but it achieved the opposite. Now Hilderic's obsessed with getting McCauly free, but because he has no means to do so, he takes out his frustration on Brome. I fear for his life, Payne.'

The young Earl folded his arms across his chest and glanced around the room. Nobody was paying them any attention. The tap room was half-full of grim individuals, all hunched over their own greasy mugs, while an extraordinarily bad fiddler was groaning away in the corner.

'I can't promise you anything,' Payne said after a moment. 'And even if I could I wouldn't advise you to tell Hilderic a word about it. Nevertheless, I'll have a word, see what we have before us, test out the possibilities. I believe we have the time. No move against McCauly has been made in months and I believe the King is content to leave it as such. He's voiced no plans to the council.'

'But do you think you can do something?' Godfrey's voice was hushed against Payne's confidence. 'You won't risk your own position, will you?'

He received a charming smile in response as Payne leaned forward and clapped him on the shoulder. 'I'll risk nothing until I know what we'll be up against. Drink up, we're supposed to be having a good time.'

Vaughn waited until the supper plates had been cleared away. Then he rose from the table and crossed the room to take his favourite seat beside the fireplace. There were no flames glowing on the hearthstone. Only the light of a few candles warmed the room, occasionally flickering in the gentle evening breeze.

He glanced back at the table to where Governor Lewis still sat. 'Come, find yourself a comfortable seat. I have a small job for you.'

Lewis looked surprised at the invitation but as usual, he said nothing. Instead, he joined Vaughn in the chair Osbert would normally have taken. Vaughn wanted to smile.

'How do you think my speech went down this afternoon?'

'Well,' Lewis spread his hands in a noncommittal gesture, 'you've given us all something to think about. I suppose you have plans already prepared for when Osbert returns with his findings?'

'A few thoughts, nothing more.' Vaughn waved his hands and studied Lewis carefully. The man had none of Osbert's illicit brilliance, nor any of his charm and personality. They'd both been made Governor at the same time and yet, while Osbert had shone in the position, Lewis had rather faded. He was a fair administrator, but lacked the initiative necessary for leadership. He was also uncommonly easy to ignore, while, at the same time, remarkably pedantic about details.

The perfect man for the job.

'What do we know about Alderman Nash?'

Lewis glanced up with a frown. 'Nash, my lord?'

'Yes. I've been reading his entry records. They state he was born in the west, in a town I've never heard of. His parents are deceased and he appears to have no other family. His means are limited, his education adequate, and yet we find he has eclipsed us all in gaining the friendship of our beloved King. At all times he exhibits nothing but the deepest humility and still manages to rise to the highest levels – without, it appears, a grain of ambition. Don't you find that a little odd, Lewis?'

'Odd, perhaps, but not impossible.'

'Not impossible – for a saint. But is Nash a saint?'

Lewis didn't answer that and Vaughn continued, 'Nash is in a unique position – and he knows it. Selar depends on him more and more as each day goes by. Soon they'll be as inseparable as Dunlorn once was with the King. We know the damage the Earl caused – dare we allow the same risk, even with one of our own?'

Lewis looked surprised at this. Obviously the thought had never occurred to him. 'Do you suspect any treachery, my lord?'

'Of course not,' Vaughn shrugged, feeling a great calm descend upon him. 'I merely wish to know more about Nash, about his activities when he's not directly involved with the Guilde. I want to know with whom he associates, who his allies are. After all, when you think about it, there's even a possibility that Nash could have very powerful friends. Friends such as the Earl of Dunlorn – but of course, I should call him the Duke of Haddon after his uncle's tragic demise.'

'Dunlorn?' Lewis struggled to his feet. 'You believe Nash is in league with Dunlorn? But what about the business at Kilphedir? Nash went there with Osbert to investigate! If Dunlorn's brother was indeed the sorcerer arrested, then . . .'

Vaughn waited for the awful possibilities to sink deep into Lewis's limited imagination. Then, moving slowly so Lewis could keep up, Vaughn began, 'I realize this sort of thing usually falls to Osbert – but as you know, he's otherwise engaged at the moment. I want you to quietly go about learning as much as you can about our Alderman Nash. I want you to subtly pass some of your current responsibilities to your staff and take care of this matter personally. Be discreet. We don't want Nash finding out what you're up to – he might well be offended. You won't need to watch him every hour, just keep an eye on him and those he associates with. Share your discoveries with no one but myself. Tell no one about this. Can you do this for me?'

Lewis's eyes bulged, but he nodded slowly. 'Of . . . of course, my lord.'

'Excellent!' Vaughn beamed. He reached out and took Lewis's arm, steering him towards the door. 'Now you go and get some sleep. Goodnight, Lewis.'

'Goodnight, my lord Proctor.'

Vaughn closed the door behind Lewis and turned the key in the lock. He leaned his back against the door and surveyed the room.

It was unlikely there was any real connection between Nash and Dunlorn. Nash had come to court a year after Dunlorn had left the country – but then again, that was no reason to assume Dunlorn hadn't set him up as some kind of spy. After all, Nash appeared to have no ambition of his own and yet grasped every opportunity as it arose to get himself closer to Selar. Couldn't that be the behaviour of a spy?

Vaughn crossed the room and picked up the letter from Brome. Hideous gushing sentiment about how the Church depended on the Guilde to achieve success in the question of Kilphedir. Vaughn twisted it in his hands and brought it to the flame of the nearest candle. Once alight, he crossed to the fireplace and poked the burning paper in amongst the kindling laid ready. He'd never liked cool summer nights.

Yes, it would be very nice if there was a connection between Nash and Dunlorn – but even if there wasn't, it didn't hurt to place the odd suggestion here and there. Who knew when he might need such a weapon?

'I hate these late summer courts,' Duke Donal McGlashen grunted, glancing around the gallery.

All of the windows were open, but no breeze entered the room. Ladies sat close to them, fans flapping like birds' wings, chatting loudly and paying no attention to the lute player before the King. A boy, dressed in a miniature of Selar's livery, sang in a high-pitched voice, but even the King looked bored. Teige Eachern stood like a church tower in the far corner, his eyes on one person only: the young lady seated beside the Queen, Lady Samah. This was her last visit to Marsay. She'd been given permission from her priory to attend her sister, the Queen, for a month before returning to take her final vows. A pity – the girl was more than a little pretty.

With a sigh, McGlashen ran his fingers around the throat of his shirt and longed to take the heavy doublet off. He shot a glance at Payne who stood beside him. The young Earl was not that tall, but was definitely considered attractive by the ladies of the court. More than one had volunteered to compromise her virtue in order to secure Payne as a husband – or so Everard claimed. Still, having seen them gather around him, McGlashen had no reason to doubt his word – or his dexterity in taking what was offered. Some men had no shame.

'I don't know why you don't just beg off and return to your estates,' Payne murmured, his eyes moving casually over the room as though he didn't have a care in the world. It was a gift he had.

'You know very well why I can't go and I wish you wouldn't take so much delight in baiting me. It does my humour no good at all and I wouldn't like to cause a scene by slitting your throat in public.'

Payne raised an eyebrow, but didn't pursue the point. 'So you have to stay in Marsay; just accept it and enjoy yourself. I do.'

'So I've heard,' McGlashen grunted. 'This is an awful risk, you know. Are you sure it's worth it?'

Payne checked to see if they would be overheard. He kept his face to the rest of the room, but allowed his voice to drop. 'We've been asked to help and we're the only ones who can. Be thankful there's at least something constructive we can do. You know Selar won't want to keep McCauly for ever. One day he'll turn up dead. How would you feel then if we'd made no effort to save him? Surely you're still loyal enough to Lusara to want her rightful Bishop free again?'

'My loyalty is not the point in question. What worries me is what the King will do when he finds McCauly gone. What will he do if we fail and are caught?'

'Then we die for our country,' Payne murmured off-handedly.

'And who will defend her then? That's my question. Who will there be left who can be trusted? We two are the only old Houses left with any power, however small. You know as well as I do what Selar plans for next spring. Neither bad weather nor political intrigue will stop him. Look at him now, sitting there gazing into eternity. Can you look at him and honestly tell me his thoughts are not on conquest?'

'I don't know, but I'm sure Eachern's thoughts are – on a different kind of conquest.'

McGlashen had to control a frown. It was so difficult for them to talk privately. These public snatches were all they had left. 'The girl is intended for the Church! She leaves in a month. Please, keep your unseemly thoughts to yourself.'

Payne smiled as though McGlashen had said something funny. 'It's not my unseemly thoughts that worry me. I'm not the one gazing at the poor girl.'

The music ended and there was polite applause. McGlashen waited until the lute began again before saying more. 'I won't argue about McCauly, if that's what you're worried about. I don't want to see him die any more than you do. He's a good man, a friend.'

'Then what's bothering you?' Payne turned a bright gaze on him.

McGlashen pursed his lips and lifted his jaw. 'I just wish

we knew where we stood. Treason's not a game, you know. If I thought for one moment that we'd get support, if we could actually make a move against Selar ... the other Lusaran magnates would follow, I'm sure.'

'Like Blair?'

'Blair was an idiot and will pay the price. He should have known better than to start an uprising without a strong figure to lead it. Somebody the people could place their trust in. Somebody they'd be willing to follow into war.'

Payne was silent for a long time, taking several sips from his cup of fragrant wine. Eventually he murmured, 'Robert won't change his mind, Donal. You and the others should get used to that fact. You don't know him as well as I do. Once he's made his mind up about something, there's no changing it. Sure, he may regret his oath to Selar – I don't know, I didn't get the chance to ask him. But even so, there's no way Robert will break that oath. He's out of it, believe me. Whatever we do, we do on our own.'

McGlashen adjusted his shirt one last time and prepared to move away. They had been standing together too long as it was. 'You may think what you like, Payne, but I tell you, there's only one future I see for this country, one future I'd give my life for. It's the only one I trust and the only one that gives us any hope. It's one, I might add, that I share with many others.'

'And that is?'

'To see Robert Douglas on the throne.'

2

The forest was warm and humid. Four days of heavy rain had left the ground soft, the leaves fresh and green, the river full. Along its banks brown bracken bent and swayed in the gentle breeze, fixed towards the lucid sun above. Birdsong sprinkled through the grove; deer paused by the water's edge, ears pricking for sounds of danger. Suddenly alarmed, they danced away into the darkened woods, oblivious to the nature of the threat.

Nash stood by the river. His light summer cloak fell in a swathe of tanned yellow and his boots sank into the forest floor. In front of him, the river ran from the cliffs, from high in the mountains of Nanmoor beyond. From this point, it was impossible to go on further, to follow the river as it cascaded down from the peaks above. But it didn't matter. This was the place he'd been looking for, the place where Finnlay Douglas had supposedly met his death.

Huge boulders embedded in the river were constantly pounded by the water as it plunged downwards. Anything falling from that height would be crushed under such power, bones would break, blood would spill, flow out and disappear into the current. Caught between the rocks, torn apart by the incessant raging water, a man would quickly give up his life and leave only a battered body behind as witness to the violence.

But Finnlay Douglas hadn't died in the river.

Shaking his head, Nash turned his back on the falls and pushed through the bracken to where Lisson waited with the horses.

'Forgive me, master, but Governor Osbert will be expecting you back soon.'

'Yes,' Nash replied, drawing his cloak back as he walked through the bracken. 'He must have finished with those woodsmen by now.'

'Will he believe their story?'

'I hope not, but knowing Osbert, he probably will.'

Lisson handed Nash the reins of his horse and together they began to walk back through the forest. 'It will be dangerous for us if he does.'

'Indeed it would,' Nash nodded. 'If the woodsmen are right and they did capture a sorcerer, I need to make sure nobody else knows about it. Not even Osbert. And as for the sorcerer himself? There's only one way I can find out more about the true fate of Finnlay Douglas.'

'You must go south, to Dunlorn. Question his brother, the Duke of Haddon.'

Yes, the Duke. Robert Douglas. Selar's old friend: the one person barring Nash's closer ties with the King. Selar's memories were still too strong, his loyalty too obscure. Despite the fact that Dunlorn had obviously no intention of being any kind of threat to Selar, the King still remembered the friendship, had unspoken hopes of rekindling the old ties. And while Selar held those hopes, Nash would never be able to get any closer to him.

Nash paused, took the reins in one hand and swung up on to his horse. With a nod, he turned to Lisson. 'I have a meeting with Pascoe tonight. We have to keep up the pressure the raiders are placing on the country. Selar is still determined to invade Mayenne in the spring and the more people fear the raiders, the happier they'll be about a war. I want you to stay around and wait for Pascoe. After that, return to Fenlock. Find a job in the village and keep a distant eye on our Lady Jennifer. Let me know if she has any strange visitors.'

Lisson smiled up at him, wide-eyed but not so innocent. 'Such as Finnlay Douglas?'

Especially Finnlay Douglas. If he was, as Nash suspected, the Enemy, then he must keep them apart at all costs. The Enemy and the Ally must never be allowed to join forces.

As the door closed behind the woodsman, Osbert sat back in his seat and folded his hands together. The little inn at Kilphedir had proved useful as a base for his investigations, though hardly comfortable. However, after three days, he was sick of the sight of this chamber above the tap room and even more sick of the smells from below.

Osbert threw a glance over his shoulder to where Nash stood by the window. The young man had his hands resting either side of it, his face turned to the cool breeze as it drifted inside. He'd changed a lot over the last year as he'd grown closer to Selar and yet, despite that, Nash still seemed to hold his place within the Guilde as dear to him. After all, with the patronage of the King behind him, Nash could afford to throw off Guilde colours and make his own way.

'Well?' Nash murmured. 'What do you make of it?'

Osbert studied again the objects on the table in front of him. A small river-washed stone and the eagle signet of Finnlay Douglas. The stone was supposed to have some power, but Osbert hadn't seen any. He only had the word of those woodsmen. But the ring?

'What would you say if I told you I believe Finnlay Douglas is a sorcerer?'

Nash hardly moved. 'Anything else?'

'Then you agree?'

'That is Finnlay Douglas's ring there before you, isn't it? You've met him. The description fits, doesn't it? What else is there?'

Osbert pushed his chair back from the table and stood. 'Well, legend has it that a sorcerer's power comes from an amulet he carries around with him – such as this river stone. If that's true, where did the prisoner find the power to escape when his guards had the stone?'

'He could have had help.'

'From whom? Or are you saying there are lots of sorcerers wandering around Lusara that we've never heard of before? Are you saying you believe the superstitions of a bunch of uneducated, backward woodcutters?'

Nash turned around at that, a brief frown marking his clear forehead. 'No, not that. I just feel I should remind you that Lady Jennifer Ross told me she saw Finnlay drowned.'

Osbert shrugged. 'She may have been mistaken. You said she'd never met Finnlay before. She has only Robert's word that the body he took home was his brother's.'

'Then perhaps our next step should be to question him?'

Indeed it should. But what would Selar say? Hadn't he told the Guilde to stay away from Robert? But surely this was different. This time it appeared the young Duke was really hiding something. 'We'll head south in the morning. I should think Dunlorn has arrived home by now – even with the floods. I doubt he'll be expecting us so soon.'

'And therefore, his excuses will not be fully prepared?' Nash smiled, his dark eyes glinting in the lamplight.

Osbert studied Nash for a moment. Then he turned and walked across the room to pour himself a cup of the bitter white wine the inn had served him. It was barely drinkable. If he'd known this was the best they could do he would have brought a cask of better stuff with him from Marsay.

Nash was watching him, with that intense air he usually only applied to Selar.

Osbert took a sip of the wine, allowed it to burn down his throat before continuing, 'Selar doesn't trust you, you know. He'd like to, eventually, but he doesn't trust you yet. You must learn to be patient.'

For the first time, there was a hint of conceit about Nash's demeanour. 'What do you know about it?'

Osbert had to smile. Skilled though Nash was at handling Selar, he seemed oblivious to others doing the same thing to him. 'I hardly think you can afford to be so arrogant so soon, Nash. Your position may be high, but you're not so high yet that you cannot fall equally quickly.'

'Are you threatening me?' Nash frowned, left the window and folded his arms.

'I wouldn't dream of it. I'm merely offering you my opinion. I've been at court for twenty years now. I've seen men come and go. Men just as capable as you. Selar has only ever trusted one man.'

'Dunlorn. Yes, Selar told me.'

'Did he tell you why he removed Dunlorn from the council?'

'I've heard that he challenged the Guilde, that he defied the Proctor.'

'Exactly. He allowed a rift to develop and never realized who held the real power in Lusara.' Osbert took another mouthful of wine and laced his fingers together around the cup. 'He allowed his pride to get in the way of his judgement.'

Nash laughed at this, strode across the room and helped himself to some wine. 'And you accuse me of arrogance! I thank you for your considered opinion, my lord, but I can't help wondering why you offer it so freely.'

'I should have thought that was obvious. When Vaughn goes, I want to take his place. I don't need Selar's help to get it – but I do want his support afterwards. I hope you'll encourage him to give it. There are few people at court who can influence Selar's opinion – you are one of them.'

For a second there was a brief fire in Nash's eyes – one Osbert had never seen before. It couldn't be from any undue loyalty to Vaughn. It had always been obvious to everyone that Nash thought the Proctor an idiot. It was an odd reaction, to say the least. Still, as long as Nash agreed to support him, it didn't matter if the fires of hell raged in his eyes.

'You have always had my support, my lord,' Nash replied, his voice dropping to a companionable warmth. 'I'll help you all I can.'

Osbert smiled. 'Good. Now I suggest you go and give our men their orders. I'll want to leave for Dunlorn in the morning.'

'Of course, Governor.'

It would have been impossible to have this meeting anywhere within the boundaries of Kilphedir. There were too many people who knew Nash, village folk who stared and moved out of his way as he walked along the street. The Guilde robes had always had that sort of effect, but now in the village the atmosphere of anticipation was almost palpable.

So he'd gone into the forest, beyond the lights of the village to a clearing dusted with moonlight. It was a good spot, wisely chosen. If only Pascoe had used the same sense.

'I told you before!' Nash snapped, glaring at the man opposite him. 'I told you to stay away from there. You paid no notice and now I've lost an entire band of men. You're a fool!'

Pascoe flinched and took a step backwards. He stopped up against a tree not far enough away from Nash's anger. 'I'm sorry, master. I warned you it might happen. I did say we needed more gold, otherwise our men might go looking for real plunder. You know villages and farms don't give up much in these hard times. Mostly these are just poor people with little to lose in the first place.'

'I know that!' Nash bellowed back. He took a few steps forward until he was dangerously close to the man under the tree. 'These raids are supposed to hit the poor and undefended. That's the whole point. You knew that when you began. So why, in the name of the gods, did you allow that band to get so close to Dunlorn? Don't you know the Duke is an able soldier renowned for his loyalty to his people? Didn't you stop to think for one minute that he might find some way to curtail the incursions on his lands? By Broleoch's breath, Pascoe, Dunlorn is about the only man in this godforsaken country who would bother!'

'I'm . . . sorry, master, I . . .'

Nash didn't wait to hear any more. 'The men are getting greedy, so if you want more money, you'll have to earn it. Pass on the word to all the raiders – I want to know the moment Finnlay Douglas surfaces. I want to know where he is, where he's going and who he is with. In the meantime, keep those men under control – and away from the likes of Dunlorn. Do you understand me?'

Nash paused as the forest behind him rustled. He turned to find Lisson emerging from the darkness.

'Forgive me, master, but I have a message for you.'

'A message? From Osbert?'

Lisson shook his head. 'No, master. From the Baron DeMassey.'

DeMassey? Here? By the gods!

Nash took in a swift breath. 'Pascoe? You have your orders. See to it I have no further trouble from your men or I'll teach them a lesson myself!'

'Yes, master.'

Nash waited until Pascoe had hurried away. He waited until all sight and sound of him had vanished into the night. He waited until his anger had abated, his thoughts cleared again. Only then did he turn back to Lisson.

'Where is he?'

'He awaits you in the churchyard, master. He is alone.'

33

'The churchyard? How appropriate.' Pulling himself together, Nash led Lisson through the forest until they reached the edge of the village. He sent Lisson ahead to stand watch, then strode down the empty street until he gained the low wall of the churchyard. Yes, there he was. Invisible to the naked eye, but easily sensed. DeMassey was taking too many chances.

'I'm honoured you bothered to come,' came a gentle voice from the darkness. 'I understand you're very busy these days. Running around after one King or another. Surely all this must make a man tired out.'

Nash stepped over the wall and joined DeMassey in the shadows of the church. 'What do you want, Luc?'

There was a flash of white teeth in the darkness, a smile. 'What do you think?'

'I don't need your help. I've told you that before.'

'If you *needed* our help, I'm not sure I would offer it.'

'And I don't want it, either.'

DeMassey let out a low chuckle, moved a little closer until Nash could see that familiar, extraordinarily handsome face. 'Are you sure, my old friend? I know you have your little coterie of helpers, but none of them can think for themselves – which I'm sure must be a real trial to you – not to mention your own fault. All that bonding must be a strain on you.'

'And you think I want Malachi interference instead? We've been over this before, years ago. You know my conditions. Are you now saying your brethren have changed their minds? Felenor – or perhaps even Gilbert? Are they willing to follow me?'

DeMassey lifted his broad shoulders in a cumbersome shrug. 'Follow, join, what's the difference? What I want to know is whether you still think you can do all this on your own.'

Ah, suddenly it all fitted together. This midnight meeting, DeMassey's sudden presence in this village – in the middle of nowhere. Nash should have seen it before.

'I might have known you'd make an appearance at some point. Though I wonder you bothered to come yourself. A man of your stature and importance? The master of the

D'Azzir, himself? Don't tell me – you heard a rumour about a sorcerer being held prisoner here and you thought you might like to take him in. Oh, come now, Luc. Did you really think you'd get here before me?'

'Actually,' DeMassey paused, his deep blue eyes catching a flash of moonlight, 'I was already nearby. Gilbert was here, in Kilphedir, the night the sorcerer escaped. What do you make of that?'

'So you did take him, then?'

'Hardly!' DeMassey laughed. 'Do you really think I'd be standing here talking to you if I had in my hands one of the Salti Pazar? By the Key, no! I'd be tearing his heart out right now, with my bare hands.'

'You're assuming he is Salti. For all you know this man might be some innocent talent, caught by accident.'

'Then he would have to be a very powerful innocent,' DeMassey replied off-handedly. 'One powerful enough to have you come charging down here from your cosy home in Marsay.'

Nash shook his head. 'Then what do you want? I can't stand here all night talking. If I don't get back soon, I'll be missed.'

DeMassey glanced around the pitch-black graveyard and back at Nash. The moon had moved enough now to endanger them both with its light. DeMassey, never the most discreet of men, wore a light summer cape of royal purple, a gold edging complementing his auburn hair. Even the white shirt underneath was of the finest cloth, embroidered on the collar and cuffs with a symbol only Malachi would understand.

Yes, he took great risks – but not without defence. DeMassey was probably the most powerful Malachi alive.

'Well?' Nash prompted. 'I haven't got all night.'

'When is Valena coming back to us?'

Yes, the same question again. The Malachi never liked losing one of their own – much less one of their best. It was a good thing DeMassey didn't know about the rebel Malachi killed on Dunlorn lands a month or more ago.

Nash shrugged. 'It s entirely up to Valena when she leaves

35

me. At the moment, she seems quite happy. I'm sure, however, that should she change her mind, she'll go running back to you.'

For once, DeMassey lost his charm and met Nash's gaze with one of ice. 'What have you done with her? You haven't turned her into one of your slaves, have you?'

It was Nash's turn to smile. 'How could I do something like that to one so beautiful?'

DeMassey drew his rich cape about his shoulders. 'If there's one thing I've learned about you after all these years, it's that you would and could do anything you wanted in order to secure your so-called destiny. I just want you to know – on a personal basis – that if anything happens to Valena you'll have to deal with me.'

Nash waited until DeMassey had walked far enough to satisfy his pride. Then he said, 'She doesn't miss you, you know. None of you. Most especially, she doesn't miss you in her bed.'

DeMassey paused, turned around and favoured Nash with a deadly smile. 'You just remember what I said.' With that he disappeared into the night.

Damned cheek of the man, coming in here, trying to find out about this sorcerer! So what if Finnlay Douglas was Salti Pazar? Did DeMassey think he had a right to every Salti on the whole northern continent? The man was a fool – a blind fool at that!

What a night! First Osbert and his surprising request. Then Pascoe – and now DeMassey. What next?

With a sigh, Nash regained the street, collected Lisson and headed back to the tavern. The tap room was almost empty, with only the most hardened drinkers still lucid. They sat around the dwindling fire like a pack of drowned rats, staring at him as he crossed the room and headed up the stairs. They'd be relieved when the Guilde left their little village. There was no trust in those glances; only fear.

Nash would have gone straight to bed, but Osbert was waiting for him on the top landing.

'I hope you've not been out wenching, Nash,' he began

with a half-smile. 'Vaughn won't take kindly to that sort of behaviour.'

'No, my lord,' Nash replied, too tired for this kind of conversation. 'I just went for a walk.'

'Well, it's a good thing I caught you. I've just received a courier from the King. It seems I'll be going south alone. Selar wants you back at court. He wants a full report of everything we found.'

'What?' Nash came to a halt. Damn him! Why now? Nash needed to go to Dunlorn himself. Osbert wouldn't be quick enough to see any lie the Duke might make. If Nash didn't go to Dunlorn – now – he might never find out the truth about Finnlay!

'He wants you back at court, Nash. Now. You can wait until morning, but if I were you, I wouldn't make this my moment to defy the King. Besides, I think he misses you. Surely that should make you happy?'

Nash gritted his teeth and tried to keep his disappointment hidden. 'Very well, my lord. I'll start out at dawn.' He took a breath and joined Osbert on the landing. 'I would appreciate it if we could compare opinions regarding this investigation – before you place your report before the Proctor.'

Osbert laughed a little and turned for his door. 'Of course, Nash. We are in this together, are we not?'

3

Deep within the heart of the Goleth mountain, Finnlay paced the corridors of the Enclave, restless, unsettled and alone.

Hour after hour he walked, going deep within the mountain to places he'd never seen before, rooms where grain was stored, cloth and firewood; smoke pits where sides of salted beef hung from beams across the cave roof, like so many thieves sent to the gallows. He sat for a long time beside the Firelake, watching fingers of steam rise from the hot pool, as prayers to heaven. Even the cloying atmosphere, thick and sultry failed to burn away his distemper.

It was his own fault. His own stupid, misguided fault. If he'd been watching more closely, he might have stopped Robert's fall from the cliff. If he'd been paying more attention, he might have noticed those woodsmen before he brought his *ayarn* out to Seek his missing brother. If he'd had any sense, he would have hidden his family ring somewhere in that dark cell so the guards might have never known the identity of the sorcerer they'd captured. Surely there was something else he might have said or done that could have prevented Robert from going before the Key.

But now Robert was banished from the Enclave while Finnlay was stuck here, because everybody in Lusara would believe he was a sorcerer if he ever showed his face again.

Slowly, eventually, he rose through the mountain again hoping to leave his mood behind him. But it followed him, like a plague, sat around his shoulders, toyed with his thoughts, shattering the peace of the early morning.

Distant, subdued, irresolute, Finnlay rested in the refectory. Without thinking, he collected a mug of steaming brew and planted himself on a trestle bench in the furthest corner of the room. There were few people up at this hour of the morning, but they kept their distance. He leaned his elbows on the table and stared into the depths of his mug.

A plate of coarse bread and cheese landed on the table before him, like salvation. Then a body – Patric – took a seat opposite and began to eat. Patric didn't look up. He just concentrated on his breakfast. He was collecting up the last crumbs before he spoke.

'You'll go mad before the month's out at this rate.'

'What?'

Patric raised his knife and casually waved it in the air. 'Take my advice, Finn. Find yourself a job to do. All this wandering around without a purpose is going to drive you insane. You know it, I know it – they all know it.'

'Oh really?' Finnlay sneered. 'And what do you propose I do, eh? I'm a Seeker, Patric. Do you suggest I turn my hand to farming? To shepherding goats? Do you think I want to be here? Hell, I've lived all my life wandering the country or at home at Dunlorn. Either way I was free – but now, I'm a prisoner of my own stupidity!'

Patric shrugged idly and tossed the hair out of his eyes. 'You could teach, I suppose, but I doubt it would suit your temperament. Then again, there's plenty of work to do in the library. Acelin is always looking for help with translations.'

'Damn it, Pat!' Finnlay slammed his hand on the table making the plate rattle. General conversation in the refectory ceased as all eyes turned towards him. He glowered back at them and hastily they looked away.

'They know, Finn,' Patric murmured softly, his pale eyes reflecting candlelight. 'They all know what happened with you and Robert and Jenn and the Key. Some heard the Key, others heard later.'

'What are you getting at?' Finnlay turned back to Patric, but now had the sense to keep his voice lowered.

'You pointed it out enough times to Robert. Whether he likes it or not, these people look to him. Now that he's banished, they're looking to you. Don't ask me what for, but you know as well as I do how important it is to everyone here that one day, sometime in the future, we can all be released from this prison.' Patric rose to his feet, gathered up his plate and cup. 'Find something to do, Finn. Something useful. You're not the only one living in a cage.'

Wilf waited all night, to be sure his mind was quiet enough, the air clear enough to abolish distraction. By the time he left his rooms, it was almost dawn. He didn't feel tired and yet he was sure if he'd lain down he would have slept.

The corridors were empty and only an occasional noise penetrated his thoughts: soft echoes from the refectory and the gentle hum of folk rising for their day's work. A nice, warm familiar touch.

He made his way quietly and purposefully down the passage towards the great cavern. He reached the balcony which looked down on the expanse and, for a moment, brushed his hand on the cool railing. Then he continued down the steps until he was on the floor. The council chamber with its panelled wall stood on his left and on his right, the ironwork frame from which hung the innocuous bell. In this place, Wilf felt small and insignificant, dwarfed by the towering roof and the power of the Key.

It was impossible to do this without somebody watching, even this early in the morning. The Key was too damned public. Wilf didn't dare close the great cavern against them all. There'd be too many questions. But if he couldn't be alone, at least he could do it in silence.

His hands began to tremble a little and he clasped them together in a prayer for courage. With his chin raised in defiance, he gazed at the black bell suspended above him. He dared not move closer for fear of waking it properly, of the bell shimmering away until there was only the black orb in its place. If it did wake, then people would come, stand behind him, hang over the balconies above and wait to see what their leader would accomplish. It had always been the way. Every sorcerer within the Enclave always knew when the Key had been awakened.

Wilf had come here every day since he had banished Robert. Come and asked the same questions. Silence had been the only reply. It was just his dogged persistence which made him return, made him plead.

Carefully, he stretched out a mental hand to the sleeping orb and felt again that presence in his mind, a presence that had both surprised and frightened him when the Key had first chosen him. He would live the rest of his days with that Other in his mind. Always there, always comforting, never alone. Always silent.

He pulled in a deep breath and focused his eyes on the bell, on the presence in his mind, willing a stronger link, his body straining every muscle, devouring, yearning for more.

What does it mean, this prophecy you gave to Robert? he begged silently. And what is this girl, Jenn, to you? Why is she Bonded to your enemy?

Fearing failure once more, Wilf closed his eyes.

Why do you torment me in this manner? The two of them have this gift of mindspeech and seem to have a destiny you

40

will not elaborate on. If I am to help, you must say how. Do you want me to bring Jenn here? Is she to take my place?

Ears straining for any murmur, Wilf waited, his heart pounding in his chest. Should he leave? Should he wake the Key properly and force it to answer? Would it?

And if it didn't, then everybody would know it had stopped talking to him. They would know that the Key put more faith in two outsiders named in its prophecy rather than trust him as well. Two people who owed no loyalty to the Enclave, two sorcerers whose powers soared way beyond his terrified imagination.

They will be the death of me.

Was that his own thought – or had it come from the Key?

By the gods, he swore silently, tell me what you want!

Fear not. She will come.

Wilf started at the faint whisper. His eyes snapped open and fixed on the bell.

More ambiguity? No further explanation?

No, nothing but more silence. Yes, the Key might have spoken to him, but there was no comfort in its words, no counsel in that hollow whisper. He would just have to wait.

It took a few hours. Longer, in fact, than Patric expected – but eventually, Finnlay appeared in his doorway. He didn't come in immediately. He just stood there, leaning against the frame, his dark brown eyes sombre and subdued. At twenty-four, Finnlay was already possessed of the kind of physical presence the Douglas men were known for. Tall and lean with eyes that could burn through oak, not even the newly healed scar on his right cheek could mar his looks. Finnlay had recently taken to wearing black. Some said he was trying to ape his brother, but others, less kind, suggested the garments were chosen more as an expression of mourning his own faked death. Patric, of course, believed neither. Finnlay was far too serious to do anything so frivolous. A pity, really.

Patric didn't look up. Instead he kept his head down, his pen still moving across the paper. Though a part of his mind concentrated on the translation, the rest was wholly focused on the dark presence half-leaning into the room.

'It's my own fault, you know,' Finnlay murmured eventually. 'I should have listened to Robert more.'

'A common failing,' Patric replied, dipping his pen in the ink. Out of the corner of his eye he could see Finnlay wander around the room, absently glancing at the piles of books.

'Very well,' Finnlay stopped and put his hands on his hips. There was a glint in his eyes not entirely produced by the candlelight. 'You want me to do something with myself? Well, I can't unless you help me. I warn you though, you probably won't like it.'

Patric paused, put down his pen and glanced up through a fringe of fair hair. 'Has it something to do with the prophecy, or Robert?'

'Only by association. This is something else. I want to try an experiment and I need your help. Will you?'

'I don't know,' Patric mused. 'I thought you'd want to talk about the Bonding or Robert or something like that.'

'I'm sick of going over it, Patric!' Finnlay snapped, then shook his head. 'Sorry, but it's the truth. It's all meaningless anyway, this Bonding. Robert and Jenn will never marry – Jacob wouldn't allow it even if Robert did believe in it – so what's the point of discussing it?'

'Well, it might help us understand . . .'

'Look, are you going to help me or not?'

Patric studied him for a moment, then got off his chair and collected a flask of wine and two cups. He handed one to Finnlay and filled it with a tangy red. He took his seat again, sipped his wine and began, 'You know, the first time I met Robert he couldn't believe that I'd never been off the mountain. He was nine years old, I a year younger – his parents believed him to be visiting a monastery. He was running away from something, down the corridor towards the still room. I came around the corner carrying a pile of books and he ran straight into me. My tutor didn't see the collision, but he did see my books all over the floor, one of them damaged beyond repair. He was about ready to whip me when Robert bowed, apologized and flashed that famous

42

smile of his. My tutor – who'd been in the cavern the day before when the Key had spoken to Robert – recognized him and sent him on his way. I got a scolding and was summarily instructed never to speak to that boy again.'

Patric glanced up to find Finnlay smiling.

'Robert didn't give me a choice. He hounded me from that day onwards, wanting to know what it was like being born in the Enclave and never leaving. Even then it was obvious how strong he was. The things he used to do . . .' Patric shook his head and drained his cup. 'Suffice to say that for the last twenty years, a Douglas has been getting me into trouble of one kind or another. I fail to see why I should change those habits now. What do you want me to do?'

'I'm still not sure I like this,' Arlie murmured, helping Martha to settle into her chair in Finnlay's room. Her condition was well advanced, so his concern was understandable to Finnlay. However, Martha herself had been the one to volunteer, and she was undoubtably the best person to help for this particular part.

Arlie straightened up and turned back to Finnlay. 'Are you sure you know what you're doing?'

'As much as I can. As I told you, Robert and I were up in that cliff following up a lead on the whereabouts of the Calyx.'

'And you found the cave before or after he found the rod?'

'Before. He began Seeking inside the cave, focusing on the properties of the Key – and that's when he discovered the silver rod, disguised as a broken jug.'

Arlie looked dubious, but it was Patric who spoke into the silence. 'I've seen this silver rod. It is nothing out of our time or place. I've no idea what it does or what it's for, but I'm positive it has something to do with the Calyx.'

Arlie appeared only slightly mollified and Finnlay reached out a hand to pat his shoulder. 'Don't worry. There's no way that any harm could come to the child, Arlie. Martha will just be monitoring my trance, no more. Both you and Partic will be here if I have any trouble. You're a trained Healer, you can stop it if you want.'

'I'm only partly trained, Finnlay, but I take your point,' Arlie's soft smile was more for his wife's benefit than anything else.

'Are we ready to start then?' Patric almost bobbed with excitement. 'You know what you're looking for? You realize that it may not even work? When Robert tried this, he was Seeking for the Calyx in a small space. I know you're a stronger Seeker than he is, but that doesn't mean you can't kill yourself by overstretching.'

'That's why you're all here.' Finnlay lay down on his bed and reached for Martha's hand. 'I'm just going for a wander. If there is something within a hundred leagues of the Goleth that has the same properties as the Key, I'll find it. If you have a better idea how to find the Calyx, speak now. Otherwise, save your objections until I get back.'

Patric pulled up a stool on the opposite side of the bed. Arlie stood guard by the door. With his arms folded across his chest, his lost hand was invisible. Even at this early stage, this little venture had to be kept secret from the council – they still knew nothing about the rod.

Now that he was ready to start, Finnlay was gripped with a sudden terror. Was he really strong enough to reach so far across the country, or would the Key try to stop him? Seeking that far – even with Martha monitoring him – could easily kill him.

'Breathe deeply, Finn,' Martha began softly. 'Concentrate on my voice. Don't push too hard this first time. We've no idea how this is going to affect you, so don't overstretch yourself.'

Midnight was definitely the best time. Most of the others had gone to bed, the sky was clear of cloud interference and a blanket of peace had descended on the Enclave. Within the darkened room, Finnlay relaxed on the bed, felt his new *ayarn* solid in his left hand and placed his right hand where Martha could easily hold his wrist.

He had to work hard to control his panic. This was going to work. It had to.

He took Martha's advice and breathed deeply, listening to her voice as she took him further down into the trance. Soon he lost all sense of the room, the others, even the bed he lay on. Then his body, too, was left behind.

Free now of all physical constraint, he went out into the night, Seeking. This part was easy, familiar. A thousand times before he'd gone like this, his mind floating. As his awareness left the mountain, he noticed briefly the Enclave guards at their posts along the approaches, their auras known, their positions predictable.

Still feeling full of strength, Finnlay looped down from the mountain and into the valleys beyond, east and further east. He could see nothing but darkness, but that was how it always was, how it always had been. There was only the aura of a known sorcerer to focus on. But he wasn't looking for a sorcerer. Instead, he concentrated on the Key, as though it were the Key he was Seeking rather than the Calyx – and now that it had spoken to him, he had some idea of the essence he was looking for. Slowly, an insistent tugging behind him warned he was on the right track. The real Key was imposing on his senses, but he had to push past it and stretch further, wider, finer, beyond that. Away to something else that had a similar aura. Perhaps he could go far enough to reach Dunlorn. Perhaps he could even touch the rod, hidden within the walls of the castle. If he could find that, then there would be no doubt left.

What was that?

Like being caught in a strong current, Finnlay found his focus snagged and torn back, west and into the darkness. Back towards the Goleth. He struggled to pull out, but he was bound entirely by what he'd found. Compelled, he brought his attention fully to that one spot within the night. It was an aura he knew, yes, but so strong he couldn't tear himself away. An aura familiar on its own, but also bound up with something he could only guess at, something intimately connected and fathomless. So very strong . . .

Jenn! She was coming to the Enclave. But Robert had assured him she wouldn't, that this was the most dangerous place for her, being so close to the Key – because it wanted her for some reason. Robert had entrusted Finnlay with keeping Jenn safe if she ever did come back – and she was obviously very important to Robert. Finnlay had given his word without hesitation.

But now Jenn was riding up the mountain. Beside her was another aura, this one pale in comparison to that glow . . . Fiona! Was she coming back, too? Jenn was riding a bay gelding, and her deep blue cloak flowed out over its back. By the gods – he could *see* her! Not just her aura, but her, in every detail. The fine-boned face, the brilliant blue eyes, the dark flowing hair. All of it. It was impossible!

He drew in a deep breath and crashed back into his body. Startled, Martha leaned forward, her eyes glued to his.

'Are you all right? What happened?'

Finnlay sat up and shook his head. Weakness drained him and for a moment, he thought he'd faint. Then abruptly, his head cleared. 'I'm not sure but I think . . . I don't know what I've done, but I think we've broken the old barriers of Seeking. I just saw Jenn riding up into the mountains. Now, tonight.'

He paused and took another breath. Then, with his eyes on Patric, he added, 'Jenn's coming to the Enclave. Coming within the influence of the Key. We have to get to her first.'

The night had started out cloudy and dark, but by the time they reached the gate, the midnight stars were well advanced, dusted across the sky in a glorious shower. Jenn tried to keep her eyes on the trail, but the spectacular heavens kept drawing her gaze up, defying her senses. How could it look so much better from on top of the mountain?

Fiona seemed oblivious to it. But then, she had seen it before, many times. She'd told Jenn all about how she'd grown up at the Enclave: her father Marcus, the Jaibir, leader of the council; her mother, Ayn, a respected councillor herself and a formidable Seeker.

Ayn. She was the one who had found Robert, had brought him to the Enclave as a boy, that first time.

Yes, there it was again. That same twisting of her insides whenever she thought about him. She knew what it was, but refused to acknowledge it. After all, what good would fear

46

do? How could she demolish her frustration and ignorance except by coming to the Enclave?

Why had he just shut her out? They'd grown so close, had worked together to free Finnlay from his prison, discovered the mindspeech they shared together. Then Robert had come back here and abruptly desired nothing more to do with her. Why?

The blackness of the gate closed in on her, compressing and feeding the fear. By the time they emerged, she was about ready to turn and run.

'What's he doing here?' Fiona murmured in the gloom.

Jenn started, flinched – then saw a familiar face coming towards them across the grassy bowl atop the mountain. It was Arlie Baldwyn carrying an oil lamp, and he welcomed them with a smile.

'Good evening, ladies. So nice of you to stop by. Can I offer you some supper?'

Martha made up the spare bed in Arlie's study. It was difficult moving around with this great bulge getting in the way, but she managed. Patric offered to help, but he was virtually useless at all things to do with organization. Finnlay was better, laying out a plate of bread and cheese, putting a brew on the fire. She could see both of them wanted to keep busy, wanted to avoid thinking of what would happen if Arlie didn't manage to get to Jenn first, before Wilf realized she was here.

More important was the thing none of them wished to discuss. Why, when he had been looking for the Calyx, Seeking out something which had a similar aura to the Key, had Finnlay received a real vision of Jenn? Why was there a connection between the Key and Jenn where there should be none?

'They're coming,' Patric murmured from the door.

Martha went back into the living room and smoothed down her apron over her growing belly. With a practised eye, she surveyed the room and the things Finnlay had laid out on the table. She had put a lot of effort into making these rooms a home since she and Arlie had arrived last autumn. A home where they would have to live for ever since Arlie had lost his hand to the Guilde butchers. Now this living room was warm with rugs on the floor, two small tapestries on the wall either side of the fireplace and hanging baskets of herbs and dried flowers in every corner. Even the ancient oak chest beside the door was draped in a blue and white rug Martha had woven herself, last winter.

'Welcome back!' Patric moved first, ushering first Fiona and then Jenn into the small living room. Arlie followed behind and gained Martha's side. He was looking very pleased with himself; she could tell. His blue eyes twinkled with that old light whenever anything interesting was going on. He gave her a quick kiss, then immediately began to take care of their guests, pouring out the steaming brew.

Martha turned to Jenn, a wide smile on her face. 'My dear, how are you? You've grown!'

Jenn smiled in return and gave her a hug. 'So have you!'

'Arlie's sure I'm having twins, but I keep trying to tell him that this is what all pregnant women look like.'

Fiona had stopped just inside the door, her glance picking up the others in the room. Without looking too hard, Martha could see she was uncomfortable, but Fiona had never been very easy around people. She had a brusque manner and a forthright mind and a tendency to voice her thoughts. As a result, she'd never really collected friends in the way most people did and Martha had often wondered if that was why she didn't spend too much time at the Enclave. For most of her adult life, Fiona had worked as a Seeker while spending most winters as a teacher within a noble household in the area she was Searching. For the last few months, she'd been with Jenn at Elita, training the girl in her new-found powers.

Putting a genuine smile on her face, Martha approached Fiona with a welcome, determined to try once again to scale those prickly walls. 'Come in and sit down, dear. You must be cold from that ride up the mountain. And hungry.'

Fiona relaxed a little and let Martha draw her into the room. It was really up to Finnlay to speak, but for a moment he seemed to struggle now that Fiona was here too. But then, there'd always been a problem between Finnlay and Fiona.

When the others sat, Martha gave Finnlay a nudge. After collecting his thoughts, he took hold of the conversation, dominating the room in much the same manner as his brother always did. But where Robert was so at ease with this kind of thing, Finnlay was less so. He lacked the same natural confidence and, as a result, often sounded abrupt and disorganized.

He began with a question for Jenn. 'How did you get away from Elita?'

'I . . . suggested to my father that in order to keep up the pretence of my taking the veil, I should go on a retreat to an abbey.'

'And you won't be missed?'

'He's expecting me to be gone for a month or so.'

'And did you have any trouble after Robert and I left you at Elita?'

'Not really.' Jenn frowned, her eyes going to each of them in turn, looking for answers. Yes, she had changed too. This was not the homeless waif who'd come to the caves almost a year ago, new in her sorcery and ignorant of the powers arrayed against her. Jenn had grown up. It was obvious in every gesture, every word. But there was also something else there. Something in the way she glanced at Finnlay – in the way he looked back at her. Even Fiona noticed it.

'Is something going on? Something I don't know about?'

In the sudden silence, Martha looked to Finnlay to respond. He nodded, accepting her prodding and folded his hands before him.

'All right, I suppose if anyone has to do it, it's up to me. Fiona, your mother has gone to Marsay. And Robert has been banished from the Enclave.'

'What?' Both girls spoke at once.

Finnlay went on, 'When Robert and I came back here, there was a council meeting to discuss that presence you sensed at court last year, Jenn. They believed it was an unknown sorcerer of substantial power and therefore worthy of an effort to bring him into the fold. You know how everyone here believes that if we found someone strong enough to wield the Key properly, it would tell us where the

Calyx is – which would in turn give us a way to live openly and in freedom outside this Enclave. Well, Robert tried to dissuade Ayn from going to Marsay, offering to do something himself, but neither Wilf nor Henry were willing to trust him.'

'Why not?' Fiona asked before Jenn could.

'They thought he was hiding something – from twenty years ago when the Key spoke to him as a boy. He's never spoken about it and so they don't trust him. Anyway, Robert was so concerned about Ayn going to Marsay, he agreed to go before the Key and let it make the decision.'

'Heaven and earth!' Jenn whispered.

Finnlay swallowed. 'With the council and half the Enclave as witness, the Key spoke to Robert again – but this time, we could all hear. It told us how he can mindspeak with you, Jenn, and gave us part of a prophecy it had given to Robert all those years before. I have the exact text written here. Then,' Finnlay paused, looking down at his hands, 'the Key shattered Robert's *ayarn* and told him not to return to the Enclave unless Jenn was with him. Wilf was so angry that Robert had lied about the mindspeech and knowing the prophecy that he banished Robert. He left telling me that the Key is not to be trusted. He won't come back here.'

Martha couldn't take her eyes from Jenn's face. It was amazing how skilled Jenn was at hiding her thoughts, even from those who knew her. She sat opposite Finnlay, her eyes glued to his face as though hoping he'd made it all up. Fiona, too, watched Finnlay, her customary frown marring her otherwise handsome face. Jenn rose from her seat and put a hand on Finn's arm in comfort, but it was Fiona who fired the first question.

'And my mother has gone to Marsay? In search of this presence Jenn felt? A presence she said was wholly evil? By the gods, what was Mother thinking?'

'Well, this is a nice little scene.'

Martha looked up to find Wilf standing in the doorway, his eyes bleary and puffed from sleep.

'I might have known you'd try something like this, Finnlay. But you must have known the sentries would wake

50

me when the girls arrived. I'm sorry I kept you waiting, but I see you've already told them what they need to know.'

Martha moved towards him, but Wilf held up his hand, making her pause. 'I have no intention of disturbing you. I've only come to tell Jenn that she must take the oath of allegiance to the Enclave or leave in the morning.'

Finnlay sprang to his feet. 'No! I will not allow it.'

'This is none of your business, Finnlay. Well, Jenn? Robert's been banished from the Enclave – by the Key. We can't trust him any more and the Key itself has labelled him as our enemy. Where does that leave you? What do you say?'

Jenn stood slowly, but Finnlay didn't give her a chance to reply. 'I said no, Wilf. Jenn will not go before the Key and take the oath. If you try and force her, you will have to deal with my sword.'

In Serin's name, where had this come from? Finnlay stood there, his eyes blazing with a determination she'd only ever seen him use against his brother. Why was he so adamant?

Jenn finally spoke. She came around the table and placed a hand on Finnlay's arm, 'It's all right, Finn. Really.'

'No, it isn't. Jenn, trust me on this.' His intense gaze held her for a moment and then she turned back to Wilf.

'I'm sorry, but my answer is no. If you object, then I must ask to take it up with the full council.'

'Really!' Wilf snapped, his eyes growing cold. 'Well, you can take it up with them right now. They're waiting in the chamber as we speak. And you, Finnlay? Don't think for one moment that your predicament will stop me from banishing you also. One step out of line and you'll suffer the same fate as your brother – and I won't care if the Guilde do find you and tear you limb from limb.' With that, Wilf turned and stamped out of the room.

'Finnlay,' Martha breathed, 'did you have to push him so hard?'

Without speaking, Finnlay stared at the empty doorway, his shoulders stiff and unyielding. Slowly he shook his head and turned back to Jenn. 'I had no choice. I gave Robert my word.'

*

They were waiting, just as Wilf had promised. This time, Jenn could recognize their faces, pasty with living beneath the ground. A cave life – what kind of life was that? Where was the joy in a summer's day or the passion of a winter's storm? These people were immune to those normal pleasures, passing the seasons with an indifference bordering on apathy. Did they have any real idea of what life was like outside? Did they even care?

Jenn didn't sit down. She didn't intend to stay long enough. Finnlay closed the door behind her and stood at her side. In profile, he looked so much like his brother she could almost believe it was Robert standing there as he had the first time she'd come into this room. Yet there were differences. Things that ran so deep she was only now beginning to see them. Like Finnlay's willingness to trust something that he could neither see nor understand. He had placed his faith in Robert and Robert had placed his faith in Jenn.

Who was there left for Jenn to believe in?

'Have you changed your mind?' Wilf came straight out on the attack. 'Or have you let this rebel sway you?'

Immediately, Jenn's anger got the better of her. 'Oh, I always let other people make my decisions for me.'

Wilf was not amused, 'Don't you dare try that tack with me, child, or I'll make you very sorry.'

'What do you want from me?'

Wilf rose from his seat at the end of the table. Placing his hands firmly on its surface, he replied, 'I want you to take the oath. If you refuse, you will leave here and not return until you do.'

'Why?'

'Because I will not be defied any more!' Wilf slammed his hand down, making the star candle jump. Henry glanced around uneasily, but neither he nor the others said a word. 'These are matters beyond either your knowledge or comprehension. I hope that you'll have the sense to take the proper counsel and give us your oath!'

As Jenn met his gaze, her anger turned cold and seeped into her bones. He really did believe she'd let Finnlay make her decision. But Finnlay had told her nothing but the truth. Would they have done as much?

'You banished Robert, didn't you?' Jenn began evenly, moving to the other end of the table. Her eyes swept over the councillors, ending with Wilf. He just sat there, a belligerent frown on his lined face. His mind was already made up, and all because Robert had insisted on thinking for himself. 'You banished him because the Key told you to. It said he was an enemy. Did it say I was an enemy, too? Did it say I should be banished?'

Silence.

'Did it even say I was to be forced to take the oath?' Not a single answer. 'What would the Key say if it discovered you were abusing your authority in such a manner?'

'How dare you speak to me like that!' Wilf bellowed. 'I'm the Jaibir, the chosen of the Key and whether you like it or not, you will do as I say!'

Her heart racing, Jenn shook her head slowly and placed her hands on the table. She leaned forward, but the words that came out of her were not of her own design. 'I could burn this place down, Wilf. Do you want to see me try?'

Wilf's eyes widened in fury and for a moment, Jenn wanted to withdraw her threat, wanted to take it back ... anything to take that look from his face. But she couldn't. She took her chance – probably the only one she would ever get now. 'I'll make you a bargain, Wilf. You let me come and go as I please with no more talk of taking the oath. You'll also leave Finnlay to live here in peace. If you throw him out, he's under strict instructions to come straight to me at Elita. I'll take his appearance to mean you've broken the bargain. In return, I promise that when the time comes, I will Stand the Circle, go before the Key and give it the chance to choose me as next Jaibir.'

She felt rather than saw Finnlay flinch at this, but she kept her concentration on Wilf. Inside, her whole body was shaking, but outside she was as steady as the mountain itself. With a tentative breath, she continued, 'There is, of course, no guarantee that the Key would choose me, but at least that would settle it once and for all. What do you say?'

Henry couldn't keep his peace any longer. 'But she should still go before the Key . . .'

'No.' Jenn stopped him before he could gather pace. She hardly knew what she was doing, but it was too late now. 'That's my offer. Take it or leave it. Before you decide however, I should remind you that now you've banished Robert, I'm the only other likely candidate who could wield the Key as it was intended. Do you really want to get rid of me, too? – for I promise you, if you send me away I will never return.'

Henry snorted, unimpressed. 'How do we know you'll keep the bargain?'

Jenn shrugged. 'I'll give you my hand on it.' Without thinking, she gathered all her anger and frustration into a single blinding streak. It soared down her left arm and into her palm. Then she lifted her hand from the table leaving behind a black mark, a perfect handprint, burnt into the wooden surface. In some dusty part of her mind, she could hear Robert's reaction: caustic, deriding and horrified.

But Robert wasn't here, was he? 'That's the only oath you'll have from me, Wilf.'

The old man sprang to his feet, his mouth open at her temerity, her wilfulness. 'You're too clever for your own good, girl! Go ahead. Do as you please. But get out of my sight!'

They were outside and running down the passage before Jenn could bring herself to stop. Finnlay was laughing, but Jenn, standing against the cold stone wall, could do nothing but shake. Robert was going to kill her, if she ever saw him again. Taking pity on her, Finnlay gave her a quick hug and they continued back to Martha's rooms.

'By the gods you should have seen her!' Finnlay almost spun around the room, filling up wine cups as he went. Arlie, Martha, Fiona and Patric were all absorbed by his story, even though Jenn was sitting quietly by the fire, none too amused. 'Wilf didn't know what to say. You'd think she'd already Stood the Circle.'

'And the hand mark?' Patric quizzed. 'Is it permanent?'

'Unfortunately, yes.' Jenn grunted. She drained her newly filled cup and reached out for more. 'Mineah only knows what got into me.'

'Well, he won't make that mistake again,' Finnlay laughed.

'Oh?' Jenn snapped, eyeing him dryly. 'And you think it was a good idea that I should challenge his authority so openly? Don't you see that I've just made exactly the same mistake Robert made? Wilf feels threatened by both of us and in his way, all he was trying to do was make us accept his leadership which, when you think about it, he has a perfect right to do. Now all I've done is alienate him – and branded all of you at the same time. Go ahead and gloat, Finn, but I'm the one who'll have to pay the price in the end. I made a promise I'll have to stand by. I can only hope Wilf lives a long time.'

Finnlay's smile vanished and he took a deep breath. He came back to her and slowly refilled her cup. 'I'm sorry. I should have helped you more. I should have said something so you didn't have to go so far.'

'It's not your fault,' Jenn glanced up at him and gave him a weary smile. 'I don't know why you're sorry, though. You once tried to convince me to Stand the Circle. You should be happy, wondering if this means I'll be able to find the Calyx one day.'

Finnlay couldn't find an answer to that one. Instead, it was Martha who spoke. 'I think you'll find that Finnlay's ambitions have changed a little. Besides, it would dent his pride somewhat if he wasn't the one who discovered the Calyx himself.'

'Oh, Martha, I never said that. Besides, if I'm lucky, I might find the Calyx long before Jenn has the chance.'

Fiona took that moment to stand. She moved to the door but paused, her wary gaze sweeping over everybody except Finnlay. 'Well, this has been very nice, but it's late and I'm off to bed.'

As she vanished down the corridor, Finnlay started after her, but went no further than the door. He said nothing for a moment, but then his shoulders dropped and he turned back to face Jenn. 'So what are you going to do?'

'You're asking me now?' Jenn shook her head and got to her feet. 'Serin's blood, Finn, haven't you done enough for one night?'

Jenn didn't wait for a reply but headed out of the room. She couldn't think any more. There was only one thing she needed right now. Sleep.

4

Micah waited atop the gatehouse tower. From there he could easily see the procession as it came towards Dunlorn: Deverin and a dozen of his best men, all wearing their livery with pride, surrounding Robert and the horse and cart he towed behind him. As they came closer, Micah could actually see the long wooden casket in the back of the cart.

In the courtyard behind him were gathered the inhabitants of Dunlorn, together with all those who lived close by. All had come to pay their respects, almost five hundred of them. They stood in silence, like Micah, waiting.

The gates were open, the guards lined on either side as Robert approached. He glanced up at Micah once. Was that a warning?

Micah turned and dashed down the steps to greet Robert. Orders were given to take the casket into the family chapel, an honour guard to stand by – and for no one to open the box.

Robert began to climb the steps to the hall. There was nothing in his face, no hint of what had happened. Just a dark shadow around his eyes, the long hair blown back from his brow, his mouth set in a line. His black clothes were muddied and his cape fell from his shoulders like a shroud. With a glance back at the cart, he murmured, 'Where's my mother?'

'Inside, my lord.'

There was no response for a moment, then Robert turned back to Micah. 'How is she?'

What could he say out here where everyone would hear him? 'She has spent much time at prayer, my lord.'

Robert nodded slowly and glanced around at the waiting people. Acknowledging their tribute, he turned and took the stairs two at a time. Once inside he strode across the hall so quickly, Micah almost had to run to keep up.

'My lord,' Micah ventured as they climbed the stairs, 'you have guests waiting in the winter parlour. Lord Daniel and others.'

'Yes, I know,' Robert grunted, passing his study door. 'They'll have to wait.'

They continued on until they reached Robert's bedroom. There he ushered Micah inside, glanced quickly down the passage, then closed and locked the door. Briskly he whipped off his cloak and strode over to a side table where fresh water, a bowl and linen had been laid out for him.

'How much time have I got?'

'Time, my lord?' Micah murmured, completely at a loss.

'Until the Guilde gets here. How long?'

The magic word knocked Micah back to reality and he sucked in a breath. 'An hour perhaps, little more. We're keeping track of them from the top of the keep.'

'Damn!' Robert swore and splashed water on to his face. He rubbed a towel over it, then removed something from inside his muddy shirt, wrapped in red cloth. Then he stripped down to his waist, his back a mess of healing bruises and welts mixed in with the old battle scars.

Micah frowned, but felt the sudden sense of urgency. He handed Robert a fresh shirt, then took a sombre black jacket from the chest by the window. As Robert pulled it on, Micah poured him some wine and stood waiting.

Robert ran his hands through his hair, then strode to the window. 'I don't suppose there's any way we can slow them down? No, of course not. An hour! Too little time. I can't bury Finnlay before they get here. I still have to talk to my mother.'

'I should warn you, my lord,' Micah ventured, 'she will not see you today.'

Robert turned back from the window with a frown. 'She blames me, doesn't she? Well, she'll have even more reason to hate me before this day is out. Still, I have to talk to her – and before the Guilde get here. I can't risk the alternative.'

'My lord,' Micah held up his hand, now completely unable to keep track of this discourse, 'will you tell me what happened?'

Robert crossed the room to take the wine from Micah. He lifted the cup, drained it in one go and handed it back. With something that looked a lot like a smile, he said, 'Yes, but not now. All you need to know now is that Finnlay is not dead.'

'What?' Micah breathed, his heart suddenly pumping madly. 'Then how . . . ?'

'I'll tell you everything later. Right now I need to tell my mother the truth. She needs to be prepared for when the Guilde arrives. They'll be asking some very dangerous questions.'

Micah took a deep breath and let it out slowly. Why? Why did he never expect these things? After all these years, he should be used to this kind of surprise. But no, once again the reality of working for a man like Robert had walked up and smacked him in the face. One of these days . . .

'Are you all right, Micah?' Robert was leaning forward, frowning in concern.

'Am I . . .' Micah took another deep breath. After that he felt somewhat better. 'Finnlay's alive?'

'Yes, but I still have to convince the Guilde that he's dead. They believe Finn's a sorcerer and they come here determined to prove it. The problem is that I no longer have my *ayarn*. The Key destroyed it. Every night since I left the Enclave I have tried to make another, but I can't. I can use my powers without it, but anything big could kill me.'

'Mineah's teeth!'

'My thoughts exactly. Now, tell me where I can find my mother. Then I want you to go down to Daniel and the others. Tell them I'll be with them shortly. After that, go to the chapel. Stay there until I come. Don't let anyone – and I mean *anyone* but me in.'

'Aye, my lord.' Micah had to wipe the smile off his face before he left the room, but for comfort, held it inside, where no one would see it.

She was in the solar, just as Micah had said. Robert stood in the doorway and tried not to flinch at the look Margaret gave him. Three of her ladies were with her and they all stood at his appearance, their hands together, their eyes downcast.

'Please leave us, ladies,' Robert's voice sounded harsher than he'd intended, but it was done now. Slowly the women filed out past Robert and he closed the door behind them.

Margaret wore the black of mourning, her face pale against such heaviness. She was clutching a trium, the one Trevor had given her for her birthday, only weeks before Selar's invasion. It was that even more than the look on her face which made Robert pause.

'I'm glad to see you're back in one piece, Robert,' Margaret said quietly and stiffly, 'but if you don't mind, I'd rather not talk today, now that you've brought Finnlay home.'

'I'm sorry, Mother,' Robert took a tentative step forward, his hand reaching out to her. She stepped back and he tried again. 'But what I have to say can't wait until tomorrow.'

'No, Robert, not today.' Her voice dropped to a murmur. 'I don't want to know how it happened or what you were doing up there on that mountain. Lady Jennifer's letter said there'd been a fall, but—' Margaret lifted her chin, '—all I know is that my son is dead. He was in your care . . .'

Her words petered out as she gazed at him. That one single look was like a knife in his chest, cutting him in two. If only she knew how much he was to blame, how greatly he had failed her and his father. Since his father's death, her great comfort had been the Church. One breath of sorcery now would only make her hate him.

Slowly now, to calm her reservations, he moved forward until he stood before her, until he could whisper the truth and not be overheard by the ladies waiting outside. 'I know you blame me, Mother. It is my fault. But I can't let you go on suffering. Finnlay was . . .'

'No!' Margaret moved to turn away from him, but he caught her hands and held them tightly between his own.

'Mother, Finnlay is alive.'

For a long moment she stared at him, her eyes wide with incomprehension, shock and horror. She didn't understand – and then she did. Slowly, like an autumn leaf, she fell into his arms. He held her tight, not wanting to let go. When she looked up at him again, her eyes were full of questions.

'Where is he?'

'Safe, Mother. He's safe.'

'Then why all this . . . Why say he's dead? I . . .' Her voice trailed off again. She was suddenly uncertain, afraid that she couldn't trust him. She stepped back. 'Tell me what happened.'

'I'm sorry I can't tell you any more. I just couldn't bear you thinking he was dead when I knew he wasn't.'

'Then this has to be kept a secret? From everybody? For ever?'

'Yes. Or at least until it's safe for him to return.'

'And when will that be?'

'I don't know. Perhaps never.'

Margaret's mouth became set in a line, anger now tumbling over the rest of her emotions. 'Why won't you tell me the rest of it? Your father trusted me with the truth. Why do I not deserve the same respect from my own son?'

She knew exactly where to hit him, to cause a wound as deep as her own. She waited for his answer, refusing to move until she got one.

'I . . .' Robert murmured and shook his head. This was much harder than he'd dreamed possible. Even if he could tell her the whole truth – even if he *could* Seal her and protect her without an *ayarn* – what would she say about the sorcery? It went against every precept she believed in. A part of her was still attached to Saint Hilary's, a part of her soul still longed to take vows. Could he live with her hate?

And all the while, the Guilde was getting closer to Dunlorn, ready to strike down the sorcerer's household.

'Sit down, Mother.' He drew her to the window seat and sat beside her. 'I know how this must seem to you, but I beg you to trust me. I keep the truth from you because it's not safe for you to know.'

Wasn't this the same argument he'd used with Jenn?

'I don't want to hurt you, Mother, and I do trust you. You deserve the truth – but I won't risk your life in that manner. I just wanted you to know that Finnlay is alive and safe. In fact, he's probably safer now than he's ever been before. I beg you not to ask me any more questions.'

Margaret watched him steadily. 'I believe that much. But it's not enough.'

'Mother, if I could tell you . . .'

'You would? I doubt it,' Margaret interrupted bitterly. 'You were always too good at keeping things to yourself, no matter the damage it did you. But don't worry, I won't tell anyone. You're my son.'

And what could he say to that? He'd already destroyed her faith in him.

Robert stood and pulled aside the drapes over the window. This part of the castle faced south and gave him no view of the approaching Guildesmen. Instead, there was just the edge of the moor and the rolling green farmland that stretched for leagues.

'I don't suppose it would do any good if I promised to tell you one day. I'm not sure I could keep my word.'

'And you never break it, do you?' Margaret replied, her tone under complete control.

Break it? No – only in ways that no one would ever notice.

'You must keep up the pretence of mourning, Mother.'

'There will be no pretence.'

Robert turned away from the window, away from his mother and all the closeness they had ever shared. 'The Guilde will be here very soon to investigate these rumours of sorcery surrounding Finnlay's death. Even though there's no truth to the rumours, we must continue to pretend Finnlay is dead – for our safety as much as his. They may want to speak to you. I'll try to stop them, but I may not have a choice.'

'They will have no satisfaction from me, Robert. If nothing else, I can promise you that. I suppose we will go through a pretence of burying Finnlay? Once everything has calmed down, I will return to Saint Hilary's for a few days.'

Robert made it as far as the door before he paused. 'Will you come back?'

Margaret didn't answer. Instead she stood and turned her back on him, held her trium and gazed out the window.

Down the stairs Robert went, trying to keep his pace even, steady, sombre. He ignored the pain, ignored the demon. He had to concentrate now.

Only minutes outside of Dunlorn waited his most dangerous challenge yet. The Guilde. Coming for blood. It would require all his skills to get through this. Lies and deception. They were the best tools he had now, his only useful weapons.

Daniel and the others were waiting in the winter parlour. Daniel, Harold, Sir Walter Mauny, Kem Raskell and Hal Talbot. They each looked at him with a strange mixture of sorrow and expectation. Harold frowned – as usual – but it was Daniel who came forward and spoke first.

'Robert. You look exhausted. Was it a difficult journey?'

'The rains didn't help any and my own injuries slowed me down,' Robert replied, keeping his expression carefully closed. 'It was good of you to come.'

Daniel nodded, 'We wanted you to know how sorry we are about Finnlay. It was a great tragedy.'

'We also wanted you to know,' Harold added with a glance at the others, 'that should you need any . . . help, we'll stand by you. All of us.'

'Help?' Robert frowned. What – exactly – were they offering?

'What he means,' Daniel murmured, 'is that we will stand by you. Regardless.'

Of what?

Oh, yes. They must have heard the rumours. But – were they serious? Did they believe that Finnlay was a sorcerer –

and would they really stand by Robert if they found out the truth?

Yes. That was exactly what they were here for. To tell him they didn't care. Genuinely touched, Robert said honestly, 'I thank you for your words of kindness and your offer of help. I shall pass on your good wishes to my mother. As for the rest?' Robert shrugged. With any luck, they might see nothing more than his refusal to take the rumoured allegations seriously.

It didn't work.

'You're in trouble, Robert.' Harold grunted, his gaze penetrating. 'We're here to help. Remember that.'

There was a movement behind and Robert turned to find Deverin waiting, Alard Bain hovering behind, obviously agitated. 'Forgive me, Your Grace, but representatives of the Guilde are here to see you.'

'Thank you.' His time was up. He returned his gaze to the others. They were watching him, waiting for him to tell them what to do. There was only one way out of this – but the risks were so high he didn't dare think about them.

'Daniel, would you do something for me?'

'Of course!' Daniel's eyes lit up.

'Would you keep my friends company for a few moments. Deverin will show the Guilde in here. Will you tell them I'll see them soon?'

'Delighted!' Daniel smiled and so, oddly, did the others.

'I must go and speak to my mother,' Robert added faintly. Where did they get this enthusiasm from? Why were they all so . . . pleased?

'Don't you worry about those Guildesmen, Robert,' Harold beamed. 'We'll look after them until you get back.'

'Thank you.' Robert nodded, still bemused – but he didn't have time to worry about it now. He had to get to the chapel before the Guilde arrived. Gesturing for Deverin and Alard to join him, he strode out of the parlour and down the corridor to the guard room. From there they took the narrow spiral staircase to the chapel.

The doors were open and muted daylight softened the incense-filled air. The long wooden box was laid out on biers, draped with the Douglas banner and surrounded by tall candles. An armed guard stood at each end of the bier, solemn, their eyes downcast. Micah waited by the door.

Robert glanced once at Micah, then turned to the two men accompanying him. 'Alard, I want you to keep watch on the rest of the Guilde soldiers. Let me know if they decide to look around at all.'

'Should I stop them if they do?'

'No,' Robert replied with a smile. 'Just tell me what they see.'

'Aye, my lord.'

He disappeared down the passage as Robert turned to Deverin. 'Have these two men stand guard at each end of this corridor. Then I want you to go back to the hall. Wait ten minutes, then bring the interrogator up here. Make sure he brings one other with him – no more.'

Deverin paused a moment, then nodded. 'As you wish, my lord.'

Once the guards had left, Robert closed the doors and turned to Micah. 'We haven't got much time so we'll have to be quick. Here, help me take this off.'

They removed the banner and placed it to one side. Then Robert took out his knife and gently levered the lid from the box. Inside was a layer of rocks and some old sacks. As they lifted the lid clear, Robert glanced up at Micah.

'I need your help and I can't ask anyone else to do this.'

Micah said, 'I'll get into the box, my lord – but I don't look anything like your brother.'

Robert grinned. 'No. But Jenn did something when Finn was in that prison. I'm not exactly sure how she did it – and I know for certain I can't reproduce it. The only way to get rid of the rumours of sorcery completely is to prove to the Guildesmen that Finnlay did die and that his body is here – right where it should be. With any luck, they'll put the rest of the story down to superstition.'

'Then what can you do? Without your *ayarn*?'

'I think I can make you look like Finnlay for a few moments. I think if I twist the Mask concept around and instead of projecting a blank wall, I put his face on your body, then that might be enough to satisfy them.'

'You *think*?' Micah murmured, climbing into the box to settle himself gingerly over the layers of rocks. There was just enough room for him. 'Does that mean you're not sure?'

'Yes, that's exactly what it means.' Robert lifted the lid back into place.

He could just hear Micah's voice through the wood. 'And if you pass out from the strain it will just be from grief, right?'

'Right.' The lid was firmly in place, the banner laid out again. Footsteps came along the corridor and Robert leaned down towards Micah's head. 'Just don't move a muscle when I open this thing, I beg you.'

There was a creak from the door and the candles jumped and flickered. Robert waited until Deverin had brought them in before turning a composed face towards the Guildesmen. Osbert! Thank the gods. For a few moments there, he'd thought it might be Vaughn himself.

'Good day, Governor.'

'Good day, Your Grace. This is a sad occasion. You have my sympathy, of course.' Osbert moved around the bier, his eyes glancing over the black eagle banner. He'd put on weight over the last three years, but not so much that he had become cumbersome and awkward. His sanguine face belied the sharp intellect and determined conservatism he was known for. His dull grey eyes and thinning hair tempted some to see him as a man beyond his best, but, at only forty, Osbert considered himself to be in his prime.

'I am honoured you've come all this way, Governor. Surely a letter of condolence would have sufficed? And in such weather?' Robert stayed by the bier, glancing once at Osbert's companion and then at Deverin, who stood by the door, his beard masking his face and hiding whatever thoughts he might have on this matter.

'Yes, the weather has been unseasonable, I admit. You must have had difficulty, yourself, returning with such a load?' Osbert was watching him carefully – and trying to

65

appear otherwise. In fact, he was trying to look as casual as possible.

Oh, yes, he was definitely suspicious.

'I returned only today,' Robert replied evenly. 'I was forced to stop several times – and my own injuries kept me from travelling too fast.'

'Of course,' Osbert nodded sympathetically. 'Would you tell me, Your Grace, exactly what happened? The details of the accident that led to the untimely death of your dear brother?'

Robert allowed his eyes to flicker to the casket and back to Osbert. 'Is that why you've come? To interrogate me? And now of all times? By the gods, Governor, I've been back in Lusara almost a year and you choose this moment to test my loyalty to the King?'

The attack had caught Osbert off balance – as it was intended to do. After all, he'd come here with thoughts only of sorcery. However, if there was no sorcery involved – and if Robert had indeed just taken his dead brother home having gone nowhere near Kilphedir – what could Robert know of the rumours?

Ah, ignorance. What bliss!

'My visit here is sanctioned by the King, Your Grace, but it is not to test your loyalty, I assure you. I come merely to find out the circumstances of your brother's death. There have been whispers, Your Grace. I seek only to find the truth.'

'The truth?' Robert arched an eyebrow. 'I'd love to know the truth myself. All I know is that I fell from the cliff. When I awoke at Elita, my memory of the incident had gone. When I did remember the following day, I took myself back to the forest below the cliff and tried to find my brother. I assumed he must be there somewhere, looking for me, perhaps afraid that I'd been killed in the fall. What I found was his broken body, tangled among rocks in the river.'

There was a bitterness in his voice that was only partially for show. Without pausing he continued, 'Did he fall trying to find me? Did he fall trying to save me? If I'd regained my memory sooner, would I have been able to save his life? I don't know, Governor. You want the truth, but I can't give it to you. I only wish I could.'

He held Osbert's gaze for as long as he dared, then deliberately looked away, giving him time to broach the next, inevitable subject.

'Forgive me, Your Grace, but these rumours – I fear there is much evidence.'

'Rumours of what?' Robert grunted, not turning back.

'Two woodsmen claim to have seen your brother in the forest by the river. They say he was working sorcery. He was imprisoned but escaped. I came here to . . .'

'Sorcery! In Lusara?' Robert's head snapped round. 'Are you mad? What kind of idiocy is this? Some trumped-up charge of the Proctor's? I told you, Finnlay died! I pulled his body from the river with my own hands – or are you accusing me of lying?'

'No, Your Grace . . .' Osbert stammered, trying to keep up.

'But you won't leave here until you've seen proof with your own eyes, is that it? Proof you can take back to the Proctor? You take the word of two woodsmen over mine?'

Osbert shut his mouth and took in a good breath. He clasped his hands together and nodded – once. 'I could lay the rumours to rest if you would allow me to see the body, Your Grace. Surely that is for the good?'

Robert shook his head slowly. 'Yours, perhaps, but not mine. No good can come to my House by opening this casket. I've already given orders that I don't want my brother's body to be seen. His injuries were terrible. If I'll not let my own people see him, why should I let you? You come here with only rumours and suspicion.'

'I come also with this.' Almost triumphant, Osbert held out his hand. There, sitting neatly in the palm was Finnlay's ring. Robert reached out to take it, but Osbert pulled back. 'I'm sorry, Your Grace, but I fear I must insist.'

Robert kept his eyes on the ring a moment longer, then there was a presence beside him: Deverin.

'My lord, it would be better to allow the governor this one concession. Then we can let Lord Finnlay rest in peace.'

'Yes, Deverin,' Robert nodded, his voice a murmur, 'you're quite right.'

Doing his duty, Deverin set about removing the banner and loosening the nails in the top of the casket. Robert used the time to focus his thoughts. This was going to be so very hard. Attempting something he'd never tried before – without even his *ayarn* for support – and in front of such a dangerous audience. What if it didn't work?

He reached down deep, brought forth an image of Finnlay. He held it tight and controlled – then began to change it. Remove the scar from his face, build up the bruises, the cuts, the bleeding. Then overlay that with broken bones, a coarse and bloody gash across the throat. Then colour, white and blue, black now for the blood. Then reach out and place it over Micah, lying within the casket.

And, may the gods forgive him, the smell of a body now two weeks old.

There was a scrape of wood as Deverin lifted the lid clear. Robert kept his face averted. He couldn't control his expression and the illusion at the same time.

There was a gasp and the scrape of leather against stone. Then the lid was moved back in place. Deverin did not knock the nails in, but instead came around to stand close to Robert. Only then did Robert dare release the illusion. He sighed and turned to face Osbert.

'Forgive me, Your Grace,' Osbert bowed slightly, clearly shaken. His suspicions must have run very deep. Or perhaps the man had no stomach for the sight of blood. 'This has been a great intrusion. I see you have visitors awaiting your presence. I will withdraw and return to Marsay. Thank you for your patience.'

Robert waited until he backed to the chapel door. 'Osbert?'

'Your Grace?'

Walking up to face the governor, Robert replied grimly, 'I would have my brother's ring back. It should be buried with him.'

Osbert hesitated – but what choice did he have? 'Of course, Your Grace.'

The ring was dropped in Robert's hand and Osbert

removed himself and his companion. The glow of yellow disappeared down the passage just as the sun peeked out from behind a cloud. 'See them off my lands, will you Deverin?'

'With pleasure, my lord!'

Robert closed the chapel door before helping Micah out of the box. He still had to get back downstairs to see his friends and assure them that they had no cause to worry about him. After the funeral service he would send them home – the fewer people involved in this madness the better.

As Micah climbed out, he smiled. 'It worked!'

'Yes, strangely enough. Deverin helped – though unwittingly.'

'No, that's not what I mean. You didn't pass out. I can tell – it wasn't even a strain, was it?'

Robert came to a complete halt, his eyes on Micah. 'No. Not even a bit.'

Micah, suddenly full of himself, folded his arms, totally smug. 'You don't need an *ayarn* any more, my lord. You're just like Jenn. That's why the Key destroyed it. Maybe you never needed it at all!'

Glancing down at the ring in his hand, Robert had to smile himself. 'Why is it that you always see these things before I do? What am I doing wrong?'

'I see them because I'm not a sorcerer, my lord.'

'Thank the gods for that,' Robert laughed. 'You'd be absolutely unbearable if you were!'

5

'Just look at him,' Hilderic hissed, 'hovering around the King like a snivelling hound hungry for scraps. McCauly still languishes in prison and Brome doesn't give a damn. He makes me sick!'

Godfrey turned away from the window and the scaffold erected outside. He glanced around the hall to check the proximity of those closest to them. Fortunately this time, they were quite alone and nobody would have heard Hilderic's venom. Nevertheless, Godfrey kept his voice low and his tone as gentle as possible. 'Be careful of what you say in here, Brother. Within this company are those who would report any trifle to the King in order to secure their own position.'

Hilderic grunted and clasped his hands beneath his cassock. His face was still full of clouds, however. Godfrey frowned at him, then turned his attention to the others. The hall was half-full of lords and ladies, magnates, Guildesmen and priests. All preparing to go outside and witness the execution like a flock of carrion ready to pick over the bones of their less fortunate brother. At the end of the hall, by the throne, stood Selar, majestic in crimson and gold. Vaughn, Brome and a dozen other men stood around, all of them conscious of the King's slightest word, all ready to do whatever he bid. The Alderman, Nash, stood out in the crowd, distinguished by his quiet dress and composed demeanour. He said nothing, spoke to no one – but Selar knew he was there. It was obvious in the small glances he threw Nash, in the slight raised eyebrow he received in return.

'They've grown close, those two,' Godfrey murmured. With any luck he might be able to distract Hilderic away from Brome. 'It's hard to tell, though, whether Nash is a good influence or bad.'

'A Guildesman?' Hilderic whispered fiercely, his white eyebrows raised in horror. 'How can that be good?'

'You heard his report to the council. He said that there was no real proof that sorcery was once again alive in Lusara. If it had been Vaughn he would already have called out the troops for a holy war. Imagine the arrests, the burnings, the hundreds of people falsely accused.'

'Osbert hasn't returned from Dunlorn yet, or even sent word. He may bring further proof with him.'

Godfrey nodded slowly. 'I doubt it. Even if there is something going on, Robert's far too clever to let anything slip. He hasn't survived this long by being careless.'

Hilderic turned a suspicious eye on him. 'Then you believe there's something to the rumours?'

'I believe in the gods, Brother,' Godfrey murmured to cover himself. 'Anything else is pure conjecture.'

'Conjecture or not,' Hilderic grunted, turning towards the doors as they opened to admit the Queen, 'there's no doubt Selar intends to go through with this. One way or the other, Baron Blair will die a traitor's death today and neither the gods nor rumours of sorcery will save him.'

George, Earl of Kandar, took up his usual position to Selar's right. There were others beside him on the platform before the scaffold, but he paid them no attention. Beyond the crowd of courtiers, the courtyard was filled with towns-people, jostling for a view of the coming proceedings. The noise of anticipation was immense: so too was the smell and the heat.

He glanced across at the King. Selar looked tired, but not remotely uncomfortable. There were whispers that he'd not been sleeping well and that he'd been drinking to excess a little too often. But it was only over the last week and George wasn't inclined to worry. Selar's moods were often difficult to read – one of the reasons why he was so feared by those who lived around him. There was no way to guess which way he would turn from one day to the next.

There was only one consistency. His treatment of Rosalind, his Queen.

Knowing he would likely be observed, George shot only a brief look at her as she sat beside her husband. In profile her lips were pressed together, her auburn beauty flushed. Her hazel eyes glittered with fearful resolve. Hardly aware of the crowds before her, she kept her children close, as though afraid they would be dragged from her. As Kenrick sat oblivious at her feet, she took Galiena's hand and turned to Selar, her voice low so only those closest could hear.

'I beg you, my lord. Please reconsider. Your children should not be witness to this. They are too young.'

Selar barely acknowledged her. 'Silence your protests,

madam. I was a child of four when I first saw a man quartered. It did me no harm.'

'And were the following years free of nightmares, my lord?'

As Selar turned his full gaze on her, Rosalind flinched, but continued, her voice shaking. 'Sire, this crowd will show your children that pain is a toy to be played with, an entertainment. Is that what you wish them to learn?'

George swallowed, hardly daring to breathe. The challenge was there in the air between the King and Queen, the kind of challenge only Dunlorn had ever dared voice to Selar.

And only he had ever got away with it.

Selar reached out and grabbed Rosalind's wrist, pressing it down hard against the arm of her chair. Rosalind gasped, but could not escape his grip. Selar brought his face close, his eyes flaring with barely contained fury. 'Remember your position, madam. This traitor despised the throne your son will inherit. Kenrick must be witness. They will both stay and you will say not another word. Defy me again and you will be sharing the scaffold with Blair.'

As Selar released her and turned away, George had to fight the urge to comfort the Queen. Sitting there with rigid back and eyes straight ahead, she looked isolated and scared. After all these years as Selar's Queen, of treatment such as this, Rosalind could still muster the spirit to fight him, even though her only recourse was words, and she found the experience always terrifying.

For the sake of her children, Rosalind regained her composure. A movement from the arch opposite drew George's attention. Blair was being led out, his hands bound, his head high. Before him was a priest, intoning the Prayer for the Damned.

'Oh, blessed gods of thunder and rain, we beseech thee to forgive us our dread sins. Though we have committed the greatest of crimes against your law, we beg you in mercy to receive our souls . . .'

From his demeanour, it was obvious Blair was begging nothing. He stuck his chin out and didn't even flinch as the crowd jeered and flung curses at him. The moment he stood on top of the platform before the noose, Selar rose to his feet, his hands raised to silence the restless crowd.

'Rupert, Baron Blair. You have been judged guilty of treason. This, the most heinous of crimes, must be punished with as much force as we can achieve. Treason cannot be treated lightly when it is a betrayal not only of a vow made unto the gods, but also unto the person of your sovereign lord. This betrayal we feel keenly. We would rather have remained your friend than become your executioner. And so it is with heavy heart that we pronounce sentence on you, Baron. We pray the gods will have mercy on your soul.'

With that, Selar nodded to the black-hooded executioner hovering beside Blair. He lifted the noose over the old Baron's head and stood back. Again the priest prayed aloud, his voice increasingly drowned out by the chanting of the crowd. Then a lever was thrown and, with a jerk, Blair fell through the trapdoor, his legs kicking at air. A shout went up from the crowd.

George's eyes went instantly to Rosalind. She sat there white-faced and rigid, her nails digging into her palms. The children, seated beside her, didn't take their eyes from the spectacle in front of them.

Then they were cutting Blair down moments before the last breath had gone from his body. All the while the crowd jeered and yelled, waving their hands in fruitless menace as Blair was laid out ready for the next stage of his sentence. A massive blade was wielded and displayed to the crowd before being slashed across Blair's belly. Red blood spurted from the gaping wound. The noise rose to fever pitch as Blair's entrails were dragged from his body and held up for the crowd to see. And then there was a piercing scream — a child's scream.

No one but the royal party even heard it, let alone took any notice. George darted to Rosalind's side. In her arms, cradled against the terror, was Galiena. She screamed again and again, begging her father to stop it, to stop killing Blair, and there was nothing Rosalind or anyone else could do to silence her.

'Get her out of here!' Selar hissed, but as Rosalind rose he turned his full glare on her. 'Not you, madam. You stay and look after my son.'

Rosalind was about to protest when George gently touched her shoulder. She turned to him with eyes full of tears.

'Let me take her.'

Gratefully, Rosalind handed him the terrified child and instantly Galiena clung on to him. Without pausing, he turned and made his way through to the back of the yard, taking long strides in his hurry to get her away from the horror. The child's screams had gone hoarse as she tried to gulp in air. Abruptly, before he could even get her indoors, she slumped in his arms. He paused only long enough to make sure she was still breathing, then hurried on.

By the time he reached Rosalind's apartments the nurse had been warned and was ready for him. However, George was not about to give up Galiena. Instead, he kicked a comfortable chair closer to the fire and sank into it, shifting the girl around until her head rested against his shoulder. The nurse hovered in the background, but said nothing. George sat there unmoving until Rosalind finally returned.

Selar was with her – along with what seemed like half the court. Still George kept hold of the child until Rosalind herself took her from him. Then he rose, stretched the kinks out of his arms, bowed and left the room. He waited alone on the landing, standing still and facing the netted window. Suddenly, his hands began to shake and he stared down at them as though from a great distance. With a bemused smile, he clasped them together and waited.

It wasn't long before Selar came out with Vaughn, Eachern and Nash all murmuring their pleasure that Galiena was well. Selar merely grunted. George said nothing but met, without hesitation, the steady gaze of the King.

After a moment the gaze shifted away and Selar replied to something Vaughn was saying. Without even addressing George, Selar led the others down the corridor, leaving him alone. Slowly, George turned back to Rosalind's door. He stood there for a long time, studying every line of the oak panel, every nail and stud holding it together. Then, with a deep sigh, he wandered away down the long corridor towards his own rooms.

'You can't be serious!' Valena blurted. 'And what happens if Osbert comes back with evidence to the contrary? What will you say to Selar if Osbert proves you were underplaying the situation? You'll go the same way as Blair!'

Nash sat across the table from her and steepled his fingers together. The little house was quiet now that the crowds outside had finally drained away. The celebrations had gone on for hours, affording little peace for those who craved it. Now, in the dead time before dawn, only the church bell could be heard, calling the religious to morning prayer.

'It's not a matter of evidence, my dear,' Nash replied evenly. 'What matters is that I convince Osbert not to present it to the King. I believe I can do that. He's anxious for my support – I think he'll play along. There've already been a few arrests across the country, charges of sorcery. After Vaughn's defiant speech last week, we could be looking at a holy war against sorcerers. I can't allow this thing to get so big I can't manage it. If Vaughn has his way, none of us will be safe. We'll be frozen, unable to move or act with folk watching our every move. No. There'll be no presentation of evidence. If I have to, I'll Bond Osbert to make sure – and chance the consequences.'

'And if Osbert comes back without evidence?'

'What do you mean?'

'What if Dunlorn is telling the truth and his brother is not a sorcerer? Assuming Finnlay is dead, then it must have been another man those woodsmen caught – a sorcerer strong enough to escape prison without detection. Finnlay or not, we still have a rogue sorcerer of unknown ability roaming the land and we don't have a clue who it is. How do we catch him? How can we carry on with this doubt? How do we know that the Enemy won't turn up at the next corner, ready and able to stop us?'

'We don't,' Nash replied simply. It was very difficult to think clearly with Valena leaning over the table in such a manner. The black gown she wore suited her colouring too well, setting off the pure softness of her skin, the glints in her eyes. Even after all these years, she was still a distraction to him. It was always such a challenge – controlling his reaction and yet still allowing himself the pleasure of her. A careful balance, a delicate combination.

A dangerous choice.

'How much longer is this to go on?' Valena stood, walked over to the window to open the shutters. A bleak blue-black sky greeted her. 'When you first brought me here you told me it would take you only a year to get what you needed. That time passed months ago and still it seems you're no closer to Vaughn's secret library. How can you hope to find the Key if you cannot get near those books? What good will Selar's support be if, once his armies are at your disposal, you have no idea where to start looking?'

Nash smiled, calm and serene. 'There's plenty of time to find the library – and more important things to pursue first. You despair too easily, my sweet. Yes, perhaps this will take longer than I anticipated, but we've come a great distance. Vaughn needs me as his spy to Selar. Selar needs me as his spy to Vaughn. Neither have any idea what's really going on. When I'm ready to move, neither will be able to stop me. Besides, I may even be able to remove Vaughn and put Osbert in his place. After that, the whole thing will be easy.'

'But when is that going to be?' Valena snapped, turning to face him. 'I'm sick of this place, these people. You allow me no company other than your boys – and you won't let me touch them, either. I'm growing to hate this house and the way you must come in secret every night. When are we going to do something, Nash? When?'

'What would you suggest? These things can't be hurried, you know that.'

'Then let me do something. If you can't get close enough to Vaughn to find out where this library is, let me work on him.'

Nash shook his head, a small laugh escaping. 'He's taken the Vow, my dear. He wouldn't let you close enough to seduce him.'

Valena waved her arms in frustration. 'Then let me go to

Elita. You've said enough times that there's a lot of ground work you need to do before she can take her place. I can start that for you. She's never seen me before. She wouldn't suspect anything. I could befriend her, talk to her.'

'No . . .' Nash's voice trailed off as he felt a sudden brush against his senses. Unfamiliar and alarming.

'What's wrong?' Valena murmured.

Nash stood and wandered to the window. Focusing, he sent his senses out into the dawn-fresh morning, trying to locate the origin. It was still there, pressing and releasing, testing, no more. Somebody was Seeking, and they knew what to look for.

'I think we may have found our rogue,' Nash smiled, withdrawing. Abruptly, the brush vanished – or rather, moved on. 'Did you feel anything?'

'No.'

'Then it wasn't one of your Malachi brethren. This is wonderful!' Nash laughed. 'He's made it easy for us. Now I don't have to go out looking for him. He's right here, in Marsay.'

'But you didn't get a location, did you?'

'Not an exact one, no. But I know where to start looking. Besides, I don't need to go far. I'll just wait until the next time he tries it.' Nash laughed again and caught Valena up in his arms. 'Unless I miss my guess, he'll probably try again at dusk. Then I'll have him!'

Rosalind sat by the bed and kept hold of Galiena's hand. Only now, as the dawn began to filter through the window, did the child sink into a peaceful sleep. Her face was beaded with sweat, but her brow was clear of the dark and terrible agony her nightmares had induced. Her fair hair was laid out on the pillow, tangled and matted with her tossing in the night. Rosalind would brush it later, in the warmth of the morning. Until then, she would let the child sleep on.

Feeling no tiredness herself, Rosalind watched the sun rise over the distant hills. This was no way to treat a gentle, sensitive child of nine. But Kenrick, although only seven, had suffered no ill-effects from witnessing the execution. He'd watched the whole thing, glowing afterwards at the delight his father had shown for his strength. The more Selar praised him, the more Kenrick grew within himself. Soon the two would be inseparable.

There was a soft knock at the door and Samah crept in. The veil which usually covered her long, auburn hair was gone. Her lovely face glowed in the morning light.

'She sleeps peacefully now?' Samah whispered, coming closer.

'For the last hour. And Kenrick?'

'He's fine. I should think he'll be awake soon, ready for the day's adventures.'

Rosalind sighed. 'I wish you didn't have to leave. I understand your vocation – but I'm selfish and I would much rather you could stay here, with me. I wish you could help me with the children. They have such need of your love, your kindness.'

Samah knelt beside her and took her other hand. 'They already have a loving mother, Sister.'

'By the gods, Samah,' Rosalind breathed. 'How long is this to go on? In a few years, he will have Galiena betrothed and sent away. Kenrick will move from the nursery and out of my influence. Then Selar will bully and mould him into the very image of himself. How will our beloved Lusara fare with another King who cares nothing for her people?'

'But Kenrick is also Lusaran. Perhaps he will not be like his father.'

'Selar will make it so, believe me – we have his father to thank for that. A vicious bully will always sire another. Selar's father was the making of him. Where does that leave my little boy?' Rosalind paused and brushed a strand of hair from Galiena's eyes. 'I should have worked harder to keep Selar's favour. Back in the beginning when I had the chance. Dunlorn was the perfect example of what could be achieved by those methods. If I'd had any wits, I would have done the same. But I was young and innocent, with no knowledge of survival. Now it's too late for me to do anything to stop Selar.'

'Perhaps you won't need to,' Samah replied, searching for

hope. 'Perhaps the people will rise up against him. They would – if somebody they trusted would lead them.'

Rosalind shook her head. 'There's only one man they would follow – and he'll never break his oath. And even if they did remove Selar – where would that leave my beautiful son?' Squeezing Samah's hand, Rosalind sighed, 'No. I fear there is no hope for any of us.'

Godfrey wandered out of the cloister on to the sun-warmed grass. With slow footsteps, he reached a stone bench and sat, by habit bringing his hands together within the sleeves of his robe.

Hilderic was getting worse. Even now, an hour later, Godfrey could still hear his angry ravings about Brome's discourse at mass. He'd spoken about the evil of treason in the wake of Blair's execution – enough cause to send Hilderic into a flaming rage. More than a few of their brothers had heard the curses and threats as they'd echoed through the corridors. It was now only a matter of time – and very little time at that – before Hilderic would find himself arrested. That once-formidable mind was now entirely consumed with a hatred that would in turn consume him.

And there was nothing Godfrey could do to stop him. The more he tried to calm Hilderic, the colder the distance grew between them. After today it was unlikely Hilderic would even speak to him.

Godfrey sighed and tilted his head back to gaze at the frail clouds streaked across the sky. If only there was some way to get McCauly free – but there'd been no word from Payne yet and even if there had, Hilderic couldn't be trusted.

Damn him! Why, after so many years battling Selar alongside Domnhall, did Hilderic choose this moment to falter under the strain?

'Forgive me, Deacon. I'm sorry to disturb you.'

Godfrey turned to find Father John standing behind him, quiet and tentative.

'Is something wrong?' Godfrey murmured, waving him closer.

John came around the bench and stopped before Godfrey,

his hands clasped together. He paused before speaking, as though trying to sort his words. 'No, Deacon. But . . . Father Hilderic. He's causing some concern amongst the brethren. I'm worried.'

Godfrey nodded. 'Me too. You know I've tried to stop him – and he won't listen to me, let alone anyone else. In some ways, I think he's courting disaster deliberately. Guilt will do that to a man.'

John frowned. 'Is there no possibility that Selar will release McCauly? After all this time, without charges being brought against him, Selar could believe Brome sufficiently secure in his position not to worry about opposition from McCauly.'

'Opposition is not the issue, John. The simple fact is that McCauly was anointed Bishop and legally holds the position until he dies. There's nothing Selar can do to change that. The best he could hope for is for McCauly to voluntarily renounce his vows of priesthood, and we all know he'd never do that.'

'Then why hasn't Selar done something before now?'

Godfrey shrugged. 'Because he doesn't need to. Why stir up the pot when it's bubbling away nicely on its own?'

John was silent for a moment. Then he came and sat beside Godfrey, his expression enigmatic. 'Deacon, may I make a humble suggestion?'

'If you have any idea how to silence Hilderic, I'd be delighted to hear it.'

John met his gaze steadily, his usual meekness for once absent. 'It has been many years since Hilderic went on retreat.'

Godfrey's heart almost stopped. It was the most he could do to prevent himself from jumping up.

'Archdeacon Francis,' John continued, 'spent six months on retreat last year and only came back for Domnhall's funeral. Archdeacon Ohler was gone for four months the year before. Hilderic refrained because he said his workload was too heavy in Domnhall's last years. Now, however . . .'

'Brome's directing more of Hilderic's work to others every day. By Mineah's heart, Father, you're a genius!' Godfrey sat up straight. 'Tell me, where did Hilderic spend his last retreat?'

'St Austell's, in the west.'

Godfrey nodded slowly and even smiled. 'Perfect. I agree, Father. Hilderic is long overdue for a long period of rest and contemplation. After all these years, I should think six months would settle him down – or at least . . .' No. Best not to mention anything of Payne to John.

Coming to his feet, Godfrey beamed his approval at the young priest. 'I'll have a word with Ohler. He can put the proposition to Hilderic and leave him no room to refuse. With your support, we can have Hilderic out of the capital within a couple of weeks!'

As John joined him on the path, Godfrey added, 'Father John, I think you've just saved our friend's life.'

Murdoch held the cloak for Ayn as she slipped beneath its warm folds. With summer drawing to a close, her old bones needed the extra protection. She tied the laces up under her chin and turned to face him. 'I won't be gone too long. The city is still excited after the execution yesterday. There'll be too many people roving around and that will hamper my work.'

'Perhaps you should rest a couple of days before you do too much,' Murdoch replied. 'I know you're a powerful Seeker, but even you need your sleep. Ben is still washed out and he's thirty years younger than you.'

'Ben is washed out because he was in the taverns last night, drinking,' Ayn murmured with a gentle smile. 'I don't blame him with this being his first trip to Marsay – but while he was out, I was asleep. I admit I was up early, but I've done nothing all day, so please stop worrying, Murdoch. This morning's effort produced nothing, so I can hardly stop, can I? I'll be back in a couple of hours, no more.'

Murdoch held the door open for her and she left the warm comfort of his tailor's shop. She turned left and walked up the slight incline towards the main avenue. On the brink of evening, the streets were almost empty. They would fill again later as people ventured out in search of entertainment.

Ayn crossed the avenue and took a busy street which wound along the city wall. This was a favourite haunt of traders and hustlers and consequently filled with every type of establishment possible. This was just the kind of area an unknown sorcerer would keep to, his identity hidden in the constantly changing crowds. Although Jenn had apparently sensed this presence within the castle walls, there was no need to assume the man belonged there. Besides, Ayn was in no real hurry. It took some time to scan a city of this size from wall to wall.

The street dipped down towards one of the lesser city gates, then turned up again, towards the castle. There was a branch off to her right which opened out on to a small courtyard. In the centre was a well and on each side, a tavern. Neither was particularly busy, though there were plenty of people about. Yes, this would do nicely.

Ayn wandered into the courtyard and paused by the well. With her back to the wall, she dropped her left hand and allowed her *ayarn* to slip from her grasp. Her foot nudged it close to the well where it would remain unnoticed. Then she entered the nearest inn. With a silver coin she took the only private room which looked out on to the courtyard. The innkeeper brought her ale and a bowl of stew, but Ayn was not interested in eating. The moment he was gone she sat within the shadows of the window and focused on the *ayarn* below.

How many years had she been doing this? How many had she brought into the fold in this manner? It had always been so easy for her to reach out to the small stone, to channel her senses through it and create a vibration only a sorcerer could feel. Affected so subtly, that sorcerer would come looking for the source of the vibration. They would find nothing – but their search would reveal them to the one who watched. Even as she extended her senses now, the faces of those she'd found in this way came to her, one by one. More than fifty. All except Robert. She hadn't found him by Seeking him – he had found her – and that was only because he'd had that accident.

Dear Robert. If only he'd listened to her, believed her,

trusted her. Then he wouldn't have taken that terrible load
on to his shoulders alone. She would happily have shared it
with him, helped him, supported him.

But now it was unlikely she would ever see him again. Not
that Robert was likely to go along with the banishment if his
purpose was strong enough. Wilf was the Jaibir – but in
reality, he had no power to stop Robert from entering the
Enclave. The gate could be tuned to prevent entry of a
particular sorcerer, but that wouldn't keep Robert out.

No, the one thing that would keep him away was the Key.
He saw it as his enemy. He was convinced it was working
against him and had been since he was nine years old. He
would not go near it again.

Ayn sighed and, keeping her link to the *ayarn* open,
reached over for the ale. She took a deep swallow and turned
back to the darkening courtyard below. A mother was
herding her two children towards the well, carrying buckets.
They drew water, argued about who would carry it back,
then disappeared into the house opposite. Then a man
approached the well, drawing the glove from his right hand.
He pulled on the rope and brought the ewer up to his
mouth. He sipped the water, then let it fall back with a
splash.

Before he replaced his glove however, he bent down and
picked up the small stone.

Ayn leaped to her feet. How could he know what it was?
He was gazing at it intently, turning it over in his hand. She
could feel him now, bearing down on her senses, making her
heart pound, her head spin. This must be him!

He turned to face the tavern. Unremarkable features were
graced by a neatly trimmed beard and eyes of coal black. His
blue cape was enormous, falling from a tall, lean frame. He
smiled.

Ayn shrank back into the shadows. The stench of evil
invading her senses was almost overwhelming. Robert had
warned her, but she hadn't listened. Well, it didn't matter
now. Now she knew what this man looked like. With
Murdoch's help they could find out who he was and with
the council's help, decide what to do about him. Either way,

she had to get away now. If he was powerful enough to sense exactly where the *ayarn* was hidden, then he was stronger by far than Ayn could ever hope to be. Perhaps even stronger than Robert.

She gathered her cloak up and headed straight for the door. She pulled it open, but there was somebody there, standing before her. A young man, handsome, fair, but without any expression. He moved forward, making her back away into the room. She stumbled against the table, but the young man said nothing. He just waited.

Seconds later the dark stranger came to the doorway. He stood in the frame for a moment, his mocking smile making her stomach turn. He shut the door gently, then turned to face her. Moving slowly, he crossed the room. Ayn moved too until her back was against the wall, her chest heaving for denied air. The dark stranger dropped his smile and instead raised his hand. There was her *ayarn*, held between his fingers.

In panic, Ayn thought of the window. If she could throw herself out, perhaps she could get away . . . but his gaze held her frozen, like a tiny bird. Then he smiled again and brought his fingers together, closer and closer until suddenly, her *ayarn* cracked. He kept squeezing until it was nothing more than dust falling through his fingers.

Ayn screamed. Pain like lightning flashed through her, driving the life from her body. Desperately she tried to hold on, but blackness fell in upon her mind and she sank to the floor as consciousness slipped away.

6

Jenn sat on the grassy slope and watched the cows as they grazed in the midday sun. Huge clouds danced overhead, disappearing behind the needle rocks hemming the Goleth field. Here and there, the grey rock was interrupted by a black tunnel entrance, each one framed with a double wooden door.

Jenn brought up her knees and wrapped her arms around them. The stone at her back was cold and, even with the sun shining, she couldn't help feeling chilly.

She glanced over her shoulder to find Finnlay approaching, full of purpose and energy. 'You've been avoiding me,' he said.

'Have I?'

Jenn's lacklustre response slowed Finnlay down. He sank to the grass beside her, turned his gaze to the contented animals before them. 'Did you sleep well?'

'No, not really.'

He paused, not looking at her. Then, 'Look, Jenn, I'm sorry, all right? I'm sorry I dragged you into this, but really, I had no choice. Robert . . .'

'Robert told you to trust me, yes I know.' Jenn frowned. A long journey, a very late night, a terrible battle with Wilf and a rotten sleep had left her drained. The last thing she wanted right now was an argument with Finnlay.

There was another long silence. It seemed Finnlay was determined to have this conversation. 'Jenn, I probably shouldn't ask but – is there something going on between you and Fiona? Something I should know about?'

'Such as?'

This time Finnlay didn't respond. Instead, he turned and faced her, waited for her answer.

Very well. 'Yes. There is something going on, but I don't think you want to hear about it.'

'Yes, I do.'

Jenn had to glance at him. Where did he suddenly get all this patience from? A gift from heaven? 'I'm sure Fiona is a talented teacher and very successful in her own way, but to be honest, she drives me crazy.'

She was rewarded with a smile. 'Me, too. What else?'

Jenn shrugged. 'She's shown me how to place a warning and sharpened up my short-range Seeking, but she can't teach me anything important. Like setting a Seal or making a Mask. With things as they are, I'm getting to the point where I really need to know.'

Finnlay nodded calmly. 'I'll have a word with Patric, later. He's the best teacher I know. Or perhaps I could try. Is ... er ... is that the only reason you came here, now?'

'Yes.' She tried, but she couldn't hold his gaze. Instead, she closed her eyes and turned her face back into the cool breeze.

'We need to talk about this, Jenn.'

'What's the point? Will it change anything? The Key has spoken, Finn. Why should anything I have to say make a difference?'

'Do you blame me?' This was asked so quietly, Jenn thought for a moment she'd misheard.

'Blame you?' She turned and looked at him and for the first time, saw the hesitation in his face, the respect in his eyes. It was most disconcerting. 'Why would I blame you? I came here of my own free will. Sure I trusted you about not going to the Key, but nobody forced me to make that oath to Wilf.'

'Then why did you?'

'Oh, hell, Finn, I don't know. Look, what do you want from me? I've already said I'll Stand the Circle. Can't you just leave me alone?'

'Is that what you want?'

'By the blood, Finnlay,' Jenn suddenly snapped, 'I want to understand! I don't know what the hell is going on here. Everybody's watching me. What am I? A piece of flesh to be torn apart by everybody who comes near me?'

'I'm sorry.'

'Yes, sure. That's what your brother said, too. I believe neither of you!' Jenn turned away, afraid her bitterness would turn to tears. She wouldn't – couldn't – give in that easily. 'I seem to be involved in a prophecy nobody understands – and only your secretive brother knows anything about it. I'm an ally? He's an enemy? Of what? And what's Bonding? Your experts have all talked about it, but are you any closer to an answer?'

'I . . .'

Jenn ignored the interruption. 'But there was something else the Key told Robert alone. Something dangerous that he'd never tell anyone even if he could. But, I have to say that the way he's behaved, you'd think the entire bloody thing was dangerous.'

'Perhaps it is.'

'Oh? How?' Jenn took in a deep breath and turned to look at him. A look of confusion flitted across his face and disappeared as quickly as the clouds.

'If Robert was told – at nine years of age – that he was Bonded to somebody, then, as a child, he was bound to believe it. I think until now, he believed that person was Berenice. And she died.'

This was getting nowhere. 'Yes, a fever killed her. So what has that to do with me?'

There was that look again. Pained, this time.

'You know something, don't you?' Jenn demanded, a memory of something tugging at her. 'Or are you going to tell me that stupid rumour of him killing Berenice is true?'

Finnlay glanced away to the grazing cattle and shook his head slightly. 'Robert is convinced the Key intends no good with its prophecy. Your life may be in danger, I don't know. We all have a lot of questions and no answers. All I do know is that we have to work together – you and I. If we don't, we're all lost.'

Without meaning to, Jenn smiled. 'You know, Finn, sometimes you really surprise me. I know we've had our differences in the past, but if you keep talking like that, I may even be able to have a civil conversation with you more than once a year.'

Finnlay fought to control a smile. His head dropped while he glanced sideways at her, almost shyly. 'I was practising all morning, while you were asleep.'

'Now don't go and spoil it, please.' Jenn shook her head, stretched her legs out again on the soft green grass. For the first time since she'd left Elita – since Robert had sent her that last message – she began to relax a little. Maybe it was Finnlay's honesty, maybe it was just the sunshine and the nice honey-coloured cows munching away. It didn't really matter.

She folded her hands in her lap. 'The point is, Finn, I don't know how much I can help. I don't know why Robert told you to trust me.' If Robert trusted her, why wouldn't he answer her calls? How could just mindspeaking with her over a great distance be dangerous?

Finnlay shrugged, but didn't give her the first answer he thought of – she could see that much. 'Perhaps he thinks that you can give the questions a fresh look.'

'Oh, yes,' Jenn replied with a laugh, only slightly bitter. 'You are getting much better at this. Well, since you're doing so well, perhaps you could answer a few important questions for me. For example, why would focusing in on the properties of the Key help Robert find that silver rod? Are the Key and the Calyx connected in some way? Were they made by the same person – at the same time?'

'They are connected, but I'm not sure how. The Key is supposed to know where the Calyx is, so I guess Robert assumed there had to be some similar properties. The Key was made shortly before the founding of the Enclave. The Calyx has been around for many centuries prior to that.'

'How do you know?'

'There are two books which describe it. One is the *Flail an Feer*, a compendium which dates back almost a thousand years. There were several copies made originally, but I've only seen the two in our library here. The other book is a kind of mystical examination of why sorcerers have powers in the first place. It's called *The Homily of Karastican*, which some believe is older than the *Flail*. Most of it is sentimental rubbish, but there are a few interesting themes. Neither, however, really tell us what the Calyx looks like, nor how we're supposed to find it. It's only in later books that there is mention that the Key will reveal where the Calyx is.'

'But they do tell you it's important?'

'Absolutely. In the *Flail* it says "the Calyx holds all we would hold powerful". The *Homily* terms it differently, referring instead to our sacred right to its wealth and treasure. Most of all, they both state without ambiguity that within lies the way we can live with normal people and leave this mountain prison.'

'But . . .' Jenn's voice trailed off as she frowned, pointing a single finger in Finnlay's direction. 'If both books pre-date the Enclave – how can the Calyx tell you to be free of a prison that hadn't existed yet?'

'Well, that's simp—' Finnlay came to a complete stop. He shook his head, crossed his ankles and leaned back on his elbows. 'I have no idea.'

'Unless it referred to a different kind of prison. I can't see that it matters. After all, the Key's prophecy hasn't even mentioned the Calyx. What I want to know is why it would conceive a prophecy in the first place? Isn't there supposed to be some purpose behind prophecy?'

'Not necessarily,' Finnlay smiled. 'Prophecy is supposed to be a blind statement of faith that something will happen. If it's going to happen anyway, we wouldn't necessarily need to be warned.'

'Except that we have been, haven't we?' As the smile left Finn's face, Jenn nodded slowly. 'Look, I don't know about you, but I'm hungry. Where can I get some decent food around here?'

'Well, that's easy. You can't. However, I can tell you where to get some reasonable food. After that, I suggest you get some more sleep.'

'Why? Do I look so bad?'

'No, not at all. It's just that I think exhaustion is wearing down your defences. You've started being nice to me.'

Jenn swung her arm and punched his shoulder. With a mock cry of pain he scrambled to his feet and held out his hand to help her up. She looked up at him, at the resemblance between him and Robert. In some ways, talking to Finnlay was like talking to Robert – except Finnlay didn't avoid all the difficult questions. But there was still one she had to ask him.

She took his hand and stood, brushing her skirt down. 'Perhaps I shouldn't ask, but is there something going on between you and Fiona I should know about?'

His eyes went wide – and he actually blushed. 'What do you mean?'

'You didn't have to include her last night. You could have waited until she'd gone to her rooms before telling me the whole story. But no, you wanted her to be there, to be a part of it. Your first questions to me were about her. What's going on, Finnlay? Come on, tell me.'

'Nothing's going on. Absolutely nothing. You've got it all wrong. Fiona's been in love with Robert for years. Oh, he never knew, really. You know how he is – he treats everyone equally. But Fiona absolutely hates me. She's always blamed me for scaring Robert away from the Enclave. Then Robert married Berenice. It didn't seem to matter to Fiona that the marriage had been arranged when they were just children. Now I'm sure Fiona blames me for getting Robert banished. Trust me, she would never even look at me. She just thinks I'm a pale copy of my glorious brother.'

'Oh really?' Jenn enquired, 'and I suppose that's why she never takes her eyes off you when you're in the same room. Nor am I the only one who's noticed. Still, I'm sure you're right. Well, I'm going to eat. Bye, Finn.'

Finnlay liked the new library principally because it was nothing like the old one. Instead of being dark and musty, this room was long, light and airy. The ceiling of the cave sloped up sharply, like the arches of Saint Bastion's Church in Ballochford. Ventilation shafts had been chipped out of the stone centuries before, wide enough for a man to crawl through and covered by gauze frames. Along the walls were dozens of tables, large and small, with a bewildering array of chairs and stools arranged around them. Running down the centre of the room were two enormous racks of books. There were three doors, one at either end and a third in the centre of the south wall. Beyond that door was the map room, Acelin's private hobby. Not that there were too many maps in there at the moment, but he had hopes.

And as Finnlay suspected, Acelin was in attendance, perched on a ladder, changing the wick in one of the oil lamps which hung from the high ceiling on a long chain.

Finnlay came to a halt beneath the ladder and squinted up at the shadowed ceiling.

'Why don't you try that design Patric drew up for you? If you put the chain through a pulley you could bring the lamp down to the ground to do that kind of thing.'

Acelin barely glanced at him. 'It works fine the way it is.' With big hands already blackened with ancient ink stains, Acelin finished replacing the wick, lit it with the candle perched on top of the ladder and screwed the glass back down. He blew out the candle and slowly descended the ladder. His long wiry frame seemed to suit the equipment, his legs almost as long as the supports, like a tall, grey-haired spider.

'What do you want, Finnlay – apart from trying to tell me how to do my job?'

Finnlay backed out of the way as Acelin folded up the ladder. 'I . . .' he began, but Acelin just hefted the ladder on to his shoulder and disappeared into the map room. Well, he had to come back. There was no other way out of the library.

With a shrug, Finnlay turned into the double row of bookshelves. He wandered along the silent passage until he reached the end. He was about to turn back when a movement caught his eye. He stopped, took a step back and looked again. It was Fiona, curled up on a big chair with three books laid out in front of her.

Finnlay glanced over his shoulder, but Acelin hadn't reappeared yet. He cleared his throat and said, 'What are you doing?'

Fiona didn't even look up. 'Reading.'

'Oh?' Finnlay came around the corner a bit more. 'What?'

'Books.'

Stupid question. He tried again. 'Look, Fiona, I wanted to apologise for last night . . .'

Fiona snapped her book shut, collected the others together and dropped her feet to the floor. 'By the mass! Finnlay Douglas apologizing? Well, I knew it was a good idea to come to the library at this time of day, when most good folk are busy at work. I thought it was just because I could get some peace and quiet. Little did I know the honour that would befall me.'

She was already packed up and walking off before Finnlay could form a complete sentence. He took one step after her. 'Fiona?'

She stopped. 'Yes?' He faltered, and she took the opportunity to speak, her voice level and completely without inflection. 'Forget it, Finnlay. Jenn's not here so you can stop pretending we're friends.'

'No, I . . .' But she was already walking away and he could do nothing to stop her.

'Well?'

Finnlay turned around to find Acelin standing behind him polishing his eyeglass with a grubby cloth.

'What did you want? Or did you just come in here to scare my customers away?'

'Patric has been at me to put my time to some use. He said something about you needing help to translate some of the older books because nobody can read them any more.'

Acelin eyed him derisively. 'And you've come to volunteer?'

'Well, yes.'

'And how long will this last?' Acelin turned away and began striding up the aisle. Finnlay almost had to run to keep up with him. 'Do you really think I want to be giving you some of my most valuable manuscripts just so you can play with them until you get bored? You've never stuck with anything in your whole life. I know you.'

'Look, just wait!' Finnlay grabbed a sleeve and brought the tall man to a halt. 'It's up to you, but I would like you to give me some work. I will finish it, I promise.'

Acelin studied him for a second, then nodded. 'Very well. How's your Saelic?'

'Well . . .'

Wilf wandered into his bedroom, pulled off the dull grey robe and let it drop to the floor. He didn't even bother to remove his shirt. He just tore back the bed covers and sank on to the pillows, drained of all energy. He felt far older than his sixty-five years; in every bone of his body he ached with defeat. After last night, he needed a nap. Sleep. Any rest at all.

It was too much for one man to have to deal with. Jaibir or not, the Key had chosen the wrong person for this responsibility. He'd handled it all wrong, charged at the poor girl like she was a proven criminal and in the end, he'd achieved absolutely nothing.

Would just asking her have made a difference? Would she have been prepared to take the oath?

Probably not. Not after Finnlay had spoken to her. Damn him. Damn them all!

Most especially, damn Robert Douglas.

For twenty years Robert had been lying to them. Every time he'd come within the caves, his very presence had been a lie. It didn't matter whether the Key had forbidden him to speak about the original message. What mattered was that for twenty long years, Robert had insisted that the message was private. For him alone. It had nothing whatsoever to do with the Enclave.

And he was supposed to be a man of honour! That's what everybody always said. Robert Douglas – couldn't even bring himself to break his oath to the King. No, couldn't go about saving his own beloved country because it would betray his sense of honour. But he certainly could go on lying to people who were supposed to be his friends, people who relied on and trusted in him. But Robert's honour was nothing more than an abstract concept. When applied up close, he saw nothing wrong in breaking his own rules.

Wilf turned on the bed, trying to get comfortable, but there were lumps in the mattress and the pillows kept squeezing out from under his head. No matter which way he went he couldn't even get close to that cool dark place where sleep dwelled. The only comfort he could feel was the abstract touch of the Key.

'I did it wrong, didn't I?' he asked of the air, of the Key. He knew it wouldn't hear him, but continued anyway. 'I just wish I understood what you want from me. Am I supposed to lead these people or am I supposed to just stand by and watch as those two fulfil some prophecy I can't even comprehend?'

He lay there for a long time, simply not thinking. Then, his mind still wide awake even as his body craved rest, Wilf rose again and got dressed. He left his rooms and stepped out into the passage. He kept going until he reached the great cavern.

It wasn't empty. Two of his fellow councillors sat on a bench in the far corner, quietly chatting. People walked along the balconies, down the steps, across the floor. There were also two boys playing near the door of the chamber. They shouldn't be there, but Wilf said nothing to them. He just walked up to the Key and gazed at it for a long time. Then, his mind only half-focused, he spoke aloud.

'Well? If you can't give me what I want, what can you give me?'

The two in the corner stopped their conversation and looked at Wilf as though he were a madman. He paid them no attention. He just stood there, waiting. He would wait all afternoon – all night if he had to. Yes, that's exactly what he would do. Give the Key no choice but to speak to him.

And then it happened.

Like the passage of a cloud across the moon, the entire cavern went dark. Not pitch black, but a half-dazed grey, close to sleep, like the dreaming of a child. Wilf felt a pressure on his back, on his shoulders. It wasn't unbearable, but it did hurt. And there was a sound. No, lots of sounds. Something like voices chanting, but the words were meaningless, just noises out of the darkness.

Suddenly the grey was swept away by a searing light. Wilf fell to his knees, choking for air. It was too hot. Stifling, draining heat. Burning his throat, his eyes, the flesh from his bones. He gasped, unable to breathe. Then just as suddenly, it stopped.

He was looking down. On a room. Round, with walls so high the people standing there were tiny, like a circle of ants on a dirt floor. They were chanting. Wilf was stuck high above them, a hanging effigy. Then things began to move, slowly at first, but then faster and faster until he couldn't begin to take it in. Something appeared on the floor between the people. It was black and round, but before he could reach out and touch it, it was gone, the room with it. Once again he was beaten back by the heat and a sun so scorching it could incinerate him in seconds. Again images flashed by him too quickly to grasp and abruptly the darkness folded in on him again, cool now after the heat. Calm again like that other presence in his mind.

This was our beginning. We have shown you our birth. Be content, my chosen.

The Key.

Wilf opened his eyes to find he was still standing in the great cavern. The boys were still playing, his friends once more chatting. He opened his mouth to tell them what he'd seen, but the moment he moved, a great wave of dizziness knocked him down and he collapsed on the floor. There were cries of horror and faces peering over him. Wilf just smiled, closed his eyes again and let his body sink into sleep.

By the gods – what an incredible bore! Finnlay escaped the library barely awake, but at least Acelin had grudgingly accepted the proof of his sincerity. Now Finnlay could go back when he wanted and begin his research without Acelin asking unnecessary questions.

He ambled down one corridor after another until he reached a modest door in the older part of the caves. He knocked briefly. 'Jenn?'

'Come in, Finnlay.'

He opened the door – and came to a halt. Jenn was sitting on the bed, her back up against the wall. She had a blanket around her shoulders, her hair tossed over one shoulder, in a mess. She'd been asleep – but he hadn't woken her. Instead, her eyes were blank pits, staring at the floor as though looking into a great distance.

'What's wrong?'

She turned her head slightly. 'I don't know. I . . . just had the strangest dream. At least, I think it was a dream.'

He pulled up a chair and sat. 'Tell me.'

'I'm not sure I can. Some of it's so vague, while other

parts are terribly clear. I don't know . . .' Her voice trailed off. She sighed and began again. 'I was in a place I couldn't recognize. It was light and there were windows around the walls. Long windows much taller than me. The walls were red stone and very sharp – and yet the room was circular. I couldn't see a door from where I was. I think . . . I was on the floor. There were people standing around, in a circle.'

'How many?'

'Ten, perhaps fifteen. Some had their eyes closed, others were looking at me. It's really strange . . . I felt completely numb.' Jenn turned and looked at him quizzically, like he would be able to answer her questions. She blinked a few times and there was less of the blankness to her stare.

'This is so hard to describe. I was numb at first but as the dream went on, I began to feel things. Heat and dryness and the cold floor. After a while I could feel – no, sense – other things and that's when I started to hear the voices. A chant of some kind. I couldn't understand it.'

Finnlay reached over to a shelf by the fireplace and poured Jenn a cup of wine. She took it, drank and returned to her story. Now there was clarity in her gaze as though she was seeing the dream before her, as clear as the cave wall.

'I know it sounds stupid, but I could swear these people around me were pressuring me, just like the council did on my first night here. I couldn't move, couldn't speak. I just had to be there – not exactly sitting or lying or anything. I was just there. But the longer I was there, the more I could sense, the more I understood. I know after a while I could understand what the chant meant. I mean, it made sense in the dream to my dream self. Then . . .'

'What?'

Jenn glanced at him, then dropped her gaze. 'I remember one of the people started to gasp. He went red in the face, but the others did nothing. I don't think they could. The man fell to his knees in front of me, reached out to touch me – then died. And Finnlay . . .' She frowned, her pale face haunted by the memory. 'I think I killed this man.'

She was so caught up in her story, so wounded by the threatened reality, that there were tears in her eyes and her hands shook, spilling the wine. Finnlay moved forward, took the cup from her hands and knelt beside her, keeping a hold of her hand. 'It was just a dream, Jenn. You didn't really kill him.'

'But it feels like I did. And after that, everything changed. The people stopped chanting. Somebody came and picked me up and then I realized how small I was. But—' again Jenn's eyes changed, coming to life, '—I felt so powerful and I knew these people. Each one. They'd told me things, during the chanting, and now I knew everything they knew. Not just one mind but fifteen – and then, hundreds before them. Even the man who'd died.' Jenn stopped suddenly, holding her breath.

Finnlay waited. Eventually, Jenn glanced down to where their hands were joined, then up at him.

When she spoke again, her voice was firmer and her face had regained some of its colour. 'There's something else I just remembered. Finn, I don't think this was just a dream.'

'Why?'

'At the end, as I was being carried outside I heard this voice – but the voice wasn't inside the dream. It was like somebody outside the door.'

'What did it say?'

'*This was our beginning. We have shown you our birth. Soon you will show us our death.*' Jenn's eyes grew wide and for the first time since he'd met her, she looked terribly, terribly vulnerable. 'Finn, it was the Key speaking to me.'

The crackling fire put dancing shadows on the walls and burned away the ghosts of Jenn's story. Still, Finnlay felt haunted by something he couldn't name. Arlie and Patric had come and were even now asking Jenn questions. Fiona should have been here too, but after that scene in the library Finn couldn't bring himself to approach her again. After a while Arlie and Patric sat back and looked to Finnlay for answers.

His response was uncompromising. 'It seems there's already a link between you and the Key. I'm just glad Robert isn't here.'

'Oh, Finnlay!' Arlie groaned, 'surely you must see the importance of what's happened here? Jenn has never Stood the Circle and yet the Key can access her dreams as though she were Jaibir. More than that, we have before us the first eyewitness account of how the Key was formed. Until now we had only stories handed down through the generations and thrown together in sketchy records. For instance, I'd never heard that anyone died in the procedure, and from what Jenn says, the Key may have been responsible for his death.'

'Well, I have to say it answers a few awkward questions,' Patric said. 'Such as why the Key has an affinity with the Calyx. I know you'll all call me a fool, but I'll bet the man who was killed told the Key where the Calyx was hidden.'

'And so he had to die?' Jenn murmured.

'To keep the secret safe. Think about it. From what Jenn says, the Key was made by the combined powers of all those men, all their thoughts and memories. Apart from the power, the process would also have put into the Key a host of minute details never before collected together. One of those details could have been the whereabouts of the Calyx. What I want to know is what else the Key was told.'

'You mean the prophecy?' Arlie whispered.

'Exactly. The prophecy told us that Robert and Jenn were Bonded – without saying exactly what that meant. It revealed the fact that they could mindspeak – which they'd kept secret from the rest of us.' Patric glanced at Jenn in half apology before continuing, 'The prophecy called Jenn the Ally, Robert the Enemy and someone else the Angel of Darkness. They each have some sort of part to play in a destiny the Key claims Robert has been avoiding all his life. After Jenn's dream today, I think these creators may have given the prophecy to the Key.'

'But was it told in bits – or in one piece?' Arlie asked. 'It makes a difference. We've had lots of different prophecies over the centuries, but never one like this before. I was there. I heard the Key. The way it spoke, the patterns and every-thing – didn't sound much like prophecy to me. And this one was never written down, it seems. Perhaps this is why.'

Jenn reached out and put her hand on Arlie's arm. 'You mean it's possible that the Key has made this prophecy up, all of its own accord?'

Arlie shrugged. 'I don't know. It's just one theory.'

'And another theory,' Finnlay added, his voice low, 'is that the Key was given the prophecy as a whole – by the man who was killed. Perhaps it was kept secret all this time because ... because ...'

'What?' Patric asked dryly.

'Hell, how should I know? There are lots of prophecies – and most of them speak about some creature of evil.'

Jenn nodded. 'Remember that one we heard last year? From the hermit in Shan Moss? He said that a dark angel would come and tear the Church in two.'

Finnlay stared at her. She seemed completely ignorant of what she'd just said. She just turned to the fire and held out her hands, rubbing them together.

'A dark angel did come to Lusara and tear the Church in two.'

'Oh, who?'

'My brother.'

Jenn froze at that, then turned slowly. Finnlay continued, knowing they were all looking at him. 'It fits. We know the Key told Robert something dangerous. What if it told him he was the Angel of Darkness. And after all, the moment Selar heard about Robert's return, he threw McCauly in prison, effectively splitting the Church in two. And if you think about it – that could be the real reason why Robert would never Stand the Circle. If he'd been told something like that, he'd never put himself in the position where he would have that much power. It even explains why he refuses to stand against Selar.'

'Except that you're forgetting one thing,' Jenn said. 'The Key named three people. The Angel of Darkness, me as the Ally and Robert as the Enemy. Now I'm willing to concede Robert could indeed be the enemy of the Enclave – but we've no guarantee of that. Either way, Robert cannot be the Enemy and the Angel at the same time. Not in the same prophecy.'

Finnlay was about to argue, but at that moment, Patric sprang up and stood between them. 'No. Not Robert. The Angel is somebody else – but he does exist.'

'What do you mean?'

'The Angel of Darkness. Don't you see? If the Ally and the Enemy exist now – then the Angel must also. Here and now. I think ... I think that was the presence Jenn felt at court. Remember you said it was wholly evil?'

Jenn sucked in a horrified breath. 'And Ayn's gone there looking for him!'

It was barely dark this time, but it didn't matter. Jenn sat beside the bed and held his hand, monitoring his trance. The others kept back, watching, waiting. Finnlay could almost feel their dread. He couldn't tell what they feared more – his success or his failure. He'd broken all the old boundaries of Seeking when he'd seen Jenn riding up the mountain, but there was no guarantee he would find anything useful at all if he tried to stretch as far as Marsay. If he could just get a glimpse of Ayn's aura ...

He closed his eyes and let his body relax. Deeper and deeper he went, just allowing the process to form on its own. It was easier this time. Was it because Jenn was here, or because he'd already done this once?

Now he went out into the darkening sky. Out into the land he could visit only in this manner. He floated, soared, lingered. He kept no track of how far he went. There were no maps for this journey, no guides, no rules. Here, in this world, he was entirely free.

There, what was that? A presence? Yes. Down and down he went, spiralling towards an invisible quarry. Ayn!

In Marsay. She was standing in a room ... clutching something ... a cloak? But her face? Terror. Nothing less. By the gods, what was happening—

Ayn opened her mouth, screaming silently – then a mist formed as she sank to the floor—

—and Finnlay slammed back into his body so fast he almost blacked out.

'Finn!' Jenn urged, leaning over him. 'What happened?'

'I saw . . .' Finnlay struggled for air, then there was a cup brought to his lips, cold water going down his throat. He swallowed and dropped his head back to the pillow.

And then he told them. The whole vision. 'I think somebody destroyed her *ayarn*.'

Jenn glanced at the others. 'Do you know exactly where she was?'

'In a room somewhere. It looked like a tavern, though I could be wrong. There was a window behind her, but it was dark outside. Jenn,' Finnlay paused, grabbing her hand, 'we have to help her. This man, this sorcerer she was sent to find. He's got her. I know he has. And he's strong. Who else can destroy an *ayarn*?'

'Me?' Jenn shook her head. 'I'll have to go to Marsay.'

'Impossible!' Arlie strode forward. 'You can't risk it. Your training is incomplete, you've only just learned how to do a Mask. On top of that, you know nothing of combat skills and, forgive me, but your Seeking ability is low at best. If this man is as strong as he appears, he'll surely be an expert. Besides, your father is expecting you back home. It could take weeks before you find Ayn.'

'By which time she'll be dead!' Jenn snapped, coming to her feet.

'There is another option,' Patric ventured. 'Robert.'

'Yes!' Finnlay sprang off the bed, his mind whirling. 'Can you mindspeak him, Jenn? Tell him Ayn's in trouble? He could get to Marsay quicker than we could.'

She stared at him a moment, then nodded slowly. 'I'll try.' She sat again and they waited in silence. Soon however, Jenn shook her head. 'I'm sorry. I can't get through to him. I know he's there, but he can't or won't listen. Perhaps losing his *ayarn* has something to do with it. I don't know.'

She dropped her head, but Finnlay didn't need to ask. Robert had shut her out. How was he to know that this was important? If only he wasn't so damned stubborn.

'There's nothing else for it,' Patric murmured, a strange smile on his face. 'I'll have to go to Dunlorn and tell him. In person.'

As one, they all turned and looked at him. He gave them

a sheepish grin. 'Well, I always promised him I'd go and visit one day. I guess this is a perfect opportunity.'

'But you've never been off the mountain before,' Finnlay objected.

'Well, you can't go, can you? Nor can Jenn. Arlie would be in trouble the moment somebody saw his missing hand – and we can hardly expect Martha to spend three or four days in the saddle in her condition. I certainly don't want to mention any of this to Fiona yet, since we really have no evidence that Ayn's in trouble. I don't see that we have a choice – unless you want to try telling somebody else within the Enclave about all this.'

There was silence.

Finnlay coughed a little. 'I'm not happy about keeping it from Fiona. It's her mother we're talking about. She has a right to know.'

Jenn looked at him levelly but said nothing. Trying not to sound like he was making an excuse, Finnlay added, 'We brought her into this, Jenn. It's not fair to shut her out now.'

'And I'm sure she would take the news very calmly, not worry and do nothing rash or impulsive to fight something that was strong enough to defeat her mother.' Jenn's voice was gentle and Finnlay could only nod in response.

Then Jenn stood up and folded her hands together. 'Fiona's not returning to Elita with me, so I'll leave tonight and take Patric down the mountain. Once in the valley he should be all right. Finn, can you organize a map – and show him how to read it? He'll need a horse too. You can ride, can't you Patric?'

'I've practised a little, but only in the field up here. I'm afraid I'm not very good.'

'It will have to do. I also need one of you to give me some sort of history of sorcery. I'm sick of working in the dark.'

Arlie nodded. 'Leave it with me, Jenn. I'll get Martha to send you what you need via one of our couriers. I'll give you the details of how to unlock the code before you go.'

'Thank you,' Jenn nodded. 'Let's get moving.'

The others filed out of the room, leaving Finnlay alone with Jenn. He paused by the door, his hand on the latch.

'Are you sure you want to leave so soon? Anybody could take Patric down the mountain.'

Jenn began collecting her things together and stuffing them into a saddlebag. Her shoulders were stiff and her voice strained. 'I'm a bit worried about Fiona. If she gets wind of this she'll be worried sick.'

'Jenn,' Finnlay growled.

She stopped packing and slowly turned to face him, her eyes dark in the candlelight. She didn't look at him, but instead focused on the crackling fire. Again she looked tiny and vulnerable and, for a moment, utterly lost. 'I just don't know what to do, Finn. He won't talk to me. Not even with all this distance between us. Not even when it's so desperately important. He just won't talk to me.'

'There was a time when he wouldn't talk to me either,' Finn said. 'Don't worry, Jenn, he'll come back to you.'

'And in the meantime?'

'Have faith.'

7

Micah hefted the axe high in the air and brought it down with all the force his tired muscles could muster. The blade sank deep into the wood and stuck there.

Grunting, Micah pushed it back and forth until it came free, then pressed his thumb to the edge. With a sigh, he turned back to the shed, put a handful of water on the whetstone and began to sharpen the blade. Before he could finish, however, his ears were assaulted with childish screams of laughter and two young boys tore into the shed and immediately began chasing each other around his legs.

'Uncle Micah,' Peron, the youngest screeched, 'tell Savin to stop chasing me!' This was instantly punctuated by another yelp as Savin reached around Micah's knees for his brother's hair.

'All right, stop it, both of you!' Micah left the axe and swept an arm around each boy. In one movement, he picked them both up and carried them outside, struggling and kicking. He strode over to the well and laid the boys stomach down on the well wall, their heads hanging over the side. The screams of laughter echoed down the well as Micah continued, 'The more you struggle the more likely you'll fall in – and don't think I'll climb down there and rescue you. It's far too dark and dangerous for me. You'll miss your dinner and your mother won't know what's happened to you.'

'And what do you think you're doing to my sons?'

Micah glanced at Lanette as she came across the farmyard, a clay pitcher in her hands. The hot sun made her auburn hair light, her pale skin glow. She grinned and shook her head at him. Matching her smile, Micah turned back to the boys and leaned forward so they could hear his whisper. 'See what you've done? Now I'm in trouble too.'

Instantly the boys stopped struggling and Micah set them back on the ground. They took one look at their mother and scampered off into the field behind.

'They're supposed to be bringing the milk cows into the byre,' Lanette began, handing Micah the pitcher. 'But on a day like this, they'd rather be playing. As should you.'

Micah put the pitcher aside and drew some water up from the well. He took the bucket and emptied it over his head and bare chest. The sudden cold made him gasp and Lanette laughed at him.

'It's too hot to be chopping wood, Micah. Surely there is other work you could do around here to expiate your sin?'

With an ironic laugh, Micah took up the pitcher again and sat on the stone wall. 'Father won't let me do anything else and you know it. The only reason he allows this much is because of Mother.'

Lanette sighed and sat beside him. 'You should be grateful he gives you that much.'

'Grateful? You know he still hasn't said a single word to me since I returned. Not one. Not even a greeting.'

'What did you expect? A warm welcome? A return to the

fold? You were gone a long time, Micah. He needed you then and you weren't here. You were off with the Duke in distant lands for reasons Father cannot understand. Even less can he understand why you came back.'

'He's never given me the opportunity to explain,' Micah grunted, and drained the rest of the ginger beer. 'Every time I walk into a room, he leaves. Whenever I try to say something, he glares at me and walks off. How am I supposed to make him forgive me?'

Lanette reached out and touched his face, took his hand in hers. 'I'm not sure he can forgive you, my dear brother. I know you've tried hard all these months, but I'm not sure it will do any good. You were always his favourite, Micah. He watched you grow with such pride. Right up until the day the Duke took the King's oath. From that day onwards, you were in the service of a traitor and Father cannot forgive that. Your refusal to leave the Duke since has only made it worse.'

Why did it have to be so complicated? Why couldn't they just accept his decision? 'You're telling me I have to leave Dunlorn before Father will forgive me.'

'It would be the first step.' Lanette gave him a tentative smile. 'I'm sure he'd listen to you after that.'

'He would have me break my oath just to please him? I can't do that.'

'I'm sure the Duke would understand.'

'Of course he would,' Micah growled. 'He would release me instantly – but that's not the point. I don't want to leave his service. I believe in him.'

'But you see, that's the problem. Father cannot understand why you give your loyalty so freely to the Duke and not to the family. The Duke is loved by the people, even now. He has many powerful friends who'll stand by his side. You may believe he deserves your loyalty, but surely we are deserving too?'

'Why do you think I'm here now?' Micah frowned in the harsh glare of the midday sun. 'I'm trying to prove just that.'

'But tonight, when the sun sets, you'll leave us again and return to the castle. Every time you turn your back on this farm, you betray Father.' Lanette squeezed his hand. 'I want you to be reconciled, Micah. This has torn the whole family apart. Our brothers are too close to taking sides, and then there'll be no peace. Do you really want to see that happen? Surely it would be best if you left the Duke's service.'

Micah carefully released his hand from her grip and came to his feet. There was only one answer he could give, but she would never understand. 'I'm sorry, Lanny. I just can't.'

She was about to protest when her husband Ian came striding out of the farmhouse. 'Lanny? Is Micah ... Oh, there you are. You'd better come inside, Micah. There's somebody asking for you. A beggar, by the look of him.'

Lanette gave him an odd look, but rather than answer, Micah swept up his shirt and headed indoors. His eyes took a moment to adjust to the sudden darkness. When they cleared, he found his parents waiting by the hearth. Before them, draped over a stool, was a figure from the depths of poverty. A thin, ragged cloak lay over his shoulders, shrouded his head and was caked in mud, bits of straw and the gods knew what else. From his hunched shoulders and bare, bleeding feet, Micah guessed the man was exhausted.

'Can I help you?' Micah asked, moving forward.

At that moment, the man lifted his head and fixed his gaze on Micah.

'Patric!' Micah gasped, his breath taken completely away. 'But what . . .'

Patric's pale grey eyes spoke a silent warning; Micah sank to his knees, throwing a comment over his shoulder. 'It's all right, Father. I do know this man.'

David Maclean shook his head and turned away. 'Lanette, would you bring some ale and food. The stranger must be hungry.'

'Of course, Father.'

'No,' Micah murmured, studying Patric carefully. The bruises on his face, the cuts on his feet were real. This was no disguise. There was only one reason why Patric would leave the safety of the Enclave. He came to his feet with an apology. 'I have to get back now anyway. The Duke has a council meeting I must attend. I'll take my friend with me.'

Even as he said it he knew the damage those few words would inflict. His father had made the first move by offering hospitality to this odd friend, opening the door for Micah to share some part of his life with his family. But all Micah could do was deny his father the opportunity – slam that door back in his face. By taking Patric to Dunlorn, Micah would only re-open the wound that might have been healed.

With a sigh, he helped Patric to stand. Ian opened the door for them and held Micah's horse while Patric mounted. As they left the farm, Micah couldn't bring himself to look back. He already knew what he would see.

Subdued sunlight streamed across the floor of the council chamber from a sky overburdened with clouds. The morning's sun had disappeared but the heat remained, undiminished by the threatened storm.

Robert sat at the head of the table, his hands resting lightly on the papers laid out before him. All of his councillors were there, intent on the discussion, but Robert's attention strayed as he gazed around the familiar room. It had once been a royal bedchamber, sixty years ago when King Edward's grandfather had spent a summer at Dunlorn. Robert had long ago removed the bed and in its place had put this long ebony table.

The grey stone walls were hung with tapestries, one depicting a battle fought three hundred years ago in which a Douglas had been victorious. Beneath the twinned windows was a long wooden chest, carved in relief and dark with age. Beside the table lay the blue and gold carpet given him by Oliver as a wedding present. And over the fire—

The sword: resting on ornate oak arms within a scabbard of oiled black leather and gleaming silver. Trevor had died with that sword in his hand. Robert had fought the Sadlani in the north with that same blade. He had placed it, hilt-first, before Selar in vowing his allegiance. And when Berenice came he'd placed it over that fire, swearing it would not come down again except for battle – or to put in the hands of his son.

'What a mess,' he breathed.

'My lord?' Deverin paused and looked at him with a frown.

He'd spoken aloud – and now they were all looking at him, waiting for him to speak. But he had nothing to say. He couldn't even remember what they'd been discussing. But Deverin's frown abruptly dissipated and he nodded.

'I agree, my lord, it is a mess. In the last month, there've been only two sightings of raiding parties within our borders. The first was high on the moors in the northwest. Two weeks ago, they were seen again, this time in the south. If it is the same party, they've been travelling fast.'

'Any casualties? Damage?' Robert gave himself a mental slap and tried to focus on the subject; it was, after all, very important. At that moment, the door at the end of the chamber opened and silently, Micah slipped in. He said nothing, just stood by the door with his hands folded in front of him, his expression – for once – entirely unreadable.

Something was wrong.

'None reported, my lord,' Deverin continued with a glance in Micah's direction. 'These men may have just been passing through. I have had word from other places, however, where they continue to burn farms and villages. None of your manors have been touched. On the whole, I believe the problem is getting worse rather than better. That one success we had is the only one I've heard of. Nobody else has got close enough to find out where these men come from. They could just be the usual robbers and thieves roaming the countryside, but with more organization. I'm afraid I have no further ideas about what we can do.'

'Nor have I,' Robert replied grimly. 'Unless they strike again, we've nowhere to look. Keep up the patrols, Deverin, and let me know of any further movements.'

'Of course, my lord.'

'Any more business?' Robert glanced down the table but to a man, his council shook their heads. 'Then thank you all for your attendance.'

Chairs scraped on the stone floor as they all rose and filed out, murmuring to each other about the business of the day. As the last one left, Robert turned to Micah, his eyebrows raised in question. Micah raised a hand, motioning Robert to follow him.

They went out into the corridor and along to the spiral staircase at the end. Up one flight and they were at the door of Robert's study. Still Micah had said nothing. What was going on?

Micah opened the door and ushered him in. 'I'm sorry to do this to you, my lord, but it was necessary.'

'What was necessary?'

Micah almost smiled. 'You have a visitor.' With that he turned and indicated the chair by the fireplace. Sitting there was—

'Patric?' Robert bounded forward. 'By the gods, what are you doing here?'

Patric struggled to his feet, but he was obviously in some pain and immediately Robert pushed him back down.

'I'm just fulfilling a promise, my friend,' Patric replied with a smile. 'I swear though, by the look on your face, you didn't believe my word.'

Shock swept away Robert's earlier dark thoughts. 'No, I admit it. But . . . how did you get here? And what happened to you? Didn't you even ride?'

Patric held up his hands, 'I did to begin with, but yesterday I was beset by robbers. They took almost everything I had – including the map your brother gave me. I was forced to continue on foot and I got lost. All I could remember was your description of Micah's farm. I asked the way and, fortunately, found him. I didn't dare go about asking where I could find the castle of Dunlorn.'

Sinking to a chair opposite, Robert took in a deep breath. It was so strange seeing this face – in this room. They had always been so far apart, but now the two very different parts of his life had become twisted together, like strands of rope. 'Was it worth it?'

At this, Patric laughed. 'You live in a very strange world, Robert. So many people – the country is so big – I never dreamed . . .'

'Micah, could you organize some food and a bath – and some fresh clothes?'

'Of course, my lord,'

But Patric wasn't finished. He held up his hands again, his smile vanishing. 'Wait. I'm sorry, Robert, but this isn't entirely a social visit. I've come with some news and to beg your help.'

'My help?'

Patric nodded, his face clouding over. 'It's Ayn, Robert. She's been taken.'

'Ayn?' Robert's enthusiasm abruptly dried up. No – not that . . .

'Finnlay was trying a new method of Seeking in the hope of finding the Calyx. Instead, he got a clear vision. He saw Ayn in terror, her *ayarn* destroyed. At the end, she collapsed unconscious. He's positive that the man who did it is the one she was looking for. When I left the Enclave, Finnlay was certain Ayn was still alive.'

Robert sprang to his feet, his left hand automatically flexing to release his *ayarn* – but he didn't have it any longer. He strode to the window, pushed the shutters wide and flung his senses out across the land. Where was she? She had to be alive. She had to be.

'I . . . can't tell . . . without her *ayarn*, I may not even be able to find her.' He drew back in and snapped an order. 'Micah, have Deverin prepare my horse, food for the journey. I'm going to Marsay.'

Micah frowned, but he knew better than to argue. As the door shut behind him, Robert turned back to Patric. 'All right. What else have you got to tell me?'

'That's it.' Patric said, pulling off the filthy cloak.

'Oh?' Robert raised an eyebrow. 'You've always been a terrible liar, Pat. Tell me the rest. What's this new method of Seeking my brother was attempting? How did he manage a proper vision? Why is he certain that it's accurate?'

'Because . . .' Patric began – shot Robert an apologetic look and paused.

'Well?'

'He . . . tried it the night before and got a vision of Jenn coming up the mountain.'

'Jenn? She went to the Enclave?' Robert's breath faded away and he sank into the nearest chair.

'Don't worry, Robert. She didn't go near the Key. Finnlay kept his promise. She left with me, showed me how to get down the mountain. She'll be back home in a few days. She was quite safe the whole time, really. You've got nothing to worry about.'

'Worry? You have no idea what you're talking about! Every time she goes near the Key she's in danger. What was she trying to do, going to the Enclave like that?'

Patric shrank further into his seat and swallowed loudly. 'She needed help. Apparently Fiona couldn't teach her some important things: setting a Seal, making a Mask. Finnlay showed her before we left. He had no trouble at all and . . .'

'And?' Robert prodded. Did he really want to hear the rest?

'By the gods, Robert,' Patric shook his head and stiffly leaned forward, 'I just wish I knew what was going on with all this. Finnlay taught Jenn these things so quickly you'd think she was already a master. She's amazing. She faced down the council when they wanted to force her to take the oath. But I have to tell you, warn you, really. Finnlay didn't want me to say anything, but Jenn herself said I should. She said that if we were all going to work together you must always be told the truth. Of course, I had to agree, but I also think Finnlay had a point. I'm not sure you really want to know all this, do you?'

Patric was rambling – probably with exhaustion, but also because he was avoiding something. Robert didn't even want to guess what it was. Three shocks in one day was enough for any man. Still, it had to be done. 'Go on. Tell me.'

Taking another deep breath, Patric said, 'Wilf threatened to throw Finnlay out of the Enclave and banish Jenn if she didn't take the oath. Like an old warrior, she refused to be threatened but . . . in return for Wilf's co-operation she vowed to Stand the Circle next time.'

No.

Like the first breath of winter, Robert trembled with an icy shiver and he could feel the demon shake within him. If she Stood the Circle . . . if she did that . . . Oh yes, she would be Chosen. And then . . . then . . . he would have to stand against her.

'Serin's blood!' It was all going wrong: the whole point of his sacrifice, his banishment. He'd given up the Enclave so this very thing would never happen. He was Jenn's only real link with the Enclave and he'd been so sure that with him gone, she would never go back.

He had to see her, talk to her, find some way for her to renounce her vow . . .

But – how could he, of all people, try to talk someone out of a solemn oath?

Then how else to stop her?

A knock at the door and Micah entered with Deverin close behind. Robert stood, put a reassuring hand on Patric's shoulder and turned to face them.

'Your horse is ready, my lord,' Micah said quietly. 'I suggest however, you may want to leave after sunset.'

'I agree.' Robert felt as pale as the veiled sun. 'Deverin, would you take my friend to a room near my own. Take good care of him, he's had a hard journey.'

Deverin nodded and helped Patric out of the room. Micah closed the door behind them and once again waited patiently. Robert moved back to the window and gazed out.

So much of this room was exactly as his father had left it. The warm oak panelling, the thick padded chairs by the fireplace, the bookshelves by the door. No fewer than four windows completed the gallery, looking out on to the court-yard and the moor beyond. On a clear night he could often see a glow in the sky from the town of Loch Feer, half a league away. On market days when the wind was southerly, he could smell the bread being baked, the smoked fish on sale.

Closing his eyes, Robert relaxed his breathing and let his senses drift out of the room high in the tower. Behind him he could sense the empty space hidden behind the panelled wall and the secret passage which led out of the castle. This was how he'd first found the room, some sixteen years ago. Wandering in this study when his father had been out, he'd toyed with his powers and caught the feeling of vacancy behind the fireplace. It had taken him three days to work out the lock on the panel, with Finnlay's help. The room beyond was a nightmare of cobwebs and broken furniture. No windows, but instead, another door leading to a damp spiral staircase. At the bottom was a tunnel.

He'd used that exit before, to get Finnlay out to the Enclave when his powers had first manifested. They'd only been back a week before Selar had come. What would have happened if Selar had come and Robert had not been there?

'You said you would never go back to Marsay.'

Robert started. He'd forgotten Micah was standing there. 'No, you can't go with me. Not this time.'

Micah shrugged and moved over to stand beside the window, his shoulder leaning against the stone support. 'It was just an idea. Do you think you'll find her?'

'I don't know. I only hope she's still alive when I get there.'

'And if Finnlay is right? What if it is this rogue sorcerer who's taken her? What will you do then?'

Robert frowned and glanced at Micah. 'If he is evil as Jenn said, and if he has destroyed Ayn's *ayarn* – then surely he must be the Enclave's enemy – not me.'

Micah shrugged again. 'Well, perhaps we don't fully understand what the Key means by enemy. If you find him, you'll fight him, won't you? I should come with you.'

'You can't. This is too dangerous. Besides, I need you here. My mother sent word she would be returning tomorrow. You'll have to find some excuse for my absence. On top of that, you're the only one I can trust to look after Patric. Keep him out of trouble. You're bigger and stronger than he is – he'll do what you tell him. If he doesn't . . .'

'I'll throw him in the dungeon.'

Robert laughed involuntarily. 'We don't have a dungeon!'

'I can arrange something.' Micah smiled briefly, then lapsed into silence. His eyes turned towards the window, his thoughts obviously elsewhere.

Yes, there was something wrong – and it wasn't just

Patric's sudden appearance. Robert turned to the table and poured them both some wine. 'Your father?'

'Aye,' Micah said, taking the cup. 'My father. Lanette thinks if I left your service he would at least listen to me.'

'Then,' Robert hesitated only a moment, 'you must go.'

'Either that or you must take arms against Selar.'

'Which you know I won't do.'

'And you know I won't leave.' Micah folded his arms and turned a troubled gaze out the window. 'You're not the only one who's stubborn, my lord. Given enough time, my father will see the truth – I'm sure of it. He's just waiting to see how determined I am.'

'Then he's already fighting a lost cause. Perhaps I should write to him and tell him what a nuisance you are in that regard.'

Micah fought it, but his smile won. Before he could reply, there was a discreet knock at the door and they turned to find Deverin standing there.

'Is something wrong?'

'No, my lord. I . . . er, just wanted to ask you something,' Deverin began, clasping his hands in front of him. 'Something of a personal nature.'

It was obvious that the big man was bothered about something. Robert glanced at Micah, but he was equally mystified. Nodding, Robert closed the door and turned back. 'Go on.'

'I would know, my lord,' Deverin spoke quietly and carefully, 'how I have failed you that you no longer trust me.'

Robert frowned, completely thrown. 'Failed me?'

'Aye, my lord. I've done my best to serve you, but I know I have had little effect on those raiders. Is that the problem?'

Robert shook his head. 'I don't understand, Deverin. Why do you think I don't trust you?'

Suddenly uncomfortable, Deverin shot a glance at Micah before replying, 'I know what you did, my lord. When Governor Osbert was here. It was Micah in that casket, not Lord Finnlay. I don't understand how you did it, but I do understand why.'

'You do?' Robert asked faintly. Why did the world suddenly feel like it was spinning around him, out of control?

'Aye, my lord,' Deverin nodded with subtle confidence. 'You are a sorcerer.'

A failure, incompetent – and now a fool into the bargain. He should have seen this coming. He should have known Deverin would have put the pieces together. By the gods, what an idiot!

Robert walked to the end of the table. 'It is I who have failed you, Deverin. I should never have placed you in a position where you could guess the truth. My only excuse is that I was not thinking clearly. If I'd had time to prepare before the Guilde arrived, we could have buried the casket before Osbert got here and then no Guilde law in the country could have opened the grave. I am sorry.'

'No, my lord,' Deverin grunted. 'You did what you had to do. I would rather that than go on believing that Lord Finnlay is dead. As it is, I know he's safe.'

With a smile, Robert asked, 'And how do you know that?'

'You wouldn't have left him otherwise.'

Robert nodded and glanced at Micah. 'So what do I do now? He's too big to beat into submission.'

'Well,' Micah replied, folding his arms with something like a self-satisfied smile on his face, 'I can't offer you any suggestions, my lord. You know I can't say anything about this in front of him. You also know why.'

'Which in itself is a suggestion, right? But I don't know if I can Seal him. Without an *ayarn* . . .'

'May I respectfully remind you, my lord, of something you're always telling me? You don't know everything.'

Deverin was staring at them both, unable to comprehend either the conversation – or Micah's lack of respect. It was time to put him out of his misery.

'I should really ask you if you want to do this, Deverin.'

'Do what, my lord?'

'There's a process I can perform, to protect you from the knowledge you hold. It's called a Seal and Micah has just displayed how useful it is. He's completely unable to mention anything about my powers in front of anyone who's not also

Sealed. That way you can't say anything by accident – nor be forced to admit the truth. Of course, it also protects me in the process, but whereas I might one day be found out, you'll always be able to say you knew nothing about it.'

'Very well, my lord.'

Robert frowned and took a step closer. 'I have to ask this – are you not bothered by all this? You've known me a long time. Doesn't it worry you to find out that I'm a sorcerer?'

'Why should it? You are a good man, my lord. This power is no better or worse than the way you wield a sword. You've never used that for ill – and I bear the scars to prove it. I trust you to use your other weapons in the same way.'

If only everybody in Lusara could have the same attitude. The Enclave could open up, Finnlay could come home and sorcerers could once again walk the country without the threat of certain death. All this could be achieved without ever finding the damned Calyx. Hell, that would really make Finnlay's day!

'I warn you, serving a sorcerer is no easy task. Just ask Micah. No, don't bother, he can't answer you. At least, not yet.' Robert held out his hand, hoping he could empower the sequence without the aid of his *ayarn*. Deverin glanced once at Micah, then reached out and touched Robert's hand.

Robert felt nothing different to the way a Seal usually felt – but that was no guarantee of success. 'Micah? You're the best test I have handy. Go on, say the magic word.'

'Oh? Which one is that?' Micah tried his best to look innocent. 'Could you perhaps mean the Enclave?'

'That's the one!' Robert laughed and clapped the bemused Deverin on the shoulder. 'Congratulations. You're now one of the damned.'

Deverin was smiling now and shaking his head ferociously. 'I don't think so, my lord. Far from it. However, I should warn you that you may have to go through this ... process again quite soon. I think old Owen may have put a few pieces together himself.'

'Has he said anything?'

'Not directly. I can sound him out if you like.'

'Go ahead, Deverin.' As the big man reached the door,

Robert added, 'And since you asked – I've always trusted you.'

Deverin bowed. 'Thank you, my lord. If you'll permit me, the feeling is entirely mutual. I'll wait with your horse. If you go out with our patrol tonight, no one will think it unusual.'

8

Selar paced up and down, dragging his robe behind him. The candles had burned low, leaving thick yellow lumps of wax on the table by the bed. Every time he turned, they shimmered and jumped, but they never spoke back. Just like his court. Back and forth he paced, with such precision he could almost predict how the candles would flicker. They were so pathetic. One blow would send them flying. One puff of air would extinguish them for ever. His power over them was complete, his dominance total.

Osbert had said Finnlay was dead. He saw the body with his own eyes. There was no sorcery in Lusara. Those woodsmen had been drunk, the villagers fooled. There was nothing for Selar to worry about. The little stone they'd kept was nothing. Completely useless. He'd even given the ring back to Robert. It was now surely buried with the boy's body, deep beneath the stones of that pretty chapel at Dunlorn. No sorcery . . .

So why couldn't Selar sleep? Why were his dreams so invaded with images he wanted to forget? Why did Carlan's face keep reappearing? The old traitor was dead. He had to be now, fourteen years later. Nobody had seen him, heard of him, since the night of the battle. He had disappeared. He had already been old, probably past eighty. How could he be alive now?

Well, he wasn't. That's all there was to it. And these dreams were just some part of his memory resurfacing with those rumours of sorcery. Now that Osbert had declared them dead, he would be able to sleep. Perhaps not tonight, but soon, when the truth sank in. Yes.

Selar stopped pacing and sat on the end of his bed. He should call Nash and get the man to make him one of those potions to help him sleep. At least they worked. But how long could he keep doing that? What would happen to his authority if his court discovered he was so close to breaking? How could he keep control if he was always afraid to shut his eyes at night?

He had to lay the ghost of Carlan to rest. He had to make sure the old magician was not now working against him. He could have survived, changed sides and befriended Tirone. Together they could be behind these raiders, deliberately destabilizing the country in preparation for an invasion.

But there were no troops along his borders. No escalation of hostilities and nothing his informants could tell him was proof that Tirone was ready to invade Lusara.

There were just the nightmares: the night of his triumphant battle, his mentor, Carlan, had gone missing. Selar found him by the river. Then Carlan admitted he was a sorcerer. His wizened face leered over Selar, laughing at him, devouring him. Selar would become Carlan's tool, his zombie, mindless, obedient. He'd known that in a moment. He'd felt such an overwhelming stench of evil he'd stepped back, his foot slipping on the muddy river bank.

Then Carlan had pushed him in.

Then he'd almost drowned.

Then Robert, a mere boy, had saved him, not knowing the man he saved was . . .

The nightmare was always the same. In truth, Robert had saved his life – but in the dark depths of his sleepless nights, the boy's face turned into a twisted copy of Carlan's. Selar would never be free of him. Never . . .

Selar stood, walked the length of the room and opened the chest with the ivory inlay. He lifted out two flasks of wine and went back to bed. There was one other way he could make sure he slept tonight.

*

118

The past, like a demented beast, came back to haunt him every step of the way. From the high moors of Dunlorn, across the flat fields of harvested wheat and once again into the hills. Every league he travelled brought him closer to Marsay. As his horse climbed the final plateau which would eventually drop down to the river Vitala, he found it more and more difficult to believe the last four years had gone at all. In three weeks it would be the anniversary of Berenice's death: a few days after that would mark the day he had left Lusara, determined never to return.

And now here he was, stealing his way back into the city in exactly the same way as he'd left it. Under cover of darkness, in disguise and unseen by anybody.

The irony of it all was laughable.

Godfrey hurried through the torchlit courtyard, trying to keep up with Payne. 'Are you sure about this?' he murmured, nodding to a passerby.

'Positive,' Payne said without checking his pace. 'There's almost no way to get to him without Selar's permission, let alone get him out. You've seen the cell, you know where it is. The whole idea of a rescue is out of the question unless Selar decides to move him. It's just too dangerous. Too many things could go wrong.'

Godfrey reached the door and pushed it open, waiting for Payne to enter first. 'Then you can't help.'

'I didn't say that. Just give us some time. With Hilderic on his way to a retreat in a week or so, there's no urgency.'

With a sigh, Godfrey shook his head. 'That's assuming I can get Hilderic to actually leave. You have no idea the pressure we've had to put on him to go. Fortunately the other Archdeacons are adamant – and completely impervious to every argument Hilderic comes up with – and there've been a few.'

'He's a tough one, that's certain.' Payne paused long enough to flash Godfrey a smile of encouragement. 'Don't worry. We'll find a way to solve the other problem – if I have to forge the papers, myself.'

*

'Well?'

Nash glanced sideways at Valena as she poured water out for him to wash his hands. Her eyebrows were raised in question, her sensuous lips pursed in apparent disapproval. Despite the fact that it was his money which paid for this house, Valena moved around it as though it were her own private castle, and he were just a guest.

'He'll be looking for me. I have to go,' Nash replied, plunging his hands into the cold water. Immediately the bowl became stained, but he took no notice.

'Don't you ever get tired of playing the faithful servant?' Valena murmured, handing him a linen towel.

'Don't you?'

'I'm not your servant, Nash!' Valena snapped back. Abruptly she smiled, 'Oh, I see – you do like it. You love running here and there at his every command. Your tail wags like a little puppy every time he so much as glances in your direction. Oh, how it must feel to be wanted so, needed and loved so by a King. Most men only aspire to a glimpse – perhaps even an audience. But not my Samdon. No, you want to be his . . .'

'Stop it!' Nash reached out and snatched her hand, drew her laughing into his arms. 'Why do you delight in provoking me? Do you love danger so much?'

'Why,' she murmured sweetly, 'it is because you are so easy to provoke. You're so sensitive whenever I mention Selar. Even more these days. I cannot help wondering . . .'

'Then don't. You know why I need Selar.'

'Yes, yes, I've heard it all before. But we're no closer, are we? Even now.' Valena reached up and placed her fingers over his lips, deliberately teasing. 'It's quite an achievement to have Osbert eating out of your hand, but after seeing Finnlay's body with his own eyes, it couldn't have been too difficult to convince him to underplay the situation at Kilphedir.'

Nash frowned and disengaged her hands from his body. 'We've still got problems. Selar's deteriorating slowly, Vaughn is begging to be allowed a witch-hunt and Osbert is no closer to making Proctor than he was a year ago.'

'But surely the Guilde realizes how unstable Vaughn is?'

'They may realize it but they're all equally terrified of sorcery. One breath of it and they panic. They want a pogrom – and in his current mood, Selar might just say yes.'

Valena stepped back. 'Then you have to stop him!'

Nash held up his hands, quietened her before Keith downstairs could hear. 'Osbert's report has given us a few extra days – however, it does mean that I'll have to take the next step with Selar. I've been putting it off, but I don't think I can afford to much longer. He must be made to realize the consequences of a hunt for sorcerers.'

It was hopeless. No matter how many people John asked, no matter how deep into the city he travelled, no one had heard or seen anyone going by Ayn's description. He'd quizzed all his contacts, walked the halls of every hospice and tavern in search of her, but she'd disappeared. After two weeks, it was impossible to believe he would find her – alive or dead. There hadn't even been any pauper's funeral for a woman looking like Ayn.

Disconsolate, John headed back to Murdoch's little shop. The street was dark. Unseen, he slipped through the front door and made his way up the stairs to the dwelling rooms above. He knocked once and opened the door.

'John!' Murdoch was standing in the centre of the room. 'I hadn't expected you tonight.'

His friend looked startled, but it wasn't until John had closed the door and come further into the room that he saw why. Murdoch had a guest. The man stood by the window, the shutters open a crack. He was looking out and hadn't moved when John came in.

John opened his mouth to apologize – then stopped abruptly. The stranger . . . that face . . . familiar, and yet . . .

'In Serin's name!' John breathed, clasping his hands together.

At this, the stranger turned his head away from the window, smiled and shook his head. 'I'm afraid you're mistaking me for someone else, Father. I apologize for startling you. If it makes you feel any better, Murdoch here

121

went white when I walked into his shop tonight. I don't know, you men working here in the city, day after day, I'd have thought you'd be used to a few surprises now and then.'

Murdoch took John's arm and steered him to a chair, placed a cup of warmed wine in his hand. 'Perhaps I should introduce you two. Father John Ballan, meet Robert Douglas, Earl of . . .'

'Dunlorn and Duke of Haddon.' John nodded violently, almost spilling his wine. 'I'm sorry, I just never thought I'd meet . . .'

Dunlorn raised his eyebrows, producing a curious mixture of expressions. There was irony there and self-mockery, too. But something else as well. John tried to pull his thoughts together. Of all the people he had expected to find here, Robert Douglas was definitely not one of them.

'John?' Murdoch prodded, 'were you out searching? Did you find anything?'

'What?' John murmured, unable to take his eyes from Dunlorn. For some reason, he'd expected Robert to look more like his brother, but the differences were, upon examination, both stark and yet subtle at the same time. Sure, the basic features were the same, but Robert was a handspan taller than Finnlay, his shoulders broader and more powerful. But that wasn't all. The face itself was different, more solid – yes, a little older – but also more . . . oh, it was impossible to put a name on it.

The eyes, however, spoke volumes. The deepest green John had ever seen, now glinting with reflected candlelight. They watched John with a combination of curiosity and wariness.

As though sensing John's unease, Dunlorn smiled again, left the window and came across the room. He gave Murdoch a gentle nudge, then pulled a chair out from the table, faced John and sat. 'I've come to find Ayn, Father. I believe she's still alive. Have you seen anything, heard or sensed anything that might help me?'

Dunlorn hadn't taken his eyes from John, but the gaze had changed again, now deeply intense. 'No, I'm sorry. I've been out every night now, but I've no idea where she might be. I was about ready to give her up for dead. How do you know you can find her? How do you know she's alive?'

Suddenly John felt like a fool. Here he was, sitting in the same room with the most powerful sorcerer ever to walk the lands of Lusara, a legend on the battlefield, a hero to the people, a former King's councillor and peacemaker in the country – and John was asking damn stupid questions!

He blushed and tore his eyes away. Fortunately, Murdoch came to his rescue.

'I don't understand, Robert. We sent young Ben back to the caves only two days ago. He wouldn't even be there yet. How did you find out about Ayn?'

Dunlorn shrugged and reached out for the jug of wine. 'It doesn't matter. If I were you though, I'd keep my appearance here quiet. I'm not exactly welcome at the Enclave these days.'

Murdoch nodded slowly. 'Yes, Ayn told us what happened. But you're here to rescue her. Surely that makes a difference?'

'We'll worry about that after I find her. In the meantime, I need you to tell me everything. Had she sensed anyone yet? The man she was looking for. Did she know where to look?'

Robert's voice was low but determined. John burned to question him, ask him all sorts of things – but there was no time. Instead, he told everything he knew, Murdoch filling in the remaining details. At the end, Dunlorn sat back, drained his cup and placed it back on the table.

When he said nothing, John took a deep breath and said, 'Do you know about Baron Blair?'

But Murdoch interrupted, 'He knows, John, he knows.'

'Oh.'

Robert said nothing, only ran his finger around the rim of his empty cup. Murdoch frowned at the silence, glanced once at John, then said, 'Well, what do you think? Is there any hope? Will you be able to find her?'

'Oh, I'll find her, I promise you,' Robert replied standing up. He moved back to the window and nudged the shutter open again. 'At the moment, however, I'm more concerned about what else I'll find. After all, Ayn didn't just disappear on her own, did she? Somebody has her – and that somebody

123

doesn't want to let her go. How many people in the city like that can there be?'

Selar strode across the courtyard; Vaughn, shorter and older, scurried to catch up, but Selar kept going. There were going to be no further arguments from the Proctor today. A constant barrage over breakfast and a further hounding as Selar dressed for his ride was enough for any man. Perhaps a few hours in the dungeons beside McCauly would cool Vaughn's ire for a bit.

He wanted to seek them out, hunt them down and kill the last of them.

Sorcerers.

Despite what Osbert had reported, Vaughn believed there were more of them. Everywhere. But the idiot had no idea what he was letting himself in for. All he had to go on was superstition, hearsay and a pile of jumbled history both unreliable and unsubstantiated.

But Selar knew.

Was it possible that Osbert's investigation had failed to bring out the truth? Had even Nash, the most perceptive of Guildesmen, missed the vital clues that would lead them to an answer? The whole Kilphedir story was fantastic – but it could also be a sign. After so many years, just when Selar was laying the seeds for war, a story surfaces of sorcery within his borders.

And what if Carlan was behind it? What if his evil powers had let him live so long? What if he'd been waiting around, hiding and planning?

Perhaps it was time to give Vaughn what he wanted – but not this morning. Right now, all Selar wanted was a little peace.

Selar reached his horse, glanced a greeting at Nash, then swung up into the saddle. Deliberately, he waited until Vaughn was almost with them and then he kicked the flanks of his mount and cantered off towards the gate. Nash and the guard followed behind.

It was yet another hot and sultry day, the last of the summer squeezing out sunshine like juice from an apple.

The city stank, a polluted and rotting carcass beached on the shores of the Vitala. He was glad to be rid of it – if only for a few hours.

The hills were cooler, browned by the sun and forgiving. As the land opened up before him, he let the clean air soak into his flesh. As he had practised over the last few weeks, he allowed the pounding rhythm of the horse and the wind blowing through his hair to wipe away the cobwebs of his sleepless night, the effects of the wine – and the nightmare.

He slowed as they dropped into a narrow valley where four or five trees drank the life from a struggling stream. He left the soldiers above, keeping watch, and jumped down from his horse. Nash joined him, his faithful, undemanding companion.

'Vaughn won't leave it alone, you know.'

Selar wandered down to the water's edge, then glanced over his shoulder at Nash. The young man was dressed sombrely in brown trousers and a deep green jacket. He never liked to draw attention to himself by dressing in gaudy colours – or in rich cloth. Simple clothes suited him, too. That sharp angular face, half-hidden by a beard, those black silent eyes, always watchful. Very little passed this man entirely unnoticed.

'I enjoy turning him down,' Selar replied with a shrug. 'It's his own fault. He's too excitable. Saying no to him is one of the few pleasures I have left. Now he has hours to wait until I return. He should be well stewed by then.'

'So, you intend to give him permission?'

Those eyes were watching him carefully. 'Vaughn says he knows things – ways to tell if a man is a sorcerer. He could be exaggerating, but even so, I don't think he would make the claim if he couldn't back it up. Either way, I don't want sorcerers wandering around my country!' Selar caught himself up, took a breath. If only it could be that simple. Perhaps that could be his cure. If he burned them all away, then wouldn't that burn away the memory of Carlan?

'Sire,' Nash interrupted his thoughts so softly, Selar hardly noticed. 'What if I told you your court already has a sorcerer?'

What was the man talking about? 'What do you know? Tell me! Now!' demanded Selar.

Nash appeared completely relaxed – but that only meant he was trying to hide something. 'Please, Sire. Be calm. I will tell you all.'

'I am calm,' Selar said through gritted teeth.

Nash continued, 'There is one who has the powers you seek. But he is no enemy to you. He's been with you some time and has proved his loyalty.'

'Who is it, damn you?'

Nash's face was completely devoid of expression. He stood so his back was to the guards above and brought his hands together. He then drew them apart and between them crackled tiny arcs of lightning. 'I am a sorcerer, Sire, but I am not evil.'

Selar gaped, his heart racing. He was frozen to the spot, unable to take his eyes from those black pits. 'You . . . a sorcerer?'

Nash said nothing, but dropped his hands. He made no move towards Selar. He just stood there waiting.

For what? What, in the name of the gods . . .

'What do you want from me?' Selar gasped. Should he call the guards down, now? Would Nash be powerful enough to overcome them? In the name of Serin, Nash could kill him where he stood!

'I desire only to serve you, Sire.'

'What kind of answer is that?' Selar spat, anger now reaching out to drown his terror. He took a step backwards, shot a glance at the guards on the hill. They'd noticed nothing. Would they come to his rescue if he called? He turned his attention back to Nash. There was still no threat – merely patience. He must think Selar would just accept this revelation and let him remain at court. Taking another breath, Selar sneered, 'And what would you do if I threw you in prison, eh?'

'I would go wherever you sent me, Sire.'

'Then get out of my sight! Out of my city, my country. You have lied to me. You've betrayed me just like every friend I've ever had. You claim to be better than the others, but you're worse – not even Dunlorn kept something like this from me. If you mean what you say about serving me, obeying me, you will do as I say and leave Marsay and never return!'

Yes, this was the city he remembered. It had hardly changed. Sure, after a day of wandering around in the borrowed robes Murdoch had given him, Robert had seen some differences. But on the whole, four years had done little to this city. The people, on the other hand, had changed. There was something decidedly brittle about the way they laughed, the easy way they quarrelled, the wary step of every man who passed the castle gates.

In the more commercial areas, there was wealth and prosperity – but the names above the shops were not Lusaran. These were traders who had come here in the wake of Selar's conquest, happy to make the most of this new market, of the laws which favoured them. Down by the walls, along the older parts of the city the division was clearer still. Here, beggars vied for space in the narrow streets, frequently trampled under the bustle of visiting tradesmen, courtiers and Guildesmen. A few taverns, shops and the odd market still survived – but there were also many derelict buildings, vacant windows and collapsed roofs. Some had even been burned out. One, a farrier Robert had once favoured, was shut up completely, its windows boarded up for some time. The butcher next door was reduced to selling a few scraps. In this forgotten part of the city, existence was eked out by the grace of the gods alone. No earthly help was forthcoming.

Robert didn't actively Seek Ayn. He had to get to know the city again, feel for its warmth, its weaknesses. The best place for this was the old haymarket. With the heavy rains, grain prices had soared and the bidding was desperate. Fights broke out every few minutes and the city guard did little to stop them. Robert kept to the sidelines, hunched over in his forest-green cape and matching cap. When he walked, it was with a deliberate limp, his face grimy and muddied. It was unlikely anybody would recognize him – even if he were to go near the castle – but there was no point taking chances.

He wandered the perimeter of the market, listening to the odd conversation here and there, just like he had done years before. It was the best way to find out how the people felt and thought. But even here, their conversation was stifled, as though they feared the Guilde was listening to every word.

He was about to leave the market when a rider came up the alley. He was moving too fast and was immediately jostled by the crowd. The horse reared and backed away, forcing Robert up against the wall. Somebody shouted a warning and the horse reared again, throwing its rider.

The man fell in a heap at Robert's feet and he could do nothing less than help him up.

Fury boiled in him like iron in a furnace, searing, white and blinding. First Selar's banishment and now this damned market chaos; he was ready to burn them all. Nash kicked his horse forward, but there was no room. The stupid animal reared in panic, scattering people in every direction. He fought to control it, but only made it worse. He felt his feet slip from the stirrup and he tumbled to the ground. Instinctively he rolled away, but then a pair of hands grabbed him, pulled him to his feet.

'Are you all right, sir?' his helper asked.

'Yes,' Nash snapped without looking. Instead he reached out and grabbed the reins, sending his senses forward to calm the animal as he should have done before. He turned back to thank the stranger, but he'd disappeared, his cloak a mere splash of green in the throng. Swearing, Nash pulled his horse out of the square and back along the alley. He took a longer route, but finally arrived at the little house, his mood no better – in fact, much worse.

The demon was coming again. She could feel him. He was outside even now, invading her senses, shutting everything else out. The others didn't know yet. The boy, the woman. They couldn't tell when the demon was near, but Ayn could. Like a wrenching of her flesh, tearing her apart piece by piece, she could feel him come nearer. Any moment now he would come close, close enough to touch her, close enough to torture her again.

A door slammed somewhere above. Feet scattered down the stairs. Another door opened, crashed back against the wall.

The demon spoke. 'He's banished me!'

'Why?' the woman answered, 'what did you do?'

'I revealed myself. Now he wants me gone. Blasted fool!' This seething fury rattled against Ayn's bones. With her eyes blind, all she had left were her ears – and her too-heightened senses. Why couldn't the demon just let her die?

'I thought you said you knew how to handle him this time?' the woman cried, horrified. 'How can you have ruined everything a second time? What were you thinking of?'

There was wood scraping as the demon replied, his voice rising, 'He wants to set Vaughn free on a witch-hunt! I was trying to stop him. He thinks Carlan is still alive.'

'But he is.'

'Selar doesn't know that – and he won't – not until it's too late. No,' the demon paused, his voice dropping so low Ayn wouldn't normally be able to hear it. Now, however, she could hear everything. Too much. 'No, he's just terrified. But it's not sorcery he's afraid of – only Carlan. The more his fear controls him, the more he'll feel alone. In the end, he'll remember that I was his friend. He'll call me back.'

'And if he doesn't?'

'He needs me. Just like he needed Carlan. He's not a man who can live his life entirely alone. He was always like that – that's why I chose him in the first place.'

The woman laughed, an ugly sound in the darkness. 'And he still doesn't know, does he? That the man he's so terrified of and the man who has become his closest friend are one and the same? You didn't tell him that, did you? You didn't tell him that you are Carlan?'

'No, of course not! Enough of this. I haven't got much time – perhaps an hour before he sends soldiers to make sure I'm gone. I must squeeze some truth out of the old woman before I go. Keith can get rid of her tonight, after we've both gone. Make it late. Have him take her downriver and dump her body. I don't want anyone in the city finding she's been murdered. After that, I suggest you stay low for a while. Send the boys away. I'll be in touch by the usual means.'

That same laugh again, low and horrible. 'You sound so sure of yourself. Why? How can you Bond Selar now that he's banished you?'

Bond? What did that mean . . .

Ayn's heart pounded. Dry mouth, searing breath dragged in and out. In vain she struggled against the ropes holding her to the pallet, but she was too weak now, too old and frail to free herself and warn the others. She didn't even have the strength to pray.

'Go on,' the demon grunted. 'Give Keith his orders. I have work to do.'

And then he came close to her again. Close enough for her to feel his breath on her beaten face. Blind, weak and helpless, Ayn couldn't move away.

'Now, old woman, this time you will tell me. You'll tell me if there are any other sorcerers still alive in this putrid country of yours. Tell me all about the Salti Pazar. Most of all, you can tell me who the Enemy is and where you have hidden my Key.'

'Are you sure you won't be missed?' Robert asked. 'Will no one be asking awkward questions later?'

Father John shook his head and gave Robert a strange look. 'I have many and varied duties. I'm often away from the cloister in pursuit of that work. How else would I be able to serve my own people as well as the Church?'

Robert nodded and continued up the hill towards the market square. Hawkers were packing up now and heading for home. It was almost dusk and time to start the real work. He paused at the corner to give the young priest some last instructions. 'Remember, no matter what happens, I don't want you to interfere. Even if the Guilde come upon me, recognize me and haul me away. You are to do nothing. I only want you to keep watch and make sure I'm not disturbed.'

'But . . .'

'You must understand, if I'm taken, there's nothing you can do to help me. I'll be much better off knowing that I only have myself to worry about. Do you understand?'

'Yes,' John murmured unhappily. 'Where do you want me to wait?'

Robert glanced around the market square. 'No less than thirty yards behind me at all times. I'll be walking and stopping. Just don't look as if you're following me.'

The young man brushed his sandy hair back under his hood in a gesture that reminded Robert of Patric. Was it possible the two were related? Hardly. There were very few families that had more than one sorcerer among their number.

Robert steered John into the street, then went off on his own. People passed him by without a second look. His limp was rhythmic, his hunched shoulders convincing. Nobody here would ever recognize him, because nobody would ever believe he'd come back to Marsay.

His senses reached out into the seething mass of the city. Focused and full of energy, Robert swept over all the mild, pale and misty auras he felt, none of whom possessed power. Instead, he kept the setting high, looking for one aura in particular.

Nothing.

He could feel John behind him, aimlessly following his every move, just as he'd been told. But in front was nothing but an empty city, vacant of even the friends he had once loved.

With an inward sigh, Robert changed tactics and turned into the nearest tavern. He took a table by the door, open to let in the little sunset breeze. He ordered a jug of ale and took one mouthful. Then he hunched himself down over it, his elbows resting on the table, his eyes closed. Now John had to earn his keep. This was the moment when Robert was at his most vulnerable.

With the bitter ale taste in his mouth, Robert concentrated, blocking out everything but his single purpose. Ayn's aura. He blocked out John. He blocked out Murdoch. Even . . .

What was that?

Hardly daring to breathe, he brought his focus into a solitary point. It was an aura he knew and it was—

In one movement he was on his feet and out the tavern door. Without pausing, he ran down the street, forgetting even to limp. He left the first alley and almost slid down the next. He scrambled to a halt at the corner and, with his heart pounding, he peered around the edge of the building.

Across the narrow street was a small house. Two windows on the street level, two more above. The door was set a little crooked, but it closed neatly into its place, aided by the hand of an extraordinarily beautiful woman.

Valena!

9

'I'm sorry, Robert, I don't understand.' Murdoch pulled the shutters closed and quickly lit a lamp. 'Are you telling me that last year you had a Malachi within the walls of Dunlorn – and you *didn't* kill her?'

Robert nodded and tried very hard to stop pacing up and down the small loft room. Father John waited by the door, looking entirely helpless in the face of Robert's sudden energy.

'There were too many people about at the time, too many possibilities for real disaster. If I'd challenged her she could easily have brought the combat into the full view of several hundred people. You must sense Malachi coming through Marsay every now and then, but you don't go about challenging them, do you? You don't need to tell me it was a mistake. I know. I failed to kill Valena when I had the chance and now I'm sure she's got Ayn in that house.'

'But I thought you couldn't Seek her?'

'Not directly, no. An *ayarn* always makes an aura easier to focus on and hers has been destroyed. On top of that, she's injured – unconscious. The weaker she gets, the harder it will be to find her. I can sense she's in Marsay and on the same side of town as that house, but no more.'

'Robert,' Murdoch's voice was emotionless, 'only three or four sorcerers have ever been able to sense an unconscious aura. Are you certain she's still alive?'

'Positive. The gods alone know what they've done to her. The point is, we need to get her out of there. Tonight.'

Murdoch ran a hand through his shaggy beard and glanced across the room at John. 'It'll be tricky. We'll need some help.'

'No,' Robert said. 'Nobody else. We've endangered too many people in this venture already. Just you and me. John can keep watch. If anything goes wrong, we'll need somebody to warn the Enclave.'

John sighed unhappily, 'And what am I supposed to tell them?'

Robert paused at this. What indeed? To avoid Marsay at all costs? But where would that get them? And besides, there was one person who would pay no heed to a warning like that. 'What do you know about Valena?'

'Nothing,' Murdoch admitted. 'I can't say I recognize her from your description. Perhaps if I see her when we go in I'll be able to tell you more.'

'Let's just hope you don't see her,' Robert grunted. 'I don't want a fight. I just want to get Ayn free. If we call down hordes of Malachi on us, we'll never get out of here alive.'

'That's fine, except that there aren't hordes of Malachi in Marsay.' Murdoch opened a cabinet near the door, throwing a grimace in John's direction. 'I would have known if there were. One, I could miss. No more.'

Murdoch strapped on his sword. Robert adjusted his disguise and picked up his own weapons. As he slipped the slim dagger into his boot, his hand shook and he clenched his fist to control it.

It was happening again.

He could feel it, deep down. Disquiet, frustration. Why

hadn't the Enclave council listened to him? Why had Ayn volunteered for this mission? She must have known it was dangerous, must have known there was some truth in his warning. Had he destroyed her trust in him so much that she hadn't listened at all?

Yes, there it was, rumbling away inside him, boiling with . . . with . . . anger.

Robert turned stiffly to the window but didn't push the shutters open. Instead, he closed his eyes and drew in breath after breath. Steady. Steady. Grab hold of the demon and control it. It could be controlled, he knew it. Was certain of it. He'd been controlling it for almost twenty years now. He could do it again. He would do it again. He would continue to control the demon until the day he died.

'You didn't say what you want John to tell the council,' Murdoch interrupted, 'in case we get ourselves killed.'

Involuntarily, Robert laughed. This was so stupid. The more he tried to stay out of things, the more he became embroiled in them. What should he tell the council? What did it matter since they wouldn't believe him anyway?

'You can tell them . . . that the only person who should approach Marsay is the one who can wield the Key properly. Otherwise, the same fate will await them.'

John stared openly, his mouth agape. 'But that could take centuries.'

Robert picked up his long black cloak and threw it around his shoulders. 'I hope so.'

The sun set very slowly on the Vitala river. Great globules of molten sunlight dangled across the water like so many ships on the sea, for ever moving, until the last had faded away leaving only a faint glow in the sky, purple and orange, blood and fire.

Nash couldn't leave the view until it was completely dark. He couldn't bring himself to turn his horse away and ride west until all sight of the city was lost to night.

Selar must recall him. He had to.

Everything was in place. A position in the Guilde, physically close to that secret library. A unique and close relationship to the King. The Ally, waiting right where he could find her. Why, not even the old woman's unbreakable will could threaten him. She'd told them nothing – not even her name. But it didn't matter. None of it mattered.

None of it would matter if Selar didn't recall him.

It was a pity the Bonding could only be done voluntarily. If it wasn't for that, Nash could go back tonight, sneak into the castle while Selar was asleep – or drunk. Nobody could stop him . . .

But it was pointless thinking along those lines. Selar had banished him for the moment, and he would go home. Visit Bairdenscoth for the first time in some months.

With a grim smile at the dark city, Nash turned his horse away and spurred it down the hill.

'Can you see him?' Murdoch murmured, his face hidden in the dark shadows. 'If he's in position he should be somewhere by the corner.'

Robert didn't bother stretching his senses, he could see John quite clearly – though few others would. 'Yes. He's ready. Are you?'

Murdoch shook his head disparagingly. 'Have you any idea how long it's been since I used a sword in battle?'

Robert smiled in the darkness, his eyes returning to the little house a few short yards up the street. 'Don't worry, my friend. You'd be surprised how much you remember.'

Murdoch grinned. 'Oh, I remember lots of things – like that night on the Sadlani border. And look what happened that time.'

'That was entirely different,' Robert also remembered. 'We weren't facing sorcery then.'

'That didn't stop you using it.'

'No.' He shot a glance at Murdoch and smiled again. 'You're not still annoyed about that, are you?'

Murdoch grunted and let out a chuckle. 'Nowhere near as much as the Sadlani. Look, are you sure Ayn is in here?'

'No – but let's face it, where else is she going to be?'

Robert waited a few minutes longer until the Basilica bells struck midnight. This area of the city was deserted now, not

135

a soul in sight. Further down towards the wall, taverns were still open and most revellers would flock there. Even better was the fact that there was no moon. It was hidden behind a curtain of fleecy cloud.

What would he find inside? Was Ayn still alive?

If only Jenn was here. Her Healer's sight would be invaluable. Her other talents . . .

Robert hissed in a breath. *What was he doing?*

'What is it?' Murdoch jumped, ready to move.

'Nothing,' Robert grunted. 'Let's go.'

Rosalind rose from her knees as she heard the outer door open and close. Her hands were still clasped together, her eyes still on the modest trium high on the wall above her prie-dieu, but her heart and her mind were far from prayer.

Selar had ordered a search for sorcerers. Even now, Vaughn was organizing his men, gathering together his host of soldiers to go through the land, to arrest and burn every person suspected of the arcane. Vaughn said he would know how to find them – but what else would he find in the process? Who else, innocent and inconvenient, would be burned at the stake as a sorcerer?

Rosalind heard Samah enter the room behind her and came slowly to her feet.

She tried hard, but she couldn't hide her distress from her own sister.

'What is it?' Samah asked, moving quickly to take Rosalind's hands.

'The King has forbidden me to visit McCauly again.'

'But why?'

'Selar came back in a terrible rage this afternoon. And now this business with the Guilde . . .'

'I know,' Samah murmured, joining her by the window. 'I was jostled as I came back from the Basilica. His Grace the Duke of Ayr was kind enough to escort me back.'

Rosalind nodded, letting her mind go blank. 'Perhaps it would be best if you return to your priory. I fear the city is no longer safe.'

Samah squeezed her hands, a warm smile on her face.

'Sister, I will not leave you until this is over. My final vows will await until I get back. Now come, let's get you settled into bed. You need some sleep.'

There was no light coming from the house. It was silent. Robert scanned the surrounding streets carefully before he put his hand anywhere near the latch. Strangely, it was unlocked, and quickly they slipped inside.

It was very dark, but he didn't dare raise a light, not until they were certain the house was empty. Murdoch began to climb the stairs before them, his feet padding silently on the wooden steps. Robert moved forward into the front room, but it was empty. A little furniture spread around, expensive but sparse. He stretched his senses to encompass the whole building, but apart from Murdoch above, he still couldn't sense Ayn – and fortunately, no one else either.

Was he too late?

He stood still, held his breath and listened. Yes, Murdoch was good at this. Years of practice collecting information at the capital had bred in him a superb ability for silence. Either that or he'd been discovered.

Robert continued to listen—

There! The smallest sound . . . coming from . . . the cellar!

No longer caring about the noise he made, Robert strode to the back of the house and threw open the cellar door. The steps were lit by a single lamp hanging from the roof. Yes, now there was more noise from below – and from above as Murdoch started down the steps.

Robert moved down into the cellar, drawing his sword as he went. He placed his hand on the door at the bottom, but still his senses failed him. With a quick breath, he opened the door.

Something slammed into him from the side, pushing him up against the wall. He instantly brought his sword arm up, countered the blade held perilously close to his throat, and thrust back. His attacker stumbled, but immediately countered with another blow. Steel clashed against steel, but Robert had the advantage of size and weight. Every blow he exchanged sent his attacker further back into the room. He heard Murdoch clatter down the stairs behind him, but concentrated on finding a weak point to make use of.

Suddenly the moment came and Robert swung his sword, knocked the blade from his attacker's hand. As he stumbled to retrieve it, Murdoch sprang forward and raised his dagger. With a blow to the head, the young man fell to his knees and then to the ground, unconscious.

'Well timed,' Robert murmured. 'Let's find Ayn. We can question him later.'

Without pausing Robert clenched his hand and brought forth a clear white light. This room was tiny, but there was another door to the right. Fearing what he would find, Robert pushed it open, brought the light up to bear.

'Ayn!' He bounded forward, dropping his sword. She was lying on an ancient pallet, her eyes closed, her face puffy and bruised. Caked blood surrounded her mouth, nose and ears and she was completely still.

'Is she alive?' Murdoch hissed as Robert fell to his knees beside Ayn.

'Yes – just.' He put his hand to her face, tried to wake her up. 'Ayn? Can you hear me? Ayn?'

She stirred, her head moving so slightly he could have missed it. Murdoch found a lamp and lit it, brought it close. Robert killed his own light and cut the bonds holding Ayn to the bed. Again he tried to wake her.

'Ayn? Please say something. Can you move?'

'Robert?' A tiny sound, barely audible, barely understandable.

'Yes, I'm here. It's all right. You're safe now.'

'No,' Ayn said, the whisper stronger now. 'Too late. He'll come again. To kill me. You must go. Evil.'

'We have to get her out of here, Robert. There's no telling when Valena will come back. We've been lucky so far, but we can't afford to push it.'

'I agree,' Robert nodded, his eyes still searching Ayn's face. Her eyes were still closed and she was rambling, not making any sense. He brushed the side of her face again to comfort her and she was quiet again.

With gentle hands they lifted her from the bed. She was so light and frail Robert was afraid they would break her.

'I'll carry her,' Murdoch murmured, putting one arm beneath her shoulders, the other under her legs. 'You take care of the menace in the next room. You're better qualified.'

Robert nodded, but as they came to the door, the boy was ready for them, his sword raised to come down on Ayn—

The demon rose. Full-blooded, stretched taut against Robert's control, seething fury and hatred. Robert's hand shot up and a bolt of blinding white light blasted across the room. It hit the young man and smashed him back against the wall, dead.

'By the gods, Robert!' Murdoch hissed. 'How did you do that?'

Horrified, Robert stumbled across the room and fell to his knees beside the body. He gulped in air, but nothing could stop the tremor in his hands. It was gone now, the demon. Vanished with the life of this boy.

'Robert, come, we have to move.'

'Yes . . .' The boy was dead, there was no denying that. There was a gaping wound across his chest, burned and blackened. His blue eyes stared through a fringe of blond hair. He couldn't have been more than seventeen.

'Murdoch, come here. Does he look familiar to you?' So familiar . . . in the same way Jenn had when he'd first met her . . .

Robert reached down and tore the shoulder of the boy's shirt open. There, as though etched in blood, was the Mark. A House Mark. Campbell.

'By all that's holy, what have I done?'

'Robert, please,' Murdoch insisted. 'I can't hold her for ever. We must get out, now.'

'Yes, yes.' Robert swallowed his horror and came to his feet. He turned away from the body of Keith Campbell and led Murdoch up the stairs. The moment they were back in the street, they turned up the hill to where John waited.

'She's alive?'

'Yes, but she's very sick. We have to get her to a Healer.' Robert glanced back down the street, then ushered them around the corner. They had to keep moving away from the house.

'We'll never get her all the way across town without being noticed,' John said, frowning up at Robert. 'Murdoch's place is too far away. I know somewhere close.'

'Is it safe?'

'Safer than these streets.'

John led them higher up the hill, turned down a short alley where the end was blocked by a wall. A wall that looked oddly familiar. In the centre was a door. Without pausing, John pulled out a key and opened the door. He showed them through, down a short passage and into an empty cloister.

'Wait here,' he whispered. 'You shouldn't be seen. This part of the abbey is kept for visiting clergy. I have to go and get a key for one of the rooms. I won't be long.'

The bells of the Basilica struck the half hour as John disappeared. Had it really only taken that long to go into the house, find Ayn and get her out? Had it really been so quick a task to go in and lose control of the demon?

Keith Campbell. Dead. Latham Campbell's grandson, abducted during the Troubles – just like the McGlashen boy killed with the band of raiders. Just like Jenn.

Murdoch was eyeing him warily. 'How many times have you done that?'

'What? Killed?' Robert replied dryly.

'No,' Murdoch frowned, unamused. 'Used that . . . power?'

Robert shook his head and looked away. 'Too many times.' Far too many. But always before he'd used it in full control. Never before had it just leaped out of him. Never before had he simply struck out of rage.

Was the Key right after all, would his anger win in the end? Was this demon so strong that he would never be safe – and how many more people would he kill before the Key's demands were satisfied?

John appeared suddenly out of the shadows, a smile of triumph on his face. He led them to a door, unlocked it and ushered them inside, closing the door behind them. Murdoch laid Ayn down on the bed while John pulled rugs out of a chest. Robert knelt down beside her, lifted a cup of water to her lips. She took a few drops and swallowed noisily.

'How do you feel?' Robert asked, trying desperately to See her wounds.

'Doesn't matter,' Ayn whispered, her eyes still closed. 'You must get out of here, Robert. All of you. It's not safe. He will come for me again. He'll find me. He knows me now and he will find me.'

'Who? Who took you? Was he Malachi?'

'No. Not Malachi. The woman, yes. Not the demon.'

Demon? Who was she talking about? Why had she used that name?

'Tell me about him, Ayn. Do you know his name? What he looks like?'

'Evil. He looks like evil.' Ayn tossed her head about, her breathing going ragged. 'Please, he will come for me. You must leave me and go.'

'We're safe here, Ayn. I won't let anything happen to you.'

Ayn's hand abruptly reached out and grabbed his sleeve. For all her injuries, there was still some strength there. 'Robert, please. You must listen to me. It's you he wants.'

Robert shook his head. 'It's all right . . .'

'No! You don't understand. I can't remember his face, can't even remember what he said to me. All I know is that he is the spirit of Broleoch and he is looking for you.'

'But why?' Robert glanced at Murdoch and John. Both were equally mystified.

Ayn let her head rest on the pillow, her lips opening in a painful smile, 'You, my dear, sweet, Robert, are his enemy. Remember? The Key told us. You are the Enemy. But not the enemy of the Enclave. You are the demon's Enemy – and he knows it. He just doesn't know who you are. As long as he doesn't know, you are safe.'

She lapsed into silence then and Robert coaxed a few more drops of water between her lips. 'John, how long can we stay here before somebody notices?'

'You'll have to leave before dawn. You could stay the whole day in here, but I would never get a Healer in without being seen. I think she needs help urgently.'

'I agree. Murdoch, can you arrange horses and a litter? If we can get her to Parly's farm, we can nurse her in safety. It's only a league from the city walls. If we go slowly she should be all right.'

'No, Robert!' Ayn found his hand, forced her blind eyes open. 'You must listen – the demon will find me anywhere I go. I can't even go back to the Enclave. If you're with me he'll find you, too. I'm dying, Robert. I know. Please, leave me and go. I cannot bear to be responsible for your destruction. We need you too much. Only you are strong enough to fight him.' She paused long enough to take a ragged breath. 'Give me Convocation.'

Robert snatched his hand away. 'No! Never.'

'You must, Robert. You cannot refuse. Though no oath binds you to the Enclave, you are still one of us, subject to the same laws. You have no choice. This is the only way all of us can be safe from the demon. Give me Convocation, Robert. I ask out of pity and of love. It must be your hand and no other.'

She was right. He had no choice. Once asked, Convocation must be given. He dropped his head and nodded. He took her cold fingers between his and squeezed gently. 'Very well. I give you Convocation with the love and honour I owe you. May your gathering be all you richly deserve.'

'Thank you, Robert,' Ayn breathed, relief removing the frown from her lined face. 'Go in peace with the gods.'

With that, Robert leaned forward and kissed her forehead. Then he set her hands together and sank back on his heels. He could hear John murmuring a prayer in the background. Murdoch came close, kissed Ayn's bruised cheek, then stepped back against the wall, his hands folded together in front of him.

Robert reached out with his left hand and traced a triangle on Ayn's forehead. Then he touched the point between her eyes, summoning up the power from deep within himself, a power wholly unlike that which he'd used to kill the boy. He held it tightly in his hand and waited for it to merge with Ayn's dwindling reserves. A filmy blue light appeared as his hand moved down to her shoulder and followed across to the other, two sides of the trium. As his hand moved to complete it, Ayn smiled. His finger touched her forehead again and the triangle was complete, the merging finished. Under his control now, he twisted and snapped. Ayn stiffened, let out a breath – and vanished.

Robert stared at the empty bed for a long time. All that was left of her was a narrow line of ash on the clean linen, the remnants of a long and rich life.

A hand squeezed his shoulder and John's voice came to him. 'It was her choice, Robert. She's with the gods now. With Marcus. These ashes are but the remains of her body, no more. I'll scatter them under the oak that stands within the cloister, on hallowed ground.'

'Thank you.' Robert's voice was a harsh whisper. Empty and void, he came to his feet but he couldn't bring himself to look at Murdoch.

'John's right. Convocation was her choice. Much better she go like that than at the hands of this demon.'

From one demon to another. Was there really a difference?

Robert didn't argue. There was no point. They wouldn't understand what he was talking about.

'We'd better go, Robert.'

He heard John turn for the door, heard it open – then heard John gasp.

'I hope you have a very good explanation for taking the keys, Father.'

That voice . . . so very familiar. Robert stiffened and didn't dare turn around – but he had to, slowly, until he faced the door and the man who stood within the frame, his clerical robes falling to the floor like the wings of an avenging angel. Yes, it was Godfrey. He was frowning, extremely unhappy. He looked from John to Murdoch and then to Robert. His eyes glanced over the disguise without recognition and returned to John.

'Well . . .' his voice trailed off and slowly his gaze came back. The frown deepened, his mouth opened and he took a step forward. 'Is that . . . Robert? Is it you?'

It was so good to see a friendly face, Robert couldn't help smiling. He pulled his cap off and nodded. 'I'm afraid so.'

Godfrey strode into the room to give Robert a quick violent embrace. Shock made his voice shudder, but his mind was working just fine. 'I know I probably shouldn't ask – but what are you doing here? And within the cloister?'

'Would you believe I'm thinking about entering the priesthood?'

'Then it's time I left it. And I suppose Father John was giving you instruction?'

'Unwillingly.' Robert met Godfrey's even gaze. 'I wish you hadn't found us.'

'And you want me to say nothing about your secret return to Marsay, is that it?'

'I'm afraid so.'

'And you won't tell me what you're doing here. Do you plan to stay?'

'No, I'll be out the city gates the moment they open at dawn.'

'I see.' Godfrey glanced at John, then back at Robert. 'I don't suppose I could convince you to remain? Even for another day?'

'The gods themselves couldn't make me spend another night in this city, my friend.'

'Very well.' Godfrey nodded. 'In that case, I'll let you go. But I warn you, next time I won't be nice about it. We have a lot of catching up to do. I heard about Finnlay. I'm very sorry. How is your mother?'

Robert swallowed. 'She's well enough.'

'Perhaps I'll come and visit you one day,' Godfrey said, standing back to let him go. 'I've missed you.'

From nowhere, Robert produced a chuckle. 'Then you're getting soft in your old age, Deacon. Missing me is easy – having me back is the hard part.'

144

10

The doubled guard changed at midnight and patrolled the walls of his castle. They were wary and jumpy – and why not? Hadn't they been told by the Guilde Proctor himself that the country was full of sorcerers?

Selar sighed and gazed down into the courtyard from his bedroom window. Only the night guard was awake now. And the King. Another night without sleep. Another perilous night battling a shade he could neither forget nor forgive.

And now Nash was gone, too. Banished in the flesh more easily than the sorcerer in his dreams.

But he'd even admitted it! Calmly. Without so much as an apology. No hesitancy, nothing. Just: I am a sorcerer, Sire – as though he were remarking on the quality of the horses!

Lies. Damned deceit, betrayal, and all of it coming from that all-pervading evil.

Would Nash come back?

Had he even left?

No. Vaughn would find him; hunt Nash down without ever knowing that it was one of his own beloved Guilde who broke their sacred laws with his hell-born powers. Serve them both right!

Selar turned away from the window and paced up and down again as he had so many nights recently, a prisoner in this waking hell.

And Carlan? Selar had never even guessed that he was a sorcerer. Just like Nash. Not until that awful moment by the river. Only then had the truth come out. Only then had Selar understood how he had been used, fooled, duped – almost consumed. Would Nash have done the same thing? Would Nash . . .

Exhausted, Selar fell to his knees. The rich carpet beneath him felt like straw, his soft robes like hessian. No penitent pilgrim had ever suffered like this, plagued by something he could not stop, could not even control. People would notice soon and then his power would begin to fade.

By the gods, why could he not shake off this shade?

With a groan, he reached for the nearest table, where a bowl and jug of water had been laid for him to wash in. He grabbed the jug and up-ended it over his head. There was no refreshment.

He lifted his head and bellowed. 'Forb'ez!'

The door opened instantly and his servant stuck his head in. His ghostly white hair and colourless eyes accompanied a face as immaculately composed as ever. 'Yes, Sire?'

Selar stared at him for a moment, then grunted, 'Bring me some wine. Not that sickly stuff from Banderyn, but the stronger one. The dark red from last night.'

'Of course, Sire.'

As Forb'ez vanished, Selar was alone again. Alone with a distant memory and a terribly close present. It seemed there was to be no rest again tonight, just the nightmare – without even Nash's potions to ease the hours by.

'By the gods, why aren't you here when I need you?' he moaned into the silent night. 'Why did you force me to stand against you? Why won't you swallow your damned pride and come back to Marsay?'

But there was no answer in the darkness. Just an empty silence.

He'd said he wouldn't return. He'd stood downstairs in the council chamber and told Selar that he would never come back to Marsay. And then he'd gone.

Selar hadn't stopped him. Selar hadn't believed him. But he should have known. Robert never made a vow he didn't intend to keep.

Then, one after another, the years had gone by and even though he was back in the country, he made no attempt to come to court – even unofficially. Was his condemnation so great that he could not even bring himself to look upon his old friend? Or was it something else? Fear, perhaps.

No. Not that. If only it had been that – but Robert had never been afraid of Selar. Not even afraid of his power, the power he wielded over the country Robert loved so deeply. The country he'd sold his honour to serve.

And there'd been no fear in his eyes on the bloody field of Seluth in the aftermath of the battle. Just a moment of surprise as he recognized the man he'd dragged from the river only hours before. He'd stood there, bloody and exhausted, beside the body of his father. Surrounded by the last of his Dunlorn men, Sir Owen Fitzallen crouched at his feet, seriously wounded. Sir Alexander Deverin, massively tall and solid, stood just behind him. Robert had held his father's sword in his hand, still covered in gore from the fighting.

Selar had said nothing – but those green eyes still gazed at him steadily, waiting for the victor to move first. Then, abruptly, as though the idea had just occurred to him, Robert moved forward, landing on his knee before Selar. Without breaking the gaze, he lifted up the sword and offered it hilt-first to Selar. A surrender of sorts. By every movement, every defiant line of his body, Robert Douglas, newly made Earl of Dunlorn, had offered up his sword like a man who expected execution.

It was the greatest of double-bluffs. Selar couldn't execute this young man, this boy of fifteen or so – not after he'd saved Selar's life in the river.

And the boy knew it.

So he'd sent them away. Had Robert and his men escorted back to Dunlorn. Kept Robert prisoner for two years until he decided what to do with him.

Perhaps Selar should have executed him after all. Then he would have had no idea what it felt like not to be alone.

A knock on the door shattered Selar's memories. He glanced up briefly to find Forb'ez bringing bottles of wine into the room. He placed them down on the table and left. Selar stared at the wine for a long time, then, feeling ancient and overused, he got to his feet and picked up the first bottle.

It was the voices in the hall outside that first warned Rosalind. Before she could even get out of bed, there was a crash, breaking glass and a deafening bellow. She threw the covers back and jumped out on to the wooden floor. At that moment, the door banged open and Selar stood there, his eyes glazed, his shirt askew and stained with wine. Behind him stood two guards. He waved his hand, sending them away, then kicked the door shut, his eyes burning into Rosalind.

'Good evening, madam.' Selar lurched into the room, banging against the small table by the door. He looked at it, then swung his hand and sent it flying.

Rosalind flinched and took a step back.

'What's wrong, wife?' Selar spat contemptuously. 'You're not afraid of me too, are you? I would have thought such a feeling beneath your mighty pride.'

Rosalind didn't dare answer. Instead, she kept her ground and watched him warily.

'What are you standing there for? Fetch me some wine, woman!'

Wine, yes. Give him more wine and with luck, he might just collapse and sleep it off. Rosalind grabbed the nearest flask and held it out. He snatched it and took a deep draught. He wiped his mouth on the back of his sleeve and took another step towards her. His eyes running up and down her nightgown, he sneered and said, 'Where's your sister?'

'In bed, my lord.' Rosalind tried to keep her voice steady, but it was impossible. A trembling began at her knees, worked its way up to her hands, her throat.

'Is she alone?' Selar leered, then burst out laughing. 'Your family are all the same. So high and mighty. So bloody proud of your pathetic history, and what have you got left, eh? Your brother, the puling Duke, thin and weedy, a weakling if ever I saw one. Then his lovely twin, your dear sister Samah, destined for the Church – or so she thinks.'

Rosalind stepped back as Selar came around the bed, sat on the side.

'You won't even ask what I mean, will you?' Selar swallowed more wine and belched. 'You should. Yes, the sweet sister, Samah. I would have taken her myself, but I have other plans for her.'

'Plans, my lord?' The trembling was worse now, much worse.

'She thinks to leave us soon to take her final vows, doesn't she? Well, I have to tell you, dear wife, that I have requested Bishop Brome for a dispensation of her postulate's vows so that she might marry.'

'What . . .'

Selar snapped to his feet. 'Don't whine, woman! Do you think I can allow her to bury herself in a nunnery? She's the sister of the Queen, aunt to my heir. She's far too valuable for me to let her run off like that. With beauty like hers I can buy the loyalty of a whole army. Just be glad I'm buying the loyalty of one man only. He will marry her right and proper, be sure of it. I should think you'd be pleased, having her around more. But no, you aren't pleased, are you?'

'My lord, please, do not do this . . .'

'It's already done. She marries Eachern in a fortnight.' Selar waved his hands, dismissing the subject completely.

Rosalind fell to her knees, reached out her hands. 'Sire, I beg you. My sister has a vocation, she has been called to the gods. She must marry no mortal man. You must not force her . . .'

'I can do whatever I like, and damn the gods!' He swept up his arm and pushed her away. 'Look at you, weak and snivelling. Just like this hopeless country of yours. You lie there weeping and wailing and do nothing!'

'What can I do, my lord?'

But he wasn't finished. He threw the flask to one side and fell to his knees in front of her, his face coming close to hers. 'Nothing. That's your lot in life. To do nothing. It's all you're good for. Serin's blood, I only married you to get an heir. Then you give me nothing but a girl! What use have I for a girl? Two years I had to wait for my son. Two years! But what blood has he in him, eh? A weak, snivelling pathetic mother from a weak, snivelling pathetic family. Why, even your father was quick to be rid of you. But I have your measure, madam. I saw the way you cosseted my boy during Blair's execution. You would have him just as weak, to do your bidding, not mine. You would have him be kind and

149

generous and sweet to your carping, mindless country. But you're wrong. Very wrong indeed.'

Rosalind lifted her head, afraid to look at him. Instead, he snatched her hands, dragged her upright. Frozen with fear, she now could not take her eyes from his face.

Selar nodded slowly, a smile ugly and vicious growing. 'You don't think I know, do you? Young George? His attentions to you? My cousin treats you like a lady, panders to your sense of nobility. Makes you feel like you're worth your crown. Yes, I know all about it. But he wouldn't touch you, would he? No, no real courage in that one. But then, he didn't have my father to help in his education.'

Words, forced, urgent, desperate came out of her mouth. 'No! My lord, your father was . . .'

'Wrong? Hell, I know that!' Selar spat, dragging her closer to him so she could smell his breath, his sweat. 'My father was a monster. All my life he made me believe I was his favourite. My sickly brother Tirone looked like he wouldn't survive, so for twenty years my father taught me, trained me, put me through all the trials of a warrior until I was fit enough to succeed him. And then, Tirone began to grow stronger – and I was dropped, just like that. Dropped as though I was worthless. It didn't matter that Tirone wasn't fit enough to rule Mayenne, it didn't matter that his arms were barely strong enough to hold a sword. It didn't matter that he knew nothing of battle tactics, of diplomacy, of history. No. All that mattered was that he was the oldest and he would become King. I was relegated to the background. My father, successful teacher in the end, had made me in his own image. Ruthless, ambitious, determined. Such wonderful gifts for a son to have of his father. Who could ask for more? Me. And what I wanted was the crown. A crown that was my due.'

He stared at her for a moment then shook her, like a doll. 'Don't look at me like that, wife! I mean to do it and you'll not stop me. I will have that crown from my brother if it costs me my life! And I'll give it to my son. Yes, the son you gave me in all your innocence. Do you think I give a damn about your pathetic country? You must have known that I

150

only wanted her armies, her riches, in order to take back what was rightfully mine. Don't look so shocked. You've known it all along, tried to thwart me at every turn. But no more.'

Rosalind pulled against his grip. 'My lord, I've done nothing to harm you! I have done all you have bidden, given you two children of whom you can be proud.'

'You've given me a girl I can only marry off and a boy you would coddle and protect. I had thought to get rid of the girl at the end of the year. I've already arranged her betrothal. Now I think she'll go at the end of the month. Yes. Out of your reach, madam.'

'No, Sire...' Tears streamed down Rosalind's face, her throat constricted so she could hardly breathe. His grip on her hands tightened as his smile grew.

'And as for my son? He'll move out of your nursery. It's time he was trained properly to succeed me. After all, he'll have two crowns to wear by the time I'm gone. You should be proud. Fear not, you will still see him from time to time, but only in public – where you can't suborn him. Don't doubt that I know how to make a King out of him. He already worships me.'

Rosalind struggled against his hold. Drunk as he was, his grip slipped and she jumped back, looking for something to use as a weapon. Suddenly his eyes flared with rage and he swung his arm, his hand hitting her head so hard she fell sideways against the bed, her senses reeling. Before she could recover, he was dragging her up again, holding her hands, swearing at her.

He hit her again, harder this time, on the face. Her lip began to bleed as she scrambled away from him, desperate to cry for help, but knowing it would do no good. Selar laughed, enjoying her helplessness, enjoying his rage.

'You can't get away from me, you Lusaran whore! I'm the King. There's not a man in this castle, this city, who wouldn't run a sword through you at my command.' He grabbed her again and with a grunt, threw her back on the bed, held her down, his hand over her mouth. 'Yes, you are good for something. I still have only one heir. I could do with another, should something happen to my boy.'

In vain she struggled again, but his answer was another blow. Her head spinning, she felt his hands rip her shift apart and the weight of him on top of her. Gasping for air, she closed her eyes and screamed silently.

No one heard. No one but the gods.

'I'm sorry, my lord, but the Queen is not receiving visitors today.'

George frowned down at the girl standing in his way, trying to see through the crack left open in the doorway. 'The Queen is well, I hope.'

'She is well enough, my lord, but asks to see nobody today. I will tell her you came.' The girl fidgeted – and tried not to. Something was amiss. Rosalind had never refused visitors in her life – she received too few of them.

'Then I'll see her for just a moment, long enough to assure the court that she is well.' Without waiting, he reached over the girl and pushed the door open. Before she could stop him, he was in the room and looking around for Rosalind.

She was seated by the window, as far from the door as she could get in her meagre apartments. She started at his approach, glanced in his direction, then quickly away. But he had seen enough. He ran to her side, fell to his knees. 'My lady, what has happened? Who has done this to you?'

With her hands clasped firmly on her lap, Rosalind kept her eyes averted, her voice a steady murmur. 'It does not matter, my lord. Please go and leave me in peace.'

'I will go, of course, but only when I know that you are well.' She said nothing more, but George already knew what had happened. Only one man would dare hit the Queen and get away with it. 'The King did this? To you?'

In answer, Rosalind dropped her head. 'Please, go. It's not safe for you here.'

George glanced over his shoulder, but the serving girl had gone for the moment, though she was probably close by, perhaps even listening. He dropped his voice to a whisper.

'Please, Rosalind, let me help you. I don't care if it's not safe. He cannot be allowed to mistreat you so.'

Now she looked at him and he saw the bruises, the cuts on her face, the red marks on her wrists. Her eyes were steady. No tears, no shadow, no weakness. Just a calm that took his breath away. 'Would you really help me? Even when you know the King did this?'

Taking his courage by the throat, George reached out and touched her hand. 'You must know I love you, my lady. And loving you, I have no choice but to help you.'

She glanced down a moment at his hand on hers, then back to his face. She searched it for a moment, looking for something. Then she said, 'Even if it cost you your life?'

'My life is yours, my lady. I would do anything for you.'

At this, she smiled, lighting her injured face with a beauty he'd never seen before. 'Very well then, my lord. I accept your offer.'

Osbert waited in the council chamber along with the others. His supper sat heavily in his stomach; eating quickly like that always gave him a pain. But when Selar called a council meeting, everyone must obey. It was a pity Selar couldn't bring himself to have these meetings in the morning, like he used to.

Osbert glanced across the table where Vaughn sat chatting with Chancellor Ingram. The Proctor almost looked happy – and why not? Hadn't Selar promised him his pogrom?

So, where was Nash?

With a casual turn of his head, Osbert switched his attention to the King. He was looking even worse now. Dark rings circled his eyes, black against the pallor of his skin. The gods alone knew what he'd done the night before, but he'd not woken until midday, and then in a rage. He'd snapped at everybody and even had one of his pages whipped for forgetting extra water for the bath.

What was eating away at him? Nash had hinted Selar was plagued by bad dreams – but if Osbert could see the damage they were inflicting, how long would it be before their enemies heard? It would take very little for the barbarians across the Sadlan border to mount a few incursions. In this condition, Selar would be hard-pressed to form an armed response.

And still they waited. The meeting could not begin until the last councillor appeared. Selar frowned at Vaughn, jerked his head towards the door. The Proctor took the hint and rose to his feet. Before he could get very far, the doors crashed open and Governor Lewis stood at the end of the table, his face white with shock, his chest heaving for air.

'Sire! I come with grave news.'

Selar rose to his feet immediately. 'Well, what is it?'

'I went to fetch Earl Kandar as you commanded, but I could not find him anywhere. I searched his rooms but found them empty. I sent out guards to find him and—'

'What?'

'The Queen, Sire. She's gone.'

'Gone?' Selar repeated with disbelief.

'Yes, Sire, with your children. Her sister and a couple of Kandar's personal guards have gone as well. There's no sign of them anywhere. I fear . . .'

'Eachern!' Selar bellowed, 'call out my men. Get them mounted up and in the courtyard in ten minutes. Vaughn, raise your forces, too. They must not get away! Do whatever you must to get them back. I don't care who you kill, but bring my son back alive!'

It was not until Vaughn had finished issuing orders to his soldiers that he realized Lewis was waiting behind him. The Guilde entrance hall was still full of people and the noise was incredible. Glancing at Lewis, Vaughn pushed open the door of a dark antechamber and waited for Lewis to follow him inside. Then he closed the door and waited in the light of a single small window, high on the wall.

'Is this about the Queen?'

'No, my lord,' Lewis replied, obviously nervous. 'You asked me to observe Nash. I did my best but I . . .'

'What?' Vaughn snapped.

'I was not prepared for what I would find, my lord. On two separate occasions I spied him in the company of a

certain woman of extraordinary beauty. I'm told she fre-
quents his rooms in the castle.'

'A woman?' Vaughn gritted his teeth. This was too much.
'Who is she?'

'I've not yet been able to discover her identity, my lord,
but I will. I found the house where she lives and . . .' Lewis's
voice trembled as he delivered his report.

'Out with it, man!' Vaughn ordered. He didn't have time
for this.

'Last night, as I was coming back to the castle, I passed by
the woman's house. I saw two men enter and I swear one of
them was the Duke of Haddon. He had a cap on, perhaps in
an attempt at disguise – but I'd know that face anywhere,
my lord.'

Lewis waited for Vaughn's explosion. Vaughn stared at
him for a long time, almost unable to believe this news. Nash
– the woman – Haddon. All connected in some way.

'Why didn't you tell me this last night?' Vaughn
whispered.

'I couldn't find you at first then . . . I was worried my eyes
had deceived me.'

'And now today you are sure?'

Lewis nodded, 'Yes, my lord.'

Vaughn watched the man for a moment longer, then
turned his gaze up to the small window. Without any
warning at all, he began to laugh.

11

Finnlay started awake, lifting his head from the pile of papers
strewn across the table.

'You're supposed to be working, not sleeping!'

Acelin was standing over him with a lamp in one hand
and a steaming cup in the other. There was no other light in
the library – all the candles had long since burned out.

'I was just . . .' Finnlay's mouth felt like soggy clay, his head like sand. He sat back too quickly and lost his vision for a moment.

'Here, get this down you.' Acelin lifted Finnlay's hand and wrapped his fingers around the cup, hesitating until he was sure it wouldn't drop to the floor. 'How long have you been sitting here? All night?'

Finnlay took a mouthful of the brew and immediately burned his mouth. For a moment he sat there, uselessly fanning his tongue and then threw a grimace up at the librarian. 'What time is it?'

'About an hour after dawn.'

'Then, yes, I've been here all night.'

'And how is my translation going?'

Finnlay closed his eyes. Acelin was a slave-driver, never satisfied with anything Finnlay did. It was a good job that the librarian didn't know what Finnlay had spent the entire night working on — or the night before. 'I told you at the start. Saelic is not my best language. It's going to take me time. Do you want me to finish it quickly or do you want it correct?'

Acelin straightened up, thumped the lamp down on the table. 'So high and mighty for one so ignorant of Saelic grammar. You've been working on this for days and yet you still won't show me your progress.'

Hunching over the table with the cup between his hands, Finnlay grimaced, but didn't look up. 'Is there any wonder with the way you stand over me? I'm only here to help you, after all.'

'Well, don't expect gratitude from me, Finnlay Douglas,' Acelin grunted. 'You have a lot of work to do before I'll forgive you for what you did to the Jaibir.'

Finnlay stared at Acelin's back as he loped away to his precious map room. After a moment a yellow glow flooded through the door and on to the cold stone floor as Acelin lit a lamp ready to start work.

With a sigh, Finnlay lifted his arms from the table and surveyed the mess. The last few lines of his notes were unreadable and he'd managed to spill wax all over two of

Patric's drawings. Still, the loss of sleep had been worth it. There was no precedent, no record of anyone ever having had a proper vision during a Seeking, but his research had turned up one interesting fact. Once, long before the birth of the Enclave, Seekers had sometimes worked in tandem to search a greater distance. There was supposed to be some way to link the focus. Although there was no actual instruction on how to achieve this link, it was obvious to Finnlay that this was the starting point for some explanation of how he'd managed to see both Jenn and Ayn.

But how to take it further, that was the problem.

'Finnlay?'

He looked up. Fiona came through the door, her eyes reflecting the light from the candle she carried. For once, there was no frown on her face. In fact, she was smiling.

'Be careful Acelin doesn't catch you with that in here.'

'I'll be gone before he sees me. I just came to tell you. It's Martha.'

Finnlay would have sprung to his feet if his legs hadn't been half-asleep. 'What's wrong?'

'Nothing,' Fiona laughed. 'She's had a little girl. They're both fine.'

'That's wonderful! How's Arlie?'

Fiona glanced down at his papers. 'Why don't you come and see for yourself?'

He didn't need further encouragement. He scraped his books and notes together in a bundle and tucked them under his arm. He paused long enough to blow out the lamp, then followed Fiona out the door.

Wilf trotted down the steps into the refectory, waved a breezy good morning to the cook and collected his breakfast. Thick oat porridge and cream, two wedges of brown bread and honey and an enormous mug of lemony brew. He called out a few more greetings as he wound his way between the tables and took a seat opposite Henry. Immediately he tucked into his food, relishing every mouthful.

'Go on, give me the report,' he said through a mouth of bread.

'Those traders reached the saddle before dark last night, but by dawn this morning, they'd moved on west without stopping. Callum followed them for a while until he was sure they wouldn't come back this way. Apart from that, there's been no traffic through the Goleth in the last day.' Henry looked tired. His breakfast plate was small and although he'd obviously finished eating, there was still a lot of food remaining.

'Anything else?'

'Sebastian has cleared the heating vents ready for the cold weather. I think he wants to open them up early this year so he has time to trace back any problems to the Firelake before we really need them.'

'Good idea. I remember what happened last year. Those gears are getting too old and worn. Perhaps it's time we thought about replacing them.'

Henry sighed and ran a hand over his face. 'Grolandy has taken a turn for the worse. They had to send for a Healer in the night. They think she won't last another day.'

'Oh. I'll stop by when we've finished here.' Wilf stuck his spoon into the porridge and lifted forth a lump of creamy grey stodge. 'And what's the good news?'

'Sorry?'

'You always finish your nightly reports with good news. What is it?'

Henry actually smiled – though slowly. 'Martha had a little girl just after midnight. I'm told it was an easy birth – but having witnessed one of those, I'm not exactly sure how to take that.'

Wilf grinned and lifted his cup to Henry. 'It always happens on your watch. Have they given her a name?'

'Not that I know of. However, I believe Arlie's already had a word with Father Vernon. The Presentation is to be this afternoon – so make sure you're around for that. I'll be sleeping.'

Henry picked up his plate and cup and stood to leave. His eyes left Wilf for a moment – then widened in shock. 'By the gods!'

'What?' Wilf twisted around in his seat, but he couldn't see anything unusual. 'What is it?'

Henry dropped his dishes and tore off through the rapidly filling refectory. By the time Wilf gained his side he could finally see what had caught everybody's attention. Young Ben, white-faced and on the verge of collapse, sat hunched on a bench by the wall.

'I saw him come in,' Henry murmured, now wide awake. He crouched down as somebody put a cup to the lad's lips. 'Ben? What's wrong? We hadn't expected you back for weeks. Has something happened?'

Ben lifted his head. His eyes were glazed, but he could speak. 'It's Ayn, Master Henry. Murdoch sent me back to tell you. She's disappeared.'

The Enclave chapel was awfully small for such a population; that didn't mean it wasn't pretty. As Finnlay waited for the ceremony to begin, he stood in the centre of the cave and stared up at the painted ceiling. There in the foreground was the famous scene where Mineah and Serinleth were born out of the fires of creation. Further along, a depiction of the Dawn of Ages where the gods first discovered their place in the world. Then, closer to the altar, was the most popular setting, when Serinleth and Mineah joined together to drive out the evil Broleoch and douse the fires of hell on earth.

Along the walls were some more spirited interpretations of the various legends of incarnation of the goddess. Even today, a number of these were accepted to be mythological only. But the theme remained the same. She was always with them. No matter how bad things were, Mineah would never leave them alone.

Candles were lit in all four corners of the chapel – within the Enclave, these were dedicated to only four of the saints – those who had, for one reason or another, some special relationship with sorcerers. The only chair in the room was the one used by Father Vernon during mass. While the choir sang the liturgy, the old priest sat; his legs barely capable now of taking him up and down the myriad stairs within the caves.

Yes, it was a nice chapel. Certainly nice enough for Arlie, Martha and their baby. He could hear them coming now. The little girl was crying – or rather, screaming at the sudden change of surroundings. Martha entered the chapel with the child in her arms. Arlie hovered beside her, a stupid grin on his face. Father Vernon brought up the rear, leading the other witnesses into the chapel.

With a twinkling smile at his congregation, Father Vernon turned to the altar and began the first prayer. The ceremony of Presentation was the only really informal religious ritual Finnlay could think of. It was also quite possibly the most important. Every child born had to be Presented to the gods so that Mineah and Serinleth would know there was now another soul to be loved. It was imperative that the child was Presented before it was a day old. One of the best parts about it was that the actual Presentation itself was done not by the priest, but by the child's father – or closest male relative. The presence of a priest was not required, but it did add a little grace to the occasion.

Father Vernon completed his prayer and turned around to face the proud parents. Martha smiled and handed the baby to Arlie. The man's face became serious at that moment and his hands trembled as he took the tiny bundle and lifted it towards the trium above the altar.

'Blessed Mineah and Divine Serinleth, I call upon you to witness a new soul amongst your flock. This is your child. This is my child and the child of my beloved Martha. I Present you to my daughter, Damaris. I pray you keep her safe within your love, the love you hold for all our souls.'

Then, his hands still trembling, Arlie held the baby in the crook of his arm and traced a trium on her forehead. She'd stopped crying now, only letting out the occasional muffled gurgle. When he turned back to Martha, he smiled to find she had tears in her eyes.

Finnlay was the first to congratulate them, then others moved forward, kissing Martha and slapping Arlie on the back. Finnlay couldn't help taking a good look at the child. She was lying in Arlie's arm, her face screwed up like a sun-dried apricot.

'Are you sure that's your baby?' Finnlay whispered to Martha. 'She's ugly!'

'No, she's not!' Martha laughed back and gave his arm a playful slap. 'And she's got talents, too.'

'How can you tell? She's only a few hours old.'

Martha gave him a wise smile. 'Mothers know these things.'

They all filtered out of the chapel and headed towards the refectory where there would be almond cakes and spiced wine in celebration. Finnlay began to follow them, but before he could get too far, an arm shot out of a side passage and pulled his sleeve. He stopped. It was Fiona.

'Where did Patric go?'

Finnlay frowned. 'What do you mean?'

'Patric left the Enclave two weeks ago. Where was he heading? Was he going to Marsay?'

'I don't understand.' Finnlay glanced over his shoulder at his departing friends, then stepped further into the other passage. What could he tell Fiona? She was obviously suspicious.

'Don't play the fool with me, Finnlay Douglas!' Fiona hissed. 'My mother's gone missing and I think you know something about it. I think that's why Patric went off. There's no other reason why he, of all people, would just up and leave the Enclave. For pity's sake, Finnlay. Patric was born here, grew up here. He's never been more than a hundred yards from the gate. Now tell me, where has he gone?'

Finnlay swallowed. 'To Dunlorn.'

'Why?'

'I . . . saw your mother – just like I saw you and Jenn coming up the mountain. Ayn was in trouble.'

'So you sent Patric to get your brother to go and help her?' Fiona stared at him a moment longer, then turned away, hissing a curse. 'Why didn't you tell me?'

'We didn't want to worry you.'

'When has that bothered you before, eh?' Fiona closed her eyes, pain and fear at war on her face.

Hesitantly, Finnlay reached out to touch her shoulder, but she jerked away.

'Could you do it again?'

'Do what?'

'Seek my mother. Could you get another vision of her like you did before? Can you find out if she's still alive?'

Finnlay stepped back, half-afraid to answer. 'You must have tried yourself.'

'Finnlay,' Fiona groaned, 'you're a much more powerful Seeker than anybody else. Just tell me, could you do it again?'

'Not if she's unconscious . . .'

'Or dead?'

'And if I was right,' he continued, without acknowledging her interruption, 'then her *ayarn* has been destroyed. I might be able to find her, but without that to focus on, I could never do it from this distance.'

Fiona almost smiled, but the expression got twisted into a grimace. 'Then we'll have to get you closer, won't we?'

'This is mad, Finnlay,' Arlie whispered, pulling the last saddle strap tight. 'When Wilf finds out you've gone, he'll kill you.'

Finnlay glanced over his shoulder to where Fiona was tying a bag to her saddle. 'What choice have I got? She's right. We should have told her. We included her at the beginning, then made the decision for her afterwards.'

'But what if somebody recognizes you?'

'Who's going to know me? We're only going to get close enough to Marsay so I can try this tandem link with Fiona's *ayarn*. She can get a lot closer to Marsay than me. I'll still be a hundred leagues away. We'll stay away from any villages, any people at all. There's no danger, Arlie, really.'

Finished with the saddle, Arlie straightened up and held the horse's head so Finnlay could mount. 'You just be careful, Finn. I don't want to have to try explaining to your brother how those rumours of your death were not false after all.'

'Don't worry, Arlie,' Finnlay replied, swinging up into the saddle. 'Everything will be fine. We'll be back inside a week, no more. By then, you'll probably have heard from either Robert or Patric. Tell Martha I said goodbye.'

With that, Finnlay kicked his horse and led Fiona through the gate.

Getting down from the mountains was easy. Making a passage through the boggy moorlands immediately north of the range was not so simple. All the heavy late summer rains had drained into this one area, turning it into a quagmire. They tried to keep riding, but for long stretches they were forced to walk, pulling the reluctant animals behind them. Through the whole journey, Fiona only snapped at Finnlay when he tried to make conversation.

On the other hand, it was good to be out of the Enclave – if only for a few days. Finnlay found himself stopping every few hours to smell the peaty air or to stare at the wide open plains, bare of any trees but graced with extraordinary rock formations. Although it had been only a few weeks since his arrival at the Enclave, it had felt like months to his wandering heart. These few days were a balm and he was determined to enjoy every last minute of them.

By the time they'd crossed the worst of the moorlands they were both tired and worn out. Finnlay found a spot and made camp where shoulders of hard rock leaned over a small river, one of the tributaries of the Vitala. From here, heading due east, Marsay was about three days' journey. But Finnlay wouldn't go that far. He would stay here, where the only sign of civilization was the tiny village of Bairdenscoth, two leagues upriver.

'It'll be hard going in places,' Finnlay said, standing on the rock overhanging the water, 'but you can virtually follow this course all the way to the Vitala. If you start out early in the morning and find a place to stop before dusk, we can try it then.'

Fiona stood beside him, frowning into the darkening sky. Her hair was pulled back from her face, making her expression hard and uncompromising. It was as though she did it deliberately, afraid that Finnlay wouldn't take her seriously. 'Very well. But how will I know if it does work?'

Finnlay raised his eyebrows. 'That's a good question. I'm not sure. The first time I tried it, I was holding Martha's hand. She's a pretty good Seeker, but she said she didn't sense anything unusual. The second time, Jenn helped . . .'

'But Jenn can hardly Seek to the end of her nose.'

'But she does have a link with the Key,' Finnlay added, trying to keep his temper. 'Even though she doesn't work with an *ayarn*, she did have some influence on the Seeking. She didn't notice anything unusual, but perhaps, because she's not much of a Seeker, she didn't really know what to look for.'

'And I will?'

Fiona was watching him now, waiting for him to falter. Finnlay stuck out his jaw. 'If you have all these doubts, why are we here?'

'Because your stupid antics got my mother into trouble and I expect you to help get her out of it.' With that, Fiona turned away and began to build a fire against the chilly evening air.

Finnlay sighed. There was just no talking to the woman. No matter how hard he tried, he couldn't get past that wall of stubborn dislike – not even now, when he was risking his life to help her. And now she'd found something else to hate him for. Not directly, but his association with Jenn and her discovery of this presence at court had put Ayn in danger. It didn't matter to Fiona that Finnlay had fought alongside Robert to stop Ayn from going to Marsay. No. With Fiona, everything was always straightforward. Black and white. No grey to be seen anywhere.

They ate supper in silence, allowing the dusk to descend upon them like a calming blanket. After the dishes were packed away, Finnlay banked up the fire and sat down with his back against a rock. Fiona sat opposite him with her eyes closed, shutting out conversation once more.

Why did he keep trying? What was he trying to prove? That he was just as good as Robert?

But he wasn't and he knew it. Robert was taller, stronger, more powerful than he – and always had been. Finnlay didn't mind. He'd never wanted to be the same, never even imagined the possibility.

So why did Fiona keep comparing them? Was she still in love with Robert?

Not that Robert had ever known about it. He'd always been the kind of person who found it impossible to believe that anyone could have so high an opinion of him. But just about everybody else knew. Perhaps that's why Fiona was so prickly. It must be very awkward to have everyone around you knowing your heart's desire was out of your reach.

'Are you asleep?'

Fiona opened her eyes and looked at him warily. 'No. Why?'

Finnlay came to his feet, glanced up at the stars and replied, 'Because I think we should have a try at this tandem link. To see if you can sense anything now, while we're still in the same place. It would be pointless trying to find Robert because he doesn't have an *ayarn* either. We could try to find Murdoch.'

Fiona nodded. 'Very well. What do I do?'

Forcing a casual smile, Finnlay sat cross-legged on the rock beside her and held out his hand. 'Just monitor my trance, make sure I don't drop my *ayarn* – and, I guess, keep your mind clear.'

Without waiting for her to reply, Finnlay closed his eyes and concentrated on steadying and slowing his breathing. Then he felt her hand in his, her cool flesh gripping his with surety. For a second, he was distracted by her touch, but then he regained control and sent his senses way out into the night.

He didn't try to go too far, nor to stretch himself. He just wandered in the darkness, trying to capture every single nuance of Fiona's aura. The next time they tried this, that's what he would focus on, placing his Seeking within the sphere of her *ayarn*. The more he knew her, the stronger that link would be.

After a while, he struck out again, trying to relax, but finding it difficult. He moved east, further and further, but there was no sign of Murdoch – nor even of Robert. Finally, disappointed, he came back to himself and opened his eyes.

'I'm sorry. I couldn't find him.'

Fiona tilted her head sideways. 'How well do you know him?'

'Well enough to Seek him.'

'Then perhaps it did work.'

Finnlay frowned, but couldn't catch her train of thought. She was still holding his hand and he didn't want to move in case she let go. 'I don't understand.'

With half a smile, Fiona said, 'I've never met Murdoch. If you linked through my *ayarn*, perhaps that's why you didn't find him.'

She was right. If he'd been Seeking on his own, even from this distance, he would probably have found a shadow of Murdoch's aura. Obviously it was necessary for both Seeker and link to know the object of the search – at least, Finnlay prayed it was that and nothing else. 'Let's hope you're right.'

Sombre again, Fiona retrieved her hand and got to her feet. 'Well, we'll find out tomorrow night. I'm going to bed.'

Nash took a deep shuddering breath and opened his eyes. Where had that come from? Was it really as close as it had felt? And so very, very strong! It had to be the Enemy. Nobody in the world could Seek that strongly. And in what direction? Towards Marsay. Yes, definitely east. Who was he looking for?

The old woman? So she had known the Enemy!

With a smile, Nash climbed to his feet and walked the length of his tower room. He stopped before an angled desk covered in maps, some illuminated, others no more than sketches. Nash pulled one out from the bottom of the pile and placed it on top. With a finger on the vellum, he traced the Vitala backwards until it diverged into a dozen little streams. Bairdenscoth village sat beside the westernmost of these, his home lying just outside the village.

The Enemy couldn't be more than a few leagues away. He'd been Seeking towards Marsay – in the opposite direction. It had been the sheer strength of that Seeking that had caught Nash's attention in the first place.

The Enemy was out there, close by.

Nash turned his head and shouted, 'Stinzali!'

A moment later, the small, wizened figure appeared in the doorway, his bald head shining in the bright lamps. 'Yes, master?'

'Bring my supper in here. I'll be working through the night.'

It had been a long day, waiting for sunset alone by the river. Finnlay had spent his time reading, swimming and going for little walks along the bank, until the clouds drew over the sun, threatening rain. Then he spent the rest of the afternoon hunting for something to make a shelter out of. The pickings were lean and the shelter sparse at best. If the rain turned into a storm, the whole thing could fall down about his head.

The first shower came an hour before sundown. He scrambled under the lean-to and wrapped his cloak around him. It was cold, too. In a few weeks the worst of autumn would be upon them and the weather would close in for months. And once the snows came he really would be trapped within the Enclave – along with everybody else.

Would Patric be back by then? How long did he plan to stay at Dunlorn – had he even got there?

A rumble of thunder rolled across the sky, heading south, but there was no lightning. Finnlay huddled under the shelter, but he was getting wet anyway. If it rained too much, it would make the journey back to the Enclave even more difficult. Perhaps even impossible.

The gods must have been listening, because after only half an hour the rain stopped, leaving the air fresh and revitalized. Finnlay brought the fire back to life and settled down, ready.

Fiona must have stopped by now. She should be in place a day's journey closer to Marsay. Finnlay breathed a silent prayer to Serinleth and closed his eyes.

Fighting against the storm activity took a few minutes, then he was free and moving east. He took his time, ranging north and south of the river, testing his strength by catching every little aura he could taste. Further and further he went until—

Yes. There she was. Glowing in the night, familiar and warm. For a moment, he allowed himself the indulgence and wrapped himself around that aura. Then he concentrated again and focused his Seeking through her *ayarn*. There was still a long journey ahead of him.

It wasn't until he was some distance away from Fiona that he noticed the difference: he was sensitive to it this time. There was more power at his command, a better reach. There was also a different . . . colour? Tone? What was it . . .

He couldn't breathe.

Suddenly, all the power, all the strength vanished, like a door slamming shut. He struggled, gasping, but the glow behind him where Fiona waited began to dim. He'd gone too far. He should have brought somebody else along to monitor his trance . . .

'Come back to me, boy!'

The voice screeched across his fading senses and dragged him back into his body. Aching, searing pain wracked him as he opened his eyes. He could see nothing but the fire, a pile of glowing coals in the night. He tried to move and instantly felt the cold steel at his throat.

'Yes.' The voice came again. 'That's right. One move and your throat will be cut so deep you won't live long enough to watch your blood soak into the ground.'

Finnlay froze, desperately trying to get some air into his lungs. His vision kept fading in and out and his heart was racing. Frantically, he tried to gather his wits together, to remember something of his combat training, but for some reason, his mind wouldn't work properly.

'So very easy,' the voice continued, lazily, contentedly. 'You astonish me. I would have thought you'd have more sense than to try something like this so soon after your notorious arrest and untimely death.

'You are Finnlay Douglas, aren't you? And you didn't die in some silly fall from a cliff.' The blade drew closer to Finnlay's skin, drawing blood. He could feel it trickle down his chest.

'Tell me, does your brother know you're a sorcerer? Did he play along with the trick you used to make Osbert believe he saw your dead body? Or does the poor Duke really think his baby brother has passed on to the next life? I can't imagine he would know and just let you carry on. The great Dunlorn would never be a party to anything so low as sorcery.'

Finnlay began to lose the strength to move. The sneering voice grated against his senses, pouring evil into every corner of his soul. Yes, this is what Jenn had meant. If only he'd understood back then.

'Yes, that was very clever what you did with Osbert. A pity too many people saw you captured in Kilphedir. If you'd been a little more discreet, I might have been convinced the whole thing was a hoax. As it is, you've only made me more curious. Now get up.'

Struggling, Finnlay forced his legs to move. He wanted to turn around and see the face of this Angel of Darkness, but he was held completely, his life draining away with every breath.

Again the voice spoke, a whisper now, close and terrifying. 'Just when I thought everything was falling apart, you come to me. Easily and foolishly. Take a final look at the sky, Enemy. It will be the last time you see it.'

With that, Finnlay gasped as pain seared his whole body. He stiffened, then darkness folded in on him and he lost sight of everything.

12

Jenn picked her way through Elita's forest, her eyes fixed on the ground at her feet. Thick carpets of fallen leaves obscured the sprouting green she was searching for and the bottom of her gown kept catching on twigs. The ground was damp but not too wet, from autumn rain the day before. The morning had dawned cool and grey, as though awakened to the sudden change in season; not a good sign for the winter to come.

Voices came to her through the trees and she paused long

enough to look down the hill. Keagan and Shane, two of her father's men, were busy digging in the rich earth, arguing some point she couldn't quite make out. Shane was doing most of the work, his sun-bleached hair picking up what light bled through the half-naked canopy above. Keagan held a sack between both hands, taking the roots as Shane dug and pulled them up. It had taken Jenn an hour to show them what she was looking for and although they worked easily, she knew neither man really understood what they were doing.

But they were all she had; those two and Addie, her faithful maid: all she had dared to Seal in the weeks since she'd got back from the Enclave to find the awful news about the hospice in nearby Fenlock. Some time ago, the Church had handed over control of hospice work to the Guilde, thereby denying the poor free healers to see to their needs. The changeover had taken a long time, and at Fenlock longer than most, but she'd known the day would come when Guilde soldiers would march into the village and Brother Benedict would be forced to stand idle as the most needy would be forgotten.

Jenn refused to stay idle, however. Convincing Benedict had been difficult to begin with, her father even more so, but eventually she had persuaded both to allow her to co-ordinate a secret coterie of Benedict's healers to go out at night and see to those who needed them. Elita's gardens provided the necessary herbs – with the help of Shane and Keagan – and Benedict was able to continue his efforts without interference from the Guilde.

And Jenn went with him; partly to learn, partly to use her powers to shield him from discovery. So far, she'd only had to put up one Mask to avoid detection, but more were sure to be needed. She didn't know how long they would be able to keep doing this, but something was better than nothing, at least as far as healing was concerned.

With a sigh, Jenn turned to the durmast oak in front of her. Taller and slimmer than its brother oaks, this tree still had a cover of leaves and the brown marks of a few acorns still trapped along its branches. With a quick glance back at the men to make sure they weren't watching, Jenn lifted her skirts and stepped up on to the lowest branch. Within seconds, she'd climbed high enough to gain a view of Elita through the trees.

Even overcast, the castle appeared golden against the autumn backdrop. Unbidden, a great welling of love and affection filled her. To think that, once, she'd never known that this place was her home.

But thoughts of her life before brought back others of Finnlay and the Enclave. That dream she'd had, sent without doubt, by the Key.

And the prophecy.

It was ridiculous to think she, of all people, had been singled out like that – but there was no doubt the prophecy referred both to her and to Robert. No doubt at all.

And Robert alone knew the rest of the prophecy, had kept it secret since the age of nine, claiming it was personal and had nothing to do with anyone else; that he was prevented from talking about it by the Key. He had told Finnlay as much; along with a warning that even if he could talk about it, he wouldn't, because it was dangerous.

So Robert was banished from the Enclave, cutting himself off because he feared the prophecy so much. But what could possibly frighten a man like Robert to such an extent that he turned away from his own brother, his friends at the Enclave, his own country? Jenn?

Was ... was it the fear that was at the heart of the darkness she had seen in him? He'd given it a name once: the demon. It seemed she was the only one who could see it, or was even aware that it existed, and yet she knew it was the driving force behind so many of his decisions.

He kept an iron control on it – but what would happen if he lost that control? If only he wasn't so damned stubborn; if only he would talk about it, give her the opportunity to help—

'My lady?'

With a start, she looked down to find Shane and Keagan coming up the hill towards her, a full sack suspended between them. Quickly, she scrambled back down from the tree, ignoring the disapproving look from Keagan at her unladylike behaviour. She picked up her herb bag from where she'd dropped it and turned a smile on them. 'All finished?'

'Aye, my lady,' Shane nodded.

Jenn turned and led them down the hill towards the stream. The men behind her were silent. She knew they had questions about sorcery and other things, but she was prepared to wait until they were ready to ask. She too had needed time to think when she'd first found out about her powers. To those without them, the questions were that much harder because they had no first-hand experience.

She paused as a cry from above reached her through a clearing in the trees. She looked up. An eagle soared and dived, feinted and soared again, each time playing a deadly game with the pigeon that was its prey. Desperately the small grey bird flapped its wings and darted left and right, narrowly missing the eagle's talons. Tiny white feathers drifted down towards Jenn to land on the forest floor.

With a cry, the eagle dipped again and abruptly both birds were lost to sight behind the wood's thick cover. The forest was silent again, but Jenn kept her eyes on the sky, hoping for a last glimpse of the brave pigeon.

'The eagle must eat, too, my lady.'

'I know, Shane, but I'm not sure this one's really hungry. He's young and testing his strength, his hunting skills. The poor pigeon only knows that his life is in the balance. He must fight with all he has and that may not be enough.'

'In that case, I understand your empathy, my lady.'

The birds did not reappear and Jenn turned to look at Shane. 'And with what does my empathy lie?'

'With the pigeon, my lady. You feel you have little power, little strength to withstand the grand eagle, but are determined to fight it nonetheless.' Shane seemed pleased with this statement, but Keagan only gave a grunt.

Jenn held her bag in front of her. 'Or I could be the powerful eagle, testing my own wits against those who would duck and dive at every turn. Readying myself for the day when my skills would be really needed.'

172

Shane pursed his lips, stuck out his jaw, lifted his head, trying to hide a smile. In the end, he lost. 'I think perhaps your testing is of me, my lady, not the Guilde. I already quake on their behalf.'

Keagan chuckled dryly. 'Don't be such an ass, man!'

Jenn had to laugh at the two of them. 'Go on, you two, get back with that load. I'll be along shortly.'

They hesitated only a moment before taking off towards the castle. Alone now, Jenn took the path down to the stream. As the ground dropped before her, the trees thinned out, the green moss turning to brown and she arrived at her favourite place: the ruined mill. This was where she had been playing, the day she had been abducted, the day her life had changed for ever. For some reason, this place still held a powerful fascination for her, as though it was still the dark, mysterious playground of her childhood. She stepped through the arched doorway and into a room which had no roof, only the remnants of four walls. Green with moss and black with age, the grey stone had almost melted into the forest. One day it would vanish altogether and the mystery would be gone.

Why did she feel so at home here? The only childhood memory she had of Elita was of this place, of the men who had ridden towards her, engendering terror in her child's heart. But there was a warmth here, in the air, and a freshness to the scents of the forest that pricked at her senses in a way that brought comfort against the memory of fear. As though, in this space alone, could she really be herself.

A child's fancy perhaps, but this ruin, more than any other part of Elita, was the spot she really thought of as her home.

Neil was waiting for her when she returned to the castle. He held open the garden gate as she came through, taking the bag from Shane.

'Forgive me, my lady, but your father is asking for you.'

'Is something wrong?'

'We've been receiving reports all day about soldiers across the countryside. They're stopping carts and merchants and all sorts of people. They appear to be looking for somebody.'

Jenn swallowed, suddenly unable to speak. Had Robert gone to Marsay to find Ayn? Had something terrible happened?

She threw a warning glance at Shane, then headed into the keep. Jacob was in his study and looked up from his desk as she entered.

'Did Neil tell you?'

'Yes, Father. Are there many soldiers? Do you know who they're looking for?'

'I've no idea. I've sent Keagan out to take a look. It's not an invasion, though, if that's what you're thinking. It's mostly King's soldiers, though there are a few Guilde colours in there.'

Jenn took in a deep breath, but it did nothing to soothe the tension inside her. Robert must be safe – he had to be. Yes, if the soldiers were looking for him, they'd go straight to Dunlorn, wouldn't they?

'I want no further contact between you and Benedict until they're gone,' Jacob continued. 'I know we don't know what these soldiers want, but I'm not exactly in a position to ask.'

'No, Father,' Jenn murmured, wandering behind him to stare out the window.

Jacob turned his chair around to face her and reached out to take her hand. 'Do you realize that it's almost a year since you returned to us?'

Jenn shook her head. 'Is it really so long?'

Jacob laughed. 'A year is not so long, child – not after so many without you. I intend to hold a celebration for all our folk to mark the anniversary.'

'A celebration?' Jenn couldn't help smiling. Jacob was obviously very determined. 'Are you sure that's such a good idea?'

Jacob nodded vigorously, suddenly serious. 'You know you have very little time left. Up until now, Selar has been happy to leave you be, content to think you might enter orders. And while I was glad to see you back from the priory early, I cannot help thinking the King will have heard by now. His spies are everywhere. He's left you alone because he still feels secure. Should anything change that, you'll be taken away again.'

'It doesn't have to be like that, Father,' Jenn said. No, it didn't. She could always run away and, like Finnlay, spend the rest of her days living in the caves, shut away from the sunlight and all the things she loved most. What would be worse? An unwanted marriage – or a living prison?

'No,' Jacob said, 'I could find a husband for you myself. But unless I chose somebody close to Selar, he'd find some way to destroy the arrangements. Even if we did it all in secret he would assume subversiveness on our part and that would be the end of us.'

Jenn nodded. 'Perhaps I *should* take the veil. I'm not sure I want a husband.'

'You're a child, my dear, a romantic at heart.' Jacob replied softly. 'I'm sure you'd find marriage and children more preferable to a life in the cloister. I doubt you'd find a Mother Superior as indulgent as I.'

'Perhaps Selar will find me a husband as indulgent as you. After all, I wouldn't want to deprive you of having something to worry about,' she said with a smile.

Jacob's gruff laugh echoed through the room. 'All that education and the best you can do is find ways to thwart your own father!'

Jenn giggled. 'I did hear a rhyme about a lady from Fenlock – but I don't think you want to hear that one.'

'Certainly not – and especially not from you.'

She bent down and kissed his forehead, then left him alone. That way she didn't have to promise not to go out with Benedict tonight.

The sun set almost invisibly behind the hills lining the lake, so it was with some surprise that Jenn realized she needed to light a candle to continue reading. She got up from her window seat, but before she could get too far, Addie came in with a candle already lit.

'I had a feeling you might be needing this, my lady,' Addie began with a smile. 'Your father has just lit his in his study. The way you two read those books makes me wonder what you do with all that learning.'

'Not enough.' Jenn took the candle and placed it on the

175

round table she had put in here last week. Already it was covered in books, vellum and pens. Fortunately, Addie couldn't read, and wouldn't know what to make of the subject matter anyway. 'You know what to do tonight?'

'Yes, my lady. I've already seen Shane. I'll be ready when you go. I've laid out your clothes in the dressing room – and I even remembered to lock the door this time.'

'Good,' Jenn laughed. The poor girl was absolutely entranced by Shane and had been mortally wounded two nights ago when he'd found out she'd forgotten something so important. It wouldn't happen again. 'I'll call you before I leave.'

'Be careful, my lady,' Addie said from the door, her plain, pudgy face creased in a frown of worry. 'I heard about the patrols. You should stay well clear of them.'

As the door closed behind her, Jenn returned to the table and pulled up a chair. Before her were several books on history, some on land management and a rare copy of Tilkor's *Battle of Fire*, a Lusaran account of the conquest of Lusara. Jacob had given it to her with his own hands. There were few Great Houses who dared to keep a copy of this book.

What caught her attention, however, were the five sheets of paper laid out flat and covered in a fine, intricate text. The promised letter from Martha. When she wasn't actually touching it, the signs and symbols were unreadable, a language unknown to any scholar, no matter how learned. When her hand picked up the first sheet, the scrawl abruptly clarified and she could read it perfectly.

She brought the candle closer, settled into her chair and picked up the next page.

Of course, by the time things had deteriorated with the empire, our sorcerer ancestors, the Cabal, had already built up a large following. There were Cabal palaces from one side of the southern continent to the other. Every court had a representation, every Prince, a skilled teacher. Sorcery was a feared but respected skill – no less thought of than good swordsmanship. It was no secret that every petty King or

176

greedy Baron desired his own pet sorcerer – or better still, for his son to develop the powers himself. This was never the case. In those days there was no division within the Cabal as there is today between the Enclave and the Malachi. Certainly there must have been good men and bad men, but the structure of the Cabal kept a balance and crimes were punished within and by our own laws.

Unfortunately, very little writing survives to tell us about the deeper reasons why the empire turned on the Cabal. Yes, I know common history tells us that it was the Cabal who betrayed the empire, but there are unarguable facts that cannot help but make us question. A palace burned down because help was refused in a local war. Sudden taxes were raised on certain books and instruments used only by sorcerers. Many other seemingly minor but pertinent events. All of these happened before the Cabal so much as raised a hand in its own defence.

The rest of it you already know, though I'm sure a few details will have been left out of your instruction. For one, every palace, every building constructed by the Cabal was destroyed – with the exception of the Palace of Bu. We have no idea why that was left standing; until recently, were never even sure it was a house of the Cabal.

The war with the empire had been going for some time. It appears there was some dissension within the Cabal about the advisability of continuing the war since the sorcerers were terribly outnumbered; less than half of their population had real combat ability and it was unlikely they could ever win. There is some argument within the Enclave that the Cabal was much more powerful than we are today, but there is no way to prove this.

The dissenters within the Cabal gathered together in secret and, with some of their most powerful minds working together, they created the Key. This small group then gathered their people together and left Bu, heading across the sea to Mayenne, which was then a collection of small Dukedoms. It was at this point the group split in two. Our forefathers founded the Enclave, while the others became the Malachi.

Most of us have never seen a Malachi, so you may wonder why we kill them. The truth is, the Malachi want the Key. They know more of its power than we do and might even be able to wield it properly. Every encounter we have had with Malachi confirms that their intention is to take the Key from us by force, and wipe us out in the process. They want the Word of Destruction from the Key. They desire only to dominate – to make the world pay for having driven sorcerers into the dust five hundred years ago. When questioned, Malachi always admit as much. We make no attempt to exterminate them, but we cannot afford to ever let one of them survive with knowledge of us. Should they ever find out where we are, we will all be destroyed.

I know this story is incomplete in many areas, but I thought to give you an overall picture this time. Please let me know your questions and I will attempt to address them. I can do little more today as the baby is kicking wildly and upsetting my concentration. Arlie is hovering by and complaining that I'm not getting enough rest. Men worry so! I have enclosed a brief summation of the first few generations of the Enclave and marked those whose marriages were brought about by Bonding. As you can see, by the time the third generation appears, there is no Bonding at all. I can only assume that it was either impossible to continue, or deemed unimportant. Or it is possible that after that amount of time, people had simply forgotten the process involved.

This letter may take some weeks to reach you, as our couriers must be very careful. I pray that by the time you receive this, my unruly baby will be born. Take care, Jenn, and keep yourself well.

> *With love,*
> *Martha*

No Bonding at all after the second generation? Surely there must have been some folk still alive who knew about it – and why it was important. And surely it had to be very important, otherwise why would the Key, now . . .

Jenn dropped the paper and buried her head in her arms.

This was so difficult, so impossible. If only that man wasn't so damned stubborn . . . if only she could have stayed at the Enclave longer . . . if only she could talk to Patric, to Finnlay . . . to . . .

Damn you, Robert, answer me!

She punched the table in frustration, knocking books sideways. There was no response, of course. No, he wouldn't bother with something as inconvenient as having to answer her childish questions. He would just stick to his principles and damn the consequences. He knew he was right.

But he would never say why.

And what if he was wrong? What if the Key did have a plan – and one that was necessary they follow? What if the Key knew how they could find the Calyx, or the survival of the Enclave depended on her – or Robert – Standing the Circle?

The Key had named Jenn as the Ally, Robert as the Enemy. It had known about their mindspeech, said they were Bonded. What else did it know?

What *was* Bonding?

Jenn stood slowly and made her way to the window. There were no stars and no real clouds to speak of. But the air was chilly and there was enough wind to make the candle flicker.

Patric had assumed that Bonding had something to do with marriage – that it was a method of choosing partners. But . . . what if it was something else? After all, the Key had said that she and Robert *were* Bonded – not *would* be. So that meant that whatever it was had already happened. But they weren't married, so Bonding couldn't just mean that. Not if the Key could be believed.

Then what?

Mindspeech.

What had Robert said? She'd managed to do something sorcerers had only dreamed about. For how long? Had they been able to do it once and lost the ability? And why had they been dreaming about it if nobody had ever done it before? Perhaps it was that those who could mindspeak were Bonded and married simply because of that talent, hoping it would breed in the next generation. If mindspeech was so

179

valuable and desired, wouldn't sorcerers do everything they could to increase the number of practitioners?

Jenn moved back to the table. She drew a fresh sheet of paper close and began a letter to Martha.

Sweetheart, she began with a wry smile, *tell me all you know about the legend of mindspeech . . .*

Shane kept close to Jenn all the way to Markallen's farm. Brother Benedict travelled ahead, alone in the night. He knew she rode behind – but had no idea of the watch she kept for any kind of approaching danger. Benedict had long since given up objecting to her taking a real part in their nightly activities: her determination to make this plan work ran deeper than providing a little material help. The priest was not happy, but assumed her desire to accompany him on these trips was a symptom of her growing vocation – and he was not a man to discourage something like that, even if it was so oddly demonstrated.

The night was dark, but not at all peaceful. Twice, a patrol had come close and they'd had to stop and wait in silence until it was safe to move on. Then, just before midnight, they saw the lamp suspended on the inky horizon. Markallen's farm.

Remote, perched on a rocky hillside, the farm eked out an existence with goats and a few pigs. There was little for the chickens to peck at but they still managed to survive – mostly. They had started out with eleven children, but hunger, poverty and several harsh winters had reduced that number. Markallen, a man of wiry determination, kept his mother, two daughters and young son by the sweat of his body and a blind unwillingness to give up.

Markallen's wife had died giving birth to the boy, but his mother had worked hard to fill the void. She was old and had been ill for some time; the evidence was clear to Jenn as she dismounted in front of the farmhouse. Things were not quite as orderly as they had once been.

Markallen was waiting at the door. 'Brother Benedict, it was good of you to come so far.' He stepped aside, then caught sight of Jenn. There was surprise on his face, but also something else. Was it satisfaction?

'My lady! We . . . are honoured!'

Jenn gave him a smile and quickly took off her cloak to reveal the old and worn dress. This was a meeting to be kept secret. Markallen nodded, but still appeared a little nervous – and Shane noticed. As Markallen led Benedict through the front room, Shane leaned forward and whispered for Jenn's ears only, 'I hope the man's nerves are set about for his mother's sake only.'

Jenn shook her head. 'He's an honest man, Shane. His mother would have died weeks ago if it hadn't been for Benedict. He won't betray us.'

Without waiting for a reply, Jenn followed Benedict into the back room – and came to a complete stop. Benedict was kneeling beside a pallet bed, but this was no sick old lady. This was a young man, barely in his twenties – and he wasn't sick, but wounded.

'I'm sorry, my lady . . .' Markallen stammered, almost twitching now. 'I had no choice. This was the only way I could get help for . . . for . . .'

'There's no point in hiding the truth,' said a quiet voice from the door. 'Jennifer Ross is of the Lusara blood royal and will not betray us.'

Jenn and Shane whirled around at the same time to face the woman who stood there. Jenn opened her mouth in shock, but no words came out.

'Forgive me,' Rosalind murmured, moving forward. Her eyes were dark with fatigue, black shadows marring her pale beauty. 'I would have come to you directly, but I knew of no other way to contact you without discovery. I know I place your life and all these good people in the gravest of danger, but I am here to beg of you your help.'

'Forgive me, Your Grace, but . . . are you mad?'

Rosalind sat on a stool by the poor fire, clasped her hands together and lifted her face towards the young woman who stood before her. Having retired to the front room to give the monk space to work, Rosalind was now prepared for the barrage of questions. The wary guard Jennifer had brought with her stood by the door, his arms folded as though expecting trouble.

Still, Jennifer was waiting for an answer. She stood there, hands by her sides, her face open with shock. Her eyes, brilliant blue, were the brightest thing in the room.

'Perhaps I am mad, or perhaps I was driven. Does it matter? The simple fact is that I am here and I need your help.'

Jennifer's gaze narrowed and she glanced over her shoulder. 'Shane, would you take a stroll outside, just to make sure it's all peaceful?'

'Yes, my lady.'

He left quietly but unhappily and Jennifer turned back, her eyes now dark and intense. 'Have you come alone?'

'No, my children and my sister are upstairs asleep. The Earl of Kandar helped us escape and he now keeps watch over them.'

'And the man in there, wounded? How did that happen?'

Rosalind swallowed. 'We were discovered two nights ago, by a small patrol. Kandar and his men managed to kill them all, but Dien was killed and Hugh wounded. We fled, but it was soon obvious we could go no further without getting help for Hugh. We made it to this farm and Markallen said he could get us a healer – one who was not of the Guilde. I questioned him further and he admitted that you were involved. When I heard that, I felt that at last the gods had heard my prayers.'

Jennifer frowned, her fine brows coming together in a movement almost at one with her sigh. She was indeed beautiful, this strange girl, thought Rosalind. With those extraordinary eyes, light smile and the raven hair, she was enough to turn any head. But rarer still was that this beauty was lit from the inside with a fire that seemed unquenchable. A fire which drove her to take such terrible risks with her own life in pursuit of her principles. It took some courage to set herself against the Guilde in order to help Brother Benedict – more to actually come out at night to visit Markallen's mother in secret. If she'd been a man, coming from the house of Ross, she would have been a formidable adversary for Selar.

Jennifer took a few steps up and down the tiny room, then stopped, her mind obviously working furiously. 'Markallen knows who you are?'

'Yes.'

'And you want to get out of the country? Without being discovered? You know what will happen if you fail?'

'Yes.' Rosalind had had more than a week to ruminate over every single detail of that possible outcome. 'That's why I have come to you. Only you can help me.'

Again, Jennifer shook her head. 'Why? How can I be of service to you?'

How best to explain the inexplicable? A feeling, an instinct? Impossible. Only reason would suffice here. 'I know of your past. You were not brought up delicately, as most ladies of your station. You have survived alone and unaided in the land. You've overcome difficulties before and I'm sure you can do so again. You are also of the blood royal; your father one of the few alive who fought against my husband, the only one alive who continues to defy him in any measure at all. I dared not approach the borders near to Marsay. They would be patrolled too closely. My only hope is to get as far south as possible, perhaps even find a ship. When I heard of your aid to the healers, I was convinced you could help me. My only question is, will you?'

Jennifer glanced up at this. 'That's not a question.' She turned for the door and raised her voice slightly. 'Shane?'

The handsome young man reappeared instantly, shutting out the cold night air.

'We'll need horses and food for a week. We can't use my father's stock or he'll know. We'll also need Keagan to accompany us – and Addie will have to provide an excuse for me tomorrow. Once we know how quickly Hugh will be able to travel, we'll set off home.'

Briskly, Jennifer turned back to Rosalind, the shock and surprise having been replaced by a calm efficiency. 'We'll go tomorrow night. I'll be back to collect you. Be ready to leave an hour after dark. Until then, don't even think about going outside. Oh, how is Markallen's mother?'

Rosalind was happy to smile, 'Upstairs asleep. She's been improving over the last few days, I hear. I think she'll outlive all of us.'

'At the rate we're going, that's entirely possible.'

The day was sheer madness. Making arrangements in secret, trusting that Shane knew what he was doing, keeping Addie under control, and her own worry at bay. Writing the letter was even worse: it was the only plausible excuse Jenn had for leaving Elita, the only way her absence would be missed by no one.

How would Bella receive it? Her attitude had softened a little over the last few months, to the point where Jenn actually felt comfortable talking to her, asking questions. But would she go along with this lie? Would she agree to pretend that Jenn was visiting Maitland?

I beg to you trust me in this matter. I cannot explain here, but you must keep this secret even from Father, and I promise I will answer all your questions. Lives depend on your faith. Please, do not fail me.

It would have to do. Jenn didn't have the time to go all the way north to Bella and explain in person. Addie would take the letter and tell Bella the details Jenn couldn't risk being written down.

They left in the morning with Keagan, heading north. The moment they were over the ridge, Addie rode on alone towards Maitland. Jenn took Keagan down through the forest, riding slowly. Shane met them by the river with the horses and together they wound their way towards Markallen's farm, taking the most circuitous route Shane could manage. They were not stopped by any patrols, but they saw many. By dusk, Jenn's nerves were raw. Shane remained completely calm and Keagan said hardly a word.

Finally, the farm emerged from the darkness and Markallen's appearance at the door signalled all was well.

It seemed the gods were listening to prayers that night.

They travelled in silence until the first glow of dawn peeked over the horizon. They saw no patrols, no one. As a light rain began to fall, they made camp in a narrow gully. Exhausted, the children settled down to sleep immediately. Keagan stood first watch, but Jenn dared not trust to that alone. She stood at the head of the gully, her senses stretching as far as possible. She could detect nothing unusual, but felt no comfort. If only she were a better Seeker.

'You are brave, my lady.'

Jenn turned at the sudden intrusion as Kandar climbed the steep slope to join her. 'There are few folk in this country who would risk so much for the Queen.'

'You did.'

Kandar shrugged and pulled his cloak around his shoulders. The nights were getting much colder now. 'I'm a soldier, accustomed to taking risks. It's easy for me to lay down my life for what I believe in.'

'Your cousin will kill you if he finds you. Your death will be particularly horrible.'

At this, Kandar smiled. 'Every death is horrible. And besides, he won't find me. Not now.'

He sounded so sure it made Jenn quake. Where did his faith come from? He had turned his back on his own flesh and blood, his own people, in order to help a Queen who would never love him in return. Jenn had seen the way Kandar looked at Rosalind, his attention, the very way he carried himself when she was near. And yet, it appeared he expected nothing from the Queen – except to help her.

'Will you tell me why?' Jenn murmured, her gaze drifting down to the bodies close to the fire. The morning sun was blanked out by a caravan of clouds and the rain was getting heavier every moment. 'Why did she run away?'

Jenn glanced at him, but he only shook his head. 'You'll have to ask the Queen yourself. I cannot speak for her. I think she'll tell you if you ask.'

'Selar will stop at nothing to get his son back.'

Kandar smiled a little. 'And we will stop at nothing to prevent him.' He turned away then and took the path back down the gully.

185

Blind faith. All of it. Simple, blank, trusting, deep-welled faith. Where did it come from? And not just Kandar. It was Rosalind, too. And Shane and all the others. Finnlay and Martha. Patric. Where did it end? Why were they all so certain she knew what she was doing? Didn't they realize that she was just reacting to a need? There was no courage involved – and certainly no foresight. Just a rather childlike inability to say no when faced with a crisis.

Yes, Jacob was right in a way. She didn't really understand danger. At least, not until something went wrong.

'Look out!' Keagan cried above the black storm. Jenn jumped out of the path of the rearing horse and slipped in the mud. She came crashing down on her ankle, but the slope was too much. She couldn't stop herself. With her hands scrambling for something to hold on, she began to slide. It was too dark. She couldn't see the bottom of the ravine. Down and down she went, mud slithering beneath her until she landed with a splash at the bottom. Dead heather and rotting wood caught on her dress as she struggled to stand.

Someone landed beside her, hands reaching out immediately. 'My lady! Are you all right?'

'Yes,' Jenn gasped as she stood on her twisted ankle. 'The others?'

'Safe at the top,' Shane replied.

'But the patrol? Are they getting closer? Did they see us?'

'I don't know.'

'Well, you should know!' Jenn shouted, angry with herself more than him. 'Just be quiet a minute.'

The wind and rain lashed around them as the ferocious storm whipped itself up. Thunder bellowed above, sending flashes across the sky. Jenn tried to concentrate, to focus her senses and send them out, but it was impossible. There was too much chaos, too much noise.

Why wouldn't it work? Hadn't she kept them hidden from patrols for the last week with the aid of a simple Mask? Hadn't she brought a bridge back together in such conditions – and long before she'd even learned how to use her powers?

Damn it!

She reached out to Shane. He took her hand and she closed her eyes again. Focus. Nothing but focus. Forget the storm and focus. Reach out. Sense . . . yes, the others above. Looking down. Yes, that's it. Now further . . .

If she were a better Seeker, she'd know, she'd be able to tell if the patrol was on its way up the hill. But there was nothing. Just the storm-tortured moor and the evil sky. Did that mean the patrol had gone?

'I can't do any more,' Jenn breathed, opening her eyes. 'If they find us we'll just have to fight. Come on.'

They had to search for another way up, and for the last stretch, Shane had to almost carry her, her ankle was so bad. He put her on her horse, then led them on foot until they reached the crest of the hill. Suddenly the wind blasted them from the south, as though it would force them back to Marsay. The storm had followed them from the north, pestering their sleep during the day and haunting this black night.

'We can't go any further like this!' Jenn shouted, leaning down so Shane could hear her. The others were scattered behind, huddled down over the horses. Kandar shielded the Princess beneath his cloak; Keagan had the boy. Hugh's injuries were not healing and Galiena had developed a fever from too many damp forest beds, too many nights spent travelling. Samah had nursed her, but had to stop when her own fever developed. She was older, stronger, but she'd also fallen from her horse two days before and her right arm was broken. They would have to stop and rest before fatigue and illness beat the patrol's mortal danger.

Why had Jenn thought she could do this? Every day when they'd rested, she'd been kept half-awake by a need to be ready to set up a Mask should anyone come near them. Twice they'd taken shelter in remote abandoned huts and she'd found a few hours of undisturbed slumber as Shane, Keagan and Kandar took turns at keeping watch. But every night was like this one, bleak and icy and needled with dangers. She had to Seek for hours on end, changing their path when she picked up even the faintest hint of a pale

187

human aura – an effort almost beyond her fragile Seeking abilities.

And so far they'd been lucky. Any more nights like tonight and they could be lost.

'There's some shelter over there, my lady,' Shane bellowed over the storm. 'That wood – a patch of darkness. Do you see it?'

'Yes, just. It won't be dry, but we'll be out of this wind. Let's go.'

Rosalind sat quietly with her arms around Galiena and watched the purposeful activity going on in front of her. After the raging anger of last night's storm, this peace was welcome, if disconcerting. Keagan stood in the centre of the clearing and held the horse's head while Shane brushed it down and placed a cleaned saddle on its back. Each movement was crisp, familiar, precise.

Beyond the tiny clearing, the wood disappeared into greyness, making the trees nothing more than ghostly shapes in the morning's fog. Kenrick was poking a stick into the fire and jumping back. He laughed and looked to Rosalind for approval. She smiled and nodded and he picked up another stick. Galiena slept on, her breathing now little more now than a laboured rasp.

Kandar had built a shelter using some young saplings and a length of rope from the saddlebags. In its shadow lay Hugh, his chaotic rambling audible to everyone. Samah was trying to feed him while Kandar held his head. Jennifer stood at Hugh's feet, murmuring something. With a nod, Kandar stood and together they came back to Rosalind.

'I'm afraid we have no choice, Your Grace,' Jennifer began, picking up her cloak from the forest floor. 'Either we leave Hugh here to die, your daughter with him, or we find some help. As far as I can tell from Kandar's map, we covered just a few leagues last night, and the weather will only get worse now. We cannot continue on like this. If we try, we'll be found for sure.'

Rosalind took a deep breath. 'I would rather die here in this wood than risk involving any more in my folly. You and your men should leave us and go home. You've risked too much already.'

Jennifer sighed with exasperation. 'We're not beaten yet. We can get help. If we can find somewhere safe to rest for a few days, somewhere where we'll not be discovered, we can continue on.'

'But do you know anybody you dare trust?'

'Trust?' Jennifer frowned at that and swirled her cloak over her shoulders. 'I'm not sure I know what that means. On the other hand, you'd be surprised at the number of people in this country who'd be willing to help you. I'll go alone. I'll be asking directions and I can travel faster on my own. In case you need to fight, Shane and Keagan would be better helping you than me. If I don't return by sunset, assume the worst. Head for that priory we saw yesterday and ask for sanctuary. That's your best hope.'

As Jennifer turned for the horse, Rosalind handed Galiena to Kandar and followed after her. She took Jennifer's hand and spoke quietly. 'And if you return and find we're gone – or dead – remember what I told you of the King's plans. Tell your father. He'll know what to do. I've done all I can to stop Selar; the rest is up to you.'

She said nothing more as Jennifer climbed on to the horse. Shane handed up the reins, his eyes never leaving her face.

'Be careful, my lady.'

Jennifer nodded, then pulled the horse aside. She disappeared into the forest and soon all sound of her was gone.

'Don't worry, Shane,' Rosalind murmured into the silence. 'She will return. Your mistress is a lady of immense courage and strength. If she were a man, my husband would have much to fear.'

Shane met her gaze steadily for a long time. Then he nodded. 'The King has already been struck down by one lady of courage. Two would be the ending of him. I'll gather some more firewood and put some breakfast together. With a little luck, I may even catch a rabbit we can dine on this evening.'

13

So much pain! In his head, in his stomach. He kept retching, coughing and choking, but he couldn't move, couldn't lift his head, or even turn it. He was so thirsty. His lips were cracked and dry. He tasted blood. His eyes were open, but all he could see were some vague shadows on the vaulted ceiling, dark and ominous.

How long had he been lying here? Hours? Weeks? It was impossible to guess. There was nothing he could use to gauge the time. It never got any colder or darker – or any lighter. There were just the same shadows above him – and the unceasing pain.

The Angel of Darkness had caught him. That was all he knew. A figure out of some half-imagined prophecy had overpowered him and brought him here. But why wasn't he dead? Why was he kept here, left to slowly starve to death?

There was a noise. To his right. Footsteps, slow and deliberate. And light, a flickering candle dancing shapes on the vaulting. Finnlay struggled to turn his head, but a rope crossed his forehead, tied to something he couldn't see. The footsteps came closer, bringing the blinding light. Then a face, ancient and wrinkled, leaned over him. Was this the man?

'You're awake, you're awake!' the old one cried. His eyes were flat and dull, the voice creaked with age. This was not the Angel of Darkness.

Abruptly the old man scurried away, calling out to somebody else. 'Master, master! He's awake now! The Enemy is awake!'

Finnlay held his breath and tried to concentrate. His hands were bound to the bed, his feet also. He squirmed a little to feel his left wrist – but his *ayarn* was gone! The Angel must have taken it.

'Yes, Stinzali, he is awake.' That voice again, cold, dominating and utterly terrifying. 'I wonder if that means he's ready?'

'Shall I get the orb, master?'

Finnlay couldn't see either of them, but he could feel their presence. They were close. He strained against his bonds with what little strength remained, but achieved nothing.

'Look, there's still some fight in him. No, Stinzali, don't bother with the orb just yet. There're a few things the young Douglas and I must discuss first.'

The old servant scuffled away, leaving Finnlay alone with his nemesis. His stomach tightened against hunger and fear. He would have done anything for a few drops of water. Anything but give in . . .

By the mass! Fiona – had she been captured too?

No. Impossible. She'd been too far away. By now, with any luck, she would have returned to the camp by the river and found Finnlay gone. She should already be on her way back to the Enclave. She would be safe – even if she never knew what had happened to him. Not that she would care.

'How are you feeling?'

The voice came close once more, close to his ear. Deliberately out of sight, though. Finnlay didn't answer – couldn't. His mouth and throat were too dry.

'Thirsty, perhaps? Here, have some water.'

Something moved at the edges of his vision – and he was abruptly doused with a bucket of icy water. Desperately he licked his lips, trying to drink as much as he could. The shock of the water cleared his head too. Whether it had been deliberate or not, Finnlay felt a little better.

'First of all, you can tell me how you got out of the prison in Kilphedir without being seen by the guards. I realize it must have been an illusion of sorts – but I don't understand how you could have operated without your little stone, nor why you waited for the second night before you tried something. Did you work it all out by yourself – or have you a cohort who aids you in such things?'

Finnlay swallowed and took as deep a breath as his bonds would allow. His voice croaking, he replied, 'I have a hundred thousand cohorts at my command.'

Laughter. The Angel of Darkness fancied himself to have a sense of humour.

'Funny, I didn't think you'd tell me, but I just thought I'd begin with an easy question. Now, I should warn you, I've waited a long time for this moment. Longer than you could possibly imagine.'

How much worse could it get? Finnlay was going to die. That was the only fate left to him. All this monster could do to him was kill him slowly, with a lot of pain. At least he would get no other satisfaction from Finnlay. Finnlay relaxed back as much as he could and focused on his Seal. For the first time in his life he was truly glad to have it: one of many gifts Robert had blessed him with over the years.

'So, I take it you were Seeking for the old woman when I caught you,' the voice began again, all businesslike. 'I'm not sorry to tell you that she's well and truly dead by now. And just in case you were wondering, I had my people dump her body in the Vitala. She was stubborn and wouldn't tell me anything – but the old and infirm can often be like that. Did you know her well? Was she important to you?'

'Go to hell!'

Laughter again, and then a blinding bolt of pain shot down the right side of his body. For long seconds, Finnlay creased up against the agony. Gasping for air, he closed his eyes, focused once again on his Seal.

'I did warn you.'

The monster moved around the pallet Finnlay lay on, lighting candles. Now Finnlay could see more of the room. Stone walls on either side, covered in tapestries, bookshelves, lances and swords. Part of a siege arm and something that looked like a bridge support stood up against a window on his right. Decorations he couldn't even recognize hung from the ceiling. Rich and ancient, all of it. A clutter of hoarded wealth.

'Who are you? Are you Malachi?' Finnlay grunted, his eyes straining to see the face of his torturer.

'Who am I?' The voice was light this time as the Angel moved back to his former position, to Finnlay's right and just behind his field of vision. 'My name is Carlan. I am the son of Sistema who was the son of Eina, the son of Edassa who was the one who created the Key. His father, the great Bayazit of Yedicale, was the sorcerer who made the Word of Destruction. I am the last of the greatest line of sorcerers who ever lived – and I am no Malachi.'

The Key . . . The Word . . . But . . . so few generations! Five hundred years. Was this man serious? Had he really lived so long?

'What do you want from me?' Finnlay kept his voice steady, though his heart was hammering in his chest.

'I would have thought that was obvious. I want your blood. You will die here, Finnlay Douglas, and you won't even scream. The Enemy will die and there will be nobody left who can stop me.'

The Enemy? But . . . the Key had said *Robert* was the Enemy! Thank the gods! As long as Carlan thought Finnlay was the Enemy, then there was still a chance. Robert would crush this monster without a second thought. Robert would . . .

'I must say, though, I hadn't thought you'd be so easy to catch. A little careless, weren't you? Still, that's nothing now, and since I don't have all day, I suggest you start answering my questions – unless, of course, you prefer the pain?'

That terrible voice came closer again. 'Tell me how you know the Ally.'

Finnlay crushed any reaction. 'Ally? I don't know what you mean.'

'Your brother knows her. He helped take her back to her damned father. What have you had to do with her? Did you help awaken her powers? Come, tell me.'

Steeling himself against the inevitable onslaught of pain, Finnlay replied, 'I don't know who you're talking about.'

It came like lightning, fast and powerful, blinding and burning. When it was gone, Finnlay could hardly see the banners hung from the ceiling.

'My patience is wearing thin, Enemy. I want some answers. You can try protecting her all you like, but I will know what you've had to do with her.'

The pain came again and this time Finnlay let himself

drown in it. He dropped so far below the surface that everything went black and he stopped feeling altogether.

Nash strode through the door and up the spiral staircase which ran to the top of the Round Tower. Tiny windows flashed daylight at him, but he paid no attention. When he arrived at the first floor, the door was already open to the anteroom. Stinzali was sitting at his table, spooning an evil-looking broth into his mouth.

'Well? Is he awake yet?'

'Yes, master. Just now. Should I get the orb?'

Nash shook his head and drew the cape from his shoulders. 'I told you, not yet. He's not ready.'

Nash tossed the cape into a corner, then grabbed the wine flask from the table and took a large swig.

'Is he strong, master? Strong enough to refuse to answer?'

'There's some little will left in him. That will die quickly enough. His problem is that he has no idea of his destiny – or rather, the destiny he might have had if he hadn't been so stupid. I must say, I expected more of a fight out of him.'

'But he's not answered . . .'

'No, you idiot! Sorcery. He's supposed to be very, very powerful, but apart from the strength I sensed while he was Seeking, he hasn't moved a muscle to stop me.'

Stinzali smiled, a toothless gape. 'Then you will surely succeed, master. I am honoured to be the one to serve you at this time.'

'Yes, yes,' Nash grunted, planting himself down at the table. 'Stop fawning and get me something to eat. I can't face that weakling on an empty stomach.'

Finnlay awoke to a terrible calm.

He hadn't given in. His Seal would stop him talking involuntarily – but if he wanted to, he could have told Carlan everything he knew.

But he hadn't – and he wouldn't. If that pain was the worst the Angel of Darkness could offer, then Finnlay could stand it. He knew it would kill him – and soon – but in this world, with such evil free to roam, death was the preferred path.

Oh, if only he could tell them all: the Enclave, Robert and Jenn. They would find Carlan. They would hunt him down. They would destroy him.

But the truth would die with him. There was no escape from this place. Only more pain and, finally, death.

Something snatched at the edge of his awareness. That presence, coming again. Carlan. Sweet Mineah, it was starting again!

'Very well,' Carlan began, taking up his familiar position where Finnlay could only hear him but never see him. 'I'll make this very simple for you. One question. That's all I have for you today. If you give me an answer, I promise to make your death painless. I can't, of course, offer you your life. I'm sure you understand. But if you give me an answer you will feel nothing as your life slips away. You'll get no better offer from me.'

'Can I . . . have some water?' Finnlay struggled to speak, lifted his head – then deliberately sank back down, feigning collapse.

'Certainly. Though I suppose you actually want to drink it this time. Well, all right – but only a little. It would spoil things otherwise.'

Finnlay waited until the cup was at his lips. Took one swallow – then hit out with the only power left to him. The blast was hopelessly ineffectual and only engendered laughter from Carlan.

'Oh, how pathetic! If that's the best you can do, then I wonder why I bothered to find you in the first place. Now, enough of these heroics. Answer my question.'

'What?' Finnlay whispered, no longer feigning collapse. What little he could do he had done. He'd failed. Now there was nothing left.

'Tell me where the Key is.'

Now he was beyond reacting. His response was murmured and entirely lacking in purpose. 'Key? What key is that?'

More pain. This time it lasted so long, Finnlay almost blacked out again.

The voice came so close to his ear, he could feel the breath on his face. 'You know damned well what Key I'm talking about! You're Salti Pazar. You must know. Your people stole the Key from my ancestor and vanished into the land. The Malachi have hunted you down over the centuries, vainly trying to get it back, but they're such a hopeless bunch they've failed again and again. Their bloodlust is too great. They're more interested in wiping out every Salti in the world. If they had any sense, they'd get the Key back, discover the Word of Destruction and get rid of the lot of you in one go. Now—' Carlan paused, taking a deep breath. His anger was seething now, reaching out to course through every bone in Finnlay's body. '—you will tell me where the Key is. I don't really care how long it takes you to die. I have all the time in the world. Not just days, but weeks, months. Every day like this one, filled with pain. On and on. All of it for you. And I won't give up, believe me. My family has waited five hundred years for this. You will not stop me. Where is the Key?'

This time, Finnlay did pass out, but for only a few moments. When he opened his eyes again, the room was lighter and the old man was moving around him, draping something over his legs.

'As soon as you've finished that, Stinzali, go and get me the orb.'

'Yes, master.'

Finnlay burned with curiosity. That was about the only thing left to him now. His whole body was numb, beyond feeling anything at all. Even the pallet beneath him seemed insubstantial.

The old servant came back. He moved close to the bed with an insane smile on his creased face, holding something up for Finnlay to see. A black ball – orb. Almost exactly the same as the Key, but smaller, with a dulled surface as though worn by time. It was held reverently between the old man's hands.

'I suppose you want to know what this is?' Carlan began again, all civility. 'And of course, you're curious as to how I can live so long, how my father and grandfather lived so long. Well, it's very simple. A process discovered by the D'Azzir – but of course, you wouldn't know them either, would you? That's what you get for being Salti – you've missed out on so much of your heritage. Anyway, the D'Azzir discovered a way to heal wounds using the blood of their dying adversaries. My ancestor, Eina, perfected the technique. You wouldn't believe the difference it makes when you use the blood of a powerful sorcerer.'

A sharp pain dug into Finnlay's right arm. Quickly he could feel the wound begin to bleed. The old man placed the orb on the ground, beneath Finnlay's arm. He grinned again and disappeared. Carlan leaned close.

'Your blood will drain very slowly, Enemy. I don't want to kill you too quickly. The longer it takes, the more your body will try to replace it – giving me more blood to use. Pure blood, untainted by food or water. I will keep it here and use it when I need to bring myself back to life again. Think on that, Finnlay Douglas, as your life drips away from you. Your blood will help secure another seventy years of my life. You will help keep me alive for ever.'

The afternoon rain stopped before Nash finished climbing the stairs. By the time he pushed the last door open there were only puddles of water on the tower roof for him to splash through. Even the clouds had given up, whipped away from the sun by a hard wind.

Nash dried the water from a stone rampart and sat down to think. Finnlay Douglas would not give in. His powers might not be as strong as Nash had expected, but his will was. Much stronger, in fact. Stronger even than the old woman. Nash hadn't pushed her anywhere near as hard and he'd almost killed her in the process.

So the Enemy would tell him nothing. Well, at least Nash would have his blood – and the satisfaction of knowing there was now no one to stop him. He would have to find the Key by the only means left to him: Vaughn's secret library.

He'd as much as admitted its existence to Selar – the first time Nash had heard of it. Vaughn had said he had ways of finding and knowing sorcerers. There was only one way he could know such things. He must have records going back centuries: books that had been written by sorcerers, for sorcerers. Somewhere in those volumes would be some word, some link that Nash could use. Somewhere in there he would discover where the Key was hidden. It wouldn't be easy to find, that clue. It would be cryptic, hard to decipher. It might even take him years.

Nash stood up and frowned in the direction of the village. Rain had flattened the grass beside the road where a dozen soldiers cantered towards his tower. They wore no blaze, no marking at all, but the man in front had the whitest hair Nash had ever seen.

Instantly he turned, ran down the stairs and arrived in the small courtyard as the first riders came through the gate.

Yes, it was him. Forb'ez, Selar's most trusted servant. The coldest killer Nash had ever known. The man brought his horse to a halt, but didn't dismount.

'Good afternoon, Alderman.' Forb'ez bowed from the saddle, his colourless eyes hard and flinty.

Nash surveyed the others as they lined up behind their leader. Then he turned back to Forb'ez. 'Well? Is it good news or bad?'

'You are to come with us, Alderman.'

'Oh? Where to?'

'The King has sent us. He commands your return.'

Commands? By the blood of Broleoch!

Nash almost burst out laughing. So, Selar did need him after all. He'd been right. Well, Valena would have to eat her words now, wouldn't she?

'We have little time, Alderman,' Forb'ez added. 'There have been ... developments. The King requires your presence immediately. You're to come with us under armed guard.'

Nash nodded, keeping his face tightly schooled. It wouldn't do for this grim man to discover how delighted Nash was. 'Is the King in Marsay?'

'No. If we start out now, we will gain him by tomorrow night.'

Nash turned to go back inside, preparing to pack – but

what about Douglas? He paused. The Enemy wasn't going anywhere. The orb was already set up. Stinzali would be able to keep watch on him until that Douglas strength ebbed away. It was just a pity Nash couldn't be there to see him die. But Selar was too important. If there was something wrong, then he needed Nash – and Nash might finally have the opportunity he'd been waiting for for fourteen years.

'I'll be back down in a minute. Have one of your men saddle my horse.'

Finnlay couldn't tell what was different about the place. He was still surrounded by candlelight; the curtains were still pulled across the windows. It was day rather than night. Some cracks of sunshine bled through on to the walls and the vast collection crowding the room.

He must be feeling faint from the loss of blood. The cut was made an hour, two hours ago? His fingers already felt numb; his toes were cold. His heart raced so fast he could hardly keep track of it. Sweat trickled down his forehead. How much longer would it take before his vision went?

How long would it take him to die?

For the first time, Finnlay allowed his mind to approach that thought. Death; his death. Here, on this pallet, leagues from everyone he cared about. They would never know his fate, never know the evil that had killed him.

He was afraid.

'By the gods, Robert, I'm so sorry,' Finnlay breathed to the empty room. 'I should have helped you more. If I had, none of this would have happened. You would have stayed in Lusara and been around to notice this evil as it was growing. I'm sorry, Robert. I wish . . . I wish I'd never called you a traitor.'

His feet were cold now. Cold and numb. Would Carlan come back and laugh at him as he died?

Finnlay sucked in a breath and held it. Carlan wasn't coming back because he was no longer in the tower.

That's what was different! That shadow of evil for ever hovering in the background of his awareness was gone.

No. Don't wonder why or how or anything. Think fast. Now, before it's too late.

Finnlay focused hard. He could operate without an *ayarn*; all sorcerers could. But there was always a danger of backlash, of draining energy so quickly the body couldn't recover.

Well, if he didn't try something, then he was dead anyway. He could worry about the old man later, once he managed to get himself off this damned pallet.

Finnlay gathered together all the power he had in his whole body. He pulled it in, focused entirely on one thing. Then, as though he was using his *ayarn*, he let the power go, aimed at the rope binding his left arm. He couldn't even tell if it was working at first. Then ... the smell of burning hessian assailed him. He began to strain against the rope, willing it to break. Suddenly it snapped free. He'd done it!

He flexed his numb fingers, forcing the blood back into them. Once done, he reached up and pulled back the rope holding his head. He lurched up – and almost blacked out.

Slow down, Finn. Do it slowly. You've lost too much blood to hurry.

With his head still on the pallet, he undid the rope binding his right arm. He grabbed the loose sheet the old man had covered him with and bound it around his elbow to stop the flow of blood. He could fix up a proper bandage later.

Again, very slowly now, he gripped the sides of the pallet and hauled himself up. His vision swam, going black and white. He stayed there until it steadied, gasping as a throbbing pain beat against his temples. It took a long time, but eventually he could sit up enough to reach down and untie his legs. He pushed them over the edge of the cot and prepared himself for the worst part: standing up.

He waited a bit longer, until his feet had warmed enough for him to have some control over them. Then, gritting his teeth, he pushed himself up until he stood.

With a shudder, his legs folded beneath him and he fell with a thud. His chin hit the floor and he bit his tongue until it bled. Great! More blood!

He tried again. Bit by bit he regained his feet. He felt so weak he could hardly move, but he was running out of time.

There was no telling when the monster would come back, when the old man might come in to check on him.

Holding on to every support to hand, assailed by waves of dizziness, Finnlay shuffled to the doorway as quietly as he could manage. Hidden by the frame, he put his head around the corner and found the old man sitting with his back to the door.

Finnlay picked up an earthenware water bottle from the table. Creeping forward, he held his breath, lifted the make-shift weapon and brought it down with every ounce of force he could muster. Stinzali collapsed at his feet without utter-ing a sound.

For a second, Finnlay stood there, then he lurched back into the other room and cast around for his *ayarn*. He found it on the desk by the window, untouched. As he made for the door, something else caught his eye.

The orb.

He stumbled his way back to the pallet and raised the bottle high over his head. Then he dropped it on to the evil contraption, which cracked down one side. He lifted the bottle again and split it in two. Dark blood flowed out on to the carpet: his blood – and in that orb it had nearly killed him.

Now all he had to do was get out of this place.

The castle stood separate from the village. It was little more than a round tower with a small courtyard in front, guarding the door. It seemed only the old man lived there – he and the Angel of Darkness he served. There were no animals in the yard, no plants in the tiny garden. The storeroom had food, but it was almost empty of anything Finnlay could eat. Worse still, there was no horse for him to ride. Carlan must have left Finnlay's mount back by the river. He would have to continue on foot.

Stumbling with every step, Finnlay passed through the gate and headed away from the village. He wavered – but it was too dangerous. Someone might see him, someone who served Carlan. He was on his own.

Still feeling light-headed and very dizzy, Finnlay wandered

on, soon losing track of the direction he wanted to keep. The land before him kept swaying, lifting up and down and every time he tried to focus, nausea swept over him. Evening drew in and cold seeped through his shirt, making him shiver. Then the rain came, pounding down as though it would drive him into the ground. He fell into mud, struggled to rise and fell again. He looked up at the sky and for a moment revelled in the triumph. Carlan had said he would die. Well, he still might – but at least he would die free, and that monster would not be able to use his blood.

He must have slept because he woke up with water running over his mouth. He coughed and sat up. It was pitch black and the rain fell still. His bed had become a tiny river as the water flowed down from the hilltop. This was it: the end of his strength. If he lasted the night, he might live. If not?

He closed his eyes.

'Finnlay!'

A voice from his dreams. Calling him again and again. Always far away. Yes, it had to be Fiona's voice, plaguing him to the last. That lovely voice, so rich and full, the voice she used to carve pieces out of him at will.

'Finnlay!'

No closer. But then, she would never get any closer to him. She would always keep him at a distance, even if he could somehow find the courage to tell her how he felt. By the gods, that would only make it worse! If she hated him already, that would finish him completely. The greatest insult possible: the love of the brother she despised while the one she loved rejected her.

'Finnlay!'

Something was shaking his shoulder. Must be more water – or a mudslide. He should move. Should get up and find somewhere safe and dry to rest.

'Finnlay! Answer me, damn you! Open your eyes and look at me! Don't you dare lie there playing dead!'

The shaking got worse and he finally summoned up the strength to move, to open his eyes. He saw a vision to match his dream: fiery eyes, hazel and green. A frown, yes, but concerned, worried. She was holding his face, peering into it. What a wonderful dream.

'Where have you been?' she demanded. Of course she would demand. Had she ever spoken differently to him? 'I've been looking for you for days. I thought you'd been captured. For pity's sake, Finnlay! Talk to me.'

She shook him again, rattling his bones. 'Hey, stop it,' he murmured, his speech slurring. 'S'no need for that. I was with the Angel of Darkness.'

The vision frowned in either disbelief or horror — he couldn't tell which. Then she took his hands, pulled on his arms and forced him to stand. 'Come on, there's shelter down this way.'

Half-carrying, half-dragging him, this sweet image of Fiona forced him to walk. It wasn't far. Just to the end of the gully where a rock ledge overhung a small dry space surrounded by bushes. She dropped him there in the shelter, grabbed some wood and tossed it together. With barely a flick of her hand, a fire roared up, almost searing him with its heat.

This was no dream.

Finnlay blinked at the light, tried to sit up. Fiona turned to him, her hands reaching up again to tend the cuts and bruises on his face. There and in that moment, she'd never looked more beautiful to him.

'What happened to you?' she whispered, an edge of fear in her voice.

He said nothing. Instead, he leaned forward and kissed her. He took her by surprise and so it was a moment before she reacted. She pushed him away and stared at him in shock and . . . something else. Now, what was that?

'Finnlay Douglas, if you weren't already at death's door I would slap you for that!' She turned back to the fire, but it was too late. Finnlay put back his head and started to laugh. Weak and exhausted, he reached out for her hand. This time she didn't struggle. She let him pull her close, let him wrap his arms around her. With her head against his shoulder, Finnlay closed his eyes and waited for sleep to conquer him.

14

'No, don't lean forward in your stirrups, you fool!' Robert laughed. 'Sit back. Only go forward when the horse is climbing a hill.'

Patric bounced back on to the hard leather saddle and tried to gather up the loose reins. These riding lessons were bad enough as it was, without Robert having given him this bad-tempered, ill-mannered stallion for a mount. Sure, it was a beautiful horse – from a distance. Trying to control the grey from on top of its back was a nightmare.

'I never had these problems at the Enclave,' Patric grumbled, getting a better grip on the reins. 'And I rode from there almost to your door. You make me sound like I don't know what I'm doing.'

Robert laughed again and brought his horse alongside. Walking now, they entered a quiet glade only just beginning to turn a golden brown with autumn's first touch. 'If you're sitting on a quiet little animal who is required to go in no more than a straight line then, yes, you can ride. But as Collie there is teaching you, not all horses are the same. Who knows when you'll have to jump on the first one to hand and ride for your life? It has happened, you know. If you intend to make any more trips away from the Enclave, you'd best be sure you do know what you're doing.'

'That's easy for you to say.' Patric pulled again as the horse tossed its head. 'You've years of physical training behind you. Your muscles are like rocks. Me, I'm just not strong enough for a horse this size.'

'Strength is not the issue. It's your will alone which controls the horse. As soon as he realizes that you're the smarter one, he'll be like butter in your hands. Don't keep pulling on the reins like that. He's a big animal, he needs his space. Let him have it. He knows what he's doing. Only instruct him when you want to change something. Work together with him. But when you do want a change, make sure he knows that you're the one making the decisions. It's that simple.'

Patric glanced at Robert and saw the suppressed smile accompanying the prodding tone. 'Simple, eh? If it's so simple, why can't I do it?'

'Because you keep trying to rush it. That's all. Take your time. Practise. Sometimes you can be as bad as Finnlay.'

'And how long did it take him to ride a horse like this?'

Robert raised his eyebrows and pursed his lips. 'About an hour – but don't be discouraged. You'll learn, eventually.'

'Sure, after I've fallen off another dozen times.'

Robert laughed again as they left the glade. They followed a trickling stream up out of the trees and back on to the open moor. There was warmth in the sun, but the snapping wind whipped it away before it could sink in. Heather rustled in a whispering chime, all purple and brown like a moving carpet. There was not a soul in sight.

'I think it's time I was getting back to the Enclave,' Patric said, bringing his horse to a stop. The view was enormous, empty and yet full, a bleak reminder of his old enclosed life. 'I do have work to do and if I don't leave soon, the weather will play against me.'

Robert was silent and when Patric turned to look at him, he saw only a profile. His expression was impenetrable, a look which had appeared with increasing regularity since Robert had returned from Marsay with the news of Ayn. To the casual observer, Robert appeared to be his usual self, but underneath, there was a hardness that had never been there before.

'What do you know about prophecy?' Robert's voice was low, and so quiet Patric could hardly hear it above the wind and the heather.

'No more than you do.' Patric kept his gaze on Robert, his tone level. 'We have hundreds of prophecies, churned out over a thousand years. Prophecies about the weather, the gods, great battles, saints, everything. They rarely come true and when they do, there's no proof that the prophecy had anything to do with it.'

'And what about a prophecy given to us by the Key? How many times has that happened?'

Patric didn't have an answer. This was the first time Robert had broached the subject, but the way he spoke, his tone, the set of his shoulders – he'd already made up his own mind. He just wanted Patric to argue in order to prove to himself that he was right.

'Well?'

Patric formed his reply. 'To my knowledge, the Key doesn't prophesy. But then, I haven't read all the older books in the library. For all I know, it once could have been a daily occurrence.'

'Don't dissemble, Pat. I want the truth.'

'Very well. I read about one, once. Only one reference was ever made to it – at least, that still survives.'

'And?'

'It was very vague. So vague, I can't even quote the exact line. It had something to do with a particular event that was supposed to happen at a particular time. It never said what it was supposed to be – but from the date of the book and the other references, my calculations indicated the expected event was to happen some two hundred years ago.'

'And did it?'

'How should I know?' Patric said. 'As I said, there was only the one reference to it. What do you want from me, Robert? I'm not an oracle.'

'A pity.' Robert looked up, a wry smile on his face. 'Tell me what you think our prophecy means, Pat. Your honest opinion, now. Don't mind my feelings.'

Patric stared at him a moment and shook his head. This man was more changeable than the Lusaran weather. He swung his leg over the horse and jumped to the ground. As Robert joined him, they walked along the hilltop, ignoring the autumn breeze and its chill.

'I don't know what it means. Until we find out more, it's impossible to guess. The Key has never done anything to harm the Enclave, only to protect it. You're the only one who thinks the opposite.' Patric paused. 'I think the Key wants you to do something that must keep you out of the Enclave.'

'Well, you're right, there,' Robert grunted, making Patric glance at him in surprise.

'What does that mean?'

Robert didn't answer, only smiled bitterly.

It was more than Patric could stand. It was time he knocked some of that bitterness out of the old renegade. 'If you'd stayed at the Enclave, even Stood the Circle, it would mean you wouldn't be out here in the real world. And if you're not out here, the Bonding will never happen.'

That wiped the smile off Robert's face. His jaw became set, his eyes hard as steel. 'The Bonding will never happen anyway, Pat, regardless of what the Key says.'

'And why is that?' Patric stood his ground.

'If I told you to ride into the nearest town and reveal that you're a sorcerer, would you do it? If I told you to tell everyone you saw that there's an Enclave of sorcerers in the Goleth mountains, would you do it?'

'But what has that . . . ?'

'Would you?' Robert snapped.

'No.'

'Why not? You said you trusted me. You said you believed in me. If that's so, then you should, by rights, do exactly what I say. Would you just do as I say without using your own judgement? Would you ask no questions, just take what I say as an irrefutable truth?'

There was no answer to that. Patric dropped his head and played with the reins in his hands. Robert stood close for a few seconds, then turned away, his gaze returning to the horizon.

'How is Finnlay dealing with living at the Enclave?'

'Not well. He wouldn't mind it if it wasn't forced on him.'

Robert smiled a little. 'Poor Finn. It's so at odds with what he's always loved. What he's always wanted.'

Patric watched him a moment. 'But Robert, what about . . .'

'No, Pat, no more prophecy. I'll keep fighting the Key.

There's more than one kind of demon to be fought, Pat, and that one is enough for me.'

Robert moved around his horse and leaped up into the saddle. As Patric scrambled on to his horse, Robert added, 'Wilf did me a favour, banishing me. It's better this way. Better that I cut all ties to the Enclave. I know my brother is there and I wish he wasn't – but wishes have got me nowhere. It's the only way to reduce the risk of—' He broke off and turned to face Patric. 'I'm sorry you have to leave, Pat. I'll miss you. But if you do go, don't come back here. Ever.'

The smell of fresh hay and dried oats filled the stable with a rich, pungent perfume. The animals within the stalls nestled contentedly in the warmth, their thoughts on physical comfort alone, peace and quiet.

Patric squatted on a mounting stool, his feet dug into piles of sweet hay. He kicked them around as he waited.

Micah finished with the grey stallion and emerged from the stall, a saddle across his arm, bridle over his shoulder. Patric sprang up and followed him down the length of the stable.

'I tell you, Micah, he's cutting himself off from everyone. From me, from Finnlay – even his mother. I'm sure he'll find some excuse to get rid of you too.'

Micah lumped the saddle over a bar, hung the bridle on its hook. 'He's already tried once.'

'Oh?' Patric came to a halt. 'Then you agree with me?'

'How can I not? But what can we do about it?'

Patric slumped against the wall, his arms folded. 'Not much, I'm sure. It just worries me to see him like this. I have to return to the caves, but I'm terrified of leaving him alone.'

'He won't be alone, Patric,' Micah murmured. 'We must just pray that something happens to ease this . . . thing that's going on in his head.'

'You don't think he's right, do you? And what about that business of there being more than one kind of demon? The only demon I know of is the one who took Ayn. Robert's supposed to be his enemy, not ours. What is he talking about?'

'I don't know.'

'But you don't seem to be that worried by it all. Do you know something?'

'Nothing more than what you've told me, what he's told me.' Micah shrugged. 'I can only watch from the sidelines. All I know is that he never gives his word about something unless he knows he can keep it.'

'And where does that leave me?' Patric said, only a little comforted.

'Late for dinner.' Micah grinned. 'If you want to stay on Lady Margaret's good side, I suggest you go and wash now.'

Patric nodded and left the stable. There was hot water and fresh linen laid out for him in his rooms, but in his haste, he knocked the water all over his clean trousers. Changing again did make him late and he arrived downstairs, breathless, to find Robert and Lady Margaret waiting for him in the winter parlour. It was still light outside, so there were only a couple of candles lit on the table. Robert wouldn't meet his gaze, but Margaret did.

'You didn't rush on our account, did you?'

'No, my lady – or rather, yes, I did. Robert is always telling me that my manners are terrible. I'm sorry I kept you waiting.'

'Please, sit down, Patric. You're our guest and we wait upon you.' With that, Margaret smiled and poured him some wine. Plates of steaming longfish were brought in, swimming in a sauce of basil and thyme. Suddenly Patric realized how hungry he was. All that fresh air this afternoon had done real damage to his appetite.

'I had a letter this morning, Mother, from Flan-har.' Robert said between mouthfuls.

'Grant Kavanagh? Why didn't you tell me earlier?'

'You were busy. He asked me to pass on his regards and his hopes of your good health.'

'Oh?' Margaret didn't appear impressed. 'What did he want?'

'News, nothing more. He's still annoyed I haven't been to visit since I came back to Lusara.'

'Why don't you? He's only three or four days' travel away.

Now that the old Duke is dead, I'm sure you two would be able to enjoy yourselves in peace.'

Was there an undercurrent here, something between the words mother and son exchanged so politely? Who was this Grant Kavanagh and why would the old Duke's death make a difference – and why did Margaret want Robert to go away for a while?

Patric didn't have the chance to ask. Margaret was addressing him directly. 'I apologize, Patric. Has Robert never mentioned his old friend from our neighbouring state? The two of them were quite inseparable at one time. Grant Kavanagh was sent here for a year by his father – supposedly to enhance his education. As the heir, Grant was expected to sit by my husband's side and learn all he could of courts, assizes and government.'

Margaret paused, waiting for Patric to say something. He glanced at Robert, who continued his meal as though the conversation was not even happening.

'Should I take it that his education was not improved?'

'Oh, I'm sure he learned a great many things,' Margaret replied lightly, 'when he was around. What he did at other times, I know not. I'm sure my son would be able to enlarge on that topic better than I. What do you say, Robert?'

Without even looking up, Robert replied, 'Grant has ruled his independent dukedom with wisdom and competence for the last seven years. I can't see how his year at Dunlorn harmed him in any way. Perhaps I will go and visit him, as you suggest, Mother. If nothing else. I can bring you back further news of his exploits.'

If it was intended as a barb, Margaret ignored it. She turned back to Patric. 'Robert sees little of his childhood friends these days. I am pleased you, at least, have kept in touch with him. You never did tell me how you met.'

Patric paused as another plate was placed in front of him, this one with roasted beef surrounded by thick white almond milk and slices of onion.

'We met many years ago, Mother. I'm not sure Patric even remembers.'

Patric ignored him. 'I could never forget it, my lady. Your son knocked me down.'

'He knocked you down?'

'Quite by accident, he insists. My teacher, Brother Boniface, was not impressed, however. We were both punished, as I recall. Fortunately, your son was not long at the abbey, otherwise we might have ended up real enemies. As it is . . .'

Margaret was generous enough to smile. 'This was when you were nine or so? When Robert went to Saint Mark's?'

'That's right.'

'But you did not stay and take holy orders?'

Patric shrugged, digging into the succulent beef. 'I had no vocation. I work as a lay brother now, teaching.'

'And you enjoy it?'

Patric nodded. 'I prefer to contribute what I can rather than profess a vocation I don't feel. The little I can do helps inexorably towards the greater wealth. I feel it's my duty to give back in return for what I received. Who knows what great mind I may help in developing?'

'An admirable principle,' Margaret said. 'And if you found you'd developed a vocation? Would you take vows?'

'Without hesitation.'

Margaret smiled, but Robert put down his knife and stood. 'If you will excuse me, Mother, I have something I must attend to.' He didn't spare a glance for Patric, leaving the room in complete silence.

With a sigh, Margaret hung her head and murmured, 'I keep praying for him but nobody seems to be listening.'

Patric reached over to refill her cup with sweetened wine. With as much confidence as he could voice, he replied, 'Then now is not the time to stop.'

Robert took the last few steps two at a time and came out on to the battlement in the remaining evening light. He greeted the guard standing watch and moved along the stone path, a steadying hand against the rampart. The air was cool but fresh, almost welcoming.

'There you are!' Robert called to Micah, who was leaning over the edge of the wall. 'Don't jump. It's a long way down.'

Micah straightened up and fought off a smile. 'But you're always telling me I should try new things, my lord. What if it turns out I can fly?'

'And if you can't, you'll never get to spend the silver sovereign I owe you.' Robert joined him on the corner tower. 'For what use have birds for silver?'

Micah raised his eyebrows. 'I was right?'

'Once again, yes. Here, listen.' Robert reached into his doublet and pulled out the letter from Grant. By the last of the fading daylight, he read, 'Robert my dear friend, you have, of course, my deepest sympathies on the early and tragic demise of your dear brother. No doubt he will live on in our memories as a passionate but incomplete sorcerer, weighed down by the pressure of the Guilde's demands. I suspect they will use this as an excuse to go on another pogrom to clean your country of such filth. Do say, my dark angelic friend, if you need the services of an independent army, one which owes allegiance only to me. There are such dividends to be enjoyed in ruling my own state. Perhaps you would consider joining me in that condition? With our borders joined, no King or Guilde would dare cross and we would both be safe to enjoy whatever pleasures we chose.'

Micah's eyebrows rose. 'Does he know something, my lord?'

'No. He's just fishing. He's trying to tell me that I can trust him with whatever secret it is that I'm hiding. He's already made the assumption that there is one – as you accurately predicted. Here's your silver.'

Micah took the coin, examined it, bit it between his teeth – Robert had to laugh.

'Well, you never know these days, my lord. Nothing is sacred any more.' The coin disappeared into a pocket and Micah leaned forward over the wall again.

'What are you looking for?'

'Last time I was up here I dropped that knife Deverin gave me. I tried looking for it this afternoon, but I couldn't see it anywhere. Now he's asking me about it and I thought I might be able to see it from up here. He'll kill me if he finds out I've lost it.'

'That's if you're lucky,' Robert agreed, leaning over next to Micah. 'Let me see if I can find it.'

'I didn't know you could find something like that. I thought it was only people you could Seek.'

'It is,' Robert grunted, straining in the growing dusk to see anything hidden in the deep grass below.

'What's that?' Micah murmured, straightening up.

'What? Where?'

Micah tapped his shoulder and pointed further out to where a rider approached the castle. 'Who'd be arriving at this hour? Are you expecting someone?'

'No.' Robert frowned. In this light, with the sun setting behind him, the rider's identity was impossible to guess.

'By the gods!' Micah breathed suddenly. He took an involuntary step backwards, his face white with shock.

'What is it, Micah? Do you know who that is?'

'Don't you?'

Robert took another look; while there was something subtly familiar about the stranger, he couldn't put a name on it. 'No. Who is it?'

Micah looked at him, eyes wide with something bordering on fear. 'My father!'

By the gods, indeed! David Maclean? On his way to Dunlorn? Impossible – and yet, there he was, approaching the castle gates without a hint of hesitation.

'I don't like this,' Micah whispered. 'I'll go down and meet him.'

'I'll come with you,' Robert began, but Micah paused on the steps to the courtyard, his hands raised.

'Please, my lord. I beg you to wait here. You know how he feels about you.'

'Of course,' Robert said. Micah took the short steep steps down to the courtyard while Robert stayed above and watched him disappear around a corner, then reappear by the gate, just as David Maclean was ready to dismount. The two men exchanged a few words and Micah's fidgeting abruptly stopped. He took a step back and turned to look up at Robert.

Then Micah took his father across the courtyard and

around the corner. Soon Robert could hear both men climbing the steps to the battlements. What was Robert to say to this man? He had virtually disowned his youngest son because Micah had refused to leave Robert's service. And now he was here?

'My lord . . .' Micah stammered breathlessly, a thin film of sweat on his furrowed brow. 'My father, Master David Maclean. He . . . wishes to speak to you.'

Robert felt Micah's discomfort keenly and tried to make this meeting as easy as possible. 'Good evening, Master Maclean.'

Maclean bowed slightly. 'Good evening, Your Grace.'

Yes, he was Micah's father, all right. He was as tall as Robert, broad-shouldered and strong from years of farming. The hair was a darker hue of red, but the forehead was the same, as were the eyes, though older and lined by age. The gaze was nothing if not stony.

'How may I be of service, Master Maclean?' Robert asked as evenly as possible.

The older man glanced at his son then at the nearest guard, who was too far away to hear anything. He took a breath and said, 'I must ask you to come with me, Your Grace.'

'Where?'

'I cannot say.'

'I see.' Robert didn't see, but that didn't make any difference. 'Now?'

David Maclean nodded. 'With as little attention as possible.'

What could possibly drive this man to come here with such a request? It must be very important indeed to bring him here, to make him actually speak to his son – to ask something of Robert. How could Robert refuse?

'Micah, have Deverin saddle us some horses quickly. I'll go and make my excuses to my mother. I'll see you at the gate in ten minutes.'

The sun sank beneath the horizon, leaving only a washed-out glow behind the evening clouds. Robert frowned up at

214

the sky, then across at Micah, 'It'll rain again tonight. Remind me to send someone down tomorrow to reinforce the bridge across the river. At this rate it'll be washed away before winter.'

'Yes, my lord,' Micah nodded, his voice belying the tension in his shoulders. He rode between his father and Robert, but not a word passed between father and son. Micah was obviously torn.

'How long will it take us to reach this place?' Robert asked genially.

Maclean glanced up, his eyes invisible in the darkness. 'Another hour, perhaps more.'

'Then we are likely to get wet?'

With a stiff nod, Maclean replied, 'If Your Grace says so.'

'My Grace would happily defer to one with greater knowledge of the weather,' Robert replied without pausing. 'One such as a master farmer.'

'A poor master farmer would have little knowledge to improve upon that of an educated man such as Your Grace.'

Robert grinned. 'Then it will rain! Wonderful. I love getting soaked to the skin. It makes me feel all young and irresponsible.'

Maclean turned and watched him steadily. Micah was shifting his head this way and that, his face twisting in silent plea to both of them.

Maclean ignored him. 'Why have you come with me? Is it only to mock me?'

Robert dropped the smile and held up his hand. 'I mock only myself, Master Maclean. No one else is fair game. Come, let's put on some speed.'

The rain did come, but, like a delicate mediator, it was little more than a gentle mist, dusting the horses with a faint sheen and leaving Robert's face moist and refreshed. By the time they reached the hilltop, the rain had all but ceased, the clouds thinning and allowing some moonlight to filter through. It was damned cold, though.

'That's the place,' Maclean said heavily, 'down there.'

'And what awaits us?' Micah asked, bringing his horse around to face his father. There was an unbridled challenge between them – one Micah was not going to back down from. 'Tell us what this is all about.'

Maclean stared at his son, neither angry nor bitter. He shook his head. 'I don't know.'

'You don't know! Then why are we here?'

'I was asked to bring His Grace to this wood. That's all I can tell you.'

'But . . .'

'It's all right, Micah,' Robert interjected. 'I trust your father. For all that he despises me, I doubt there's a trap down there. He wouldn't have allowed you to come, otherwise.'

Maclean directed his horse around Micah's. 'I would not have been able to stop him.'

Robert nodded encouragement to Micah. 'That makes two of us.'

They entered the wood where the floor was darkened by moonshadows and damp bushes. It was almost silent; only the odd skittering here and there spoke of animal life. Robert rode beside Maclean, his eyes searching for danger despite his earlier words. This was no time to become complacent.

A small drop in the ground brought them out into a clearing. A makeshift shelter stood to the right, where a tall, blond young man guarded another lying beneath. A poor fire warmed other folk, huddled around. They all stood as Robert dismounted.

He moved forward, scanning the faces for some answer, some meaning – then one face caught his eye. Robert instantly went down on his knee. 'Your Grace! What are you doing here?'

'Please, my lord,' Rosalind moved forward. She brought him to his feet and closer to the fire. 'We are in dire need of your help. I was afraid you wouldn't come.'

Robert frowned. This was unbelievable. He glanced over his shoulder at Maclean. He stood to one side, no surprise on that gruff face. He just watched Robert with that same stony expression. He must have known the Queen was here, but he'd said nothing. Typical Maclean.

Robert turned back to Rosalind. 'What help do you need? Why are you here?'

She clasped her hands together, her expression one of profound peace. 'I have run away, my lord. I have left the King's side just as you did. I need your help to leave Lusara. We are exhausted, injured and much in need of rest. I throw us on your mercy and pray you will be kind in return.'

Left? Just like that? Did she realize ... Of course she did. No one knew better the King's wrath. She was watching him, trying to hide her fear of his rejection. He turned away and looked over the others surrounding the fire. The children! They, too? And ... was that Samah? And ... 'Greetings, Kandar.'

'Your Grace,' George nodded.

'You find yourself in interesting company.'

'The best, my lord.'

'And who is that injured?'

'One of my men as we overcame a patrol out hunting for the Queen.'

'I see.' Robert walked over to the little shelter and gazed down at the sleeping man. He looked close to death. 'How long have you camped here?'

'Since last night,' Kandar replied, joining him.

'Then it's amazing you haven't been discovered ...' Robert's voice trailed off as a figure emerged from behind the shelter. Small, cloaked and silent. Hands rose up to pull the hood down.

'Hello, Robert.'

By the gods! Why hadn't he noticed? Why hadn't he sensed her aura? Of course, that's how David Maclean had been involved! Jenn knew where to get help. Get Maclean to find Micah – Micah could bring Robert ... Oh yes, it all made sense now.

And here she was, standing before him, her eyes steady on his, waiting for his reaction.

'What are you doing here?' Robert said.

'Helping the Queen, as you are.'

'What kind of fool answer is that?' he hissed. 'You could have got yourself killed! What the hell were you thinking?'

Jenn's eyes flashed. 'Probably more than you. After all, I at least knew what I was dealing with. What kind of idiot leaves the safety of his own castle on the word of a man who openly despises him?'

'A man you sent to get me here.'

'Well, it worked, didn't it? I knew you'd fall for it.' She took a breath, then her face was composed again, though her eyes still brimmed with anger. 'The only thing left is for you to decide where your loyalties lie. Make your choice.'

Robert moved close, towering over her. 'And what if I choose not to help?'

'I'd rather you didn't.'

He had to laugh – because if he didn't, he would have hit her. 'Then I won't, will I? After all, how could I refuse such a gracious invitation? A pity I wasn't allowed to make a free choice. Now you'll never know what I would have said.'

Confusion warred across her face like clouds in a stormy sky. 'Why did you give in so easily? You know I have no power over you.'

'Then why make the threat, Jenn?' Robert leaned close so only she could hear him. 'Did it make you feel good?'

He didn't wait for a response. He turned quickly and strode back to the fire. 'Pack your things up. The sooner we get to Dunlorn, the sooner we can get warm. Micah, you and your father will accompany the Earl of Kandar back through the gate. He'll wear my cloak, ride my horse. With any luck, everyone will assume it's me returning. The rest of us will take another route.'

Kandar quickly gained Rosalind's side, his stance utterly defiant. 'I will not leave Her Grace. Send another to go back with your men. I'll stay here.'

'George,' Rosalind murmured, 'please do as he says. He's our only hope now.'

'I'm sorry, Your Grace, but I don't trust him.'

'That's all right,' Robert gestured expansively, 'I don't trust me either. Nevertheless . . .'

'My answer is no,' Kandar repeated, standing firm.

Robert took a step forward, meeting Kandar's defiance

with a steady unflinching gaze. Then, with his voice low he said carefully and precisely, 'You will do exactly as I say.'

Kandar met his gaze for a long time. A time in which nobody in the clearing moved. Then abruptly he looked away, a wry smile on his face. 'Very well,' he nodded. 'I'll go. But if . . .'

'Make no threats,' Robert shook his head, 'that's already been done for you. Now come, we need to get moving.'

15

By the time they got back through the gates, Micah's hands were freezing, although it probably had more to do with the way he'd clenched them up during the ride home than the actual cold of the night. Nobody challenged them, or even noticed that the man accompanying him was not Robert but a stranger. Maclean said nothing, but simply accompanied him through the castle and up to Robert's study.

Micah closed the door, but didn't dare lock it. It would have been much easier if he could have fetched Patric to put a warning on it, but there was no way of knowing if Robert wanted Patric to know about all this. And what would Patric say — not just about the Queen's sudden appearance, but about Jenn?

Once inside, Kandar threw off the cloak as though it were a devil on his back. He strode around the room like a wild animal on a leash. Maclean waited quietly by the window, his hands clasped behind his back.

'So what do we do now?' Kandar demanded.

'We wait,' Micah replied, stoking up the fire.

'For what?'

'For my lord to return.'

Kandar stopped pacing. 'And what if he doesn't bring the others with him?'

'He will.' Maclean said this without moving from the

window. In the ensuing silence, he glanced over his shoulder at Kandar, not Micah. 'The Duke will return, my lord, and he will bring the Queen with him. Safely.'

'And how do you know that?'

'Because he has no choice.' He returned to the window. 'The girl will make sure of that.'

She should have known he'd react like this. Storm-walled, defiant and utterly unreachable. Stubbornly proud and totally convinced that he was right and everyone else was wrong. What was she doing involving herself in something so dangerous? Didn't she realize she was just a foolish child, incapable of doing anything right?

Jenn glared at Robert's back where he rode in front of her. It was almost impossible to travel in complete silence. The children were crying, Hugh gasping out in tortured pain, Rosalind and Samah murmured, trying to soothe them all.

That he should humiliate her in front of them all – in front of the Queen. She'd done the job, hadn't she? She'd brought them safely to Dunlorn without being detected – and here he was treating her like the village idiot! Unreasonable, insensitive, intractable, rotten . . .

'Quiet now as we move down here.' Robert's voice came out of the dark, the shadow of his arm indicating where they should go. The others trailed down the incline, but as Jenn went to pass him, he stopped her. Once they were alone he turned to face her.

'There's something down there they can't know about: they'll know it exists but not how it works.'

'Then why tell me?' Jenn snapped.

'I would have thought that would be obvious, even to you. There's a secret entrance to Dunlorn and the tunnel opening is at the bottom of this ravine.'

'So?' Jenn interrupted.

'The only way it can be opened is with sorcery.'

'What's wrong, Robert? Lost your powers? Don't tell me you need my poor pathetic help. Oh, how the mighty have fallen!'

'Stop it,' Robert growled. 'Do you want to spend the rest of your short life out here in the open?'

'Well, it might be better than going in there with you.'

Robert hissed in a breath. 'The door requires two hands to operate it. I've only ever used it when Finn was around. You'll have to take his place. While you're at it, try to remember you're the daughter of an Earl – not a whining serving wench from the forest of Shan Moss.'

He wheeled his horse around and descended without another word. Fuming, Jenn followed. Her twisted ankle ached as she put pressure on the stirrup, but she bit her teeth and said nothing. She also managed to get her temper under some control by the time she reached the bottom. There would be other chances to tell him what she really thought.

The tunnel was hideous: dark and black and slimy. And the smell! At least they'd left the horses behind, to be collected later, some time before dawn. Robert led the way, Jenn following behind, holding Kenrick's hand. This had long since stopped being the adventure his mother had promised; now Kenrick was just sick and tired and weary and bad-tempered. He kept stopping abruptly so that Jenn would walk into him and stumble. Once she even fell flat on her face. Kenrick had just watched her, no apology forthcoming.

For what seemed an eternity, they stumbled and sloshed along the tunnel until they came to a corner. Robert stopped to listen.

'What is it?' Jenn asked.

'Ssh! I think I can hear water. Can you?'

'Coming from where?'

'There's another branch down that way. It could be a problem if we have to leave in a hurry.' He turned right.

'How long has this been here?' Jenn felt the need to whisper. Every sound in the tunnel carried back and forth, doubling and redoubling until it returned to the speaker. It was horrible.

'I have no idea. I found it by accident.'

'And why is the door locked . . . in such a fashion?'

'Quiet, we're going under the castle wall now. Any sound could easily be heard in the kitchens.'

Jenn shut up. Kenrick slipped and opened his mouth to scream. Prince or not, Jenn felt no compunction about slapping her hand over his mouth. He tried to bite her, but she'd played this game before. His struggling stopped when Robert came to a halt in front of another door.

'Jenn?'

She gave Kenrick into Shane's care and moved forward. 'This one too?' she whispered, afraid he would snap again.

'No,' Robert replied sarcastically. 'I just thought you might like a closer look – for posterity's sake.' He grabbed her arm and brought her hand up to the wall, pressing it hard against the slimy stone. 'Don't let go until I tell you.'

He released her and stretched high above his head, his hand invisible even to her sight. She felt something click, but couldn't say where. Then Robert pushed the door open and there was a staircase before them, narrow, spiral and blessed with a breath of light.

'Take them up, but keep them quiet. Don't do anything until I get there.'

Jenn began to climb the stairs. The others followed behind, now so exhausted only their breathing could be heard. At the top was another door – this one light wood. Jenn pushed it open to reveal a room without windows. Was this a prison?

There was some light, coming from under a door to her right. She didn't investigate it, however, just ushered the others into the room. Eventually, Keagan and Robert arrived, carrying Hugh between them. Robert kicked the door closed and laid Hugh down by the empty fireplace.

'You'll all have to keep back from the door and stay very quiet. Jenn, come with me.'

Robert put his hand on the door in a gesture that reminded Jenn of the night they'd rescued Finnlay. Robert had been so different then. What had changed him? Why was he being so cruel?

But she knew why he touched the door – to check who was on the other side. He glanced at her to say it was safe, turned a latch she couldn't see and pulled it open. Jenn slipped through behind him. She stopped abruptly when she realized where she was.

'Kandar, you'd better go in with the others.' Robert began without preamble. 'Master Maclean, thank you for your help. If you like, I'll send word with Micah when we have them all safely away from Dunlorn.'

Maclean nodded and looked like he wanted to say something more. Instead, he glared at Micah, then turned for the door. Before he'd even gone, Kandar had slipped past Jenn and into the secret chamber. Robert turned to Micah. 'Let's get to work. Get Deverin and Owen moving. We'll need blankets, fresh clothing, water and firewood. Food, too. Preferably hot. Bring everything up in small quantities – just enough for tonight. And do it all very quietly. Impress that on them, will you?'

'Of course, my lord.' Micah nodded and headed for the door. He paused, turned and flashed Jenn a smile. Then he was gone.

'Well, it's nice that somebody's glad to see me.' Jenn limped to the fireplace and sank into the nearest chair.

Robert went back to the door in the panelling and pulled it shut. There was now no sign that any opening had ever been there. 'Are you injured?'

Jenn shook her head. 'No.'

'Then why are you limping?'

Jenn couldn't answer. She knew what he'd say if she told him about her fall. Unfortunately he took her silence as an admission of guilt.

'What do you think you're playing at?' He approached slowly, but Jenn didn't want to look at him. 'Do you think this is some kind of game? Have you no idea what it's cost me to protect you? What it would cost your father if he lost you? And you vowed to Stand the Circle? Why? After everything that's happened, why?'

Jenn clasped her hands together and studied her dirty fingers. She needed a bath, but it was unlikely she would get one in a hurry.

'Well? Answer me, Jenn.'

He didn't shout, even the earlier sharp tone was gone. He

223

really wanted to know, really wanted an answer. Now she did look up. There was no frown on his face, just bewilderment. His eyes were deep green, like a forest, and just as impenetrable. Why did he have to be this way? Why couldn't he just talk to her, like he used to? Even this close she could feel his mind closed to hers. She sighed. 'I don't want to hear another lecture, Robert. You've chosen your own path. You don't rule me.'

Slowly, almost painfully, Robert shook his head, his eyes dark and troubled. 'You have no idea what you're getting into.'

This was too much. On the one hand there were people ready to follow her into hell – and then there was this ... renegade telling her she didn't know up from down. Jenn leaped to her feet and pushed past him to the panel door. 'I think I do know what I'm doing, Robert, but if I don't I have only you to blame. After all, you've never actually explained to me why this is all a problem. And you won't, will you? It's all too dangerous. Let me tell you, I don't need your protection. I can take care of myself. I have so far and I'll continue to do so. From now on you can keep your narrow opinions to yourself!' With that, she reached for the door and was surprised to find it open at her touch.

She whirled around, ready to accuse Robert, when the outer door opened and a middle-aged woman entered.

'Robert, I ...' The woman's voice trailed off as she saw Jenn. Her eyes widened as she came to a halt.

Robert sighed and nodded to Jenn to continue through to the other room. She didn't, though. There was something compelling about this woman, something entirely intriguing.

'Very well, Robert,' the woman continued, ready for battle. 'I've been patient, but I really think it's time you told me what's going on.'

'You won't like it,' Robert murmured.

'I don't care. I dislike the lies even more.'

Robert lifted his head as though in a prayer for patience. 'Very well, Mother. I'll tell you everything, but not right now. At this moment, I need your help. These people in the next room need your help. Once they're settled, I'll answer all your questions honestly.'

'And this girl?'

Robert turned to Jenn. He looked so vulnerable in that moment, she could almost forgive him. Almost.

'Mother, I would like you to meet Lady Jennifer Ross. Jenn, this is my mother, Lady Margaret.'

Margaret took a few steps forward, her keen gaze taking in every smudge of dirt, every tear in Jenn's clothing. There was almost no resemblance between Robert and this striking woman, except perhaps the grace with which she moved. This was an awful introduction and Jenn felt every inch the idiot Robert claimed her to be. Eventually Margaret favoured Jenn with a warm smile, then shot a dry glance at her son.

'I'll go and help Micah, my dear. Hurry him along. This is one explanation I can't wait to hear.'

It was past midnight before they were all settled and drifting off to sleep in makeshift beds arranged around the room. Robert stood at the door watching as Margaret moved from one to the other, checking that all was well. Jenn had long since fallen asleep and Robert was finally able to relax. At last the constant irritation of her presence had eased. He could stop snapping at her and waiting for her to snap back. As if things weren't bad enough!

Margaret left one candle burning, stoked up the fire, then joined him at the door. Robert stood aside to let her through, then closed the door after her. The study was warmer than the adjoining chamber – and very welcome: Micah was just bringing in a tray of something delicious which he laid down on the hastily cleared table to pour a cup of spiced wine for Robert and Margaret. Then he left without a word. It had been a trying night for him, too.

Margaret took her wine over to the window. The clouds had all gone now, leaving a pale blue corona around the moon. Robert went straight to the food, but after the first mouthful, his appetite left him. Probably something to do with the impending discussion.

'Hugh should be all right until morning,' Margaret began,

blowing on the hot wine. 'Nevertheless, I'll check on him in a few hours. The tonic I gave the little girl will keep her sleeping until tomorrow afternoon.'

'How soon before they can move from here?'

'I'm no healer, but I wouldn't like to see them out in the weather in less than three days. The girl is quite ill and while Hugh is strong, he needs rest to let his wounds heal. Keeping their presence secret from the rest of Dunlorn will be awkward, but I think we'll manage.' Margaret sipped her wine, her gaze floating out of the window. 'That girl, Jennifer Ross? She's the one you found in Shan Moss, isn't she? Jacob's daughter.'

'Yes.'

'She's beautiful. But how did she, of all people, get caught up in all this?'

'It's a long story.'

'I'm sure it is.' Margaret turned away from the window, wrapped her hands around the warm cup and waited.

She looked lovely with the moonlight reflecting off the silver strands in her hair and giving her skin a soft sheen. But those dark, watchful eyes were guarded. She didn't really trust him. Not any more. She wasn't even sure he was going to tell her the truth now – even though he'd promised.

Robert put down his wine, stood with his back to the fireplace and laced his fingers together. This was not going to be easy. 'What would you like to know?'

'Where is Finnlay?'

Great! She begins with the one question he couldn't answer. With a sigh, Robert shook his head. 'I'm sorry, Mother, but I can't answer that question directly. At least, not yet. Not until I've explained a lot of other things. However, what I said before is true. Finnlay is safe and with friends.'

'And you can't tell me because you're protecting those friends?'

'I'm protecting you – and Finnlay.'

'Of course.' The tension in Margaret's face, her shoulders, did not diminish. Instead she turned back to the window, as though she were afraid of him, of what he had to say. She wanted the truth, but could he tell her he was just as caught up in a tangle of confusion as she was? Even now, when he was so very sure of what he had to do, he still questioned himself at every turn. Was he about to make the biggest mistake he'd ever made?

'Mother,' Robert began, his voice low but firm. 'I am a sorcerer.'

She started so violently wine spilled from the cup in her hand. Her head dropped and a deep shuddering sigh was wrenched from her body. Robert didn't dare move. A gust of wind rattled at the casements, slipping through the cracks to chill the room.

'I was afraid you wouldn't tell me.' Margaret's voice was a whisper, frozen in the room by the midnight air. She opened her eyes, lifted her face a little. There were tears on her cheeks, glistening in the moonlight.

'You knew?'

'I wondered.' Margaret shook her head. 'With those rumours about Finnlay and your secrets and, oh . . . so many things over the years. I think perhaps I guessed, but didn't want to think about it. That . . . perhaps that was why I was so . . . content to live at Saint Hilary's.'

'Mother!' Robert whispered, shocked and saddened at the same time.

'After the Guilde was here a change came over this place. I watched Deverin and Owen and they seemed to know what was going on. They seemed at ease. I wondered how could men like that could follow you if you were involved with something so terrible.'

'But I am.'

'And then tonight? Robert, what has the Queen to do with this? With sorcery?'

'Nothing directly. But it is only sorcery that has kept her free this long.' Robert came across the room to stand before her. Carefully he reached up and brushed the moisture from her cheeks. 'I'm sorry, Mother.'

She studied him with dark eyes glinting sapphire from the moon. Her gaze wide and open, he knew she was thinking about him and sorcery together for the first time. He'd seen

that look before on others. The effect was always unpredict-
able. And he'd been lying to her for so many years now,
would she be able to forgive him?

'How long?' The words were dragged out of her, as though
she would rather have remained silent. 'How long have you
been a sorcerer?'

Robert kept his tone mild. 'Since birth. I found out just
after I turned nine. I know it bothers you, Mother—'

'Oh, Robert!' Margaret put her cup down, clasped her
hands together and turned her face back to the window. 'Of
course it bothers me. My own son . . .'

'Both your sons.'

She almost faltered at that. 'Both . . . my sons tainted by
an evil I can't begin to imagine. Are you going to tell me the
entire Church is wrong – but you are right?'

Robert took her arms and made her face him, trying to
impress the truth upon her with the passion of his words.
'Sorcery is *not* evil, Mother. It never has been. It's merely a
weapon evil people can use for their own gains. It can also
be used for good. That's all I've ever done. You've kept faith
with me this long; I beg you, don't turn your back on me
now. Please trust me. Sorcery is not evil.'

'Evil? How can you know? You can't because you have it
inside you.' Her eyes searched his face for a long time, some
shred of doubt edging her expression. 'But . . . I never
thought you were evil before I knew. I've never seen nor
heard you act in any way that could be called evil. So . . .
how can *you* be evil?' She shook her head, unable to answer
her own question. 'Was the truth so hard to tell me?'

'I was afraid you'd hate me. I didn't want to hurt you.'

'Oh, Robert. You're my son. How could I possibly hate
you?' Margaret let her face relax into the motherly smile he
loved so much. 'We all get hurt in life. You don't need to be
strong enough for all of us.'

Robert sighed and pulled her close, setting the Seal in that
moment. Her hair smelled like summer roses and reminded
him of playing in the garden as a child.

'Finnlay won't be coming home, will he?'

'Not with the way things are. It'll be a miracle if there isn't

228

some sort of Guilde hunt for sorcerers. You know their sacred duty.'

Nodding slowly, Margaret reached up and touched his face. 'My sons, both sorcerers. How can it be possible? I'm sorry, Robert, but you must understand. This is going to take me some time and a lot of prayer.'

He took her hand and kissed it. 'I know. You should get some rest. It'll be a long day tomorrow.'

'And you? Will you go to bed now?'

'No, I must keep watch in here. I'll sleep by the fire.'

Margaret smiled and pulled the door open.

'You know, Mother, you won't be able to tell anyone about this.'

'Who would I tell?'

'Your confessor.'

Margaret smiled wryly. 'I see. Very well. Goodnight, Robert.'

'Goodnight, Mother.' The door closed softly behind her and Robert returned to his chair by the fire. He pulled another one up opposite and sank into one, brought his feet up on to the other. Half-stretched out, cramped and chilly, Robert laid his head back to sleep.

One woman convinced of the impossible. Another enacting the impossible. A third capable of anything she cared to imagine. All under the same roof.

What a nightmare!

The watch was restless tonight. Every sound, every movement was challenged. As they walked the walls below his window, Micah could see the whispered conversations, the lanterns moving, the wary glances. Did they suspect something was going on? Or perhaps Deverin warned them about the patrols – three had gone by already. It was only a matter of time before one decided to request entrance to Dunlorn.

Micah moved away from the window and back to his bed, where he sat, his back against the board, his knees up. He couldn't sleep. Tonight his father had spoken to him – albeit from necessity – but he had spoken. And he had met Robert for the first time.

Nothing had changed. No one event would make his father embrace him back into the family, and if it hadn't been for Jenn, there wouldn't even have been this much.

But – there was a difference. He had come. He had spoken to Micah, and that meant that there was a degree of necessity that could force the issue. There was a way his father could be reached. It was possible!

Micah yawned, stretched his legs out and pulled the covers across. Only a sliver of moonlight escaped the window and shone across his feet. Wrapped in the blanket and the warmth of his thoughts, he finally drifted off to sleep.

Jenn woke with only the red glowing coals to light the room without windows. She laid on her makeshift bed for a few moments, listening to the breathing of the others around her. Exhausted and sick of travel and fear, they were all asleep in safety for the first time in two weeks.

She pulled back the blanket and stood, slipping on the fresh gown Margaret had given her. It fit well enough, though the hem was a bit long. Moving silently, she crept over to the fire and gently put another log over the coals, stirred them up a bit. Once the log had caught she turned around and headed to the panel door, pulled it open a crack.

The study was empty. Just moonlight through the windows and a yellow glow of fire to her left. Holding her breath, Jenn tiptoed forward and closed the door behind her. So this was the room Robert worked in. Where were his books? Put away probably, with all these strangers about. But where would he keep them? The chest under the window.

Her bare feet silent on the rich carpet, Jenn moved forward and stopped. Something in the corner of her eye. She turned her head. Robert! Asleep on a chair by the fire.

Careful to make no sound, she gained his side and sat on the floor by his head. From this angle, asleep, the hard lines had gone from his face. A strand of dark hair had fallen over his eyes, but she didn't dare brush it away. Instead she just sat there and watched him.

This was the first time she had ever seen him look at

peace. What kind of life was his then, when the only moment he could truly relax was when he was asleep?

Now she could see his face, close up, he seemed so different to the man who had saved her from the Guilde that night in Shan Moss. Then, he'd been frightening, command-ing and totally at ease with himself and the world. Or at least, that's what it had looked like. But there had always been more, even back then. The things he would half-say – and not say at all. Now it was even worse. Now he wouldn't even talk to her. And she had so many things she needed to say, to discuss with him. Things only he would understand. Everybody else, they just took her at her word. But Robert? He argued with her, caught the slips she made, pushed her to think properly. She'd only got this far because of him – and now, when she needed to talk to him so badly, he'd shut her out of his life completely.

And yet, this man was entirely responsible for everything she was now. He had saved her life, discovered her powers, taken her back to a father she'd never known. That life before seemed little more than a dream, a story told to her by another person, a tale like those she used to collect. Had it really ever happened? If he'd not found her in the forest, would she now be a travelling storyteller, delivering tales of this man, instead of keeping his secrets?

If only he would talk to her, smile at her, laugh with her. She could help him, she knew that. But he didn't want her help. He just wanted to be left alone and not have this inconvenient reminder bothering him at every turn.

She sighed and sat back on her feet. The movement was quiet, but it was enough to wake Robert. His eyes opened and instantly focused on hers. He didn't move.

Jenn's heart began beating wildly. He would tell her off again. He would snap at her, make her feel like a fool, but . . . there was no malice in his gaze this time. Only a deep green well she could almost fall into. He said nothing. He just watched her as though he were looking at her for the first time.

Jenn swallowed with difficulty, willing her voice to work. She had to say something – anything. Being pinned by that gaze was too much. 'I was just thinking,' she whispered, 'of the stories I used to tell about the Earl of Dunlorn. The one I loved most was about a battle fought on the Sadlani border. Outnumbered and outmanoeuvred, your forces were stuck in a narrow valley, pressed further and further back. Then, just as your men were ready to turn and flee, you reared your horse and rode ahead in a charge. Renewed by your courage, your men followed, defeating the enemy and making you a hero.'

'It was an accident,' Robert murmured absently, his eyes still not leaving hers. 'The horse bolted. I couldn't stop it.'

'It doesn't matter.' Her heart wouldn't slow down. 'I don't believe you anyway.'

'Why?' Robert was gently self-mocking. 'Because it's just the kind of damn fool thing I'd do?'

Jenn wanted to smile, but the muscles in her face wouldn't move. What had got into her? 'You won the battle and beat the Sadlani back to their own land. That's all that matters. Anything else is . . .'

'The truth?' Robert slowly reached out his hand to her face. For a second, he touched her cheek, softly, like a summer mist. Jenn froze, suddenly terrified. As though he sensed her fear, his touch changed and instead he gripped her face hard. 'Why are you here?'

'I . . .' Jenn gasped and he let her go.

He swung his legs down from the chair and stood up. 'You shouldn't be here. You know that. You didn't have to help Rosalind yourself. Those two men of yours are capable enough. You didn't have to risk your own life – even to save a Queen.'

'You would have done no less.' Jenn sucked in air, her fear abruptly crystallizing into anger. She scrambled to her feet. 'You have done no less.'

'But I'm a soldier, Jenn. You're supposed to be a lady!' Robert turned away to the fireplace. He reached up and put his hands on the hearthstone, dropped his head. 'You'll leave tomorrow night after sundown. Micah will go with you and make sure you go home.'

'And what about the Queen?'

'I'll get her out of the country. I said I'd help, didn't I? After all, you gave me no choice.'

Jenn was about to snap at that, but paused. Was that it? Was that why he was being so cruel?

'I'm sorry, Robert.'

His eyes glinted pale in the moonlight. 'Sorry? For what? For forcing me to break my oath to the King? Oh, don't worry about that. After all, I only let my uncle die because of it. I've only let Selar rip this country to shreds because I made a vow not to stand against him. No, it's nothing really. Nothing for you to worry about.'

He left the fireplace then, strode the length of the table to where a jug stood. He filled a cup with wine and downed the lot in one mouthful. 'I want you out of Dunlorn tomorrow night. Gone. Do you hear me?'

Jenn didn't say anything. A voice inside her told her she should be angry, but she didn't listen. Instead, she opened her eyes properly, her senses – and saw the thing she'd seen once before. Back at Elita. It was still there, inside him, eating away at him. Only now it was much bigger, much stronger and much worse. A blackness, evil and devouring. Did he still not see it? Not realize what it was doing to him?

She swallowed and kept her voice soft, unwilling to provoke him further. 'What happened in Marsay? Did you find Ayn?'

'Ayn's dead. I couldn't save her.' The words fell like rocks into the room, echoed around the fine-carved panelling.

'I'm sorry.'

Robert looked up at that. 'So am I. I killed her. She asked me for Convocation and I couldn't refuse.'

Jenn moved along the table until she stood beside him. 'I *am* sorry, Robert. I know what she meant to you.'

'There was somebody with her, guarding her. Another of your abducted fellows.'

'Who?'

'Keith Campbell.' Robert's voice was low and bitter, only now it wasn't directed at her but at himself.

'Where is he now?'

'In heaven, I hope. I killed him, too. A successful day all in all.'

'Oh, Robert, please don't do this.' Jenn reached for his hand, but he moved away.

'If you think about it, I could have saved a good twenty lives by never coming back to Lusara. Funny, isn't it? So many people look at me and see hope. It just shows you how blind they are.'

'Stop it!' Jenn moved forward again and this time made sure she caught his hand. He could have pulled away, but didn't. After a moment, he spoke again, but the bitterness was gone. There was just a quiet calm about him – the kind of calm in the middle of a storm. Jenn's stomach turned over.

'Can you see the pattern?' he murmured as her hand began to tremble in his. 'The abductions? You, Keith Campbell, McGlashen's nephew. Keith had powers, too. All children of the great Houses, with powers as though there was something special about them, something different. And Valena was a part of it. Ayn spoke about a demon who'd captured her, tortured her. The evil presence you sensed in the spring. A demon. Ayn said that I'm his enemy, Jenny. What does that make you? His ally? Why did he just leave you in Shan Moss to fend for yourself? He must have known about your abilities. About all of you. I think that's why you were all taken in the first place. He was looking for you in particular. He must have known you would be his ally.'

'Then,' Jenn whispered, breathless, 'he would have known you were his enemy. Except that . . . you're older than me – older than all of us taken . . . so . . .'

'He either couldn't take me because I was too old – or didn't expect me to be . . . well, me. Was that why he took the other boys, thinking that his enemy would be among them? How disappointed he must be. And that leaves us in a very interesting position, doesn't it? He knows about the prophecy. He knows who you are, what you are – but he's done nothing about you – yet. On the other hand, he must know I exist – who else could have snatched Ayn away from him? – and yet, he has no idea of my identity. And then you promised to Stand the Circle. Either way, Jenny, it's just like the Key said. You're the Ally, I'm the Enemy. We're on opposite sides. Don't you find that amusing?'

'Yes, very!' Jenn snapped and pulled her hand away. 'So what are you going to do about it?'

'Nothing, what else? Why should I need to do anything? After all, I've done nothing over the last year and all these things have happened nonetheless. If this demon wants me, he can come and find me. Apart from that? I don't really care any more.'

Jenn remained where she was for a moment, no longer mesmerized by his gaze. She would have reached out to him again, would have tried to ease that pain which ran so deep – but he would never allow that. She could see it in his eyes. Even as they drew her in, they pushed her away. Stubborn to the last.

Softly then, she said, 'You wouldn't have turned Rosalind away. An oath to a King is just as much an oath to his Queen, his heir. You swore to protect them all. The fact that you were protecting one against the other was never the question. You would have done all this and more whether I was here or not.'

Robert nodded. 'Yes.'

'Then why are you so angry with me?'

'Angry?' Robert laughed, short and ironic. He shook his head, turned back to the wine and poured some more. 'Oh, I'm not angry, Jenny. Trust me, this is not what I look like when I'm angry.'

'Then what are you afraid of?' The question came out without thinking and instantly she regretted it.

When he looked at her again, the bitterness and the self-loathing were written all over his face, marring his looks in a way that, again, made her want to reach out to him. Then he smiled, ugly and menacing. 'What the hell do you think I'm afraid of, you fool?'

Jenn took a step back, frowning, shaking like a leaf. Talking to him was pointless. He didn't want her here; she was a thorn in his side, involving him in things he would rather stay out of. Now she couldn't even tell him her idea

235

about Bonding and mindspeech. He would never listen. He'd shut the door on her and he would never open it again.

'I'm sorry, Robert,' Jenn murmured, backing away. Desperately, she held back tears. She wouldn't give him that satisfaction! 'I'm really sorry. I'm sorry I ran into you in Shan Moss. I'm sorry I turned out to be a sorcerer. I'm sorry I've caused you so much trouble over the last year. I'm sorry I came here and ruined everything for you. I . . . I'm sorry.'

With that she turned and fled. He called after her as she pulled the door behind her, but she couldn't stop. She didn't want to hear any more. She threw herself down on her bed, closed her eyes and took in great gulping breaths. She couldn't afford to let go just yet. There was still so much to do. Later, yes. Much later. For now, try and sleep. Forget Robert. Just go to sleep.

Why had he tried to call her back when he'd just spent the last hour trying to get rid of her?

As the door slammed shut behind her, Robert hung his head, closed his eyes and took in a dragging breath. It didn't do any good. The knife was still there, buried inside him, driven deep by the look on her face as she'd run away from him. A wound as grievous as the one he'd inflicted upon her.

Robert left the table and opened the chest under the window. Lying there before him, still wrapped in the cloth Jenn had given him, was the silver rod he'd found in those mountain caves. He took it out, lifted back the cloth and held the rod up to the candlelight.

Robert sighed and shook his head. With a brisk movement, he wrapped the rod back in the cloth and returned it to the chest. Instead, he pulled out two maps and took them back to the table. With a wave of his hand, three candles flared into life and he spread the maps out in their light.

Work. That was his only tonic, his only salvation. He had to keep working. So, if it had to be work, what was the easiest way to hide a Queen?

16

The camp was already well established by the time Nash rode in with Forb'ez at his side. A dozen pavilions surrounded a larger one; camp fires stretched out into the darkness throwing flickering light over soldiers eating and bedding down for the night. The sky was a haze of woodsmoke, laced with laughter and shouted commands. Among them were the blazes of at least twenty lords that Nash could recognize at a glance, not to mention a large contingent of Guilde soldiers.

Was this the hunt? Is that why Selar had brought him back? So it had started already.

Forb'ez had said there'd been developments, but he'd refused to be more specific on the journey here. Now, as they dismounted before the royal pavilion, Nash couldn't help noticing the guarded looks in his direction, the abrupt pauses and heavy silences.

'You are to wait in here, Alderman.' Forb'ez lifted the tent flap and ushered Nash inside. This was just the antechamber, devoid of furniture, with nothing more than a brazier in the middle of a brown, mud-stained carpet. He was left alone.

This was not quite what he'd had in mind. If Selar had brought him here only to arrest him for sorcery, then why wasn't he in chains?

Well, if he had to wait to find out, then he would do so.

A wind from the north whipped against the walls of the tent. The flapping grew louder as the night wore on. All he could hear were distant voices and the occasional booted feet as they marched past the door. Finally, just as the night watch called midnight, the flap opened and Forb'ez reappeared. At a gesture, Nash followed him out and around to the larger pavilion. Forb'ez held the door open for him, but stayed outside.

Selar was waiting for him.

He was reclining in a tall chair, throne-like and regal. He

was dressed like a King, a formal cape arranged over his shoulders and stretching out beyond his feet in a sea of blue. A gold circlet sat on his fair head and he held a jewelled goblet in his right hand, the rubies glinting in the same candlelight as the ring on his thumb. He could have been ready to receive a royal deputation from a visiting envoy.

But even with all this show, Selar couldn't hide from Nash the black circles around his eyes, the sickly white of his skin, the purple hue of his lips. He was unwell – but this was a disease of the spirit rather than the body. The commanding power was still there, but gone was the will to wield it. The change was so subtle it might take weeks or months for anyone around Selar to even notice. Selar was walking close – very close – to the edge.

Without ceremony, Nash bowed, kept his head low and waited.

Deliberately, Selar left him there long enough to get seriously uncomfortable.

'I should have you executed.'

The words came out easily and softly. He might be falling apart, but his mind was working just fine.

Nash took a chance and straightened up, clasping his hands before him.

'Why?' Selar's mouth barely moved. 'Why did you tell me?'

'To serve you better, Sire.'

Selar gestured, the contents of his goblet flying over the cyan rug. 'Don't try that on me, Nash!' he hissed. 'I want the truth, damn you, or I will order your execution. The guards are still outside that door. One word from me will bring them inside. They'll strike off your head before you have a chance to use a single evil word!'

Nash didn't move. He didn't dare. In this particular situation, it was possible that Selar could succeed with such a threat. 'What am I to say?'

'Why did you tell me? What do you want from me?' Selar's voice rose, his eyes twitching with tightly contained fear.

'Sire,' Nash began, keeping his voice steady, 'I have already

238

told you the truth, but you are unwilling to hear it so I must say nothing more.'

'The truth!' Selar spat. 'You really expect me to believe that you revealed a secret you've obviously kept all your life – just so you can serve me? I'm not a fool, Nash! Don't treat me like one.'

'If I thought you were a fool, Sire, I would not be so willing so serve you.' Nash tried not to flinch as he said it, but instead kept his gaze on Selar, his breathing steady. He had to appear servile, subservient, humble.

Selar stared at him for a long time, then slowly he arose from his seat. He left Nash waiting while he poured some more wine and took a long drink. Nash watched him in profile. Now that the first flush of anger was gone, what would replace it?

'You want to serve me?'

'Yes, Sire.'

'Just as you've done so far?'

'Yes, Sire.'

'Is that all?'

'It is all I can do, Sire.'

Selar chuckled harshly at that. 'So very humble, aren't you? But don't think I'm duped so easily. I haven't got this far by being fooled by men like you. Is it not also true that you told me because you don't want Vaughn's men going out into the countryside rounding up all your friends? You hope to get me on your side in order to protect your fellow sorcerers. Isn't that what this is all about?'

No. Selar wasn't a fool. 'Sire, my concern about Vaughn's activities only reaches to those who would be falsely accused. To my knowledge, there are no other sorcerers in Lusara.'

'And that,' Selar said, 'is a blatant lie! You've never been concerned about the people before. There are more sorcerers. That business in Kilphedir proves it.'

'But Osbert vowed it was a hoax.'

'You could have convinced him otherwise. In return for some favour.'

'Sire, Osbert takes his duty very seriously, as I am sure you know. That duty is the same as for all in the Guilde, a sacred

239

duty to rid the land of all sorcerers. It's been our duty since the Battle of Alusia.'

At this, Selar smiled, ugly and insincere. 'Then what are you, a confessed sorcerer, doing among the ranks of the Guilde?'

'How better to serve my King, Sire?'

Selar laughed outright, drained his cup and refilled it again. Now he came back across the room. 'Your answers are all prepared, aren't they? You knew I'd ask that question – and all the others. I gave you enough time to think about it. You're so very calm in the face of my anger. Every other man in this country would be shrivelled up in terror. But not you. Is it because you have all these powers? Or is it because you're so damned arrogant you don't care?'

Nash took a deep breath. This wasn't going entirely well. 'Sire, I know my revelation was a great shock, but I assure you, the truth is as I have said. My only desire is to serve you in whatever way you wish.'

Raising his eyebrows, Selar said, 'So you keep saying. But I wonder just how far your service would go. Would you serve me – in any matter – regardless of the consequences?'

'As long as there would be no harm to your person, Sire, yes.'

'Even if it conflicted with your oath to the Guilde?'

Ah, the trap! Selar too had been prepared for this interview. If Nash said yes, then Selar would say he couldn't trust him. If he said no, then Selar still wouldn't trust him. Either way he was damned.

He had to take a chance. One single chance on which everything rested. He sank to his knees, raised his hands in supplication. 'Sire, I beg you to believe me. I come from an inconsequential family of small means. I wished to serve my King and joining the Guilde was my best means. My oath to the Guilde was always, in effect, an oath to you. I read our histories of how sorcerers once stood at the side of mighty Kings during the days of the old empire. I desired nothing more than to serve you in such a way. That was in the beginning. Now, however, over the last year I have also grown to love you as a friend and was glad of your friendship in return. I am now and always will be your servant to command as you wish – in whatever capacity you choose.'

Selar said nothing. Nash had to lift his eyes to see what the effect of this speech was. The expression on Selar's face was entirely unreadable. He was silent a long time. Then he placed his cup down on the armrest of the great chair and took a step forward. 'My friendship is not so easily bought. You have lived a lie and led me to believe it. I won't trust you so easily again. I'll take you back, but you'll need to prove yourself to me. I have something I want you to do. Something a man with your unique talents should have no trouble performing. If you fail, you die. It's as simple as that.'

Nash wanted to smile. It seemed the irony of the situation had eluded Selar. He'd been thrown out because he was a sorcerer – but he'd been brought back for exactly the same reason. 'Tell me, Sire.'

'The Queen has absconded, taking my son with her. My men can't find her and her band of traitors anywhere. I want you to find her and get my son back to me alive.'

Involuntarily, Nash's eyes widened. Selar raised his eyebrows in mock horror. 'Yes, sorcerer. I want you to use your powers to get my heir back for me. I don't care what you do with that whore I married. I don't care what methods you use. I don't even care how many of your friends you employ on the venture. I just want my son. Can you do that for me, sorcerer?'

Nash let out a pent-up breath. Selar was asking the impossible – and knew it. Still, if there was no other way . . .

'Yes, Sire. I can do it. But you'll need to call off Vaughn's hunters.'

'I have already. They're all out searching for the Queen instead. But let me warn you – a search for a Queen could easily be returned to a search for a sorcerer, should I find you've lied to me again.'

The cast, the tone – everything was the Selar of old. Except that behind the menace was not the usual ruthlessness, but fear. Real, terrifying, killing fear.

Nash rose to his feet and bowed again. 'I am your servant,

Sire. With your permission, I shall retire and begin my plans.'

Selar had known he would agree, damn him. The moment Nash had stepped outside the royal pavilion, Forb'ez led him to a tent especially set aside, comfortably furnished, with a real mattress on the portable cot. Nash wandered around the room, pulling his gloves off. Forb'ez waited in the background as though he knew exactly what was going on. Well, perhaps he did.

'Can I get anything for you, Alderman?'

'Yes,' Nash tossed his gloves down on the table. There was paper and ink ready for use. He picked up a pen, dipped it and scrawled two words on a sheet of paper. He folded it up, sealed it with wax, then wrote the name of a village on the outside. He turned back to the pale-eyed man and held it out. 'Have a courier take this. He's to tell no one where he is going. He will bring back the two men with him by morning.'

Forb'ez met his gaze stonily, took the note and bowed. 'Of course, Alderman.'

As the flap dropped shut behind him, Nash drew off his cloak and tossed it over a chair. He inspected the contents of the flask of wine left beside the bed, then sat down.

So, little Rosalind had run off and taken the brat with her. How very brave of her. And how very convenient. Selar had called him back because of it. Well, a chance was a chance, no matter what guise it took.

But what kind of chance was this? Rosalind would be damned difficult to find. He couldn't Seek her. She was human and, as such, her aura was the same as all humans: pale, indistinct, impossible to pick out from a crowd, no matter how well he knew it. Seeking would show him nothing.

And he couldn't even go back to Marsay to question any witnesses. Rosalind could be anywhere by now – being helped by a people held in open contempt by her husband. Her actions would be seen as a direct defiance of the King; there would be plenty who would flock to her side, plenty who would risk their own lives to shelter her. This would take time – and all his resources.

Well, he could make a start, and perhaps in the meantime, he could get close enough to Selar to make the search for Rosalind unnecessary. Yes, this might work out for the best after all.

With a self-satisfied smile, Nash stripped off his clothes and went to bed.

'I tell you, Governor, this is something the King will want to know about.'

Osbert glanced up at Chancellor Ingram, finished his mouthful and wiped a fine lace cloth across his lips. 'What would you have me do? Charge into the King's bedchamber and tell him all his enemies are ready to pounce?'

Ingram threw up his hands and flopped down into a chair pulled out from the table. 'You're the only one I can approach, Osbert. I tried talking to Brome, but he's too afraid of the King to cross something like this. Eachern's too thick – and besides, he's off on his own tearing rage now his bride-to-be has disappeared with the Queen. Vaughn's in Marsay licking his wounds and you're the only councillor left who can think straight enough to broach the subject with the King.'

Osbert laid his napkin on the table beside his plate and waved the servant away. Ingram was a mousy little man who rarely spoke out of turn, but he played an invaluable part on the council. He'd once been a minor functionary in Tirone's court, but Selar had noticed how efficient the man was and, before the conquest, had stolen him away. Ingram had worked quietly in the background for the last sixteen years. He was no soldier, but an extraordinary administrator – able to organize the most cumbersome army, the most pompous event or the most delicate negotiations. He was no statesman, but he knew almost everyone worth knowing, and as such he held an even more enviable position.

Osbert pursed his lips. 'Are you sure of your information?'

Ingram sprang forward, spreading his hands on the table before him. 'I know you have spies everywhere, Osbert, but your people aren't going to notice the kind of things my connections see. Isolated, you can sweep it aside. Together, when viewed from a distance, I have to say I'm afraid of what will happen if the King doesn't do something.'

Osbert leaned back and steepled his hands together. 'If Brome knows about this, then he can come with us. Where is the King now?'

'You know he never rises before midday any more. His pages were bringing water for him to wash as I passed by just now.'

'Very well,' Osbert nodded. 'We'll collect the good bishop on our way.'

Nash lifted the door of his tent and glanced outside. Nobody was paying him any attention. All the better. He turned back to the two men standing in the centre of the room: Lisson and Taymar, brothers. His best men. He would need such quality before this job was done.

'Lady Valena will receive your message by tomorrow night, master, but I should warn you, Pascoe may be difficult to find at this time.' Lisson glanced at his silent brother. Only a year apart in age, they were almost identical and were often assumed to be twins. They had an almost uncanny ability to know what the other was thinking. When together, Lisson almost always did the talking.

Nash nodded and crossed the room to finish dressing. As he picked up his jacket, he glanced at Taymar. 'Pascoe is most likely to be south. The last orders I gave him were to clear up that band harassing Dunlorn lands. They're wasted there now that I have killed the Enemy. I want that band positioned no more than a league away from this camp. Let me know when they arrive and I'll come out myself. In the meantime, find out what you can about the Queen. Somebody must be helping her. Somebody very capable.'

Lisson collected Nash's sword and held it out for Nash to strap on. 'Is it possible, master, that the renegade Duke of Haddon has helped her?'

Nash chuckled dryly. 'I think not. Dunlorn is too far south. Rosalind would have been caught by now. Besides, he made a vow to Selar. He wouldn't break it for the sake of a woman. He's well out of the picture. Taymar, you get going. You've a lot of country to get under you by tonight.'

'Yes, master.' Taymar bowed and backed out of the tent.

'Stay here, Lisson. Out of sight. I'm off to see the King.'

Ingram entered the royal pavilion first. Osbert brought up the rear, keeping Brome within his sights. He'd puffed and dithered at Osbert's insistence, but eventually he'd given in. There was no doubt that he expected Osbert to do all the talking.

Selar was dressed and eating his first meal of the day – at two in the afternoon. At first glance, he appeared to have had no rest at all, but looking at the red-rimmed eyes and grey skin, Osbert couldn't help wondering if this was some kind of fever rather than some demon rumoured to plague the King.

There was no doubt at all that Selar's awesome strength was fading. Osbert glanced at his cohorts. If they'd noticed a worsening since the previous day, they weren't showing it.

'Well?' Selar barked, pulling strips off a wedge of chicken. 'How many patrols have we lost now?'

This was Osbert's area. He clasped his hands together and replied, 'There are five who have yet to report in.'

'Where?'

'All over. There's no pattern, nothing we can chase after. It's anyone's guess what's happened to them.'

'Guess?' Selar snapped. 'Just when did I give you permission to provide me with guesses, Governor?'

'Forgive me, Sire, I merely . . .'

'Don't grovel, Osbert.' Selar shoved his plate away.

Grovel? Osbert had done many things in his time, but he'd never grovelled! Nor would he, not even to this half-demented shadow!

'Sire,' Ingram stepped forward and Osbert shot him a sharp glance. So he'd found the courage after all?

'I feel I must pass on some intelligence I have just received this morning.'

'Has somebody seen that whore?'

Osbert closed his eyes briefly. To address the Queen in such a manner was not seemly – even under these circumstances. Before Ingram could do any more damage, Osbert reached out gently and touched his elbow, drawing him back. Then he turned to the King and put on his most reasonable face. That's when he noticed Nash. Standing in the corner, unobtrusive as always.

Had Selar forgiven him his alleged crime? So quickly? What had Nash done in the first place and why was he here, now, back beside the King?

'Are you going to stand there all day, Osbert?' Selar commanded his attention once more and Osbert took a deep breath.

'We have received reports from all over the country. Also from Sadlan and Tusina. News of the Queen's abduction has somehow passed our borders. Our neighbours have heard and have already begun to calculate the damage to your throne. They also speculate who is behind such a gross act. I must also add that they have assumed for themselves that the Prince was with the Queen when she was taken. This in itself has excited their activities. I have word that Borallain of Sadlan has already moved troops through the desert in an approach to our border.'

'Don't be ridiculous! How could he have reacted so quickly? Does he have spies in my court?'

'None that we know of, Sire.'

'Then look again!' Selar slammed his hand down on the table and glared at Osbert. 'What else have you? Anything from Mayenne?'

At this, Osbert glanced again at Ingram. The Chancellor shook his head slightly. 'Not a word, Sire. I must say, however, that silence in itself is not necessarily a good sign.'

'Not where my blasted brother is concerned.'

'Er . . . yes, Sire.'

Selar's gaze turned steely and he turned his head slightly to address Nash. 'Where's Eachern?'

'About three hours west, Sire.'

'Get him back here.'

'But Sire,' Osbert held up his hands. 'His Grace is needed in that area. It is not inconceivable that the Queen . . .'

'The Queen will go nowhere near the Goleth range,' Selar snapped. 'She's far too superstitious. I want Eachern back here, where I can see him.'

Osbert had no choice but to argue this. There was always the possibility, sitting on Selar's council, that a man would one day say the wrong thing and end up in prison. Look what had happened to McCauly. Then again, it was his duty to speak. 'Forgive me, Sire, but surely you don't suspect Eachern had anything to do with the Queen's abduction?'

'I never bother suspecting anyone, Osbert. I just look and know. Eachern has had his plans nipped in the bud. I don't want him getting ideas about changing sides and running off to my brother. I've already had one cousin betray me. I have no intention of chancing another. Eachern hasn't the intelligence to turn on me – but he does have the motivation now he's lost his little strumpet.'

Selar came to his feet and put his hands on the table, towering over them all. 'Anything else?'

Osbert had come this far, he couldn't leave with only half the job done. He swallowed uncomfortably, but continued nonetheless, 'Sire, with news of your heir having been abducted, our neighbours getting restless, the sovereignty of your reign will come into question.'

'My reign . . .' Selar's voice trailed off and he frowned. He was silent a long time, then said, 'Come on, out with it, man!'

'Secure yourself, Sire. Direct the patrols to cover many small areas. Send all your remaining troops to your borders.'

Brome chose this moment to voice his opinion. 'We should also round up any known opponents of your reign, Sire. Any dissident roaming free at the moment would only make heavy capital out of your troubles. There should be no alternative, no replacement ready to take your throne. Without an heir to follow you, this is what your opponents will be thinking. If you cut them off now, you confine your problems to a single concern.'

Selar stared at them each in turn, then closed his eyes slowly and dropped his head. He lifted a hand to dismiss them. 'Very well, do what you like. Draw up a list of those you would have me arrest. I want to look at it before you do anything.'

'Yes, Sire,' Osbert bowed and began to usher the other two out of the tent. Before they could withdraw however, Selar threw one final comment after them.

'I warn you, don't even dream of putting Robert Douglas's name at the top!'

Lewis dipped his pen in the ink one last time and scratched his name at the bottom of the letter. Then he folded the paper and dripped wax on to the break. He pressed his ring against the wax and waited for the impression to take.

Nash was back beside the King and still no one knew why he'd been sent away in the first place. They were very quiet, those two, almost secretive.

And now Selar had refused to list Dunlorn as a possible danger. Was Vaughn right? As each day went by, Lewis saw more evidence that there might be some connection between the dark Guildesman and the former councillor.

What could they be up to?

Taking the letter, Lewis rose and left his tent. He summoned the nearest guard and sent the letter on its way to Vaughn.

It was the commotion outside his tent that woke Nash from a deep sleep. It was black as the bowels of hell, an hour of night when nobody wanted to be awake. Somebody was whispering violently, urgently. Lisson was arguing back.

'What's going on out there?'

'I'm sorry, master.' Lisson appeared with a lantern in his hand. Following close behind was Osbert, an embroidered robe thrown carelessly over his nightshirt.

'You have to come, Nash. Now!' Osbert hissed, his eyes blinking against lost sleep. 'It's the King. He's drunk and tearing the place down. We can't control him. We have to get him quiet. If word of this should leak out . . .'

Nash was already out of bed. He threw on some clothes and strode out of his tent. Within seconds he was outside the door to Selar's bedchamber. The sound of crashing furniture was loud enough to wake the camp.

Inside, Forb'ez was trying to limit the damage being inflicted by Selar, roaring drunk and stumbling around the littered room like a wounded bear. Nash took one look at him and gestured the others back. He moved forward until Selar could see him and Nash could see his eyes.

Yes. It was there. All of it. The memory, the nightmare, the terror. This was no drunken rage. This was a man slipping into insanity from weeks – months – without proper sleep.

It was time.

'You can all go back to bed now,' Nash murmured, keeping his eyes on Selar. 'I'll take care of him.'

Forb'ez hesitated until Nash added, 'By all means, wait outside. The King needs some rest. I'll give him a tonic and sit with him until he sleeps.'

Slowly they left and Nash was alone with Selar, who was teetering on his feet like a felled tree waiting to crash. Nash moved closer, ready to catch him. 'Let me help you, Sire. I can, you know.'

'Can't help me,' Selar slurred, his eyes unable to focus. 'You jus' a sorcerer. No magic in the world can cure this.'

Nash reached out and put his hand on Selar's shoulder. 'Not magic, Sire. You're troubled. I'm here to ease your pain.'

Selar raised his eyebrows like an uncomprehending child. 'But this pain's too old. S'pposed to be gone by now, but he keeps coming back, you know? It's his curse on me. Again and again. Now he comes even when I drink myself to sleep. Why does he keep coming back when I don't want him to? Why won't he come back when I want him to?'

This was not making any sense. 'Who, Sire?'

'My friend.' Selar murmured and lurched away. He headed for a chair but missed, collapsing to his knees. Nash was instantly at his side, but Selar was almost oblivious to his presence.

'My friend. Never came back. Never betrayed me but never came back. That's a worse betrayal – leaving me alone when I needed him. His honour ... won't allow ... You know he saved my life? I killed his father 'n' he saves my life. Must've hated me but never betrayed me ... never stood ... but now he's stood by and let me ruin everything ... S'all gone wrong. Everything. And now I can't even forget when I sleep. He haunts me.'

'Dunlorn?'

'No.' Selar shook his head vigorously, totally caught up in his story. 'Carlan. Evil. Wants to suck my soul from my body. There'll be nothing left. Nothing left of me. Nothing of my realm. Nothing to leave my son ... Don' even have a son any more.'

Nash sat back on his haunches. Selar had no idea what he was saying, but the meaning was very clear. Ever since the first word of Kilphedir had reached them, Selar had been plagued by nightmares of Carlan. The rumour of sorcery was all it took. And yet, even after all this time, the image of Dunlorn was still a shining hope for Selar. Things had been good while he was around and now that he was not, everything had gone wrong. If Nash didn't do something soon, Selar would probably go to Dunlorn himself and beg on his damned knees for the renegade Duke's forgiveness!

But even Bonding Selar now would not bring him back to his former strength. There would be no bite in this lion without a son to inherit all he had worked for – all he hoped to achieve. And where would Nash be if both son and friend returned to stand beside the King?

'Sire,' Nash murmured softly, dropping his voice, 'I can help you. I can take away the nightmare so you can sleep soundly every night. All you have to do is trust me.' Trust me to Bond you to me with a tiny cord that you will never be able to sever. Put your trust in me and you will never be alone, never want another friend but me. 'Trust me, Sire.'

Selar stared at him with red-glazed eyes. His mouth hung open, lacking volition. Slowly he shook his head. 'Don't trust you. You're the same as he was. Carlan. Sorcerer.'

'Carlan was evil, Sire. I am not. I have never raised my hand to strike you as he did. You know I could have, many times. But I am here only to help you. I can take away the nightmare so you never remember it. You'll never even remember Carlan. You'll no longer be afraid of me. We'll work together as we once did, side by side. You will no longer be alone, my King.' This will be the first touch, the first level. Later, when you're ready, we'll make the final Bond. Then you will obey my every word. 'Come, Sire.'

Sweetly soothing, Nash helped Selar to his feet and guided him around the broken furniture and glass to the bed, helped him to lie down. 'All you have to do is trust me. Do you trust me?' Nash kept talking as he drew his dagger from his boot.

Selar still watched him, less drunk now than before, as though he knew what was about to happen. 'No choice, do I?'

'Just say you trust me, Sire, and everything will be well.' Nash laid out Selar's wrist bare to his blade. He could not make the cut until Selar consented. How many times had Nash done this? So why now was his heart racing with anticipation? 'Sire?'

Like condemning his soul to hell, Selar closed his eyes and nodded. 'Do it.'

Nash sliced the blade across Selar's wrist and instantly blood sprang from the wound. Selar flinched. Before a drop could hit the bed, Nash brought his garnet ring to the wetness and touched a drop of blood on the stone. It bubbled, hissed, then was drawn down into the red heart until all that was left was the shining cut stone. Selar opened his mouth to scream – then passed out.

Quickly now, Nash tore off a strip of sheet and bound up the wound. It would be healed by morning, leaving no scar, no sign at all. And no reminder to Selar of what he'd consented to.

Nash wiped the blade clean and slid it back into his boot. Selar was asleep now, properly. He would sleep for twelve hours at least. When he awoke, he would remember nothing of Carlan, nothing of that moment by the river. His memories of Dunlorn would change, too. Selar might never realize it, but his life had just changed for ever. Permanently.

'You fool,' Nash murmured. 'All this time you've had the

same dream. Over and over you've taunted yourself for having been a fool to believe in me. And now you'll never know the truth, will you? I didn't push you into the river. You slipped and I tried to stop you falling. I would never have let anything happen to you. If you hadn't been so afraid back then, we would have done this fourteen years ago. As it is, your pretty Queen has done me a great favour and, I suppose, in return I must do one for you.'

Nash unfolded his legs and stood up. He went to the door and stuck his head out. Forb'ez was there, along with Lisson. By the looks on their faces, neither had heard a word of his discussion with Selar.

'You can go in now, Forb'ez, and clean up. The King will sleep until the afternoon. Then I believe he'll be up and refreshed. When he's ready, you can tell him I've gone to do his errand. He knows all about it. I'll send word to him when I have news.'

Forb'ez jerked a nod. 'Yes, Alderman.'

Nash drew Lisson away towards his tent. When they were inside, Nash dropped into the first chair to hand. A first level Bonding always drained him. No matter how he practised and perfected this corruption of the sacred ritual, the cost was always the same: bone-draining exhaustion. He could afford a few hours' sleep now, but he'd have to be up and away before dawn. He toyed with the pen still lying where he'd left it on the table. Of all the things he'd had to do in his long and eventful life, this was, without doubt, the most distasteful. But he didn't have any choice. He had to get Kenrick back and Pascoe alone would be no use at all.

'Lisson, in the morning, I'll be meeting with Pascoe. It'll take some time to round up all the raiders and get them organized, find out if they've heard or seen anything. In the meantime, I want you to saddle up your horse and go to the Baron DeMassey.'

'Master?' Lisson moved forward, not understanding.

'You know where he is?'

'Yes, master.'

'I want you to tell him to meet me at Bairdenscoth in a

252

week.' Nash paused, the unspoken words already bitter in his mouth. 'Tell him I . . . need his help.'

17

Rosalind sat in a corner and watched. Although all these preparations were being made on her behalf, it was hard to feel a part of the organization, much less to feel she was actually one of these conspirators.

The long table was covered in papers and maps, a few books and the odd cup of wine. Along its sides were ranged a group of the most fearless soldiers she could ever hope to meet. Sir Alexander Deverin of Ankar, whose father and grandfather had served the Douglas House and whose two sons would one day follow him. Owen Fitzallen, who ruled Dunlorn when its lord was away and who had suffered near-mortal wounds in an effort to save the last Earl's life in the Battle of Seluth. Then there was Alard Bain, young, inexperienced, but with a tough streak in him. Such courage could be seen again in the forms of Shane Adair and the brusque sergeant, Keagan. Although they would return to Elita tonight, their council was still welcomed and they gave their opinions honestly.

Kandar too was there. No longer caught up in mistrust and travel-worn fear, George had allowed himself to be charmed by these companions – and had learned to listen.

Brightest of all these young fires was the flame-haired Micah Maclean, whose father had brought them to this haven. Micah showed his worth in the questions he asked, in his gentle suggestions. More than once, he made the others laugh with his deprecating wit and seemingly simple queries.

Ruling over them all, however, was the towering figure of Robert Douglas, with his commanding voice, his eye for detail and his relentless pursuit of the perfect strategy. There was a challenge there, in his eyes, in the way he looked at each of them individually. Without the others ever realizing it, Robert reached out and drew them all together into a cohesive unit. This was Robert at his best. This was when he was at his most formidable.

It was such a familiar sight, a memory of years gone by when Robert had lived at court. This same fire she saw now, raked up by his unceasing pressure to make the others think clearly, was something she'd once seen almost every day.

And how Selar had loved him.

The whole court had felt the effects of Robert's leaving, some more than others. The Guilde had almost openly celebrated. Stunned, the Church had argued vehemently for Robert's pardon. Almost breathless, the court, the city, the entire country watched as one so mighty, in the end, fell. What had surprised them all, without exception, was the speed with which it had happened.

In Selar there had been no change at all. On the surface, he appeared determined to prove that he hadn't needed Robert, hadn't desired the friendship, and didn't feel the void that remained.

Of course, everybody had assumed that once Robert had left Marsay, there would be a few months – a year at most – when he and Selar would speak little. But as the weeks went by and news of sweet Berenice's death reached court, fears began to grow deeper. When at last it was confirmed that Robert had left Lusara, intending never to return, it was as if a great silence had descended upon them all.

It was odd that one man could so heavily influence so many. For the people, it had been as if the last breath of hope had left Lusara, blown by the same wind that had filled the sails of Robert's ship, like the last glow of sunset before the whole black of night.

But even night had its own right and proper ending – with a dawn. Was this meeting, secret and unobtrusive, held high within a castle avoided by those who still held power; was this a new dawn for Lusara? Was this one man, upon whose shoulders rested the hope of a nation, ready to take up the fight against a rule which openly defied the laws of the gods and a King who callously and wantonly desired the destruction of the very thing he had vowed to protect?

Would Robert now put aside his vow and make a stand against Selar?

'Not everything is as it seems.'

Rosalind started at the quiet voice beside her. Jennifer had slipped into the room and perched on a stool close by. She wore the gown Lady Margaret had given her, soft-spun wool of a dark, luminous blue. With her dark hair brushed and plaited over one shoulder, Jennifer leaned back against the wall, calm and relaxed. Her fingers were laced together and her face the picture of patience.

'You speak as though you know my thoughts,' Rosalind began in a whisper, unwilling to disturb the plans being discussed around the table.

'I, too, have been watching. It would be impossible not to wonder if your sudden appearance here might herald a change of fortune for Lusara. You are, after all, Lusaran born, of one of the finest Houses in the country. After so many years of acting as a bridge of peace, your actions will, in some eyes, signal only the opposite – should there be one prepared to take the cause up as his own.'

'You appear doubtful. Do you know him so well?'

'I don't know him at all,' Jenn said evenly.

'But the longer he leaves it, the more the people see his inaction as an endorsement of Selar. If Robert doesn't move soon, he may well lose the support that is his by right.'

'Why do you assume he will act?'

Something in the girl's tone made Rosalind turn and look at her anew. Her face, young and yet so serious, gave nothing away. 'If nothing else, Robert is a man of honour. He loves Lusara with a passion that brought him to the edge of mortal danger. His House has always been closely allied with the crown; at almost every important battle in the last five hundred years, a Douglas has fought alongside the King. His own father was killed defending Lusara against Selar. His oath aside, there should be no reason why Robert would not stand now and remove a usurper who stains our country so deeply.' Rosalind tried to keep the bitterness out of her voice, but it was hard. Seeing Robert again only made it harder.

'But you can't just put Robert's oath aside, Your Grace,' Jennifer replied, her voice almost inaudible. 'If he is, as you say, a man of honour, then that same honour bids he keep that oath. He cannot remain the man he is – the man who would rescue Lusara – and break that vow.'

'But if he had enough reason – if I told him about Selar's plans for war against Mayenne, surely then, Robert would do something. If it is only his oath which keeps him from acting – then men have broken oaths before. The oath Selar made to this country on taking the crown makes Robert's oath void. If . . .'

'The breach of one does not assure the negation of the other. Whether Selar intends to destroy Lusara or not remains to be seen, but Robert won't break his oath of allegiance. Since he can't in conscience stand beside Selar, he has instead determined not to stand against him.' Jennifer paused. 'There are some things in life that remain absolute. This, I'm afraid, is one of them.'

'Then,' Rosalind scrambled for some hope, 'you agree? You think Robert should do something?'

'I'd never dream of telling him what to do, Your Grace.'

'But what do you think? Please—' Rosalind reached out and took her hand. The flesh was cold, even though the room was warmed by a roaring fire. '—I cannot leave Lusara knowing there is only doom in my wake.'

Jennifer looked down at their hands joined together. She stared at them a long time, then, with a small breath, she replied, 'I think, Your Grace, that the argument is far from over. Go in peace. What you've done has not harmed your country. It's only harmed the evil at its core. We will be free, one day.'

'Only when Selar is dead.'

'Yes,' Jennifer said with a shy smile, 'but regardless of what happens in the meantime, one day he will die – and then we will be free.'

Rosalind studied her for a moment, then let go Jennifer's

hand and turned back to the table. At that moment there was a pause in the conversation and Robert looked up.

'Your Grace, would you care to review our plan?'

'Well ... I ...'. Rosalind paused, suddenly unsure. What did he want her to say?

'Please,' Robert gestured her over. 'We need a little encouragement.'

Rosalind glanced at Jenn, who smiled in response. Then she stood, smoothed her dress down and walked around the table to stop at Robert's side. He flattened the map out in front of him and put his finger on a spot marked in black ink.

'This is Dunlorn and this blue line here is the ocean. As you can see, with the mountains between and especially at this time of the year, the journey to a port would take some three weeks. On top of that, by the time you reached a harbour, most ships will have already docked for the winter. Your party would be discovered long before spring and, if you'll forgive me, you'd probably not live to see the first blossom.'

Rosalind looked up at him, but he didn't appear worried. Rather, he contained a smile which made his green eyes sparkle almost mischievously. 'But you have an ingenious plan?'

Robert grinned. 'Well, it is a plan – it's up to you to decide how ingenious it is. In two nights' time, we will depart Dunlorn by the same means we arrived. We won't be seen – I can make sure of that. Once clear we'll split into two groups. Your sister, Samah and the Princess will travel in the first party, accompanied by Alard Bain and one other. They will first travel north and then east to the border of Flan-har. The second party, with yourself, Kandar, the Prince and Deverin will travel a little south and then east. The patrols out looking for you will be seeking a lady with two children and we will do what we can to disguise your face, so it's unlikely they'll notice anything strange. I've already sent a letter to the Duke to be waiting at the border to meet you. From there he will take good care of you – of that I can assure you.'

'But what about the patrols?'

'I have not as yet been approached to help in the search. Depending on how desperate the King gets, that may or may not happen. However, we can make a few arrangements to thwart that event. Firstly, I'll mount patrols of my own – I already have men out on a daily basis to keep the raiders at bay. I'll also have a patrol follow you – at a safe distance, of course. They'll be dressed as Guildesmen and King's Guard. Should any real patrol get close enough to stop you, my men will stop you within sight and deem you authorized to travel on. With a little luck, you should make it to the border within four days, five at the most. The best part is that you should be able to travel in daylight, sleeping your nights in whatever inn we encounter. Also, should things get really bad, my men will guard you on a run to the border. Once there, Grant Kavanagh will protect you.'

Robert fell silent as Rosalind stared at the map. Eventually she looked up, turning her gaze on each man in turn. In the end, her eyes landed once more on Robert. 'You said, we? Does this mean you intend to go with us?'

'Of course.'

Rosalind shook her head. 'I cannot allow it.' Feeling the eyes of everyone on her, Rosalind coloured and looked to Jennifer for help. There was none forthcoming. This was one battle she would have to fight on her own. 'You must stay here, Robert. Should you be approached to aid the search for me, it would look most suspicious if you were not to be found – especially if so many of your soldiers were gone, too.'

Robert shook his head, a frown already forming. 'My absence won't prove anything. Believe me, it's important that I go with you. I can ensure your safety.'

'It is not only my safety that's at stake here, but also that of Lusara. You're too valuable. If it should be discovered that you're aiding me across the border, then Lusara will lose everything. I forbid you to come with us, with whatever authority I may have.' Rosalind paused. She hadn't realized she felt so strongly about this until now. 'If you overrule me, then I must ask that you let us go on our own without your help or your men.'

Robert shook his head slowly and murmured, 'By the gods, not again.'

There was a movement from the other side of the room as Jennifer came to her feet. She looked at none of them and quietly walked out into the secret room. Robert continued as though he hadn't noticed. 'Very well, my Queen. As you wish. I'll stay here. Now I suggest we all get moving. We have a great deal to organize in a very short time.'

With that, the meeting broke up. Robert turned and left the study closing the door none-too-quietly behind him.

Patric heard the feet on the stairs, but before he could even get up from his chair, the door to his room burst open and Robert stood there, green eyes blazing. Patric leaped up, the book still open in his hands. 'What's wrong?'

Robert took a deep breath and closed the door quietly and precisely behind him. 'You wouldn't believe me if I told you.' He frowned and sank on to the end of the bed. It appeared the chairs by the window were more than he could deal with.

'She's here, isn't she?'

'Who?'

'Jenn.'

Robert folded his arms. 'Yes, she's here.'

'And?'

'And what?'

'Don't be obtuse, Robert. You know what I'm talking about.' Patric stood in front of him, the book under his arm. 'Have you talked to her? Have you tried to get her to revoke her vow to Wilf?'

'That would be a little rich, coming from me. If nothing else, she did do it to protect my brother.'

'Stop avoiding the question. Did you talk to her about the . . .'

'Patric,' Robert stood abruptly, his tone changing completely, 'I know you were planning to leave soon.'

Patric turned away and put the book on the little oak table. 'Trying to get rid of me early, are you?'

'Not exactly, no.' There was a hint of a smile on his face. 'I know you've not spent too much time out of the caves and your combat abilities have never been tested – but I wonder if you might consider doing me a small favour.'

'Oh? What?'

'It wouldn't take much more than a week – and you'd get an opportunity to put all that riding practice to good use. Then there'd also be a chance to flex the odd Mask here and there – in the most exalted company.'

'What are you trying to convince me of, Robert? Don't play games with me – I've known you too long. What do you want me to do?'

Robert paused and pursed his lips. With an entirely innocent expression, he put his hands on his hips and said, 'How would you like to join the Guilde?'

The garden was definitely past its best now. Working from the south wall, the gardeners had removed most of the autumn debris, leaving stark dirt clods where there had once been bright flowers. Only the fruit trees in the corners and the whitethorn hedge showed any green.

Margaret wandered along the path, enjoying what little sunshine there was and trying not to think about the disturbing things Robert had told her. His appearance by the gate did nothing to still her thoughts.

'Enjoying the peace, Mother?'

She studied him for a moment. Then she put her hand in the crook of his elbow and they walked on together. 'To the eye, this garden looks to be doing nothing, but if you could peer beneath the surface you'd see all kinds of activity among the worms and insects. Is there really such a thing as peace?'

'I'm not the best person to answer that question.'

Margaret glanced aside at him. 'They will be safe, won't they? When they leave here?'

'As safe as they can be. It all depends on how much Selar still thinks I'm no threat. I can only hope that my constant presence at Dunlorn has assured him that I'm involved in nothing. He won't believe for a moment that I'd go out of my way to help Rosalind.'

'He believes you won't break your oath.'

'Yes.'

Margaret frowned. 'Forgive me, Robert, but why won't you take a stand against him? You could so easily.'

He took a long time to answer. His eyes grew hard and a knot appeared at the side of his jaw. 'Why doesn't anybody believe me?'

'Believe what?'

'It's not a question of why I won't – I simply *can't* break my oath. It wouldn't do any good if I did. I could never muster a force big enough to overthrow Selar and I absolutely refuse to take the crown myself. I know some people hate me for making that oath in the first place, David Maclean for one – not to mention Finnlay.'

'But he understood . . .'

'No, he just went along with it. He's never forgiven me.'

They came to the stone bench in the shade of twin lemon trees and Margaret sat down. Robert stood before her, in profile, his expression troubled. Why was it that even after all they'd been through there was obviously still so much Robert wouldn't talk to her about? So much going on beneath the surface that she could only guess at.

'You miss him, don't you?' Margaret murmured softly. Robert didn't even blink, so Margaret continued, 'You miss being at court with Selar, having the influence and the power to do what you could. In a way, though, sometimes I think you miss his friendship even more. I think that's why you never talk about him – perhaps never even think about him. Did you think he would go after you when you left court?'

Robert gave a half-laugh and looked down at his boots. 'You make me sound like a monster, Mother. Why would I expect a King to go running after me?'

Margaret shrugged. 'You were the only one who ever had a good influence on him.'

'Is that what everyone thinks?'

'History has borne it out, my dear.'

He looked away and shook his head slightly. 'Then history has it wrong. We were friends, that's all. I never had any influence on him. If I had, then I would have been able to . . .' Robert paused and sat down beside Margaret. He put his elbows on his knees and laced his hands together.

'The truth is, Mother, I didn't want to leave. I just had to. I couldn't stay any longer. I can't explain why.'

Margaret reached across and took his hand. 'I'm not asking you to justify your actions to me. I just want to be sure you understand yourself. It is, after all, your conscience that you have to live with, not mine.'

Robert glanced up with hooded eyes. 'Then you think I did wrong to leave?'

'You loved Selar, gave him every scrap of loyalty the Douglas House is famous for. It doesn't matter a damn what I think, Robert. What matters is that you believe the truth. You did all you could.'

'Did I?' For a moment there was a cold glint in his eyes, and then it was gone. He lifted her hand and pressed it to his lips. 'For what it's worth, Mother, I think Finnlay was right. But whatever you do, don't ever tell him.'

Jenn stood by the open window and watched the sun set over the dusky moor. The smell of sweet heather rested on the breeze, along with the sound of bleating sheep. By the river below, trees rustled in the wind, dropping leaves in a sprinkle of colour, gold and brown. The year was coming to an end and soon winter would be upon them.

With only a deep orange glow in the sky, Jenn pulled the study window closed. It was time. There was a movement behind her, but it wasn't Robert. Nor was it the Queen. She'd already said goodbye.

Margaret approached quietly, immediately taking her hands. 'I wanted to thank you, before you left. Robert told me what you did to help Finnlay.'

Jenn frowned. 'He told you?'

'Why? What's wrong?'

'Nothing.' Jenn murmured, unable to tear her gaze away from this woman. The deep brown eyes held a steadiness that was wholly compelling, a faith in something or somebody that had not been shaken, no matter the recent revelations. 'Then you know everything.'

'My conscience is at war, if that's what you mean,' Margaret smiled gently.

Jenn's gaze dropped. 'I'm sorry.'

'For what?'

Jenn just shook her head, unable to answer.

'You take care on your journey home,' Margaret continued. 'Micah and your men will be waiting at the end of the tunnel for you. Perhaps we'll meet again soon.'

Jenn wanted to move, told her feet to take some steps, but they refused. Instead, she just wanted to stay here in the warmth of this woman's smile, in the safety of her calm assurance. As though she knew, Margaret smiled again and held out her arms. Jenn embraced her, unwilling to let go. Then she was moving through the door and down the steep cold steps to the tunnel.

Alone now, she stopped and waited for her eyes to adjust. The gloom was almost unbearable. It pressed down upon her, suffocating. Not caring one way or the other, Jenn raised her hand and brought a light into being. It was weak and tiny, but it was enough. Picking her way carefully, she began the long walk, her thoughts, like the tunnel, contained close and narrow.

'Above all, Micah, don't go out of your way to avoid the patrols. They won't know who you are, why you're travelling. Just don't let on that you've come from Dunlorn.'

Micah nodded and finished adjusting the girth strap on Jenn's horse. The others were ready, waiting for Jenn to emerge from the tunnel. Patric hovered by the dark opening, ready to help Robert close the entrance once they'd left. He was unusually silent, watchful even.

With deft hands, Micah finished with Jenn's horse and turned to mount his own. Like a sentinel in the night, Robert stood beside him, his black cloak falling to the ground, his long hair like a hood to his shoulders. He just wanted this to be over.

'One final thing, Micah,' Robert murmured. 'Take good care of her. You're the only one I can trust. She won't defy you. If I sent anyone else she'd walk all over them. But you keep to your task.. Get her home safely.'

Micah glanced up, but Robert's face was in darkness, deliberately so. In response, Micah said, 'I will, my lord. I promise.'

'Good.' Robert turned his head slightly and a glint of early moonlight caught his eyes. 'She's coming.'

Micah mounted his horse and turned to face the tunnel. A moment later, Jenn emerged, extinguishing her light. She paused long enough to say goodbye to Patric and give him a brief hug. Then, ignoring Robert's dark presence, she strode directly to her horse. She swung up into the saddle, sat tall and defiant, and then turned her gaze on Robert.

Neither of them said a word. There was no movement, no expression. No goodbyes – nothing. There was just the silence, punctuated only by the restlessness of the horses, the breeze in the gully. A film of cloud brushed over the moon and was gone, bringing them back into that pale blue glow, cold and empty.

Slowly Robert reached up and touched the neck of Jenn's horse. Then, without a word, he turned on his heel and walked back to the tunnel, disappearing inside with not even a hand raised in farewell.

Jenn was the first to move. She kicked her horse and started up the side of the ravine. Shane and Keagan followed close behind while Micah brought up the rear. Reaching the top, they turned north and headed out into the bleak shadows of open moorland.

'When you get back, Micah,' Jenn spoke suddenly, drawing her horse alongside his, 'I wonder if you would do something for me. It might be difficult. It all depends on how he'll take it.'

'Of course. I'll try. What is it?'

'Would you thank your father for me. He put a lot of trust in a complete stranger the other night. I don't know what I would have done if he'd said no.'

Micah glanced at her, but only her voice gave anything away. 'I'd love to know how you convinced him to come in the first place.'

'That was simple. I told him who I was. I suppose he assumed that I wouldn't be there asking for help if it wasn't really important.'

Micah nodded. 'He has a great respect for you. Your father stood firm against Selar, you see. Pledged him no oath of allegiance. Such things are very important to my father.'

'Oh?' Jenn murmured. 'Then I suppose you'd better not tell him that I think Robert was entirely right doing what he did. We wouldn't want to shatter his illusions now, would we?'

The land unfolded like parchment before them, brown at first, then glowing green as they reached Elita. Even the weather had been kind, with neither the nights nor the days too cold to bear. A little rain on the second day had them sheltering in a tavern. That's where Micah had asked her about life at Elita. Sitting there opposite him, with his sparkling, mischievous eyes following her every statement, it was impossible not to reply. She told him all about the hospice, Brother Benedict – even how she'd come across Rosalind. It was good to talk to him again freely, without having to watch every word she said. What was even better was how Micah, Keagan and Shane got on. Almost complete opposites in character, Micah and Shane seemed to deliberately bait each other, making Keagan either grumble or laugh in response. It was this alone which made the journey bearable. With them talking together, Jenn could sit back and watch, listen or pay no attention. They didn't require anything of her, nor demand any kind of response. Only Micah watched her from time to time.

Then, as a full moon broached the edge of dusk one day, they arrived at the ridge overlooking Elita. It was time for Micah to turn back.

'You won't go running off the moment I leave, will you?' Micah asked slyly.

'And where would I run to?' Jenn replied with a nod at Shane and Keagan. 'With these two trailing me every step of the way.'

Then he was riding back down the ridge, his hand raised

in farewell, his laughter floating on the wind, and once again she felt alone.

The castle guard was alert to their arrival. The gate was opened and Neil was waiting in the courtyard. Jenn was barely off her horse before he took her to one side. 'Welcome home, my lady. Your father awaits you in his study.'

He said nothing more, but a swell of uneasiness rolled in her stomach. She wanted to go up and wash first, change her travelling dress before she saw Jacob, but those few words from Neil stopped her. If Jacob was waiting, she had to go and see him.

He was alone, sitting in his customary chair by the fireplace. A letter lay on his lap, the wax seal hanging over his knee. He didn't look up when she entered.

'Close the door.'

Jenn did as she was told and moved closer to him. Her hands were cold and she wanted to get close to the fire, but didn't dare.

'I cannot tell you how disappointed I am in you. I cannot begin to express how much you've hurt me.' Still Jacob didn't look at her. 'I took you back into this house, despite your background, hoping – believing – that you, born a Ross, would still be able to learn, to be schooled to take your place. Instead you've brought nothing but shame and dishonour down on us.'

Jenn's stomach went cold and her hands began to shake. She wanted to say something, but knew that the moment she opened her mouth, Jacob's icy tone would turn to fury.

Now, in the silence, he lifted his head and his eyes were like steel. 'Where have you been?'

Still, Jenn could say nothing and Jacob continued, 'I sent you a letter to Maitland. I wrote to remind you to be home in time for your anniversary celebrations. But you weren't there, never had been. You've seen Dunlorn, haven't you? Even after you promised you would never see him again. But it was just a lie, wasn't it?'

Jenn broke at this. She sank to her knees, her hands reaching out to him. 'Father, please listen to me. You don't understand.'

'Listen while you fabricate more things for me to believe? I had hoped Dunlorn had some honour left!'

Jenn wanted to run – not only from this room, but from everything. Everyone. But she couldn't. Instead, she gripped her trembling hands together and tried to stop her voice from breaking.

'Father, I didn't intend to lie to you, but it all happened so quickly and Robert had nothing to do with my going . . .'

'You really expect me to believe that!' Jacob spat. 'I don't want to hear any more about the traitor!'

'But you must, Father,' Jenn whispered, swallowing the lump in her throat, 'if I'm to tell you the truth.'

And then it came out. Everything she'd not wanted to tell him, not wanted to involve him with. From the first moment she'd walked into Markallen's farm to the night she'd left Dunlorn. Deliberately, she told him how Robert had reacted at seeing her, how he had insisted she leave the next night, how he had told her off for getting involved in the first place. And then the rest came out, too. Everything except the sorcery. Everything Rosalind had told her. Selar's treatment of her, the beating, the rape – and his plans for war. Once she began to speak, the gods themselves couldn't have stopped her. When she finally came to an end she sank back on her heels, exhausted.

'Please don't blame Addie or Shane or Keagan. Punish me, by all means, but I promise you, they were just trying to look after me.' Jenn hung her head, unable to look at Jacob, afraid of what she would see.

'You . . . thought fit to help the Queen in such dire straits – and didn't stop to tell me?' Jacob murmured, horrified. 'You risked your life so that . . .'

He broke off and looked away. 'In Serin's name, Jennifer! Why? Couldn't you trust me? Did you think I wouldn't help? That I might turn the Queen over to the patrols?'

'No, Father,' Jenn looked up, her heart still beating wildly in her breast. 'But this way, if I was caught, nobody could blame you. Everyone knows I'm disobedient, unruly. They could all just blame it on my background. Both you and

Bella could be safe this way. If you knew nothing about it, then they could hold nothing against you.'

'And you sought to protect me? Your own father? By lying and putting your own life at risk?' Jacob leaned forward and grabbed her wrist. 'Has it not occurred to you that protecting you is *my* job?'

'I'm sorry, Father,' Jenn sank back to the floor as he let go her hand.

'Dunlorn was right, you are a fool!' Jacob grunted after a moment. 'And no, I won't dismiss your cohorts. I know only too well how you wrap people around your fingers, twisting them to do your bidding. And once again, you twist me around. For all I despise your methods, I cannot help but admire your courage in helping the Queen. And yes,' he added grudgingly, 'I did underestimate Dunlorn. That he's helped Rosalind escape is a mark in his favour. After so long, one such mark is welcome – though hardly enough to undo the old damage. It seems he does have some honour left. Enough to help a Queen in distress. A pity he didn't do something long before now to ease her distress, before she felt a need to run away!'

Jacob turned back to Jenn and waited for her to look up at him. He was frowning and there were deep lines around his mouth. 'But you, Jennifer? For all that I love you, I cannot trust you. You lied to me. It's my own fault. I should have taken a closer hand in your education. I should have kept a closer guard to stop you being abducted in the first place! But I can no longer accept your wilfulness. You'll not leave the castle without my express permission – and then, only to go into the village. You will have nothing more to do with Brother Benedict. Shane can carry on your work there. That's his punishment. Beyond that?'

Jacob broke off here, his eyes going to the letter forgotten on his lap. 'Beyond that, your deceit will soon be somebody else's problem. The King, desperate to head off any trouble Rosalind's defection could cause, has decreed your marriage. In two weeks, Selar will bring your intended here – with a weighty guard. He will expect to find you willing and prepared to make your vows.'

With a gasp, Jenn scrambled to her feet. 'But, two weeks?'

Almost unwillingly, Jacob softened slightly. 'Yes. Just two weeks. Hardly enough time to make a wedding gown. But it's the King's order and I'm in no position to defy him.' He paused and the hard lines left his face. His hand reached out to her, but didn't touch her. 'We knew this would happen sooner or later. I'm sorry, but there's nothing I can do to stop it.'

Then it really was all over. All the freedom, all the adventure, all the danger. Everything. In two weeks she would be married and her life would change completely again.

'Does . . .' Jenn swallowed and began again. 'Does the letter say who I'm to marry?'

Jacob nodded, his lips pursing in displeasure. 'No low-born oaf for you, my dear, only a high-born one. Tiege Eachern, Duke of Ayr. Selar's cousin. A bloodthirsty warrior of no grace, little imagination and even smaller intelligence. All in all, Jennifer, you would have been better off taking the veil.'

Jenn nodded slowly, her hands still shaking. Faltering, she said, 'I'll be ready, Father. I promise you will not be ashamed of me again.'

'No,' Jacob replied, his voice with an edge she'd not heard before. 'No – and to prove it to everyone else, I will make sure your wedding is the finest in the history of our House. I will invite everyone I know to witness the sacrifice Selar demands. This will not be done quietly and cowardly. If I can do nothing else for you, I will do that alone.'

Dropping her head, Jenn backed away murmuring something about washing and getting some rest. She couldn't stand there any longer. She left the study and walked back along the short passage to the hall. There were people there, working, lighting candles. They called out a welcome to her, but she couldn't answer. Instead, her feet took her to the staircase and she began to climb. At the top, she turned right and walked down the empty corridor to her room. She opened the door to find it just as she'd left it two weeks

269

before. There was even a fire burning in the hearth and bread and cheese on the table.

Jenn closed the door, turned the key in the lock and stumbled over to the table. She stared down at the plate, the flask of mead, the chunk of thick yellow cheese. Then she swept the whole lot off the table. As it went crashing to the floor, she stuck her hands beneath the table and with a heave, upturned it. Gasping for air, she staggered to the bed, tore off the blankets and heaved them around the room. Everything she touched she knocked aside with all the anger, frustration and venom she'd held inside for so long. Then, when the whole room was a complete wreck, she fell to the floor, crying uncontrollably. She curled up into a ball in the corner, her eyes shut tight, her throat hurting, her chest heaving.

Alone, Jenn sobbed in her corner, cradled the pain and wished that it would all go away.

A war.

Selar was going to start a war with Mayenne. He was going to take his own brother's crown. He was going to use Lusaran troops to steal something that had never been his in the first place. That's what this had all been about. The raiders, the Church – Bishop McCauly, the Guilde – all of it. All so Selar could wage a war to satisfy his own thirst for revenge. For blood.

Jacob pushed his chair closer to the window. The little wheels knocked against the stone wall, but he took no notice. Instead, he pushed the window open and rested his elbows on the sill. Outside, the dawn was just breaking, clear and crisp, all full of new hope and promise.

But in reality, the only promise was war – and the only hope?

There was one. Slim, pale, but just as clear as the dawn. A hope germinated by a Queen's defiance, a child's abduction and a nation on the edge of war.

Jacob sighed and turned his chair around until he could face his desk. He pulled against the oak until his useless legs were stuck beneath it and he could write comfortably. Feeling the warmth of the morning sun on his back, he pulled forth a sheet of paper, dipped his pen in the ink and began to write the letter. The first of many – but without doubt, the most important.

18

Finnlay started awake in a cold sweat. For a moment he couldn't remember where he was. His heart was racing and the only thing that filled his mind was an echo of the dream – a nightmare.

'Are you all right?' Martha peered over him, her face lit in profile by soft candlelight. Behind her was the familiar grey stone of a Goleth cave and an open doorway where Arlie waited anxiously.

'What time is it?' Finnlay mumbled. His mouth felt like it was full of sand, his head rattling with rocks.

'Sunrise was an hour ago,' Arlie replied, moving to the side of the bed. He glanced at Martha, then looked back at Finnlay. 'You've been asleep for almost a whole day. How do you feel?'

Struggling to sit up, Finnlay replied, 'I've felt worse. Have you got any food? I'm ravenous.'

Martha smiled, disappeared out of the room for a moment and returned with a bowl of the most delicious-smelling stew he'd ever had the pleasure of encountering. She'd barely placed it on his lap before he tucked into it with relish. Martha moved about the room tidying up here and there while Arlie just watched him. It seemed they were waiting for something. As Finnlay scraped the last out of the bowl, he looked up at them, already feeling better.

'Well? What's wrong?'

Martha came and sat on the bed, took the bowl and cradled it in her hands. 'You were calling out in your sleep. You sounded . . . terrible.'

Finnlay shook his head, rubbed his hands over his face. 'It's just the same nightmare. It'll wear off.' He paused and turned to Arlie. 'Well? Am I well enough to get up?'

Arlie shrugged. 'If you can ask the question, then I guess you must be.'

With that, he came around the bed and took Finnlay's arm as he came to his feet. The moment he let go, however, Finnlay's legs turned to water and he sank backwards on to the bed. With a grin he held his hand out to Arlie again. 'You really must get around to finishing your Healer's training, my friend.'

'I know, I know. There just never seems to be the time.'

Martha disappeared as Arlie helped Finnlay wash and dress. Finnlay hated having Arlie fuss over him, but he began to feel his strength slowly returning. Another bowl of that fine stew and he'd be as good as new.

In the living room, Martha must have read his mind. She had a place laid out for him, some bread, wine and more stew. As he took his seat, he glanced over at the crib in the corner. The baby was asleep, her tiny eyes screwed up in concentration, dreaming of the gods knew what. 'She's still ugly.'

With a laugh, Martha slapped his shoulder and dumped the huge plate on the table in front of him. 'That's gratitude for you. We take you in, nurse you back to health and all you can do is insult our child. Wait until you have one of your own, my dear. Then you'll change your tune.'

Finnlay spoke between mouthfuls, 'Speaking of changing tunes, has there been any further word from Wilf or the council?'

Arlie took a seat opposite him and sipped a cup of brew. 'Not that I've heard. I'm sure they'll want to talk to you again – you were a little shy on details when you arrived yesterday. When you can fill in the rest, I think they'll be a little more receptive.'

'I don't know why it's such a hard story to trust. As if I'd make such a thing up,' Finnlay said bitterly. After all he'd gone through, the terrible journey back to the Enclave and the trial of telling his story to the council, their reluctance to act rankled badly.

'Oh, you know how Wilf feels about you and Robert. This whole thing has just got under his skin. He does believe you – he just needs to calm down a little. You'll find his attitude has changed since yesterday—'

There was a knock at the door and Arlie broke off to open it. 'Oh! Fiona! Come in.'

Finnlay dropped his fork and scrambled to his feet. He quickly swallowed the food in his mouth, but couldn't come up with anything like the shy smile she greeted him with.

'Hello, Finnlay.'

'Hello.'

'Are you feeling any better? You look better.'

'Do I?' Probably not. Still, he shuffled around the table, sort of showing her to a seat and feeling like an idiot at the same time. Arlie and Martha were watching him with something that should have been amusement – but wasn't. But then, they'd always been good at keeping a straight face.

'Here,' Martha murmured warmly, 'have a cup with us. It's freshly brewed.'

Martha was such a natural mother – always had been, even before the baby. She was always able to make people feel welcome and wanted. Perhaps that's why she took such good care of Finnlay.

'And how's little Damaris?' Fiona ignored Finnlay and leaned over the crib. 'My, she's grown already.'

'Yes, hasn't she,' Martha replied with a smile. 'But Finnlay here just keeps telling us she's ugly. If he says it again, I'll have to get Arlie to take him outside and teach him a lesson in good manners.'

Fiona shot Finnlay a glance, but it wasn't as unkind as it could have been. Inwardly, he relaxed a bit. If only he'd had the chance to talk to her properly on their trip back. If he could have just told her . . . well, everything . . . then . . . Oh, what was the use! She'd looked after him, nursed him through the worst of his injuries and brought him back safely to the Enclave, but that was probably more because she felt responsible in some way rather than because she'd stopped hating him. Still, there had been that look in her eyes the night she'd found him . . .

Another knock at the door. Finnlay was closest, so he opened it. It was Wilf.

'Oh, good, you're up.' Wilf nodded at him, then glanced beyond to where the others stood. Finnlay moved back. There was something very subdued about the Jaibir this morning.

Wilf came into the room holding a folded piece of paper in his hand. He glanced once at Martha, then turned to Fiona. 'I've just . . . er . . . received a letter. A courier, from Marsay.'

Fiona's smile instantly dissipated and instinctively Finnlay moved closer to her.

'The courier took a long time to get here. There've been patrols out covering the whole country. The word is that there is a hunt on for sorcerers as a result of Finnlay's adventure at Kilphedir a few weeks ago.'

'And,' Fiona took a deep breath, 'is there any word of my mother?'

'Yes,' Wilf replied, his gaze dropping to the letter in his hands. 'Murdoch has written a full account. I'm sorry, Fiona, but Ayn is dead.' Ayn had been a close friend for over thirty years. This news must have been difficult for him to deliver. 'It appears Patric was successful in getting Robert to try and rescue her. Together with Murdoch, Robert got Ayn away from her captors, but she was too seriously wounded for them to help her. Ayn asked Robert for Convocation.'

'By the gods,' Martha murmured.

Fiona said nothing. After a minute, Wilf put the letter on the table. 'I'm very sorry, Fiona. Your mother was loved by us all. I personally shall miss her friendship and her wisdom. Please, read the letter when you're ready. Murdoch says she died with great courage, choosing Convocation rather than risk being a burden to them. He says she was dying and nothing short of a miracle could have saved her.'

Fiona just nodded vaguely. Wilf glanced at them all once more, then turned and made his slow way out of the room.

For a moment, nobody moved. Then Arlie stepped forward and picked up the letter, turning it over in his hands without opening it.

'My mother . . .' Fiona whispered. 'Oh, Mineah!' With that, she flew into Finnlay's arms. He held on to her as her whole body shuddered with sobs. He said nothing to her, no words of comfort. After all, what comfort could he give her? He'd known about Ayn. The Angel of Darkness had told him, but he'd refused to pass on a spiteful boast like that to Fiona, not when they'd gone out there in the first place to try and find some trace of Ayn.

But Ayn was dead, and so was Marcus. Fiona, crying uncontrollably into his shoulder, was utterly alone.

Wilf stared at his plate, but despite the appetizing aroma and the rich sauce melting across the beef, he couldn't really bring himself to eat. He sat alone in the refectory. Almost everybody else had long since finished their evening meal. He'd deliberately waited, partly to avoid having to talk to people, but mostly with some vague hope that he'd have some appetite. Neither had worked.

'I guess that's the price of being Jaibir.'

Henry had come up from behind. He walked around the table and sat on the end of the bench, in profile to Wilf. 'Not that it would have made a difference. The whole Enclave is in shock. First we get Finnlay's extraordinary tale and now this, with Ayn. All in all, it's not been a good year.'

'No.' Wilf gazed at his plate a moment longer, then put down his knife and pushed the meal away. Instead he poured out some more wine. 'I didn't want to believe Finnlay, I admit, but now?'

Henry glanced at him with a frown. 'Now what?'

Wilf sighed. 'I was ungenerous with him and he didn't really deserve it. I just found it impossible to believe that he'd actually met this Angel of Darkness – and then went on to escape. And the detail! Four generations? Back to the creation of the Key? Is it even possible that this Carlan was telling the truth?'

A movement in the corner of his eye made him pause. Finnlay. He made no show of getting food – he just spotted

Wilf and Henry sitting together and made his way across the wide, low cavern. The young man looked a lot better than he had coming through the gate yesterday morning. There was even a little colour in his cheeks now, some life in his eyes. Within a week or so, physically, he would show no signs of his most recent adventure. Even the scar on his cheek had healed completely, leaving only a pale pink line from his cheekbone to his chin.

Finnlay picked up the flask of wine and a spare cup and helped himself. Then he perched on the table, his feet resting on the bench beside Wilf. 'Well? What's the verdict?'

'Direct and to the point as ever,' Henry murmured.

'It's all right, Henry,' Wilf raised his hand. 'For once, I think Finnlay is quite right to take that tone. Even though he shouldn't have left the Enclave in the first place, I concede he only did it for Fiona's sake. How is she, by the way?'

Finnlay shrugged, his eyes going dark. 'How would you expect? She's lost both father and mother in the space of a year. Both unexpectedly. She's hurt, lost, mourning. Like everybody else, really.'

He dropped his gaze to the cup in his hands. He turned it around, toying with the liquid. 'What are you going to do?'

'There's nothing we can do. You don't know what Carlan looks like – and he's hardly going to go around admitting that he's the Angel of Darkness, is he?'

'No, but we could try getting hold of the Malachi, Valena. I'm sure she knows where we could find him.'

'And what do we do then?' When Finnlay frowned, Wilf sat forward earnestly. 'I'm sure we all had our doubts about that prophecy, but as each day goes by it appears there is more and more truth to it. If this man you encountered is indeed the Angel of Darkness, then we're not up to dealing with him. Yes, I admit, it was dangerous to send Ayn to Marsay and yes, I will even admit that we should have listened to Robert's warning – but that doesn't really make a difference, does it? The Key has given us no instructions about what we are to do.'

Finnlay groaned. 'Since when have we become only the slaves of the Key? Are we not capable of thinking for ourselves? Out there is a sorcerer of incredible power, wholly and completely evil. He named the Ally and the Enemy and tortured me to find out where the Key was. Are we supposed to just sit back and wait for him to come and get it – simply because the Key hasn't mentioned this little matter? We need to do something, if only to stop the fear which will roll through this place as easily as thunder on a winter's day. We can't just sit here and wait to be slaughtered.'

'Finnlay,' Henry turned around and faced him squarely. 'We cannot do anything. We have no weapons to fight something like this.'

'We have Robert. At least, we used to.' Finnlay frowned. 'You must bring him back, Wilf. Carlan is afraid of him – of the Enemy. Carlan thought that I was the one he was looking for, which means he'll never suspect Robert. Surely that's an advantage we should make the most of, while we still can.'

'What?' Wilf grunted, 'and you really believe your brother will take Carlan on? The man who has sworn to stay uninvolved regardless of the provocation?'

Finnlay leaned forward slightly. 'He went to Marsay, didn't he? He risked his own life on the chance that he might save Ayn. Surely that counts for something.'

'It does,' Wilf nodded. 'But not enough. No matter what you say, son, I can't trust your brother. The Key has said he's the Enemy – and for all we know, he may indeed be our only hope against the Angel of Darkness. But the point is: as long as Robert chooses to be uninvolved, as long as he refuses to trust us with the truth, he can't be our friend. Unless he changes his mind, I cannot risk rescinding his banishment.'

Finnlay held his gaze for a long time, then stood up. He pulled his jacket down and folded his arms. 'Very well, don't bring him back. But even if you won't use the one weapon the Key has given us, you still have to take this threat seriously.'

'What do you suggest?'

'Set up combat classes.'

'What?' Henry's wedge-like eyebrows shot up. 'Are you serious?'

'Absolutely. Oh, I know we all get some training at some point, but it's not enough. Not now. We're in deep trouble. Deeper than we've ever been before. We need to be ready if that monstrosity of a sorcerer ever does find us. If we're not, we will perish.' Finnlay drained his wine and put the cup back on the table. With a nod to both of them, he turned and left the refectory.

'Well, of all the . . .'

'No,' Wilf murmured, 'he's right. We must do something. I just wish I'd come to that conclusion myself, without having to be prodded into it by one of the Douglas brothers. I tell you, Serinleth was really putting us on trial when he created those two sorcerers.'

'Well, if Carlan is the Angel of Darkness and Robert the Enemy – where does that leave Jenn?'

'The Ally?' Wilf came to his feet and collected up his forgotten meal. 'I don't know. Standing somewhere in the middle, I should think. Judging by the way this whole thing is working out, I wouldn't be surprised if she turns out to be the Ally of the Angel of Darkness – and she's promised to Stand the Circle, remember? Fortunately, I'll be gone by the time that happens so I won't have to listen to a Douglas saying "I told you so"!'

'By the gods, I wish Patric was here!' Finnlay strode up and down the room like a cat stepping on hot coals.

Arlie settled Damaris into the crook of his arm and glanced up. 'Why?'

'Because he's always so full of nervous energy that when he's not around I feel like I have to make up for it.'

'Try sitting down. It does help.'

Finnlay looked around the long sitting room that Fiona had decorated herself. One entire end was covered by a tall bookshelf, but the rest of the room was almost bare of furniture. In pride of place, however, was a series of five scenic tapestries given to her by a family she'd taught for a whole winter. Aside from the chair Arlie sat on, there was only one other by the fire – but Ayn had always used that and Finnlay resisted the temptation to be the first to sit on it.

'Please, Finnlay,' Arlie urged. 'All this pacing up and down is going to wake the baby.'

Finnlay stopped and planted himself on the end of a stout wooden chest by the door to the bedroom. Martha was with Fiona and it was all he could do to keep himself out of there.

'Fiona will be fine, Finnlay.'

'Will she? Will any of us?' Finnlay strung his fingers together and rested his elbows on his knees. 'Don't you understand what's happening here? Carlan abducted Jenn and the others because he knew about the prophecy. He was looking for both the Ally and the Enemy.'

'You don't know for certain that Carlan is this Angel.'

'So why was Keith Campbell guarding Ayn, eh? How did he get there when he disappeared fifteen years ago? Ayn spoke of a demon. It has to be the same man. By the gods, why won't anybody understand?'

'Please, Finn, keep your voice down. If not for my daughter, then at least for Fiona. I think she has enough to worry about as it is.'

Arlie was right. Getting worked up about it now was not going to help. But it was so hard knowing all this and being unable to do anything about it, knowing Fiona was in pain but being unable to go in and comfort her.

'I'm going to write to Robert,' Finnlay said eventually. 'He has to know what happened.'

'Is that wise?'

'He has to be warned, Arlie. He has to know about the danger. He's my brother. Wilf may be happy to sit by and let this prophecy run its course, but I refuse to leave Robert to fend for himself. There's too much at stake.'

'My, you're making enough noise to wake the entire Enclave!' Martha came through the bedroom door and pulled it shut behind her.

'How is she?' Finnlay blurted, coming to his feet.

'Quiet now.' Martha busied herself around the fire, putting water on to boil. 'Some of her friends stopped by, but she wouldn't see them. She doesn't want to see anyone at the moment. Perhaps tomorrow.'

'Oh.'

Martha straightened up. 'No. I mean, anyone else. She's asking for you.'

Finnlay started. 'For me?'

With a smile, Martha came across the room and put her hand on the door latch. 'Finnlay, are you . . . Yes, I suppose you are. Well, you're the best person to talk to her right now. Go on, go. I'll bring a brew in for you soon.'

The room was dark. A single shaded candle stood on the cabinet by the opposite wall. Fiona lay on the bed, her hands across her stomach, clenched. Her eyes opened as he shut the door behind him. He hesitated.

'Finnlay?'

'I'm here.' He went to the bedside and he sat in the chair Martha had just vacated.

Fiona watched him for a moment, then her eyes returned to the ceiling. 'What did Wilf say?'

'Nothing much, really. He admitted it was a mistake to send Ayn to Marsay in the first place.' Too late now, of course. Too late for Ayn and Fiona.

'But he won't bring Robert back, will he? Even though he tried to save my mother?'

'No.'

A deep shuddering sigh wracked her body, but she was beyond tears now. 'It must have been so hard for Robert to give her Convocation. I know he loved her. They were very close. I suppose part of it was because he was her candidate and there's always a certain bond that lasts for years. But then, I remember him coming to visit, years later, when he could get away from court. He and father would talk for hours, arguing, discussing. Mother just sat and listened to both of them, voicing her thoughts when they paused long enough to take a breath. They loved him, both of them. And he always stood by them. Even to the point of risking his own life to go to Marsay. Even when he knew . . .'

Fiona's voice trailed off and she closed her eyes for a

moment. Only then, when she could no longer see him, did she speak again. 'Finnlay . . . what you did? That night when I found you?'

By the gods! Now he would have to explain – apologize. How could he answer with the truth when she was so vulnerable?

'Did you . . . mean it?'

He couldn't answer. He wanted to, longed to – but he couldn't. His silence forced her to look at him, and gazing into those sad hazel eyes only made it worse.

'You think I'm in love with your brother, don't you?'

'Oh, hell,' Finnlay whispered, dropping his gaze to his hands. 'I'm sorry, Fiona. I was sick that night, exhausted, injured . . . I thought I was dreaming when you found me. I don't know what I was—'

'I'm not.'

Finnlay paused, then slowly looked up.

'I never have been.'

Meeting her gaze, his heart skipped a beat. What should he say now? He let his instincts guide him. He reached out and took her hands, held them in his own. His reward was a tiny smile that went through him like lightning.

'Oh, Finnlay Douglas,' Fiona murmured gently, 'you're such a fool. Why did it take you so long?'

'I was afraid. I thought you hated me.' He smiled and shifted from the chair to the side of the bed. With his heart beating like a hammer, he leaned forward and kissed her. He let go of her hands and instantly they came up around his neck. Almost unbelieving, he swept her up and held her, kissing her again in complete confusion. After a while, he sat beside her, his back resting against the bedhead, with her lying alongside.

'I know this is not the right moment, but I have to at least ask. You don't have to answer right now. Just when you get around to thinking about it.'

'What?' she murmured, not moving from the safe confines of his arms.

'You will marry me, won't you?'

She didn't say a word. All she did was nod. He knew – he

281

could feel it. The gesture left him grinning like a schoolboy. Yes, he would write to Robert – and now he had the perfect excuse.

The most wonderful excuse in the world.

19

There was no rain, but this constant fog was even worse. Sometimes it was so deep that Nash had to ride with his senses extended just to avoid the sharp dips in the landscape. It was tiring travelling in such a manner, especially after the business with Selar. He'd had no time to rest, no time to recoup his energies. A week on the road gathering Pascoe's men together, getting them organized, had all but drained him. Still, it was all for the best. He'd finally taken Selar to the first level of Bonding – and the Enemy was safely dead, his blood in store for Nash to use when he needed it.

Now there was only DeMassey to deal with.

He'd made better time than Nash. He and a dozen of his men were waiting on the road from the village. Bairdenscoth Tower stood bleak behind them in the grey haze.

'I thought it might be you coming up behind us,' DeMassey began, gesturing in the air languidly. He wore a smile of instantly irritating proportions. He would be in a good mood, wouldn't he!

'I'm surprised you waited for me,' Nash grunted back, bringing his horse alongside.

'Now that would hardly be fitting, would it? Riding into your palace without you there to welcome us. We Malachi are well versed in all the forms of polite behaviour. Such a thing would just not be done.'

Nash ignored the jibe. He couldn't afford to snap when he had to ask something of this man.

'Your messenger said it was urgent? Important?' DeMassey

continued, obviously enjoying himself. 'What were his exact words again?'

'You don't need to go on any further.'

'But I must be sure I understood your man correctly. He said you needed my help?'

'I'm in no mood to play games,' Nash replied as they approached the tower. 'I have a job for you if you want it. But that smile might disappear when I tell you what it is.'

DeMassey opened his eyes wide in complete innocence. 'Well?'

'The Queen has absconded with the heir to the throne. She's not been sighted for almost a month. I want you to find her and bring the boy back alive – to me.'

'You want me to what?'

Nash turned his horse into the gate and indulged in a brief smile at DeMassey's reaction. Powerful Malachi he might be, but that woman could be hiding anywhere – and with the most powerful of friends. It was a task even a man of DeMassey's enormous ability would find difficult.

'Find the Queen, bring the boy back alive. That's all. It doesn't matter what you do with the others. Kill them if you like. The King doesn't really care – although I'm sure he would reward you handsomely if you brought back Kandar's head wrapped in a hessian bag.'

Nash jumped down from his horse and glanced around. Stinzali was nowhere to be seen, but he had to be here somewhere. The gate was open and the door to the stairs ajar. Leaving the others, Nash ran up the stairs two at a time, calling out for the old man. He got no response. Nor was there any sign on the first floor. Where was he?

By the time he reached the second floor, DeMassey was with him. Nash burst through the door to the anteroom and came to a complete halt.

Stinzali was here all right. Lying on the floor by the door. Dead. A pool of dried blood made a pillow for his ancient head. Already the smell was thick in the air. But Nash didn't stop. He sprang across the room and kicked open the door. Terrified of what he would – or wouldn't – find, he dashed from one end of the room to the other, but what he saw only confirmed his greatest fear.

The cot was empty. Finnlay Douglas had escaped. Somehow, bleeding, tortured and dying, the Enemy had eluded him. And at his feet lay the orb, shattered in two, the meagre blood it had collected already dust.

'Damn him!' Nash bellowed and kicked one half of the orb. It went flying across the room. He picked up the cot and tossed it end over end to crash against the wall. 'I'll pay him for this if I have to rip this land apart to find him!'

Seething, Nash whirled around, ready to blast DeMassey to cinders. The man stood by the door, waiting. For once, there was no smile on his face.

Nash strained to control his anger. DeMassey moved into the room, studying everything with a careful eye. Eventually he stopped.

'You really have kept a lot of secrets, haven't you? And all this stuff hoarded over the centuries? An interesting bequest from father to son. But Edassa never did pass it on, did he? Not this rubbish here – but the most important thing. The Word of Destruction.'

DeMassey looked at Nash, appraising and measuring. 'I wonder what you would do if you had the Word. Would you use it and destroy everything around you for a league or more? Would you go on using it, watching it gather strength each time? Would you practise with it, enjoying the power, until you had the ability to destroy the whole world?'

'I don't have the Word of Destruction, Luc, so your questions are entirely pointless.'

'They won't be if you find the Key.'

Nash turned away and wandered across the room. He picked up the cot and set it back on its legs. 'You know, when my great-great-grandfather, the mighty Bayazit of Yedicale, created the Word, he passed it to both his sons. As you know, Haliel fought in the Battle of Alusia, but died before he could test out his strength by using the Word. Bayazit was killed by Edassa himself, the night the Key was created. The only man left alive who knew the Word passed it to the Key and was struck down for his efforts.'

'Edassa was struck down months later, for trying to take the Key from the Salti Pazar.'

'And your ancestor was one who stood by him that day – so you can stop being righteous about it.'

'Then get to the point!'

'The Word was never used,' Nash said. 'We have no proof that it would ever work. Don't set too high a store by it.'

'Oh?' DeMassey smiled, 'then why do you want the Key so badly?'

'Why do you want it?'

'I never said I did.'

'You're Malachi, aren't you?'

'And though you try to forget it, so are you, deep down inside.'

Nash moved back across the room until he stood before DeMassey. 'What do you want?'

'A condition. That's all.'

'You'll be paid for your efforts.'

'I should hope so. But the condition is separate. Nothing will be done for you by any of my men – in fact, you will never receive succour from any Malachi without my condition being met.'

DeMassey stood with his hands behind his back, patient, as if ready to wait until the seas dried up and the deserts blew away.

Nash sighed. 'Very well. What is it?'

'I will see Valena.'

'She's not here.'

DeMassey laughed. 'Ah! He tells the truth at last! Still, we must be grateful for these little gems as they come to us. No, what I had in mind was something more interesting. I will help you, put all my resources at your disposal – but I will see Valena, alone. You'll make no effort to keep us apart.'

'What if she doesn't want to see you?'

'She can tell me to my face. I'll know if the desire is hers alone.'

And what would Valena choose? Once she heard about this disaster with the Enemy, would she begin to doubt

Nash's strength, his ability to give her what he'd promised? Would he risk losing her if he agreed?

It was a chance he had to take. Selar would be useless to him if Kenrick was not returned. The boy's appearance would help break down the last of Selar's armour and provide the only opportunity Nash would need to complete the Bonding.

'Very well. I agree.'

DeMassey smiled. 'Yes, I thought you might. Now, I'll get my men to clear up the mess in the anteroom. We'll stay the night and move out tomorrow. But don't expect any miracles. Finding the boy will take time. I don't want nasty messages from you about some perceived laziness on my part. Nor do I want you questioning my motives.'

Yes, this man was indeed a dangerous adversary. Nash would have to keep him in check. 'Just find the boy.'

DeMassey favoured him with a smile and a flourishing mock bow. Then he glanced distastefully around the room once more and left, closing the door behind him.

The autumn night was cold, breathing wet marsh air through the walls of the tower. Nash washed in hot water boiled by his power. He drew the cloth along his skin, dragging the dirt from his flesh and making it red and tender. He dried himself, then pulled a huge woollen blanket around his shoulders. He came to the centre of his room where the rug his great-grandfather had made formed six circles of decreasing size.

Nash stood his ground for a minute before he moved. He knelt in the dark pool at the heart of the circles and threw the blanket back. Naked, he drew the garnet ring from his left hand and held it up before his eyes.

'Well, Finnlay Douglas, my Enemy. You may have escaped, but I will find you. I know who you are now, and no matter where you are, no matter what you are doing, I will find you.'

He took a deep, calming breath and centred his concentration, pulled in his focus. The ring was buried between his hands and he closed his eyes. In his mind, the circles beneath him began to glow, each in turn, moving further outwards. He followed them, floating and charged by the power he unleashed. Enticing, it called him onwards into the dark night.

He roamed the land a free ghost, unchained by his body. He travelled high and fast, clear and deep. For hours he pulsed with the energy of a thousand thunderstorms, until at last, as dawn filtered through the tower windows, he rejoined his body and breathed life again into his ancient bones.

Nowhere.

Finnlay Douglas was nowhere to be found.

Except that he *was* somewhere. He was with the Key – and the Key, powerful and vibrant and still very much alive, was protecting and shielding the aura Nash was Seeking.

He opened his eyes and sat back. Absently he slipped the ring back on his finger and stared down at the blood colour suffused with new daylight.

The Enemy did indeed have the Key and was no more than a week's journey away from Bairdenscoth. Nash had been right all along. Either Lusara or the eastern reaches of Mayenne. One or the other. It didn't matter.

One day, Finnlay Douglas would have to leave the shelter of the Key – and when he did, Nash would find him. The Enemy was no match for him. The Enemy would take him to the Key.

With a smile, Nash pulled the blanket over himself again and laid down on the plush rug. He closed his eyes and plunged into sleep.

20

There was nothing so refreshing as washing in bitterly cold water – especially on a freezing morning like this. Still, Micah plunged his face into the bowl, shook it around for a few seconds, then emerged with a roar.

Now shivering, he grabbed a towel and rubbed it vigorously over his body. Soon his skin was red, but warm. Before he could get cold again, he threw on some clothes, ignored the waiting bed and the sleep he really needed and headed downstairs.

Robert was in the hall talking quietly to Owen. He looked up as Micah jumped down the last two steps. 'I thought I told you to get some rest.'

'I will, my lord. Later.' Micah glanced at Owen, then back at Robert. 'Any word yet?'

'What? Since you rode in this morning? Half an hour ago?' Robert shook his head. 'I don't suppose you've eaten either, have you?'

'Er . . . no . . .'

'Owen?'

'I'll have something brought up to the winter parlour, my lord. Together with a sleeping draught, I think.'

Robert laughed. 'See, Micah? I'm not the only one who thinks you're reckless.'

'I, my lord?' Micah asked innocently. Just because he'd spent the better part of the last four days in the saddle didn't mean he should immediately collapse into a bed. Of course, there were the five days immediately before that – but it didn't matter. He felt fine. 'I don't know what you mean.'

Robert shook his head, still smiling, 'Yes you do. But don't worry. You'll pay for it later. Trust me.'

'My lord?' Owen interrupted, turning to the opposite end of the hall. There, travel-stained and weary, Deverin was coming towards them, his clothes encrusted in mud.

Robert immediately strode over. The big man, a grin as wide as the sea on his face, said only one thing: 'Success, my lord!'

With a laugh, Robert slapped him on the shoulder. 'Well done, Deverin! Any mishaps? Any problems— Where's Patric?'

'Here.'

They all turned to find Patric limping into the hall, looking – if it were possible – in even worse shape than Deverin.

Micah immediately went to his aid, taking his elbow and a little of the weight off his feet.

Robert was grinning at them both now. 'Let's get you upstairs. Owen, send some food up, will you? I'm sure these battle-weary soldiers are hungry for some Dunlorn fare.'

'Aye, my lord.'

There was hot water for Patric to wash in, but Micah didn't mind. Rather, he felt a bit sorry for the man – it took years to get used to days on end in the saddle. And Patric was a mass of bruises. Micah helped him get his shirt off, washed out a few of the cuts. All the while, Deverin, ignoring the dirt, plunged into the food Owen had brought them. But, weary and bruised, Patric couldn't stop talking.

'It was amazing, Robert. You should have been there. We encountered a patrol every single day we were out. Fortunately, each time we were able to get to Rosalind first. We even stopped and shared an ale with one lot. I tell you, I almost died of fright, but Deverin here just told a few dirty stories and sent them on their way laughing. The worst night was just before we hit the border. Deverin said we should continue on without stopping, we were so close. Ouch!'

'Sorry,' Micah murmured, drawing his hands away from the cut on Patric's shoulder. The smell of hot food was getting to him and the empty hole in his stomach was growling for attention. But Patric wouldn't sit still, so Micah just handed him a woollen shirt and took a seat at the table.

'So what happened?' Robert prompted, leaning back against a cabinet. 'When you got to the border?'

'Oh, that,' Patric reached out for a piece of ham pie and stuffed it into his mouth. He kept talking through the food. 'Well, it was really dark and there was this wood we had to get through. The Queen was dubious about it, but Deverin insisted we keep moving. Then, before we could get very far, we were challenged.'

'What?'

'His Grace of Flan-har,' Deverin murmured through a mouthful of cheese and onion.

'Yes,' Patric's eyes were alight with his story, his hands

flying through the air as he spoke. 'Your old friend had sent out an advance party just in case we got into trouble. Well, this guard told us of a patrol not three hundred yards away from us. We were so close to the border we couldn't risk turning back.'

'Master Patric did something, my lord,' Deverin grunted. 'He was shaking like a leaf, but he had that stone in his hand. The patrol didn't see a thing and we got across the border without incident.'

Deverin poured himself some wine and climbed to his feet. He joined Robert by the cabinet, wiping the bread-crumbs from his beard. 'It was a good thing you sent him along, my lord.'

'Oh?'

'Yes,' Deverin nodded, 'to have kept him here for so long would have driven you mad, my lord.'

Micah ducked his head and buried his smile around his breakfast.

'Correct me if I'm wrong, Deverin,' Robert began mildly, almost curiously, 'but would I be right in suggesting that my friend actually enjoyed himself on this mission?'

Deverin nodded gravely. 'I believe, my lord, that you have judged the situation accurately.'

'And he didn't er . . . complain at all?'

'Aye, he did that, my lord.'

'What . . . not constantly, surely?'

'Aye, my lord, constantly.'

'Now that's interesting.'

Patric quickly swallowed before he started defending himself.

'What's more, my lord,' Deverin continued, bending his head towards Robert with a conspiratorial whisper, 'when he did that Mask – I could swear he was smiling.'

Micah couldn't hold it in any longer, he began to laugh.

'Leave me alone!' Patric wailed. 'I'm tired and injured. There's no need to pick on me like this.'

'Pick on you?' Robert spread his arms in innocence. 'Nothing of the kind! I'm just receiving a full report of your exploits. I would be derelict in my duty if I did less.'

'Hah!' Patric grumbled. 'That's the last time I do you a favour.'

Deverin burst out laughing and moved back to the table to slap Patric on the back before taking his leave. When the door was closed again, Patric winced and flexed his shoulder slightly. 'That man's a brute, Robert. I don't know how you put up with him. You and your friends will be the death of me! As for that Duke—'

'Who? Grant Kavanagh? He's harmless.'

'Harmless? He's the size of an ox and has no concept of degrees of excess. He treated the whole thing like it was some huge entertainment put on for him by his old and close friend, Robert Douglas. I swear, we would have been back two days ago if it hadn't been for him. He kept insisting we stay another night and drink with him. Even Deverin was in a hurry to leave – and he can really put the ale away. But for some reason, Grant took a liking to me. Kept filling up my cup and watching me drink it. I was sick for half the next day, so we couldn't leave that night. I swear he did it deliberately.'

'But you did leave – eventually.'

'The only way we got out of there was by telling Grant that you would be frantic with worry if you hadn't heard the Queen was safe. I even suggested you might come chasing after him if we didn't get home soon.'

'And that did the trick?'

'Sure did. The man's terrified of you. He even admits it – quietly.'

Robert chuckled and came over to the table. He pulled a chair around and straddled the seat, putting his elbows on the back. 'So the Queen *is* safe. What about Samah and Galiena?'

'They joined us on the second day in Flan-har. They had no problems at all. They were only stopped once, given a cursory glance and told to move on. The Princess was back to full health the last time I saw her. I should warn you, though, Grant is looking to see you for a visit very soon. He wants to know what this is all about. What I want to know is why he would help with such a thing. I know Flan-har is independent – but if Selar suspected his son was there, there would be an army crossing that border in no time, amidst talk of annexing the wealthy little state. Why would Grant take that risk?'

'He's a kind and generous soul.'

'Rubbish!'

Robert laughed. 'And he owes me a favour.'

'It would have to be a pretty big favour,' Patric murmured, polishing off the last of the bread and wine.

'It was.'

Patric looked up at this, then glanced at Micah for help. Micah just shrugged. He had no idea what Robert was talking about.

Patric leaned back in his chair, his hands resting happily on his full stomach. 'Does he know you're a sorcerer?'

Robert shook his head and helped himself to some ale. 'No. But I think he has his suspicions. Why, what did he say?'

'Nothing . . . exactly. It's just that, beneath the bluster and bravado, he really is afraid of you. Would that have something to do with the favour he owes you?'

Micah was intrigued and turned to watch Robert's response. There was obviously a story there, but Robert wasn't about to elaborate. He just shook his head, giving nothing away. 'I don't think he's really afraid of me – he was just trying to impress you. He does have a vivid imagination, which I'm sure you noticed. Anyway, we can all relax; they're safe for the moment. The only real problem now is—'

A knock at the door interrupted him. It was Owen with a tanned leather pouch.

'Forgive me, my lord, but a courier has just arrived for you. He is to wait for a reply.'

Robert took the pouch, opened it and brought out a single letter. He examined the seal, then frowned across at Micah. 'It's from Elita. Thank you, Owen. I'll be down shortly with my reply.'

Micah sat on the edge of his seat as Owen left them and Robert cracked open the seal. He read in silence for a few moments, his face hard and immobile. Patric glanced at

Micah, but neither said anything. Eventually, Robert came to his feet and tossed the letter down on the table.

'I've been invited to Jenn's wedding. My mother, too.'

A shocked silence filled the room as Robert drifted over to the window. Micah watched him go, then turned his gaze on Patric. It was Patric who spoke first.

'When?'

'In just over a week. She's to marry Eachern at Selar's order. He's in a hurry to secure all possible rivals now his son has been stolen away.'

Micah stared at the letter. He could have picked it up and read it, but he didn't want to. This was too terrible for words. But – this didn't make any sense. 'Why have you been invited, my lord? Jacob believes you're a traitor.'

'And so I am, Micah – now.' Robert's voice was flat and he spoke without turning around. 'It's ironic, but it appears that my recent . . . activities have altered Jacob's view somewhat. He's also angry about the summary direction given out by Selar. On top of that, he feels that, as I was responsible for Jenn being returned to Elita in the first place, I should be there to help celebrate her wedding.'

Patric had heard enough. He clambered to his feet, knocking his chair over. He hastily picked it up, insisting as he went, 'But you have to go and stop it, Robert. If you don't, I will. We can't let her marry Eachern. The man's a butcher! His efforts during the conquest made him the most hated man in the country after Selar. His men razed three whole villages to the ground on their own. It's inconceivable that Jenn should marry him. She must be allowed to follow her own . . .'

Robert whirled around from the window, his eyes flaring. 'Destiny? Do you really think I want her to marry . . .' Then the light abruptly died away. 'I can't stop it, Patric, and neither can you. There's no way we could get her out of there, short of abducting her, and I think she might have something to say about that.'

'But she can't want this! She can't want to marry a man like that!'

Robert came back to the table, his fingers lightly touching

the letter. 'She made her choice a year ago, Patric. It's too late to back out now. She'll marry Eachern for her father's sake. For the sake of her House. And let's face it: she'll be safer with Eachern than anyone else. He'll keep her out of trouble.'

He picked up the letter and turned for the door. He opened it, but stood with his hand on the latch, his face in profile. 'I suggest you get some rest, Micah, unless you want to stay here instead.'

'What?' Micah stumbled forward, bumping into the table. 'You're going?'

'How can I not? But I won't involve my mother in this. She's been through enough already. Be ready to leave at dawn.'

It was windy out on the higher moors, but once Robert rode down to where the hills were greener and the valleys gentle, there was little more than a breeze riffling through the trees. He didn't go all the way to the farm. He stopped on the rise above, dismounted and sat on the thick green grass, prepared to wait all day if necessary.

Below, the farm drifted in and out of cloudy shadow, quiet and peaceful in the afternoon. There were children running around a flock of geese in the southern yard. Robert couldn't tell who were noisier – the boys or the birds. He watched them for a long time as his horse grazed contentedly at his side. Then, as a last cloud left the sun shining down on the farm, a figure emerged from a building and began walking up the hill towards him. Long, purposeful strides brought the man halfway up the rise where he stopped, unwilling to go further.

'I thought you were to send my son with the news. You didn't need to come, yourself. Is it so bad?'

Robert got to his feet and wandered down to meet David Maclean. 'No, the news is good. Micah is resting after several long days in the saddle. I thought you'd prefer not to wait.'

David regarded him with suspicion only thinly veiled. 'And the Queen is safely away?'

'She is indeed.'

'Where?'

'I can't tell you that. It's safer for you to know nothing. Not just for you, but also for the Queen.'

David stuck out his jaw, but didn't argue. He turned his head and his gaze on his prosperous farm and the legacy he'd worked all his life to give his children.

Robert knew he should leave. He knew he should never even broach the subject – but David hadn't walked away. The opportunity was there and Robert had to take it.

'Can you really not bring yourself to forgive Micah?'

'Hah!' David snapped without looking at Robert. 'How can I forgive him when I can't even trust him?'

Robert's jaw dropped in surprise. 'Trust? Micah? Why he's the most trustworthy man I've ever met! How can you not trust him?'

At this, David turned a stony gaze on him. 'When my son went to work at the castle I considered it an honour. Your father was beloved of the people, a great man who stood against the usurper and died fighting him. I was proud that my son served such a House and I continued to be proud right up until the day you swore your oath to the usurper. I pleaded with Micah to leave then, but he was just a child and he idolized you. I kept hoping that as he grew older he would see what I saw, that you had betrayed your people and your country on that day – not to mention your own father. But my son was always blind when it came to you. And so I learned not to trust him. I learned not to believe anything he said because I knew that his words were your words, that your treason was his treason. Now that he's a man, he has no excuse. He's been around you long enough to know what kind of man you are. How can I trust my son when, as a man, he is blind not by accident nor from innocence, but by choice?'

Robert met David's gaze steadily. 'You are his father and he loves you. Yes, Micah stays with me from choice. I can't defend my actions to you.'

'You don't even make the attempt?'

'What would be the point? You've already made up your mind. You did so the moment I made my vow to Selar –

before I'd even had a chance to do some lasting good. You're angry with me, Master Maclean, for betraying my people and my country. But I can't see why you need to beat your anger out on your son when all he's done is follow all the precepts you yourself have taught him. Honour. Loyalty. Friendship. Micah lives by these things, breathes them as you and I breathe the air around us. He could no more betray me than he could slit his own throat. You were once proud that he served my House. You have no reason not to be equally proud of the way he serves me now – especially when it costs him your love and trust.'

David frowned. 'You have no right to tell me how I should regard my son when you yourself are to blame for his situation.'

'Perhaps not.' Robert brought his horse alongside. 'But he's my friend and I can do no less for him.'

As Robert swung up into the saddle, David shook his head again, slowly. 'Why did you come back to Lusara?'

Robert lifted his gaze to the wide valley below. 'You know, I'm not sure I know any more. And there are some days when I really wish I hadn't bothered.'

For the second time in as many weeks, Micah found himself travelling north towards Elita, but if that last trip had been quiet, this one was utterly silent. From years of custom, Micah knew when Robert would stop for the night, when they would rise, which roads they would take. There were familiar patterns to Robert's decisions that Micah could almost feel in his bones. And it was a good thing, too, because Robert didn't say a single word all the way to Elita.

The days of travelling grew long in the silence. More than once Micah worked up a conversation in his head, an attempt to get Robert to talk – about anything, it didn't matter what. But every time he took a breath to speak, every time he looked up to say something, Robert just shook his head in warning. Micah decided in the end that it was better to make no attempt.

It was not until they were riding along the banks of the

lake, with Elita glowing gold in the afternoon sun, that Robert actually spoke.

'I guess we're not too late, then.'

Micah almost fell off his horse. He stared at Robert for a long time, and, in response, Robert turned to him with a smile – just as though the last week of silence had never happened. 'The pennants are still up, Micah. The decorations? For the wedding? The castle is covered with them – so that means we're not too late.'

'Serin's blood, my lord,' Micah said. 'Sometimes . . .'

'Yes,' Robert said as he led him through the gates, 'I know, Micah.'

The courtyard was almost crowded, and bustling with activity. They were not the only ones who had just arrived. Here were faces Micah barely recognized – and others he knew very well. It appeared Robert was not the only one who had been asked to come and witness Selar's temerity. But how many would actually sympathize was another matter.

As they waited to be greeted, there were those who stopped and openly stared at Robert as if they'd seen a ghost. Fortunately, it was Neil himself who welcomed them, his quiet manner a calm breeze in this chaotic storm.

'Welcome back to Elita, Your Grace. Can I show you to your rooms?'

'No, Neil, just tell me where they are.' Robert smiled. 'You look busy enough as it is.'

'We are, I admit, filled to capacity this night and the next three. Lord Jacob has planned four days of entertainments to celebrate this wedding. Those guests who are not staying will be arriving tomorrow for the ceremony only. Tonight, however, there is to be a banquet to which all are invited.' Neil swallowed and lowered his voice a little. 'Lady Jennifer is to meet her future husband there for the first time.'

'Tonight?' Micah squeaked, but Robert took his arm, ready to steer him away.

'And our rooms, Neil?'

'In the Falcon Tower, Your Grace. You will not have to enter through the hall. I thought you might prefer it that way.'

Robert smiled warmly. 'You were always an astute judge of character, Neil. Thank you.'

'A pleasure, Your Grace.' Neil bowed slightly and turned to his next arrivals.

Robert indicated the Falcon Tower which faced the woods. 'Come on, let's get out of this. I'm attracting far too much attention.'

With a little jostling, they moved out of the main courtyard and into a smaller one. This was no less crowded, but at least there were no horses moving around and the chances of being stepped on were minimized. Robert led Micah through a maze of people down a cobbled bridge and into a forecourt where the garden wall stood on the left. Opposite, moulded into the curtain wall surrounding the castle, stood the Falcon Tower. A blazon carved into the stone far above them was shaped as a bird in flight.

'Jacob's father was a keen hawker,' Robert told Micah as they headed inside. 'He had a peregrine that was said to be unbeaten in its day. Unfortunately, the late Earl did not also like riding and used to flight his birds from the top of this tower.'

'That's awfully dangerous.'

'Not if you're a falcon,' Robert murmured. He stopped as they reached the top floor. There the room spread out before them, circular, open and spacious. A short staircase to their left led to the other rooms. Judging from the windows, Micah guessed the walls to be over twelve feet deep.

'Built for siege.'

'Aye,' Robert nodded, walking across the room. 'Remind me to thank Neil, will you?'

'Why?'

'He has a good memory. These are the same rooms I stayed in the first time I came to Elita with my father, years before Jenn was born. I used to throw paper pellets out of this window at Bella as she walked in the garden. By the gods, she used to drive me crazy. Fortunately, age has definitely improved her.'

'As I'm sure she would say of you.'

Robert threw a grin over his shoulder. 'I hope so. Serin

help me if I'm any worse. Do you think I could get away without attending this banquet?'

Micah, standing by the door, shook his head slowly. 'No. Besides, I would suggest that if you don't make an appearance before the actual ceremony tomorrow, there would be some who would say that you're afraid to show yourself.'

Turning to face Micah squarely, Robert asked, 'And what do you say?'

'Nothing, my lord.'

Robert dropped his head, but smiled, 'What did I ever do to deserve you?'

'I don't know,' Micah shrugged, 'but it must have been pretty horrible.'

He was rewarded with a burst of laughter from Robert, who came across the room and clapped a hand on Micah's shoulder. 'Come, let's unpack. Since we're here, we may as well enjoy ourselves.'

He reached out for the shirt draped over the chair. Rich and embroidered, it bore a scent of lavender which drifted on the air. First one sleeve and then the other, over his shoulders and laced together in front. Gently, he wound the ties in his fingers, lingering with each one. The silk had never felt so fine, his flesh never so alive. He sensed every fibre of it covering his body, every inch of skin caressed at the same time. Lavender and silk, smooth and sweet. Like slipping into death.

With hands powered by imagination, he picked up his sword and armed himself. Now he was ready.

Jenn tried to stand still, but the pricking and fussing over her hair was driving her mad. In the end, she pulled away from Addie. 'Please, just leave it. It will do as it is.'

Addie stood there with pins and combs in her hands, totally bewildered. 'But it's not finished, my lady. There's still the back to do.'

It was Bella who came to her rescue. 'If you give those to me, I'll finish it later. There's still plenty of time.' With calm hands, she took the combs and ushered Addie out of the room.

Jenn immediately began pacing up and down between the bed and her table. The room was littered with clothes, wash bowls and the light supper she hadn't touched. Outside she could hear the continuing rumble of guests arriving, greeting each other with pleasure. Darkness had descended an hour before and only the torches along the castle walls lit the chaos below. But she knew it was there, she could feel it.

They would be waiting for her. Waiting for her to go down and make an appearance. They would all be watching her, looking at her, judging her. Wondering if she was indeed a fit consort for the cousin of the King. Wondering if this lost waif had learned how to be a lady in one short year. Would she make some terrible social mistake? Would she show her awful manners? Would her dress, her hair be all it should be?

The memory of those women in Marsay came back to her, vicious, selfish and superior. They would be down there, wives, daughters of Eachern's friends. Oh, they would judge her, all right. Would they find her wanting?

'I wish you would eat something,' Bella murmured, pouring some sweet yellow wine into the silver cups Lawrence had given Jenn. 'You'll find it much easier if you do.'

'Easy?' Jenn snapped. 'What has easy got to do with it?'

She strode up and down without pausing, her hands twisting together until her knuckles hurt.

'Jenn,' Bella approached slowly, 'you must try and stay calm.'

'But I don't want to do this! I don't want to go through with it! By the gods, I don't even want to be here!'

'I know.' Gently, Bella reached out and caught her hands, bringing her pacing to a halt.

'I said I would and I promised Father I wouldn't make him ashamed of me and I won't, but I just don't want to do it. I can't. I know. I'll just say something or do something and Father will hate me. I've already ruined everything and I keep doing it even though I try not to. Oh, Bella, what am I going to do?'

300

Jenn gulped in breaths, unable to stop the tears which fell down her face. Bella gazed down at her. 'You're going to go through with it. You know it, I know it – Father knows it. None of us wants this marriage.'

Jenn's hands trembled within Bella's grasp and no matter how hard she tried, she couldn't stop them. With a gasp, she pulled away and stumbled to the window. There, she closed her eyes and held her face up to the breeze, tried to make it cool her burning flesh. This was so silly. She'd been fine until now. All the preparations, everything had gone on and she'd not felt this way. Why now?

With her voice barely controlled, she turned back to Bella. 'He's here, isn't he?'

'Yes.' Bella nodded, calmly. 'Neil says they arrived a couple of hours ago.'

'He shouldn't have come.'

'No. But he's here now and there's nothing we can do about it. Neil put them in the Falcon Tower. With any luck, nobody will bother them there.'

'Bella . . .' Jenn took a step forward, unable to voice the horrible confusion which battled inside her. 'I . . . Will you stay with me tonight and make sure I don't do anything wrong?'

Bella's face softened a little. She crossed the room and put her hands on Jenn's shoulders. 'Where else would I be? I know you're afraid; it's only natural.'

'I'm not afraid,' Jenn said. 'It's just that . . . I think . . . well . . . I just don't want to marry him. I can't help it.'

In answer, Bella pulled her close, stiffly at first and then gentler. Jenn held on to her and tried to still the shaking which reached to the core of her soul.

'You've come so far, Jenn,' Bella murmured, her voice low and soft. 'You won't fail now. You don't need me to tell you that you have no choice. But have no fear. I will stay by your side, no matter what. You are my sister.'

Jenn moved back a little and gazed up into that face which was so like her own. Bella had been so distant to her since the news of this wedding had arrived. Nevertheless she'd taken care of the arrangements, taken care of Jenn – and now she stood there, saying words of comfort. Would their mother have said these things? Would their mother have offered comfort like this – knowing there was no way out of this terrible situation?

Who had said these things to Bella? Who had stood beside Bella on her wedding day?

'You loved Lawrence when you married him, didn't you?'

'Yes. It took me a long time, but he was very patient. I was lucky to have such a good man.'

'Lucky, yes,' Jenn murmured. 'I'm sorry, Bella. I've been such a trial to you.'

'You're apologizing to me?' Bella let out a little laugh. 'Yes, you are a trial. But that doesn't matter any more. Come, try and calm down. You only make yourself suffer more like this. We both know you'll go through with it. You could have run away a dozen times over the last two weeks – but you didn't. Try and stop crying, Jennifer. You don't want him to see your eyes all red and puffy, do you?'

Jenn grunted a laugh and stepped back, wiping her hands over her face. 'I'm ugly compared to Eachern's real choice. Samah has ten times my beauty. He's only got me because she ran away. I should have done the same. I don't give a damn if Eachern thinks I'm pretty or not!'

Bella smiled and reached for the cup of sweet wine. She took Jenn's hands and wrapped them around the cup. With her voice barely above a whisper, she replied, 'I wasn't talking about Eachern.'

21

If there was ever only one thing you could say about Robert, it would be that he had a fine sense of occasion. Commanding Micah to do the same, Robert had put on his very best finery in preparation for the banquet. Black velvet doublet with a row of black pearl buttons running down the front, an item of extraordinary value. The remainder of his attire was also black, with the exception of the brooch worn at his throat: the Douglas eagle, hand-tooled in ebony and gold and said to be more than five hundred years old. With his dark hair falling on to his shoulders, his tall frame commanded attention. If Robert had tried to make an impression, he couldn't have done any better. There was hardly a head that didn't turn as they entered the great hall of Elita.

'I just hope there's no one here I owe money to,' Robert murmured lightly as they made their way through the crowds. Music was chiming from the gallery above, but it was almost inaudible over the laughter and conversation in the hall.

Micah tried to keep to Robert's side, but it was difficult. People kept noticing Robert, making as if to approach him, then stopping midway. At this rate, it would take them half the night just to get a cup of ale!

'Now there's a pretty lass, Micah,' Robert paused and bent to whisper in his ear. 'She's smiling at you.'

'Aye, my lord,' Micah murmured, his attention caught elsewhere. 'But there's one prettier than the whole put together.'

Robert turned his head to see where he was looking. Jenn was seated upon the dais, Bella and some other ladies close by. Jenn wore her hair up, but even so, dark tendrils fell down her throat and on to her shoulders. She wore a gown of deepest sunset blue which made her skin glow in the candlelight like the moon on a frosty night. Even her eyes shone more brilliantly than usual.

'Go ahead, Micah. She'll want to talk to you.'

'But . . .'

'Please, Micah.' Robert turned away and moved through the crowd to the other side of the room. Left alone, Micah had no choice but to approach the dais. Jenn saw him coming and smiled as much as she dared in this company.

'Lady Jennifer,' Micah bowed in his best courtly manner. 'You look beautiful. And you, Lady Bella.'

'It was ... good of you to come,' Jenn replied a little nervously.

'Yes,' Bella nodded, favouring him with a smile. She too seemed nervous, but with so many people around it was easy to see why.

'Micah,' Jenn came to her feet, stood as close as she dared, 'you have to warn him. This is not ... Please, just stay with him. I don't want him to be alone.'

With a glance at Bella, Micah nodded. Whatever Jenn was referring to, Bella made no attempt to stop Jenn's warning – or elaborate on it. He dropped his voice low so only Jenn could hear him. 'If you want to get out of this, just say so. One word. That's all it will take.'

At that, Jenn smiled up at him, her eyes sparkling with such a warmth it made his heart turn somersaults. 'Thank you for asking, Micah. But the answer is no. You know why. Now, please, go and stay with him. There will be time for us to talk later.'

With another small bow, Micah turned away and sighted Robert far away down the hall. He was talking to somebody quietly, but there was an enormous amount of attention directed at him. As Micah made his way to Robert's side, he tried to catch the odd piece of conversation, but, strangely, it all stopped the moment he came close, and sprang up again the moment he passed. The only words he did catch were 'dark angel'.

Yes, Robert did have a fine sense of occasion, with his black attire and raven hair. A pity he didn't have an equally fine sense of self-preservation.

Robert saw him coming and left his companion. 'Short conversation?'

'It appears she doesn't want to talk to me either,' Micah murmured. 'However, there is somebody who does want to talk to you. Lord Jacob.'

Waving them over, Jacob sat in his chair by the fire, surrounded by his many friends, some of whom melted away as Robert and Micah approached. Before the old Earl stretched the entire hall, glittering with important people from all over the country. His chair backed to the edge of the dais, as though, on this night, Jacob had no desire to sit above his guests, but to be one with them.

'I'm glad you accepted my invitation, Robert. If anyone should be here today, it is you.'

Robert gave Jacob a wry smile. 'Thank you for inviting me. I'll admit I was surprised.'

'The actions of both friends and enemies often surprise us. How we react to them is the important thing.'

Exuding his usual charm, Robert greeted the others surrounding Jacob. However, all of them, to a man, appeared to be waiting: it was as though there were something else going on here other than a wedding celebration. Micah was just starting to feel very uncomfortable when the room suddenly hushed. For the first time, he could hear the musicians properly – but that only made him feel worse. Turning, ready to face an enemy, Micah saw the crowd behind them part and two men walk towards them.

Instinctively, Micah moved until he was slightly in front of Robert. However, Robert put a gentle hand on his shoulder in reassurance and moved him aside. As the two men came closer, gentlemen bowed, ladies curtsied, until there were only three men left upright in the hall. Robert, Tiege Eachern – and Selar.

'Welcome back to Lusara,' Selar said loudly enough for all to hear. 'I'm sorry you have not yet had the opportunity to visit us at court. But after so long away from home, you must have had many affairs which required your immediate and urgent attention.'

After an almost imperceptible pause, Robert bowed to Selar. Although the air was thick with tension, Robert appeared completely at ease. He moved and spoke as though he'd seen Selar only the week before, rather than four years ago. It was indeed a remarkable talent, one which Micah wished he shared.

'Thank you, Sire,' Robert murmured gracefully. 'You are indeed correct. The recent death of my brother has only increased my responsibilities to my people.'

'Not to mention the death of your uncle,' Eachern grunted.

Selar turned a fleeting attention on those standing close. Instantly they moved away until only Jacob was left sitting in his chair, while Baron Campbell pushed his way through to stand close by. Both men were silent but unrepentant. They'd known this confrontation would happen. What else did they know?

Micah could hardly control the jumping in his stomach. This was what Jenn had tried to warn him about. Selar would undoubtedly want Micah to vanish, but there was no power on this earth that would make him leave Robert's side now.

The King surveyed them all with the same detached air of contempt he'd always maintained. He looked no older, despite the last four years; he appeared to be in the best of health. His fair hair shone in the candlelight, his grey eyes were bright and direct, set off by the tawny linen tunic he wore, jewelled with rubies and emeralds. Even the sword on his hip had been polished to perfection.

'Your brother's death must have been a great blow to your mother,' Selar said casually. 'It must indeed be tragic to lose a child so young.'

Robert didn't even flinch. 'It has been very hard on her, Sire. But she is well enough. She takes great comfort in the Church, as I'm sure you remember.'

Now it was Selar's turn not to flinch. Instead, he glanced at Eachern, then at Jacob. Of Micah's presence, he seemed completely unaware. The hum of conversation was almost back to normal now. Out of the corner of his eye, Micah could see Jenn and Bella still standing on the dais, no more than twenty feet away. Neither moved, but both watched, tense and expectant.

'I wonder, Dunlorn, whether you intend to come to court in the spring. Was such a thing among your plans?'

'I have no plans at all, Sire,' Robert spread his hands innocently. 'As you can see, I am here only at Jacob's request.'

'Of course.' Then Selar smiled. It was not a nice smile at all, but the kind that gave you a bad night's sleep. 'I should thank you, really, for your absence. All in all, you have been a better servant to the throne away from court than you ever

306

were present. Not that I'm sorry you came back to Lusara – not at all. But in retrospect, I can hardly think of a more loyal lord. Neither, I might add, can the people.'

He was trying to bait Robert. Even Jacob could see that. Eachern waited on the balls of his feet, hoping that Robert would react. They were all disappointed when Robert smiled easily. 'I would have no other epitaph, Sire. To be a good and faithful servant of the crown is every man's wish, is it not?'

'Is it?' Selar whipped back. 'I would have thought a heart full of courage would be a greater wish.'

'How can a man serve the crown without courage, Sire?'

Selar took a step forward. 'I don't know, Dunlorn. Perhaps you can tell me. Or should I call you my Lord of Haddon now that your treacherous uncle is dead? I can't say I have many men around me who have tried to stand in my way. Even less have I those who have so openly supported me by simple inaction.' Selar almost spat the words out. He drew up to his full height, raising his voice enough for it to be heard clearly through the entire hall. Ominously, the music came to a ragged halt.

'Yes,' Selar laughed, 'the great name of Douglas has become commensurate with that of coward. You don't know the number of times I've had men say to me, lock him up! Charge him with something – anything. Haddon is a threat, they've said over and over again. But you see, I left you alone, didn't I? I let you wallow in the hole you dug for yourself. I knew you wouldn't turn on me. I knew you were spent, tired, old and weary. By the gods, even your own uncle had more courage than you. Even when I ordered his execution, I knew you wouldn't come. And why? Because you're a coward. That's why you left in the first place. That's why you stand here now, without a single word in your own defence. Go on, Haddon. Deny it. Please. It will give Eachern a good laugh, if nothing else.'

Robert was silent, his face was entirely immobile, hands close at his sides.

'Oh? Nothing to say for yourself? Such a pity – and I was hoping this party would be so much fun. Vaughn will be

307

disappointed when I tell him you came all this way and still had nothing to say to me. All those years we had together and it's only now that I realize how little your friendship was worth to me. Come now, this room is breathless waiting for you to cast me down. You, the last hope of Lusara, the one man who has ever stood up to the usurper. Have you really nothing to say to me? Will you not strike me down, kill me on the spot? Free your beloved country?'

'I cannot, Sire,' Robert murmured. 'You will remember I gave you my oath.'

At this, Selar finally dropped the amused façade and stepped so close to Robert there was barely a handspan between them. Eye to eye, his fury almost tangible, Selar said, 'Well, if that's all that's stopping you, Robert, by all means go ahead. Let it not be said that I gave you any excuse to be a coward. You never really needed one, did you? Your surrender at Seluth proved that. What use have I for the oath of a snivelling coward when I have your entire country enslaved at my feet? Your oath served its purpose when you were still the people's hero, but now, your decaying coward-ice and apathetic inaction have dissolved that need. I release you from your vow.'

Robert, his eyes blazing with hellfire, turned stiffly around to Jacob. 'It appears, my lord, that my presence is causing your guests displeasure. With your permission, I shall withdraw.'

Jacob could only nod, his eyes as cold as ice. With that, Robert turned on his heel and walked off, the crowds falling away before him like scythed wheat.

'I told you, Eachern,' Selar returned to his banter. 'I said he wouldn't do anything, didn't I?'

'Yes, Sire, you did. A pity really; a fight would have entertained everyone.'

'But spilling blood on the night before your wedding would hardly have been a good omen – nor very pious. As an act of purification, however, it would have sufficed.' Selar chuckled. 'Come, cousin. I think it's time you said hello to your pretty bride-to-be.'

As they turned towards the dais, Jacob reached up and

grabbed Micah's sleeve. 'Go to him, boy. Now. Be quick. At this moment he needs a friend.'

As Jenn watched Micah push his way through the crowd, Bella took her hand and whispered close, 'It's time.'

Jenn could only nod absently. Micah had reached the far doorway. In a moment he was gone, but there was no relief in his absence. Would they leave now? Would he go? Would he pass through the gates of Elita and never come back?

'Come, Jenn. They're waiting for you.'

Jenn glanced up, but for a moment didn't really see Bella's face. All she could hear in her mind were the words Selar had spoken.

Coward.

That's what he'd called Robert.

A coward.

But – Robert was no coward. He was the Enemy.

The Enemy . . . of this.

'If it's time,' Jenn breathed, fury welling up inside her like a dam fit to burst, 'then I suppose we had better move.'

She let Bella lead her across the dais. She kept her eyes downcast, full of humility and modesty. She moved with all the grace she'd been taught. Her face was calm, her hands perfectly still. She breathed evenly and steadily.

She was ready to kill.

Her left palm began to itch and her oath to Wilf came back, scorched into her memory as surely as her handprint into the council table. She'd told Wilf she could have burned the Enclave down. Perhaps one day she would. But today, she would do something different. Something entirely more dangerous.

Bella brought her to the side of Jacob's chair. As she rose from her curtsey, he took her hand, his cool wrinkled flesh soft to the touch. He began to speak, keeping his voice low but courteous. Jenn couldn't hear his words. They were blown away in the wind of her anger. It was only when he paused that she realized her moment had come.

Jacob held out her right hand to Eachern. The Duke took it, bending to brush his lips over her flesh. It was only the fury which stopped her from flinching, from snatching her hand away. It kept her cool and controlled and sublimely calm. Never before had she felt so very calm.

She looked up – not at Eachern, but at Selar.

He was watching her with a mixture of curiosity and amusement. So very superior: the perfect tyrant.

And destined to die.

She let it roll around inside her, lingering over the pleasure of the power, the devastating enormity. He would never know what had happened. Never know that he had brought about his own downfall.

She raised her left hand to help focus the force she was ready to unleash.

She took a deep breath—

A hand. On her shoulder. Gripping hard.

Bella. Her voice a whisper close to Jenn's ear. 'You must say words of welcome to your husband-to-be, sister. He waits.'

The power, like a fragile candle flame, flickered and died. Disappointed and brittle, Jenn dropped her hand and murmured the words they were waiting for. She even managed a glance in Eachern's direction. He'd noticed nothing. None of them had noticed a thing.

Once again she turned her gaze on Selar, but his attention had slipped from her. As she stared at him, words unbidden came into her mind.

One day, King, be you mighty or low, I will bring about your downfall.

'Well, what do you think, cousin,' Selar murmured, utterly ignorant of the sentence she had just delivered, 'is your little bride pretty enough for you?'

With barely a flicker of her powers, Jenn reached through the contact of Eachern's hand and Sealed him. He would never be an ally to her, but she would take what protection she could get from this cousin of the tyrant.

'Yes, Sire,' Eachern nodded his thick head. He still held Jenn's hand and although his touch made her skin crawl, she made no move. 'She is exquisite. A rare jewel Earl Jacob will be sad to lose.'

'Your Grace is most kind,' Jacob grunted, only barely polite. Then, with a sudden beaming smile, he reached forward and removed Jenn's hand from Eachern's grasp. 'Please, avail yourselves of refreshments and the many entertainments we have planned. You will find Elita's hospitality does no shame to her House.'

Selar laughed outright and clapped Eachern on the shoulder. 'He means for you to leave his daughter alone, cousin. Fear not, you will have her tomorrow night. Come, let's find some wine.'

Eachern nodded, his eyes never leaving Jenn. Slowly, at Selar's urging, he turned and they disappeared into the crowd. Her stomach did a single lurch and was peaceful.

For a moment, Jacob, Bella and Jenn were alone. Only Lawrence and Baron Campbell stood close by, almost a watchful guard in these precious seconds of peace. Jacob tugged Jenn's hand until she bent her head. Then, like a hollow prayer, Jacob's words floated to her.

'I'm sorry, child. So very sorry. I was wrong about Dunlorn and I'm sorry.'

Absently, Jenn turned her head and kissed his dry cheek. Then she straightened up and looked him in the eye. 'The damage is done now, Father. Being sorry will not change it. With any luck, you may never get the opportunity to voice your apology to him in person.'

Jacob frowned, but Jenn hadn't finished. She continued, her voice still low and icy, 'What did you expect, Father? Did you think Selar would welcome him back? That they would suddenly become friends again? Did you want Robert to kill him? Here? Now? You must have known it would happen like this. It is not your legs that are crippled, Father, but your eyes. You're always telling me I don't think ahead of the possible danger. Now I suppose you know where I learned that particular trait.'

Before Jacob could even react, Jenn turned on her heel and walked away. She had to. If she'd stayed any longer she would have said something she would most certainly regret.

*

Micah pushed his way through the crowd after Robert. The hall was a chaos of moving dangers, each whispering their own treason. With his heart still pumping wildly, he reached the door, but Robert was nowhere to be seen. Panicking now, he tore across the courtyard, his boots clattering on the cobbles in rhythm with his heart. Where was Robert – packing to leave?

Micah made it as far as the Falcon Tower and glanced upwards. There was no light on in their rooms, no sign of life at all. Still, instinct guided his feet as he raced up the steps. The rooms were empty, but the door to the roof was open. He gained it, breathless, to find Robert standing there, his back to Micah. His hands were pressed down on the cold stone battlements, his gaze reaching out to the dark woods beyond. There was a stillness about his stance that was wholly frightening.

Micah gasped, trying to catch his breath, 'I can't believe Selar did that! And in public! So everyone could hear. Did he really think you would strike at him? But to call you a coward! After everything you've done for him! I just can't believe it.'

Robert didn't move. He'd never been one to show his feelings – but after something like this?

The truth dawned on Micah. 'The whole thing was deliberate, wasn't it? That's why Jacob invited you. He wanted you to face Selar, hoping you would do something. And . . . and Selar just had to destroy your public popularity . . . by calling you a coward. By the gods! You should have killed him.'

Instantly Micah sucked in a breath, horrified that he'd spoken that last aloud. Robert didn't react immediately, but then he turned slowly, his head moving up until his eyes met Micah's.

Micah froze. In those eyes was something unholy, something so dark and hideous he couldn't move. When Robert spoke, his voice was gravel falling into a pitted night.

'I shouldn't have come here. I knew it was a mistake but I couldn't help myself.'

Micah swallowed, clenched his fists against a sudden

trembling and forced himself to respond. 'Perhaps . . . but that's no reason for Selar to—'

'No,' Robert's gaze shifted slightly, the fire in his eyes taking on a different light. Still dark but no longer blindly threatening. 'But how could I do anything when she was standing there?'

He turned away again, but Micah moved closer. He frowned, knowing Robert wouldn't see it – but it didn't matter anyway. Suddenly none of it mattered now. Micah sank to the cold stone seat and shook his head. 'You're in love with her.'

There was no answer. Just a minute stiffening of the shoulders.

'Robert?' Micah reached out a hand, pulled his shoulder around so he could see that face again. 'Answer me. You're in love with Jenn, aren't you?'

The long silence was ended only when Robert's eyes reluctantly met his. 'What difference does it make?'

'But it's not too late to stop this. If you told her, you could get her away . . .'

'Oh, I can really see Selar letting me get away with that. And what would I do then? Make her live a life on the run? How could I do that to her? And what about my mother – and everyone else who depends on me? Should I just throw them all to the wolves because of how I feel about Jenn?' Robert paused. 'It wouldn't make any difference if I told her anyway. She hates me.'

'How do you know that?'

'I made sure of it.'

Uncomprehending, Micah spread his arms wide. 'But why? Did you think she might feel the same way?'

'I don't know. I just couldn't take the chance.'

'But if you love her . . .'

Robert turned away, icy in his rejection. 'It doesn't matter whether I love her or not! I can't trust anything I feel. It's just the damned Bonding, anyway.'

None of this made any sense to Micah. 'How do you know it's just the Bonding? And why would it matter if it was?'

'Because,' Robert straightened up and turned back to Micah, 'because the Key is wrong. The prophecy is wrong. It has to be. I have no choice but to fight it, Micah. All of it. If I don't . . .'

'What? What will happen if you don't fight it?'

'You don't want to know.' Robert met his gaze levelly for a moment. 'Leave it, my friend. Believe me, there's nothing you can do to help me. I only wish you could.'

22

He took the shirt off leisurely, held it out at arm's length and let it drop to the floor. His skin burned now with ice-cold and raging fever. He had faced the coward down. He had presented the coward with all his misdeeds, his inadequacies, and the only retaliation had been complete withdrawal.

All those years afraid of something that had never been real. All that time feeling the threat deep within him, a threat they had all told him was real. But he had proven them wrong. All of them. They had seen for themselves. Never again would they question, doubt. They would never ask why he protected. There would be no more protection.

The debt had been repaid. It had been no more than a weakness in Haddon to save the life of a stranger on the edge of a battlefield. Weakness. In a man he'd always thought so strong. But Haddon was weak. He'd run away. Tonight — and before. Again and again. Always he'd run away. No courage. A coward.

Haddon had deserved it.

With his arms raised over his head, he stretched out his muscles. As the pale moonlight filtered across the floor, he stepped through the misty pool and climbed into bed. He lay there, silent and still. Peaceful now, he slipped into sleep.

*

It was cold in her room. Too cold to sit still. Even under the blankets, Jenn could feel the chill in the air. She pulled the covers off the bed and sat on the floor by the fire, her arms around her knees. The flames sparked and fluttered, glowed yellow and orange, but gave out almost no heat. Huddled under her blankets, Jenn continued to shiver.

The castle was quiet now. The last revellers had retired hours ago, choosing an early night in favour of a later night tomorrow. Even Bella had fallen asleep on the cot in Jenn's bedchamber. The hall was clean, the dogs were silent. Even the chapel was ready, with flowers decorating every corner. There was nothing now to stop the ceremony tomorrow. At least, nothing short of a war.

It was curious how something so precious could fade away so slowly, so gently she'd not really noticed it until it was gone. So where was her freedom now? Blown away by time and convenience, by a desire to merely survive rather than live? Had it always been so fragile and insubstantial? So easy to destroy.

Surely it had to be more. It had always felt so real, so permanent inside her. It had driven her actions almost all her life.

And soon, in only a few hours, it would all be gone.

Jenn held her hands out to the flames, but still couldn't feel the warmth. Instead, she got up and moved around, tried to get the blood moving in her body. But nothing worked. There was a restlessness there, winding around her, binding her.

Where was he now?

Had he gone? Did she dare try Seeking him? Surely he must have left after Selar's condemnation.

Stilling her restlessness, Jenn stopped where she stood and closed her eyes. She wasn't much of a Seeker, but if Robert was within the walls of Elita, she would know.

Nothing. He was gone.

But . . .

There? What was he doing? He was out of the castle, but still within the forest, near the ancient mill. He wasn't moving.

Jenn's eyes snapped open and a moment of indecision warred within her — but it was only a moment. She threw off the blankets and quietly moved over to the chest by the door. Lifting the lid, she dragged out the old worn clothes she kept for her sojourns into the night. She pulled a gown over her head and tossed a faded cloak around her shoulders, bringing the hood up over her head. Then she silently unlocked her door, and stepped out. She crept down the passage away from the hall. The spiral staircase at the end was dark, but she didn't pause. She'd had a lot of practice lately in moving around in the dark.

Terrified with every step, she reached the courtyard and headed immediately through the garden to the gate on the other side. She felt impending freedom in every bone of her body, urging her on. Two guards marched by, but they didn't see her in the shadows. The huge oak gate was open, only the smaller iron barrier was closed. The lock clicked beneath her hand and she slipped outside, closing it behind her.

She kept close to the curtain wall until she was in sight of the lake. Then she darted out across the grass, running for the banks. She stumbled, again and again, but she didn't stop. She just had to move, energy bursting from somewhere deep, tearing through her like the wind of vengeance. Gasping and exhausted, she finally reached the wood and dropped to her knees.

Nothing made sense any more. None of it. The secrets, the mysteries, the whole web of intrigue she'd fallen into. And now Robert had been hurt again. His vow . . . gone, just like that.

What would it do to him? Would that dark part of him feed off the humiliation, the pain, the hurt?

Jenn struggled to her feet and stumbled on through the forest.

She should never have let it get this bad. And now it was too late. Tomorrow she would be tied to that brute, Eachern, for the rest of her life. She would stand there in the chapel and say words she didn't mean. But say them she would. She would not shame Jacob. Never do that. Even though the words would be a lie. Then afterwards, she would . . . have to . . . give herself to that . . . man . . . and . . . But—

Was that all she was for? Was there to be nothing more?

Foolish, stupid girl! Such an idiot to think . . . to want for anything else. Why should she be so different – why shouldn't she suffer? Why should she have the right to choose when those around her were denied that right? People like Robert, like her father.

It was too late for everything.

The forest was not silent, but certainly more quiet than the castle. There were no people around, no voices, no thoughts he could pick up inadvertently. It was about as silent as he could get.

Robert stood with his arms folded, leaning against a solid pine, its bark biting into his sleeve.He couldn't sleep, the demon wouldn't let him.

What a mess!

Poor Micah. For ever torn this way and that. Always trying to help, never feeling that it did any good. Always helpless in the wake of Robert's moods. And he had sacrificed his own father's trust in order to serve a man who was a complete and utter failure. And now there was not even his vow . . .

. . . By the gods, he'd been so close to losing control of the demon.

He should be leaving even now – but no, he would stay and finish what he'd begun. He would stay by her, no matter the cost. She was about to enter a world she had never desired, that she would loathe with every breath of her freedom-loving soul. The best thing he could do now – the only thing he could do now – was to see her up to that door safely. After that, he would turn and walk away, close that door finally and for ever behind him.

He left his tree and walked on down the hill. The dried leaves underfoot crunched with every step. The gentle breeze above sent more down to join them. Even without the moon he could see the myriad colours. But then, his sight had always been good – even before he'd known how it was enhanced by his powers. A pity they were not much use for anything else.

The ground dropped away as he approached the stream. He paused to look around. This was the place. Here. This spot was where she'd first spoken to him. The first words of mindspeech. By the gods, he'd been so surprised. But everything she'd done had surprised him. Never once had she ever been conventional or predictable. Serin's blood, how would she survive married to that monster Eachern?

He moved on through the dried and fallen bracken until he found the old ruined mill. Two stone walls still standing, tall in the night, hazy with moss and ivy. The jagged edge of one wall sloped down towards the stream on the right and ended in a rubble of stepping-stones and forest weeds. Inside was a darkness even his sight couldn't penetrate. The roofless building gaped towards the sky, an open prayer for solitude, an empty waste of hope. This was where she'd been abducted. All those years ago. This was where it had all started.

In the morning, as soon as the wedding ceremony was over, he would climb on his horse and ride away. Go home and devote himself to his work. Forget the Enclave. Forget Selar. Forget everything – or at least try to.

He had to.

Robert moved forward again until he reached the arched doorway of the ruin. His hand came out and touched the damp moss, felt the cracks in the stone, the massive strength which time and neglect had humbled. Only the counter stone sat firm within its confines, holding up the arch at the same time as its weight drew the arch down. When it did fall, however, all its neighbours would drop too and the arch would be no more.

The cavernous interior beckoned like a dream of death, but he didn't go in. He turned to go just as the moon reappeared from its cover of cloud and flooded the chamber with a dusting of seraphic white.

'Robert?'

Serin's blood – she was here! Standing by the window frame that looked out on to the stream. How could he have been so blind?

He stepped back.

'Please, Robert, wait. Don't go.'

Momentarily frozen with indecision, he then turned around to face her once more. She waited across the room, a ghost in shadow, insubstantial. Slowly she reached up and pulled the hood back from her face. He could see her eyes, but they weren't looking at him. They were fixed on the floor by his feet.

'I can't stay here,' Robert murmured, his heart beginning to pound violently. If he stood there any longer he'd bring the ruin down around him. 'I must go back. I'm sorry.'

'Robert, don't!' Her eyes lifted to his and he saw the tears fall down her cheeks. 'Just tell me. What did I do? Why did you shut me out? Was it because I tried to help you? Because I failed? Was it because of Rosalind? Did I really do wrong in asking for your help? Why did you make me feel like an idiot? Please, Robert. Tell me what I did wrong.'

It was getting difficult to breathe. He should go. He should just turn his back on her and leave. Now. Tonight. They should never have this conversation.

But how could he hurt her again? All she wanted was a reason. Surely she deserved to know that much.

Yes, he would go – but his feet moved forward, not back. Forward until he was in the moonlight, close enough to see her clearly, but far enough away to still be able to leave.

She was waiting, her eyes fixed on his.

He tried to make his voice work. 'I'm sorry, Jenny. I had no choice. Please believe me. You'll understand one day.'

'One day?' She took a single step forward. 'Which day would that be? Tomorrow, when I marry Eachern? Or perhaps next year – or maybe in twenty years' time when we've all forgotten about this. Will I understand then, Robert? Will I?'

'I love you.'

The words came out without his will, without even his acknowledgement. They just fell into the ancient ruin like drops into a pond.

Jenn stared at him, her eyes glistening with tears. 'You . . .'

When he spoke again, he did so deliberately, 'Yes, Jenny. I love you. Do you understand now?'

'No. I don't. If you loved me you wouldn't have been so cruel.'

'But that's why I did it.' By the gods, this was impossible! Go now, while you still can! Move, feet. Get away. Leave her before it's too late!

But his feet wouldn't obey his commands. Again they moved forward, not back, as though his body were ruled by some new law, created for this night alone. Clenching his fists, he managed to stop again while still a few feet from her. She looked so fragile, and yet so very strong. The heart of an oak inside the body of a willow. If only he could reach out to her, hold her just for a moment. Kill the confusion which warred inside her, the confusion he had been so careful to create. If he could just hold her . . .

But he didn't dare touch her. Couldn't risk— But fighting was so hard. It had never been so difficult. Never before had he not even been master of his own body. So much of him wanted to take another step towards her – while the same voice inside screamed at him to turn and run. He would hurt her if he did, but he would hurt her so much more if he stayed.

'You've always fought me, Robert, even when I just wanted to help you,' Jenn whispered, frowning. 'Every question I've asked has had a barbed answer. Even now, when we have this gift of mindspeech, you keep me shut out. Don't you understand, Robert? Can't you see I need you? I've always needed you. And tomorrow you'll leave.'

'Jenny, please! Don't say any more.' If he could just make her understand. 'The Key said we were Bonded. That's all this is. What I feel, what you feel. We're being forced into this.'

'The Key?' Jenn took another step forward. 'Do you think the Key has made you love me? Is it really so powerful?'

'I . . .' Her voice, her eyes, her nearness were wholly intoxicating. 'I know how powerful the Key is, Jenny. I've been a slave to it all my life. I've tried to stop . . . to limit . . .'

'Are you sure the Bonding is what you think it is? Is it not possible that it could be something else? Mindspeech, per-haps? Perhaps even the reason for my own powers? You don't know – can't know for certain. You could be wrong.'

She gazed up at him with such trust. She was so beautiful with the moonlight in her hair. She was utterly breathtaking – and she was also very, very close.

'If I'm wrong, why can't I just walk out of here?' Robert protested, but he was losing and he knew it. 'Why won't my legs obey me? Why don't you leave?'

'I don't know, Robert,' Jenn murmured. She glanced away for a moment, then her eyes met his again. 'Perhaps you do love me after all.'

'Jenny, please.' And it was impossible to fight any more. Fight required will and he had none left. 'Do you know what you're saying?'

'Yes, Robert. I do know.'

Then his hand came up and reached for hers – but the moment they touched there was a flash of light, a tiny bolt of lightning gone as quickly as it came. Just like before, when she'd put his *ayarn* back together. Startled, he tried to pull away – but couldn't.

It didn't matter. Not now. Softly, gently he touched her face, felt the coolness where her tears had been, wiped them away. He tilted her face up, brushed his lips over hers. A tremor wracked through his whole body, aching. In a daze of wonder, he kissed her again and she responded, deep, longing, yearning. Was this only Bonding? Did she want him as much as he wanted her?

As if waking from a dream, he pulled her closer until his arms were around her, hers around him. He held on to her, afraid the ghost would disappear and leave him alone once more. He trembled with the warmth of her body, the scent of her hair. Was this real?

No. She was here, in his arms. Her lips honey and soft dew. She drew him down deeper and deeper until he could see her again, standing beside the demon. But there was no danger here.

And no pain.

With angel's wings, she wrapped her arms around the

demon and made it shrink. Soon it was invisible, nothing more than a shadow of remembrance. In one moment, she had done this. Made him whole. In another moment, the image would be gone. Only now could he see the extent of the blackness the demon had created.

No, Robert, she seemed to say. I cannot make the demon die. Only you can do that. You already know how.

Peace. That's what this was. Simple peace. And in the peace, her image died away. But when he opened his eyes again, he could see her face clearly. There was more light now; they were surrounded by it. A deep, glowing blue nimbus which enveloped their bodies, but cast no shadows on the walls, no mark on the ruin to show that they were even there. What was this?

But he knew. He'd known all along what this was. Since he was nine years old he had known this day would come. Only now, when it was too late to stop, did he finally understand what it meant.

And Jenn understood, too. She smiled up at him, her fingers brushing across his lips, sending shivers of fire down his spine.

The Key had drawn them together. Now, even if he could stop it, he no longer wanted to try. With a smile, he kissed her again. *I love you, Jenny. Always remember, nothing will ever change that.*

The blue nimbus flared then and Robert closed his eyes again. This time he let go completely and lost himself in her arms.

Micah started awake as the door crashed back against the wall. Tangled in the bedclothes, he struggled to get up. He reached for a candle, but knocked it off the bed-side table. He could hear breathing coming from the door. There was a shape there, in the darkness.

Calmly now, Micah slid his hand beneath his pillow and brought out the dagger he always kept with him. He pulled back the blankets and slipped his legs over the side of the bed, but as his feet touched the stone flags, the shape in the doorway moved. One step forward. Then another.

'Micah?'

The voice was harsh, but even so, there was no doubt who it was.

'My lord? What's happened? What's wrong?'

'Wrong? Nothing.'

Standing, Micah reached for the curtain, pulled it open a little. A film of moonlight stretched into the room, a powder of incandescence that touched everything.

Robert shied away from the light. 'I ... have to leave, Micah. Now.'

'What's happened? Is it Selar?' Micah swallowed but didn't dare move. 'Or Jenn?'

Robert stepped back to the door. 'I must go. I can't stay here any more. Not now.' He stopped, no longer breathing. This sudden stillness was worse. 'I swore I'd protect her.'

Micah pulled on his clothes, his boots. All the while, he couldn't take his eyes off Robert. But when he reached for his bags, Robert stopped him, a hand on his arm.

'Will you do one final thing for me, Micah? Stay with her? I can trust no one else. Will you?'

'Yes.' The word was breathed out from the depths of his soul. 'But what about you ... ?'

Robert shook his head. 'Forget me.'

With that, Robert turned and disappeared through the door, his footsteps echoing down the stairs. Stunned, Micah couldn't move – then the cold got him. He grabbed a cloak and dashed after Robert. He clattered down the steps into the courtyard, but Robert was already far ahead of him, striding into the stables. There was no one around except the guards high on the battlements. But there was no challenge, no question thrown out into the night. There was just the silence.

Micah ran. His feet pounded on the cobbles loud enough to wake the castle. By the time he got to the stable, Robert had already saddled his horse, was leading it out towards the gate. Micah reached him in time to see the gate silently open without a hand to help it. Stunned, Micah grabbed the bridle, forcing Robert to stop.

'Must you go? Like this?'

'Be careful going back, Micah.' Robert's voice was gentle, a breath of wind amidst a gale. 'Once I go, my Mask goes with me.'

'Robert!' Micah forced him to turn and look down. In his eyes now, lit by the last vestige of moonlight, there was nothing but an overwhelming sadness.

'Look after her for me, Micah. Keep her safe.'

In that steady gaze, Micah's heart slowed and calmed. He nodded. 'What should I tell her?'

'Nothing. She knows already.' Robert leaned down and touched Micah's face. 'Goodbye, my friend.'

Then Robert was moving away, riding through the gates of Elita before even the first rays of dawn had touched the sky. The gate closed again behind him, but Micah couldn't move. All he could see was the image of Robert, riding away.

Micah stayed there a long time, staring at the gate. Then, aching in every part of his body, he turned and walked slowly back to the Falcon Tower. For the first time in his life, he walked alone.

Part Two

And so the duce in victory stands
upon the broken ashen earth.
In claim of kingship, power and lordship,
the beastly tyrant strides the breadth.
With every step Lusara weeps
and ails for every heart that bled
and aches with every tear that fell
*   and mourns and mourns for every death.*

*   Battle of Shanogh Anar*
*   by Thomas McKinnley*

23

Osbert entered the Guilde chapel through the west door, pulling it closed behind him against the spring shower. The bottom of his robe was already wet and his shoes were lined with mud. Even though it wasn't exactly cold outside, his damp clothes and the natural cool of the chapel sent a shiver through his bones. He had to stifle a sneeze before he dared move down the aisle.

Grey shadows spilled across the tiled floor, interrupted only by a muffled light from the windows above. Edges and corners were unclear and everything up to the black marble altar took on an insubstantial form, dusty and flat. Only the gold plate laid out on the marble had any colour, reflected from the presence light burning below the trium high on the east transept.

Vaughn was there, as he had expected, talking to a man dressed in master craftsman robes halfway along the north wall. As Osbert approached, there was movement by the wall as two workmen lifted a bundle of scaffolding beams on to their shoulders and carried it out. Osbert waited until Vaughn dismissed the master before speaking.

'You sent for me, Proctor?' Osbert folded his hands together and tried to banish the abrupt cold from his thoughts. His bones had seen enough of winter for one year.

Vaughn eyed him slowly, drawing his white robe around his shoulders before moving towards Osbert. 'I take it from the condition of your shoes we have another spring shower. One hopes the phenomenon will not have us flooded out before summer.'

Osbert shrugged – it was unlikely the Guilde Hall would ever be affected by floods, built, as it was, high on the mount of Marsay.

Wandering over to the altar, Vaughn spoke again, his

voice light and uncomplicated. 'I will assume your spies have had no success in finding out where the Queen has been hidden these last eight months.'

'My lord, it has been difficult to gather any information over the winter. Even now, as late in the spring as this, I've had reports of snow storms in the Goleth ranges. I'm sure . . .'

'Don't fret,' Vaughn waved a hand but did not turn to face Osbert. 'The result is not unexpected – however disappointing. How is the King on the subject of his son?'

Osbert paused before answering. That Vaughn had to ask him this question bespoke more than his natural curiosity. Ever since Selar had halted the hunt for sorcerers, Vaughn had barely spoken to the King. It had only been Selar's public humiliation of the rebel Haddon that had prevented an open split between the two. Now Osbert was the only trustworthy link Vaughn had to the King.

'Selar is still distraught and determined to get his son back, my lord,' Osbert replied evenly. 'He believes Prince Kenrick will be returned eventually.'

'But until then, his plans for war must wait, eh? After all, he can't exactly invade Mayenne without an heir to succeed him. No army nor lord would support such an effort.'

There was doubt about such support even with an heir – at least, those were the most recent whispers Osbert had heard. But he was not about to repeat them to the Proctor.

'So we wait upon the appearance of a child who might not even be alive. Tell me,' Vaughn turned to face Osbert, 'have your spies reported any further intelligence of sorcerers?'

The question made Osbert swallow hard, but he managed to answer, 'No, my lord.'

Vaughn nodded as though he were expecting exactly that response. 'Come, take a look at my new window.'

He drew Osbert back across the chapel until they stood in the centre of the aisle, gazing up at the north-facing window, still bright with new glass. Even on such a sombre day, the colours sparkled with life.

'Do you like it? I had it commissioned last year, but had to wait until today for the final installation to be completed.

You see the mountain there? On the left? That's where the shrine of Alusia stands today. In the foreground you see the bodies vanquished in battle by the glorious figure above. She, of course, is the incarnation of Mineah, triumphing in the defeat of the evil of sorcery.' Vaughn paused to enjoy the moment. Then he added, 'So topical for our times, don't you think?'

Without waiting for a reply, Vaughn turned his gaze on Osbert. 'Are you certain you found no evidence of sorcery when you visited Dunlorn last summer? No vestige of guilt in the Duke? No sign of hesitation from his men?'

Osbert frowned. Why these questions now? What was Vaughn getting at?

'No, my lord. I gave you my full report at the time. I saw Finnlay's body with my own eyes. Haddon was upset at his brother's death, but I sensed no duplicity from him – nor his men.'

'And where do you suppose the Duke is now?'

'I have no idea.' This was getting ridiculous. Why would Osbert know where . . .

'Don't you think it strange, Osbert, that the Queen vanishes from the court – apparently from the country – and soon after, the great Duke of Haddon disappears also? Do you not think it possible that the two events are linked?'

Before Osbert could even gather breath, Vaughn added, 'Especially so soon after Haddon's brother is accused of sorcery.'

'My lord,' Osbert began carefully, hoping not to offend Vaughn, 'Haddon left Elita the same night Selar humiliated him. There's no secret there. And as I said, his brother is dead and can have no relationship with sorcery . . .'

At this, Vaughn smiled. 'Except that I *know* that Finnlay Douglas *is* a sorcerer.'

For a moment, Osbert was tempted to argue this, but Vaughn gazed at him so calmly and steadily that Osbert had to take the statement seriously. 'How do you know?'

'That doesn't matter. However, I want you to bring it to the King's attention. Now that he's no longer protecting Robert Douglas, Selar might find a search for the renegade turns up news of his Queen and heir. And please, if you think it wise, don't even mention the idea came from me. Selar would only suspect my motives and not pay sufficient attention to the danger at hand. Can you do that for me, Osbert?'

How could he refuse? And yet, how could he comply? Selar had long since rejected any conversation to do with sorcery. He no longer even pretended to listen. And as for mention of Robert Douglas . . .

'I'll do my best, my lord.' Osbert bowed and turned for the door. Before he could escape, however, Vaughn called one last thing to him.

'Be sure you attend mass tomorrow, Osbert. I've asked Deacon Godfrey to deliver a homily on the new window and the evils of sorcery.'

Osbert slipped out into the shade of the chapel portico to discover the rain had already stopped. Less pleasant was the discovery that awaited him a few feet away.

Nash wore his customary grey robes and a frown of threatening proportions. Osbert swallowed and tried to contain his irritation. This day was deteriorating rapidly.

'We need to talk,' was all Nash said.

Osbert led him into the garden over wet flagstones glinting in the sudden sunshine. The borders were bristling with new spring colour while the corner-laid trees danced with pale green leaves, unsullied so far by summer's heat.

Walking with his hands clasped casually behind his back, Osbert stole a glance at his companion, whose allegiance to the Guilde was displayed solely in the new Governor's brooch he wore on his right shoulder. For the most part, Nash was seen little in his robes these days, preferring to play down his part within the Guilde in favour of the higher role he played beside the King. In only a week, Nash would be confirmed in another new position – that of King's Councillor. Yes, indeed, young Samdon Nash had risen far and fast over the last three years. Too fast, in fact, for one who appeared to have only average capabilities.

Osbert tore his attention away from speculation. He'd been over that too many times now and not once had he ever liked the inevitable conclusion. As much as he had loosely allied himself with Nash, Osbert didn't trust him as far as the garden wall.

'When did you get back?' Osbert asked lightly, looking around. They were alone.

'I have no time for small talk, Osbert,' Nash snapped. 'You told me six months ago that you were already gathering sufficient support to oust Vaughn at the next election. Now I find that you didn't even bother to stand last week. Why?'

'Because,' Osbert replied with a sigh, 'it would have been a pointless exercise. Vaughn's popularity has enjoyed a sharp rise over his stubborn position on sorcery. Most of our ordinary members feel the King was unjustified in cutting the hunt short and admire Vaughn's courage in standing up to Selar. If you'd been around a bit more often, you would have known that yourself.'

'Don't you—'

Osbert met the dark gaze without flinching visibly – though it took some effort. 'What?'

Nash calmed himself a little. 'I've spent most of the last eight months chasing after the wretched Queen, as you well know. When I've not been out combing the countryside in the bleakest winter to touch these shores in a century, I've been locked up with the King, trying to control his desire to burn down the country looking for his son. What have you been doing?'

It was always so amazingly easy for Osbert to remain calm in the face of anger, even when he admitted to some fear of the man in front of him. Now that he had risen so high, Nash was wont to show his displeasure more and more often. But, no matter how angry Nash was, he still needed Osbert.

'As it happens,' Osbert brought them to a halt before a bush of exquisite pink roses, bending to breathe in the perfume, knowing the laziness of the gesture would infuriate Nash, 'I have been trying to find out more about your secret library.'

'Oh?' Nash was visibly unimpressed.

'Answering such questions as – does it really exist?'

'Of course it exists.'

331

'And what it might contain.'

'That doesn't concern you.'

Osbert turned back to the roses. 'It's just that I might find it easier to discover the whereabouts of this famous secret library if I knew what kind of books were in it.'

'Old books,' Nash said. 'Ancient. Some written in the earliest days of the Guilde.'

'And these would be history books?' Osbert mused delicately, half-afraid the answer would be no.

But Nash was through with this game. 'Of course they're history books! What else would they be? What I want to know is, what are you going to do about Vaughn – or am I to find someone who will solve the problem for both of us?'

Osbert's heart lurched and he glanced around furtively in case somebody might have approached close enough to hear. 'You would . . . condone—'

'I've told you before, Osbert,' Nash replied in a voice of gravel. 'I need that library. I know Vaughn knows where it is. He's already hinted at its existence. It must be somewhere here in the Guilde Hall, but we can't search for it while he's still Proctor. He would burn it rather than have somebody find it. The choice is yours. Find the library for me – or lose the Proctor.'

With that, Nash turned on his heel and strode away, leaving Osbert almost breathless with horror.

There was no other explanation. His speculations had to be correct – and he had no doubt Nash meant what he said. But . . . if Osbert found the library, what would happen to him next? Would he survive long enough to see what the books contained? Or would he suffer the same fate Vaughn had just been promised?

No. Once Osbert had found the library, he too would be expendable. There was only one solution: to discover where the library was and what it contained before Nash did. He would have to find a way to get Vaughn to tell him.

Osbert left the rose bush and headed for his study. It was time he opened that bottle he'd bought last year. This was the perfect opportunity to see if it worked.

*

The tavern where he and Payne had met in secret almost a year ago was just as awful as Godfrey remembered. Then he had been uncomfortable moving around without his clerical robes; now he felt these rags were a second skin, hiding not only his identity but his treason too. The tavern's clientele paid him no attention as he took his seat in the booth opposite Earl Payne and Duke McGlashen. Conspirators all, only their unscarred but calloused hands gave away their real place in life.

McGlashen had disguised himself well, trading his usual courtly finery for the leather jerkin and hessian trousers of a blacksmith. He was a big man, tall and gruff, and the clothes suited him.

Payne looked a little more comical in the guise of a pedlar, his uncommon good looks sullied by smears of mud and clay. It was he alone who managed a smile of greeting for Godfrey.

'Is there a problem, Father?' Payne murmured, sipping on his ale.

'There had better be,' McGlashen grunted. 'I can't say I'd be happy if I found I'd dragged myself down here for nothing. You know how tenuous our positions are.'

'And they're going to get a lot more tenuous before long.'

At the frowns of both men, Godfrey patted the breast of his jacket. 'I have a letter here I received this morning. After confirming its authenticity, I came to an abrupt but inevitable conclusion.'

'Who is the letter from?' Payne asked quietly, though there was nobody within earshot.

'Archdeacon Hilderic.' Godfrey drew his mug of ale across the table and pretended to drink from it.

'But he's been on retreat since Caslemas, forbidden to make contact with anyone outside the monastery.'

Godfrey nodded. 'Except that he isn't on retreat any more. No, after months of contemplation and self-examination, prayer and solitude, it appears my old friend has decided that he has relied too much on others to do something about releasing McCauly from prison.'

'By the gods!' McGlashen breathed.

'And well you might pray, Donal,' Godfrey murmured. 'Hilderic has taken himself to Mayenne, where he plans to lay the case before King Tirone. He believes that only Selar's older brother is in a position to pressure Selar into freeing McCauly.'

'And knowing Hilderic,' Payne added, 'he'll also find some clumsy way of warning him of Selar's plans for invasion.'

McGlashen started at that, then pinned his gaze on Godfrey. 'Would he? Would he risk such a thing?'

Godfrey nodded. 'You have no idea how strongly he feels about the whole thing. Years of forced obedience to Selar have taken their toll. He hasn't been the same since Domnhall died.'

There was silence for a moment, as the two lords evaluated their own positions. In the end it was McGlashen who asked the inevitable question.

'And your conclusion?'

Godfrey took a deep breath. 'We have no more time to lose. Bishop McCauly has been in prison so long now that most people are beginning to forget that he should never have been put there in the first place. Selar has never made any attempt to bring charges of treason against him because he knew he would only make a martyr out of him. I know we waited out the winter because there were already so many soldiers roaming the country looking for the Queen. I know it wasn't safe – I accept that. But one day – soon – the guards will open McCauly's cell and find him dead of some . . . unfortunate medical condition. And who will care? Who will really notice? Now I can't tell you when that day will come, but I can tell you that the moment Selar finds that somebody has approached Tirone on McCauly's behalf, he will give the order immediately.'

'But—' Payne began, glancing at McGlashen for support, '—we dare not do anything until—'

'We don't have time to wait for Selar to decide to move McCauly,' McGlashen hissed. 'Godfrey is right. We have to move now. If we don't, McCauly will die.'

Godfrey's throat was suddenly dry, as if his courage had lasted only long enough to gain agreement. He forced himself to take a mouthful of the foul ale and swallow it. Then he stood. 'Can you do it?'

McGlashen looked down at his hands a moment and shrugged. 'His cell is almost impenetrable, but there might be a way. Hell, Father, if it was going to be easy, we would have done it months ago. I just don't know.'

'We can't wait any longer, but ... Organize what you can and I may – I won't promise – but I may be able to find something that will help you. When can you move?'

McGlashen frowned, but didn't ask any questions. 'The soonest I can arrange it will be in two days. And with any luck, I might even have a place he can be taken to where no one will give him away.'

'The Queen wouldn't happen to be there, too?' Payne murmured with some attempt at humour.

'Oh, I hope not,' McGlashen grunted. 'They wouldn't like that at all.'

Selar was in the garden playing a ball game with his squires when Nash found him. But rather than approach, Nash stayed within the oak shadows created by a refreshed sun and waited until Valena turned her attention from the game. With a simple gesture, he summoned her away from the other ladies watching the sport, drawing her deeper into the shadows.

'I don't have much time and I don't really want to speak to him again today,' Nash said by way of explanation. 'He'll only harass me again on the dreaded subject of his brat.'

'Oh, poor Nash,' Valena pouted and ran her fingers down his throat.

Nash snatched her hand away. 'I've told you before not to touch me in public. As long as Selar thinks you're a sweet innocent girl, he'll keep trying to get you into his bed. If he thought for one moment that you and I . . .'

'Oh, all right.' Valena's pout was real this time and she took a step back. 'So where are you off to now? More Queen chasing? Hasn't DeMassey done his job yet?'

'The last I heard he was pursuing his most promising lead – but he didn't say where. I just wish he would hurry up. I can't complete Selar's Bonding until Kenrick comes back. In the meantime, I must go off and do my duty.'

'Where?'

'Eachern's bleak castle. There are some council papers he must sign.'

Valena froze, her mouth framing a small 'o'. With a quick glance over her shoulder, she whispered, 'And will you see her? The Ally? She's not been out of that place since the wedding.'

Nash shook his head, running a tired hand through his trimmed beard. 'I should have kept closer watch on her while she was still within my grasp at Shan Moss. I should have been around to prevent that damned wedding.'

'But now it's too late and . . .'

'It doesn't matter,' Nash grunted, peering once more in Selar's direction. He was still wholly engaged in his game, his back to the trees where they hid. 'While she's in Eachern's grasp, the Enemy will get nowhere near her. However, the time has come when I must begin work on her. I believe the library will soon be mine and then there'll be no stopping us.'

'Not even the Enemy?' Valena asked, her eyes sparkling.

'No. Not even the Enemy.' There was no telling now where Finnlay Douglas might be. As far as Nash could tell, he hadn't once been outside the protection of the Key from the moment he'd escaped Bairdenscoth. But one thing was certain, he hadn't been anywhere near the Ally – and that was enough. By the time Nash did find Finnlay, it would be too late. The Ally would already be turned and the Enemy would not have a chance.

'I want you to send me word,' Nash continued, 'the moment you hear from DeMassey. Send Lisson – he can always find me, no matter where I am. In the meantime, you are to continue to encourage Selar to plan his war with Mayenne. If the library proves me wrong and the Key turns out to be across the border, I'll need a conquest to get to it.'

'As you wish, my love,' Valena murmured seductively. Then, blowing a kiss in his direction, she glided back to the other ladies and merged among them.

But lovely though she was, Valena would never be the Ally. Only one person could take that place. Jennifer Ross, now Duchess of Eachern.

Nash left the garden and made for the stables. He couldn't wait to see her.

Osbert stepped back from Vaughn's reclining figure and stumbled to the nearest chair. The Proctor sat stretched out in his favourite seat, his eyes glazed and dull, his mouth open and slack. That long face, so often wrinkled in contempt, now lay flaccid and weak, devoid of any expression at all. At his elbow sat the empty wine cup in which Osbert had placed a few drops of the precious liquid.

The fire crackled to his left and Osbert glanced at it before rubbing his hands over his face. He still couldn't absorb it all, the incredible things Vaughn had told him under the influence of the drug.

Vaughn wouldn't remember any of this in the morning. He would sleep and wake with the dawn refreshed and unknowing.

A tangled web of lies and secrets, all hidden in the Proctor's mind. Suspicions and fears which drove him to such desperate acts. The drug had worked, yes, but the effects seemed limited. Osbert was loath to push Vaughn any further for fear of giving him something he would remember.

Suddenly charged with unease, Osbert rose and made straight for the wall behind Vaughn's desk. There he felt along the edge of the first stone slab, his heart beating wildly against both failure and success. Abruptly, his finger stopped on a sharp point of metal protruding from a slim crack between two stones. Without pausing, Osbert moved it up and heard a click. He placed both hands on the stone and pushed forward with all his strength. With a groan as if from the depths of hell, the stone swung back, taking its neighbours with it. It was a great door, exactly as Vaughn had said.

Osbert paused when the gap in the wall was just big enough for him. Then he grabbed the nearest candle and squeezed through. The room was tiny, and icy cold. The smell of damp, dust and mould assaulted his senses. This room was as old as the Hall. It had been built entirely for this purpose. The ceiling was high and the walls covered in shelves.

But they were empty.

Just as Vaughn had said.

With a groan which bordered on relief, Osbert sank back against the shelves and tried to think.

Three times before, Vaughn had hinted at some way to find out if a man was a sorcerer – but even with his suspicions, Vaughn had tonight admitted to being too afraid, so far, to look up the knowledge needed to fight sorcery. Even so, the only source of such information had to be this ancient library. But Vaughn, fearful of Nash, had hidden the books, taken them even from this secret hideaway.

'Where none shall look, and none shall find,' Osbert repeated into the silence.

He'd tried, but Vaughn had not succumbed to the push to tell Osbert where the books were now.

Gathering himself, Osbert left the room and pushed the door back into place. Vaughn would never know the room had been disturbed. But what to do now? What was he to tell Nash?

Would Nash kill Vaughn to find these books? It was certain the Proctor was the only man alive who knew of their whereabouts – so he was safe for the moment. Nash had left the capital that day, so there was no immediate need for a response from Osbert, but even so, he would have to tell Nash something.

There was only one way to protect both library and Vaughn: Osbert would have to manufacture a lie, good enough to fool the sharp eyes of Nash. Bring books in here himself. A few innocuous, older, dusty things nobody cared about any more – and many others. He could burn them, leaving the ashes for Nash to find. The ashes, and a few useless pages as evidence, then claim that Vaughn had put a torch to the lot rather than have them fall into the wrong hands. Of course, Osbert had been too late to stop it.

Yes. A frail, thin lie, but it would be enough.

Enough to stop Nash?

Yes. He would do it tonight, while Vaughn slumbered under the drug. And when Nash came back to Marsay, Osbert would have the lie all ready to show him.

Briskly now, he cleaned up the evidence of his interrogation. He splashed the remains of Vaughn's drink into the fire, then ran a drop more wine around inside the cup. He left it beside Vaughn's chair, then straightened his robes. With one more glance at the sleeping Proctor, Osbert headed out of the room.

At last, he knew exactly what he had to do.

John collected the two books from the binder's and went back out into the morning light. Every day the weather grew warmer as summer approached. Every day John revelled as the memory of a long winter faded. He made his way through the town and up the hill to the cloister gate. He was barely inside before he realized he was being followed. He stopped and turned around: Godfrey was standing in the shadows of a great arch carved centuries ago with a vine of oak leaves.

'What have you got there?'

John glanced down at his bundle. 'Some of Hilderic's books. The covers were worn so I thought I'd get them repaired while he was away. I was just about to take them back to his study.'

Godfrey nodded slowly. 'I'll walk with you, Father.'

There was something about the careful stillness in Godfrey that made John suddenly wary. They walked in silence until they reached the study. The windows were open, the curtains away being washed. There were piles of books on the floor and tables, while the shelves were almost empty.

'You've kept yourself busy, I see,' Godfrey noted, wandering around the room. 'Dusting too? My, you are diligent.'

John placed his books on the corner of the bigger table and pretended to resume his work. He picked up a cloth and bottle of oil and turned to the nearest shelf, but the sound of the door closing made him pause. He glanced over his shoulder to find Godfrey watching him.

'We need to talk, John.'

'We . . . we do?' John stammered.

Godfrey moved among the furniture and piles of books to stand on the other side of the table. 'I never asked, did I? I never once questioned what you were doing that night with Robert. I left you alone and trusted that you were not breaking the law or your vows. Tell me, was I right to do so?'

'I . . . I'm sorry, Deacon, I don't understand . . .'

'It's simple. You once asked me if you could help. I want to know if you can.'

John's mouth felt suddenly dry and his heart leaped into his throat. He couldn't force a single word out.

'You've no need to be nervous, John,' Godfrey murmured, his face losing its hardness. 'Though I'm surprised you managed to survive so long without being able to hide your fear of discovery better. Or is it just me?'

John swallowed and shook his head.

'Oh, believe me, it's not really your fault. You didn't give yourself away, if that's what's bothering you. I had my doubts about Robert many years ago. We were close friends once – I hope we still are. But, let's be honest here, after everything that's happened lately, are you surprised I know the truth?'

'You have no idea how much trouble I'll be in,' John rushed the words out. 'No matter what you say, I'll be blamed.'

Godfrey pushed some books aside and perched on the table. 'You're a priest, John. How did you deal with the theological conflict?'

John took in a deep breath and felt his hands gradually stop shaking. He reached back and pulled a chair forward, sat down and prepared an answer. 'I'm not sure I have dealt with it. I still have days when I wonder what I'm doing.'

'As do we all,' Godfrey nodded. 'I just thought you might be able to offer me some suggestions. You see, I can't, at this moment, find it in me to condemn you – or Robert, for that matter. And since I can't, I must find another reason.'

'You're going after McCauly, aren't you?'

'Yes.'

'And you want me to help?'

'Yes.'

John sat back and studied his hands for a moment. Long ago, just after McCauly had been imprisoned, John had sent a request to the Enclave for help to get McCauly away. His request had been refused. What would the council say now if he agreed to help?

'Will anyone else know of my involvement?'

'That's up to you and how you conduct yourself. Of course, I'd rather this remain our secret. I don't particularly want to lose you.'

John looked up at this. Godfrey was watching him with thinly veiled concern.

'Very well, I'd be glad to help.'

Godfrey smiled and got to his feet. 'I was right after all, Father. We are fighting on the same side. After supper tonight, go and see Earl Payne. Tell him I sent you.'

24

The north-east coast of Lusara was perhaps the only place in the country where the natural beauty of the land faded a little. The delta valley of the Vitala river spread out over many leagues, leaving swampy groves of knotted trees and foul-smelling bogs in its wake. Only by the sea did the land rise to crumbling cliffs and dunes of reddish sand and stumpy grasses on either side of the delta. Clonnet Castle, home of the Duke of Ayr, sat high upon one of these cliffs, with a view in the distance of the cold green sea and the trading port of Jardye. Like an old and stubborn man, this place kept its own counsel and remained bleak no matter the gentleness of the weather.

Nash had been here only once before, many years ago. It had been vile back then, too, but now Clonnet had taken on another dimension, pushing into the background its unfavoured temper: it was the home of Jennifer Ross, Duchess of

Ayr, and now it would become a place Nash would visit many times in order to see her.

The welcome was cordial, but Nash was still forced to wait almost an hour before Eachern returned from a morning of hawking. He cooled his heels sipping an indifferent wine and speculating on the superb cover an invading armada would receive from this coastline. When Eachern did arrive, he made no pretence of being pleased to see his fellow councillor.

'I thought you were still in the west, chasing after my cousin's brat.' Eachern threw off his cloak and tossed it across the table, downing a full glass of wine in one swallow.

Nash climbed to his feet. 'I do have other duties to perform as well.'

'Yes, a very busy man. How do you like your new badges of office? Sit well on you, do they?'

Already tired from his journey, Nash couldn't be bothered responding to the jibe. Instead, he lifted his leather pouch on to the table and undid the laces. 'The King has papers for you to sign – but please refrain from attributing to me the role of messenger-boy. You may regret it next time you sit at a council meeting.'

Eachern was not clever enough to take the threat too seriously. Instead, he merely grunted and dragged the papers towards him. Nash brought ink and pens from the desk by the fireplace and watched the Duke as he laboriously read each document.

There was a very small resemblance between Eachern and Selar. Related on their mothers' side, both men had been brought up in the same court, subjected to the same ruthless education. But whereas Selar had a mind open to ideas and reason, Eachern had never been able to think further than the point of his sword. Fortunate, really, that it was Selar and not Tiege Eachern who had been the son of the King.

And fortunate too that Eachern was none too bright. It was all the easier to place subtle suggestions in his mind. Suggestions in place of outright Bonding. The Ally would notice such a change in her husband.

'How was the hawking?' Nash murmured conversationally, keeping a keen eye on Eachern.

'Mmm? Oh, fine, fine. Just some fun between patrols.' Eachern laid the pile of papers down and began to scratch his name across the bottom of each one, dipping his pen into the ink after almost every letter. He sanded the script, blew on it and handed the completed pile to Nash, glancing up as he did so. 'Is that all?'

'Not quite.' Nash caught Eachern's gaze and didn't let go. He'd had some practice at this now – ever since Eachern had first married Jennifer. Whenever Nash and Eachern had met at court or on patrol, he had reinforced the same message.

Keep tight control on your wife.

Aloud he said, 'I wonder how your young Duchess is? The whole court is curious about her and why you keep her locked up at Clonnet. She is well, I hope?'

Eachern struggled to tear his gaze away and Nash let him go.

'Of course she's well. Why wouldn't she be? And I don't give a damn how curious the court is. She's my wife and she will live where I tell her to live.'

Nash had to stifle a smile. 'I wonder if it would be possible to see her. She and I share some acquaintance from her trip to Marsay last year.'

Eachern's mouth opened and, for a moment, no sound came out. He appeared to be struggling against some other purpose, looking for some excuse. However, in the end, all he could do was nod. 'I'll take you to her.'

A walk through Clonnet Castle gave no indication that Eachern suffered a secret love of fine art. The furnishings were adequate, practical and looked to have been tooled by an apprentice. Only on the second floor of the main keep were there any things of actual beauty. Fine tables and tapestries, carpets and silver.

She would have brought those from Elita.

Eachern stomped along the gallery until he reached a door at the end. For a second, his hand hovered as though he would knock first, but then his thick fist came down on the latch and he swung the door open. 'My lady, I have a visitor for you.'

The room was light, much lighter than the rest of the castle. Only one tapestry graced the red sandstone walls, a landscape of greens and golds in the finest silk. Four tall windows faced south and east, shedding sunlight across a long table covered in cloth and thread. A serving girl started up from her seat, her face late to hide her surprise at their sudden entry. And seated at the far end of the table, dressed in a gown of deep ocean green was the woman Nash had waited centuries for.

She was breathtaking. Her long shining hair was unbound and fell around her shoulders as though she were still a maiden, rather than a married woman. Her eyes, of the richest cobalt blue, gazed across the room and drove a knife through his soul.

It didn't matter. He had always been fated to love her.

Eachern led him into the room, furtively glancing into each of the corners as though he expected to find robbers. Then he turned back to his wife. 'Come, my lady. I believe you are already acquainted with Alderman Nash – newly made Governor of the Guilde.'

As Nash stepped forward, Jenn drew a smile on her face which barely reached her eyes. Then she stood and came around the table, holding out her hand for him to kiss . . .

By the blood and heart of Broleoch! She was . . .

'Good day, Governor,' Jenn murmured.

'And now perhaps you understand why my wife has not yet been seen at court.' Eachern completed his search of the room and came back to stand beside Nash. 'She is disinclined to travel in this condition, nor has any wish to be in company.'

Nash scrambled to regain his composure, covering his discomfort with a deliberately foolish laugh. 'Please do forgive me for staring, Your Grace. But I had no idea. No one said a word to me about this. Otherwise I would not have . . .'

Eachern waved a hand. 'My wife is uncommonly superstitious, Nash. She would have no announcement made of the coming birth of my heir. Only her family and those within these walls know. I trust you will help to keep it that way.'

Still recovering, Nash nodded. 'Of course – but surely you are well, Your Grace? To my eyes your beauty has indeed been enhanced. I hope there is nothing wrong?'

Jennifer shook her head slightly and her smile grew more genuine. 'No, I'm quite well. As you can see, the baby grows with what I hope is an unquenchable lust for life.' She refrained from placing proud hands about her swollen abdomen as most women in her condition did and instead picked up some of the white cloth lying across the table.

'And may I ask when the event is expected?' Nash held his breath, trying very hard not to betray the tension he felt in every bone of his body. If it should be less than a month . . .

'In four weeks, Governor,' Jennifer replied lightly.

'My wife plans the child to be born at her home. She leaves in two days – against my advice – to travel to Elita.' Eachern was obviously nonplussed by this decision and appealed to Nash for support. However, Nash had another agenda – and it had nothing to do with appeasing the Duke.

'I'm sure Her Grace will travel slowly and carefully, taking no risks at all. After so much care and attention, I doubt she will endanger the baby so close to its time. Besides, the child will probably be heir to the lands of Elita as well and it would do well for it to be born within those borders.'

Eachern just grunted, but Jennifer smiled warmly.

'Do you stay with us long, Governor? My lord can show you some good hawking along the dunes. This countryside affords us little else in the way of hunting.'

'Unfortunately I must return to court this afternoon, Your Grace. However, with your permission, I'll return again, when you are more fit to ride, and see what your dunes have to offer.'

Again the warm smile. 'I look forward to it.'

He left her there, with the memory of her face burning into his eyes.

A child . . . but the child could only be Eachern's. It had to be. Finnlay Douglas had been halfway across the country and bleeding to death when the child had been conceived.

No danger there. And perhaps . . . perhaps the child would not survive anyway, despite her cautions. Perhaps the journey to Elita would cause some irreparable harm.

It didn't matter. There was no way the child could be the Enemy's, and therefore would be no threat to Nash.

As he rode away from Clonnet Castle, Nash had another comforting thought: she would be incapable of running far from him for the next few months. Plenty of time.

Yes, plenty of time, indeed. After all, just as he was fated to love her, she was fated to love him in return.

He'd been lucky. Very lucky. If Eachern and the Guildesman had come through the gallery a moment later, Micah would have been caught outright. But as it was, he was becoming extremely adept at avoiding the Duke, a skill which had come to the fore today more than ever.

As the sound of booted feet faded down the gallery, Micah pushed the stairwell door open a crack and peered through. They were gone and his charges were still safe behind him. Waving them to follow, he pushed the door open and led them to the solar. With only a brief knock as warning, he entered.

'My lady,' he murmured, hurrying across the room. 'You have some visitors . . .'

Jenn turned at his voice – then froze. A moment later, she cried in delight, 'Sir Owen! Lady Margaret!'

For a few minutes, mayhem ruled the bright little solar as surprised greetings were exchanged on both sides. Then Jenn had them all sitting down while Addie was sent for food and drink.

'We can't stay for long, my dear,' Margaret began. 'Deverin will have kittens if I am not back home by the appointed day. Still, I had to come.'

'I'm so glad to see you,' Jenn murmured, gazing at her.

Margaret smiled again and patted her hand. 'And I you. May I congratulate you? I had not heard about your condition. Have you been well? You look well.'

'Oh yes, so well, in fact, that I sometimes forget all about it. I've lost count of the number of times I've woken in the morning to plan a day out riding.' Margaret smiled at this. 'And I still keep trying to run around the place, forgetting that I've got this great lump slowing me down. How are things at Dunlorn?'

'Very well. Spring has been good to us this year, nowhere near as cold as last year. I hear there has been snow in the mountains, though.' Margaret paused and laced her hands together. 'Have you had any recent word from Finnlay?'

'None since the last I wrote to you about. Is Patric still with you?'

Margaret shook her head. 'No. He's gone ... wherever he had to go. I assume to Finnlay?'

Jenn nodded.

Margaret frowned. 'I'm not sure I'll ever get used to all this secrecy. Things I can't say when I want to and words I'm sure I know but never remember when I need to. I don't know how you manage.'

'There are worse things in life than sorcery.'

'Indeed there are.' Margaret's gaze dropped to where their hands were joined on her lap. 'You must know why I came – under such disguise. If your husband knew I was here ...'

Her voice trailed off, but she didn't look up. 'Have you truly had no word from my son? Have you absolutely no idea of where Robert might be? Where he has been all this time?'

Jenn's face betrayed nothing but concern. 'No. I'm sorry. I wish I could tell you any news at all, but I ... we've heard nothing.'

Margaret looked first at Jenn and then at Micah. 'But he's been gone so long now. When he left Lusara last time, he at least sent word. We knew where he'd gone and some reason why. Now we're left with nothing. I know his treatment from Selar would have hurt him like no other, but can that be enough for Robert to just leave us like this? Are you sure there was nothing else that could have driven him away?'

Micah tried not to stiffen at the questions, but the moment he'd had word that Margaret and Owen had arrived in secret he'd known what would happen. But they, like everybody else, had had no sight nor word of Robert since the morning of Jenn's wedding.

'I'm sorry, my dear,' Margaret was talking again. 'I shouldn't be doing this to you in your condition. It's just that I am so worried about him. With all that's happened to him over the last few years, I wonder how he has the strength to bear it. That perhaps he hasn't . . .'

'My lord has strength enough to survive anything, my lady.' Micah found the words came out without effort. 'But you know he's always needed time to sort through his thoughts and feelings. Selar's rejection hit him hard. I believe that if the circumstances had been different, he would have killed the King.'

Margaret rose to her feet.

'Then he should have killed Selar! I would have, had I been able. That that monster should defile my son's name by calling him a coward is unbelievable! All his life Robert has tried so hard to be loyal and honourable and for that he is reviled – in public!'

Ignoring Owen's hand on her arm, Margaret paced back and forth in front of the windows. 'Oh, we all know why Selar did it. He knew Robert wouldn't react in such a place. He knew he'd get away with it, believing that the people would see Robert as a coward because he would not react. Selar had to destroy the support Robert has always had across the country. I know it's wrong, but I can't help wishing Robert had just killed him there and then.'

Margaret paused, fighting back tears of rage and frustration, but before Micah could move to her, Jenn was there, holding Margaret's hands between her own.

'Please,' Jenn began softly, 'don't distress yourself so. I know this is painful for you and waiting is not easy when you have no idea of what you're waiting for. But trust me – this *is* just a time of waiting. This is not the end. It can't be.'

'Then you believe he'll return?'

Jenn lifted her chin and met Margaret's gaze. 'I don't know.'

'I do,' Micah said firmly. 'Robert will come back.'

Margaret turned her gaze on him, quizzical and hesitant. 'You sound so sure. You must know him so well.'

'I agree with Micah, my lady,' Owen joined in. 'Robert has spent these last years trying to avoid a battle that was always inevitable. One day, however, the battle will be taken to him – and he'll not fail us then. You know in your heart this is true.'

Margaret nodded slowly. 'I'm sorry ... I shouldn't have allowed myself to ...'

Jenn smiled, squeezing her hands. 'Don't apologize. Robert himself would not allow you to. He'd also be plainly irritated by your concern.'

Owen moved forward. 'I'm sorry, my lady, but we must be moving on. We need to get some distance behind us before we stop for the night.'

With a nod, Margaret embraced Jenn and Micah and then, without another word, Micah led them out of the room and down through the castle to the stables. They were on their way out of the castle before anyone could really notice. As they rode away, Micah allowed himself only the smallest pang of regret that he was not going with them.

It was routine alone that kept it bearable. Jenn ate her supper in her room, washed and changed and heaved her cumbersome body into bed. It was then that she dismissed Addie for the night and indulged in a little reading by the thick yellow candle she kept by her pillow. Only routine failed her from time to time.

A visit from that Guildesman – and Eachern had obviously been useless at finding an excuse to keep him away. Now the news would go all around the court, the subject of endless speculation.

And somewhere, somehow, the Angel of Darkness would hear. What would he do? Would he take this opportunity to further his own plans?

Did he still think Finnlay was the Enemy?

And what if he'd encountered Robert - could that be why neither had been heard of for so long? What if Robert had failed ...

No!

He couldn't be dead. She would know. She would *know*!

By the gods, Margaret had taken such a risk coming here. And why? So she could see for herself that neither Jenn nor Micah knew any more than they'd told her already? But then, if it hadn't been for the child, she would have done exactly the same thing and gone to Dunlorn.

Jenn couldn't stay in bed. Restless and weary, she got up for a while and tried to walk about, but the baby wouldn't let her. As she got back under the covers, she lay on her side and wrapped her arms about her belly. She closed her eyes and tried to imagine the other life inside her. She carefully calmed herself, breathed deeply and evenly, relaxed her whole body.

And then she could hear it. Softly and gently, like a breeze drifting across her face. Not a voice, but a presence, that had been growing stronger over the last few months. A sorcerer's presence with an aura all its own, quite unlike any she'd encountered so far – and yet, it was familiar in so many ways.

She couldn't tell whether it was a boy or girl. She couldn't even sense what it was thinking or feeling. All she knew was that at times like this, the presence reached out and calmed her, put a bar on her agitation, stopped her from pacing in restlessness.

'Another four weeks, my love,' she murmured softly. 'Another four weeks and then we'll meet.'

Nash returned to the same inn where he'd spent the previous night. For a travellers' stop, it was very comfortable and convenient, being on the main road to Marsay. With an early start he would be in the capital by sunset tomorrow.

He took a room which looked out over the road busy with carts and litters, riders and walkers. So many people so intent on their own lives that they rarely looked up to see what was about them. If they had?

Well, that's what made it so easy. The simple fact that most people paid absolutely no attention to what was going on around them. They came across small obstacles and either

350

overcame them or went around them as they chose. So few even knew the greater challenges that life dealt. Even fewer of them cared.

So Nash could move about as he liked, nudging his plans ever closer to his goal without anybody ever seeing what he was up to.

With a smile, Nash pulled his clothes off and washed. He was reaching for a clean shirt when there was a quiet and familiar knock at his door.

'Come in, Lisson.'

The young man entered, travel-stained and weary. 'I have a letter for you, master.'

Nash closed the door behind him and took the pouch from his hand. 'This had better be from DeMassey.'

Hardly able to control his anticipation, Nash strode to the window, extracted the letter and cracked open the seal. The contents were encrypted as usual, but Nash merely touched his garnet ring to the paper and the symbols took a form and shape he could read.

I honestly don't know how you're going to repay me for this. Have no doubt, however, that I have every intention of extracting just recompense. I just thought I'd tell you that now.

I have the boy. If you're sufficiently grateful when I bring him to you, I may even tell you where I found him. Since you expressed no interest in the others, I'll make you wait to hear of their fate. Suffice to say, my efforts on your behalf are far beyond what you have any right to expect.

I send this message express to you. It will take me a week or so before I'm close to Marsay. When I'm nearer, I'll send word where you can meet me. Until then I suggest you keep the news secret. I wouldn't want anybody trying to steal him away again.

DeMassey.

At last!

Nash almost laughed with delight. What a triumph. He

would hand Kenrick back to Selar, personally – and then he
would complete the Bonding.

So very close now. Very close indeed.

25

'You'd better be sure about this, Gilbert.'

'I am.'

DeMassey glanced aside at him and continued, 'Because if
you're wrong, this is going to take some getting out of.'

'Don't worry.'

'We've never ventured this far east before with a raiding
party. There are things in this part of the world we really
should try to avoid.'

'I told you not to worry, Luc. Everything will be just fine.
I know what I'm doing,' Gilbert replied confidently.

DeMassey lifted his feet from his stirrups and stretched his
legs out. Gilbert sat on his horse, with one leg over the
pommel, the image of perfect calm. They were the same age,
and yet Gilbert always assumed an older, wiser air which
irritated most people. It wasn't a façade, either. Gilbert had
been like that from a child. His ill-proportioned body had
taken years to develop any real strength. His face, never
attractive, had grown even uglier over the years. Thick black
eyebrows shadowed small eyes of a pale amber. Below them
sat a nose so large it almost had an identity of its own. There
was a crooked mouth too, with crooked teeth to match, one
of which was missing from a boyhood battle with a fighting
staff. As though to shun any attempt to hide his looks,
Gilbert wore his rust red hair long in a braid down his back
and gave every indication of being a dangerous, menacing
warrior.

He wasn't.

DeMassey sighed and glanced up through the trees to site

the position of the sun. 'Where are they? Can't Felen do anything on time?'

'If you didn't think you could trust him, why did you get him involved? You have the entire D'Azzir at your command. Why get Felen in as well?'

'I should have thought that was obvious. He'll make a good scapegoat if anything goes wrong.'

Gilbert began to laugh, then waved his hand towards the thick forest. 'He's coming now.'

DeMassey turned to look as the brush parted before the small force he'd brought from Karakham. Felenor Callenderi rode in the front.

'Good,' DeMassey said. 'Let's get this over with.'

The brook was overfull of water, though it was clear and clean in the sunshine. Rosalind walked along the bank keeping a careful eye on Kenrick as he waded barefoot in the shallows. It had been a lovely day – and such a good idea to get out from the confines of the house. Duke Kavanagh had been generous in his gift, but there was still the essence of a prison about any dwelling she couldn't dare to leave. At least she'd had a few moments like this. George had suggested this outing as a surprise. He'd even packed a lunch for them, arriving early in the morning to take them out. The guards hadn't been happy, but what could they say?

'Mother?'

'Yes, Kenrick?'

The boy stood knee deep in water and put his hands on his hips. 'When will Earl George teach me to ride? He said I had to wait until the snows went, but there isn't any snow now and he still hasn't taught me.'

'Have you asked him why?'

'I just told him he had to. He laughed. I don't like him. My father wouldn't let anyone laugh at me.'

'No,' Rosalind murmured, 'he wouldn't.'

She glanced over her shoulder to the clearing in the trees where George sat with Galiena and Samah, reading to them from a book. He'd tried so hard to replace the memory of Selar with something more substantial. Galiena had always liked him and responded well. Even Samah, her life as a nun no more now than a mourned memory, had gone with the spirit of their new life. Only Kenrick resisted. He had idolized his father and still remembered him too much. But it was early yet. Perhaps in a few years, Kenrick would learn more than his father could possibly have taught him.

And as for Rosalind? George had remained her faithful ally, yet she could see from time to time the pain in his eyes. She wanted to love him – and did, in a way. But she could never allow herself to love him as he loved her. Not while she was still married to Selar, while the children were still in such need of her. George made no demands on her and yet, at times, she almost wished he would.

'I'll speak to Earl George for you, my dear,' Rosalind smiled back at the boy. 'If you're good, I'll see if I can arrange a lesson for you tomorrow.'

A war of loyalties crossed the boy's face until he finally made his decision. He nodded. 'Thank you, Mother.'

She reached out her hand to help him out of the water. Then a noise disturbed her and she looked up. The trees across the brook rustled with the pounding of horses and instinctively she grabbed hold of her son.

Then, like a nightmare come to life, soldiers on horseback burst from the forest and splashed across the water. They wore long robes of foreign design and immediately surrounded her, waving swords from above. Rosalind screamed and pulled Kenrick behind her. She backed away, but there was no escape. Two men jumped down and tried to get at Kenrick. She kicked and flailed at them, but her efforts were in vain. One man, ugly and menacing, took hold of Kenrick and pulled him from her grasp so hard she stumbled forward.

'No! Kenrick!' she screamed.

He was thrown to another man still on his horse. As she struggled forward, unthinking of the danger, she was grabbed and thrown to the ground. While the ugly man climbed back on his horse, the other stood over her with menace in his eyes.

'Come, Felen, leave her. We've got what we wanted!'

Rosalind swung her leg and brought the man to the

ground. She fought to get to her feet and lunged again for Kenrick – then stopped.

Pain. Small and needle-like, in the centre of her back. Her legs wouldn't move. Instead, they crumpled beneath her and she fell to the ground. Kenrick was screaming for her, but the horsemen gathered together and turned back across the stream. Seconds later, they were gone, leaving only the trembling trees as evidence of their passage.

Rosalind dropped on to her stomach. It was hard to breathe and her legs were going numb. She couldn't lift her head, but from the distance she could hear feet running towards her, cries echoing in the forest.

Then hands lifted her up, turned her over, and George was whispering her name, urgently, terrified. She blinked but couldn't say anything.

Slowly she lost her body and then her sight. For a while she drifted down into the darkness until everything stopped.

As the firelight grew stronger, DeMassey got to his feet and stretched out his tired muscles. The camp was quiet now that the boy had taken the sleeping draught. Still, they'd have to keep him tied up for most of the journey. It wouldn't do for the brat to go running away.

'How long will it take for your message to reach Nash?' Gilbert asked from across the fire.

'A couple of days.'

'Are you going to tell him where we found Kenrick?'

'Why should I? I doubt he'd be interested, anyway. You know how narrow his vision is.'

Gilbert nodded, but said nothing more. He'd been unusually quiet since they made camp at sunset.

'Well,' DeMassey yawned and stretched again, 'I'm going to bed.'

'Not yet.'

He glanced back at Gilbert with a frown. 'What?'

Gilbert rose to his feet and touched his boot to the prostrate form of Felen, who lounged before the fire like a sleeping lion. 'Get up.'

Felen raised his head, his eyes half-closed from dozing. 'What's wrong?'

'Just get up.'

Felen sighed grievously and made a show of climbing to his feet. The moment he did, however, Gilbert raised his hand with lightning speed and delivered a blow to Felen's jaw which sent the man crashing to the ground. He stood over Felen, daring him to get up again, his pale eyes glaring.

Felen waited long enough to prove he wouldn't strike back, then scrambled to his feet and out of sight.

'What the hell did you do that for?' DeMassey demanded.

Gilbert didn't even look at the him. 'He killed the woman. There was no need.'

'And there was no need to make an enemy of Felen. You wait until he's licked his wounds. He won't take a humiliation like that without thought of revenge.'

Gilbert turned to him with a grim smile. 'I know. Don't worry about it. He can't hurt me. I'm going to bed. Goodnight.'

George sat in the corner and watched Kavanagh stride up and down the hall, bellowing orders one minute and pausing to ask questions the next. He filled the room with his enormous presence, yet at the same time, there was a deceptive quietness about the man that George had come to appreciate. After a while, Kavanagh dismissed his aides and wandered over to George's quiet corner. He pulled up a chair and sank into it, making the wood groan under his weight.

'I can't tell you how sorry I am,' Grant began, shaking his head in dismay. 'I have no idea how they got across the border without being seen – nor how they could come upon you without even your guards being aware. I swear, I put my best men on to the job.'

George nodded and lifted his cup to his mouth. The wine tasted like sand, but still he drank.

Grant gazed at him a moment, then added, 'I've arranged for you to head south tomorrow night. The girls should be fit to travel by then. We have to get you on a ship before word of this can get out. Who knows what Selar will do to get his daughter back – or his hands on you.'

'He couldn't care less,' George murmured. 'Galiena was always useless to him, Samah just a pawn he could use in his power games and Rosalind . . .'

Taking in a deep breath, George forced himself to continue, 'Rosalind was his means for revenge upon a country that had dared to put even the smallest resistance in his way. I know my cousin, Grant, and he won't even flinch at the news that his Queen is dead.'

Grant must have heard something in his voice because he reached out and put his hand over George's arm. 'You're not going to do anything foolish, are you?'

'Me?' George turned to look at him. 'Not at the moment, no. I'll go with the girls and keep them as safe as possible. But when the time comes, I'll return. There's something I have to do.'

'So have I.' Grant expelled a breath and got to his feet. He spread his arms wide in supplication and lifted his head towards the ceiling. 'Robert is going to kill me!'

26

It was impossible to tell where the mountain ended and the sky began. Both were laden with the same ghost-white, incandescent and unfathomable. Finnlay could have made it much easier on himself by sending his senses up the steep slope to feel with his mind exactly how much further it was to the top. But that would be cheating.

Gathering his strength for another assault, Finnlay lifted his left hand out of the snow and stretched hard. Powder rained down on his head and his face, nearly blinding him. He shook it away and sank the hand deep below the surface snow, searching for the next hold. He clutched at a rock, bound in place by ice, tested it, let his weight hang from it.

Only then did he move. More snow skittered down, dropping far below him. His gloves were frozen now, his fingers unfeeling stumps. His leather jacket was solid and encrusted with layers of ice, like glass. Diamond-sharp spikes stung his face, then numbed it as the cold gripped. Great clouds of breath sat in the air before his face.

He moved upward, his knees sinking again and again into the drifts of snow covering the last ridge. His feet stuck on things he could only imagine, for he could feel no substance. Then the sky began to darken.

'Hell!' he breathed, squinting up. 'Don't snow again now. Can't you wait just a few minutes longer?'

The sky answered with a rumble, growing even darker. The cloud sank towards him, purple and threatening. At least he could now see the edge of the ridge. Only a few more feet to go.

Controlling the desire to rush, Finnlay struck upwards again until his hands fell on solid rock. There was only a fine layer of snow here and some very slippery ice. He dragged his body on to the rock and lay there a moment, catching his breath. Then he felt the wind.

Fearful now, he sat up, straining his neck to see over the edge of the Goleth ridge. It was a mistake. A gust whipped up the other side and sent a sheet of snow into his face, covering his whole body. He stood quickly, almost slipping off the rock. This was getting very dangerous, but he wasn't going to give up now, not when he was so very close to the top. At least he could walk now.

Stumbling on the icy surface, he buried his chin in his chest, screwed up his eyes to little slits. All he could see was the blinding white snow beneath his feet, the grey encrusted stone patches here and there laid bare by the driving, icy wind. He pushed on, pressing, bending into the wind as it tried to drive him off the mountain.

He slipped and landed on his knees, his head into the wind. He lifted his eyes, but he was isolated by grey. He didn't dare move. The grey went on for ever, dismal and defiant. But then, abruptly, the wind gusted and for one single, split second, the cloud cleared, revealing the most breathtaking sight he'd ever seen.

The cliff dropped below him; the height was dizzying, but all he could see was an endless expanse of snow-capped mountains, black cavernous ripples and yawning valleys. Blinding white, the pristine view splashed itself before his eyes and was gone. The cloud sank around him again and once more the wind beat heavily. He'd done it. Made it to the top of the Goleth, the highest mountain in Lusara – and he'd done it in snow!

It was time to go back, but he didn't dare try standing again with that wind. On all fours, he slipped and slid down the top of the ridge until he was out of the gale. Then, his muscles aching, his whole body exhausted, he began the steep descent. He went slowly. It wouldn't do to gain too much speed or he would land at the bottom a broken mess.

The first part was the worst. He grew more and more exhausted with every step. It was so steep he could hardly keep his balance, but as he lost height, the cloud lifted and he could finally see where he was going. Out of the wind, his movement was just enough to keep him from freezing to death. Stumbling down the last stretch where the slope flattened out, he fell again. This time he laid there a moment, catching his breath. It was done. Finally.

'Finn?'

The voice seemed to come from nowhere and everywhere. A dead echo, drenched in snow and pale memory.

'Finnlay? Where the hell are you?'

It was coming closer, accompanied by long crunching steps in the snow.

'Damn it, Finnlay Douglas! Answer me! It's too cold out here to be playing games. Where are you?'

Finnlay tried to raise his head, but it was just too difficult. Instead, he waved his hand ineffectually.

The laboured steps halted by his head and he looked up to see the face belonging to those feet. Brown hair capped by a woollen hat, encrusted with driven snow and ice. A pair of icy blue eyes, a long nose and a mouth set thin with disapproval. 'What kind of idiot climbs the Goleth straight after a week-long snowfall? I thought you said you were just going for a short walk.'

Arlie stuck out his hand and grabbed hold of Finnlay's. Staggering together, both men stumbled in the snow until they came upright.

'What's wrong, Arlie? Were you worried about me?' Finnlay's mouth wasn't working properly and he stretched his jaw to loosen up his frozen muscles.

'I might have known you'd pull a stunt like this,' Arlie growled, throwing an arm around him to help him along. 'Just because it's your birthday doesn't mean we'll send out a rescue party if you fall off the cliff.'

'Then what are you doing here?' It was still a little hazy, but things were beginning to take shape. For instance, he could now see the black opening before him, the tunnel leading down to where it was warm and dry. 'Why did you come looking for me?'

'I just thought you might like to know.' Arlie let go of him as they reached the tunnel mouth. Sheltered from the wind and snow, it was suddenly very quiet. 'Patric's just returned. I thought, in my foolishness, that you might like to talk to him. I hadn't realized you were so intent on ending your otherwise futile existence!'

'Oh, that's nice!' Finnlay ducked his head and studied the crusts of ice still stuck to his jacket. He'd probably ruined it. Goose fat. That was the answer. Lots of rubbing to loosen up the leather again. It might take a couple of days, but he'd do it in the end.

'Sometimes, Finn, you really try my patience. Come on.' Arlie grabbed his elbow and spun him around into the tunnel. After the glare of white outside, the tunnel seemed unusually dark. The torches along the wall were little more than pinpricks of light, little voices in a whole chorus of shadow. 'What were you doing up there? Serin's breath, you didn't even tell anyone you were going! What if you'd fallen, eh? And what was the point to it? Why don't you just climb the pinnacle in summer like everyone else? You didn't even pick a nice day, did you? No view, even.'

'Oh, there was a view.' Finnlay's head was clearing a bit

now. So was the rest of him. Down here, in the tunnels, it was warm, stuffy, in fact. So warm that his frozen fingers were coming to life – painfully. And he was dripping water all over the tunnel floor.

'And you didn't see Patric coming up?'

'Patric?' Finnlay came to a halt and shook his head. Arlie's hair was stuck to his face like a frame of wet feathers. 'Patric's back? When?'

'A couple of hours ago. I've been looking everywhere for you. By the gods, Finnlay, will you please pay attention!'

'I am paying attention,' Finnlay snapped back, all fogginess abruptly dissipating. 'But what you're saying doesn't make any sense. How could Patric get up the mountain in this kind of weather?'

Arlie resumed walking and Finnlay hurried to keep up with the older man's long strides. 'Apparently our unseasonable snowstorm has only wiped out our section of the Goleth. The east ridges are quite passable. It was only bad for the last hour.'

'Well, where is he?'

'Not before you get changed. I'll not have you coming down with a fever. Martha would kill me – and I won't even think about what Fiona would do.'

Finnlay nodded slowly. 'There's no need to shout, Arlie. I got back in one piece, didn't I?'

'Did you get to the top?' Arlie asked grudgingly.

'Yes.' Finnlay couldn't help smiling.

If he'd thought the pain of entering the warm caverns was bad, it was nothing compared to the hot bath Arlie forced him to have. He bellowed his rage at the injustice of it all, but Arlie still brought in fresh pails of steaming water to refill the tub. Satisfied with his work, Arlie finally left him alone. For a while Finnlay sat there, aching in knees and elbows, but slowly, eventually, he began to laugh.

With the fire crackling away before him, he climbed out of the cauldron and stood on the rug, rubbing his body dry with a swathe of fleecy linen. Then, only because it was his birthday, he pulled on a shirt of fine fabric, lace at the collar. His breeches were mahogany brown and his sleeveless jacket forest green. He ran a comb through his wet hair, then shook it out, spraying the walls with droplets of water. He pulled on soft leather boots, gave the fire a quick stab and strode out of his rooms, completely refreshed. It wouldn't last long, he knew, but for the moment, he felt great.

Patric wasn't alone. Martha was with him, holding the baby. Little Damaris was peacefully asleep, but even so, her tiny face was full of character. Finnlay often found himself staring at her for long seconds, hoping she'd wake up. Martha had caught him once, but she'd not said anything.

'I thought you'd given up the dangerous life, Finnlay!' Patric said in greeting.

'Welcome back,' Finnlay laughed, giving Patric a brief hug. 'That was very game, coming up in this weather. You weren't to know the range was passable.'

'Oh,' Patric shoved him into a chair, pressed a cup of spicy hot wine into his hand, 'it wasn't so brave. I didn't know anything about the snow until I got too close to stop. The rest of the country is well into spring. It's only you folks up here who have had the chills put on you. I could have waited a bit, I suppose, but I didn't want to miss your birthday. Here, I have a gift for you.'

Patric hauled a saddlebag on to the table. He fished around inside for a moment, then brought out a tiny cloth-wrapped bundle. He handed it to Finnlay and stood back, a hesitant smile on his freshly tanned face. 'I hope you don't mind.'

Finnlay unfolded the cloth. Lying in the palm of his hand was a silver ring, the Douglas eagle in ebony across its face.

'Your mother gave it to me. She wanted you to have it back.'

Finnlay took the ring and held it up to the light. It was like having an old, familiar friend return from a long absence. With a grin, he slipped it on his finger, polished it against his fine shirt.

'Oh, that's a good idea, Finnlay,' Martha smiled. 'Ruin your shirt with that filthy old thing.'

'Why is everyone being so horrible to me today?' Finnlay asked in an aggrieved tone. Then he looked up at Patric.

'Thank you. You don't know what it was like losing this thing. I thought I'd never see it again.'

Patric tossed back the last of his wine. 'Your mother insisted I warn you not to go losing it again. She said that you might not be so lucky next time.'

'How is she?'

'She's in the pink of health, my friend.' Patric glanced up as Arlie returned and whisked around the room refilling their wine, sharing out a wedge of hard cheese and steaming brown rolls. 'She's an incredible woman, your mother. I swear, everyone in Dunlorn is terrified of her. They daren't contradict her. She issues an order and they jump. All except Owen. He frowns continually, shakes his head a lot – and still does as she tells him. I'll bet the place never ran so well when you were in charge.'

There was something about Patric that Finnlay couldn't quite put a finger on. Something different. Sure, he still moved like a darting rabbit, still spoke rapidly and waved his hands around left and right. His hair still fell across his face and he still brushed it away without thinking – but there was something very different about him. Something inside.

'You've changed, Patric.'

'That's what I've just been thinking,' Martha murmured, lifting the baby up so Arlie could take her. Martha then came to her feet and joined Arlie by the door. 'I like it. I think you should have gone outside long before now. What's more, I think you should go out again when the weather clears. We'll see you downstairs at supper.'

As they left, Finnlay sank back into his chair and let the warm room, the fire and toasty wine filter into his battered body. He was just getting a little drowsy when Patric moved and startled him awake.

'Why don't you just go to bed?'

'I will, but not yet. It's too early.'

Patric nodded and pulled up a chair to sit opposite, the fire between them. 'You got my last letter, then?'

'A few weeks ago now.'

'Well, the last letter I got from Micah arrived just before I

363

left Dunlorn. He's not happy with the situation, but that's only to be expected.'

'And Eachern? Is he still causing trouble?'

'You can decide for yourself. I'll get the letter out later and you can read it. It's hard to know, really, between what Micah says and what he doesn't say. Not that I know Eachern, but I'd say at a guess that he doesn't much like having Micah around. He probably thinks Micah is too loyal to Jenn – but that's only my opinion. He warned that we wouldn't hear anything from them for a while. Jenn doesn't want to risk too much communication, even with a coded letter. It doesn't matter. I plan to return to Dunlorn in late summer and I'll get some news then. If not, I might just go to Ayr myself and see how she is.'

Finnlay nodded, his eyes dropping to the rich wine in his cup. The scent of spices was heady after his exertions and every moment that passed made him even more tired. Perhaps he would have to go and have a nap.

'Then you haven't had word of Robert either.'

Finnlay's eyes snapped open. Patric was staring at him, expecting the worst answer.

'No.' Finnlay struggled to his feet, his tired muscles objecting at every turn. 'Did you expect otherwise?'

'Finn,' Patric murmured, his gaze unbroken, 'have you wondered if Robert might not just be gone . . . but dead?'

'He's not dead.'

'But he might be . . .'

'He's not dead, Patric. Robert's my brother. I'd know if something happened to him.'

'But you thought he was dead after he fell from the cliff at Kilphedir. You said so yourself.'

'No.' Finnlay held up his hands. He didn't even want to have this conversation. 'I assumed he had to be dead because I couldn't Seek him – and after I lost my *ayarn* I couldn't keep trying. This is entirely different – and I know what you're going to say next. No, I don't think the Angel of Darkness found out that Robert is the Enemy and not me, and I don't think Robert fought him and lost.'

'Why not?'

'Because Robert wouldn't lose.'

Patric nodded slowly and advanced around the table, for the moment sombre and restrained. 'I can see you really believe that, Finn. But perhaps you can tell me in that case why your sleep has been so disturbed of late.'

Finnlay grimaced. 'Martha's been talking, hasn't she?'

'Is it a recurrence of the nightmares after your brush with Carlan?'

'No.' Finnlay shook his head and ran his hands through his almost dry hair. 'It's nothing like that. Look, my not sleeping and my brother's disappearance are not connected.'

He turned and headed for the door, pausing to add, 'I think I will go and have a nap. I believe there's a supper for my birthday this evening, so I'll see you there. Welcome home.'

The refectory was decorated for the event, but Fiona would rather Finnlay's birthday had been celebrated quietly than this public display. Finnlay, of course, revelled in the attention he received, both from his friends and his students. Word had already reached them of his extraordinary attempt on the Goleth peak that day. Astonishment had been the general reaction.

Fiona had been horrified but unsurprised.

All through the supper she watched him move about the room. Every now and then he would glance back with a smile just for her, making her cheeks burn. Surely everybody would notice such a look. They would wonder why he would give her so much attention, why he had chosen her: Fiona, gruff and determined. Unpopular. So very different to the charming and entertaining Finnlay, who no doubt had learned a lot from his brother.

But Fiona didn't care what the others thought of her. She knew they respected her abilities, but she also knew that they didn't really like her. It didn't matter. What mattered was that Finnlay loved her and she'd waited a long time for him to realize she loved him in return – and as long as he did love her, the opinions of others were unimportant.

However, Patric's arrival and the absence of news about

Robert had disturbed her more than she cared to admit openly. She remained quiet throughout the evening's festivities, determined not to worry Finnlay on this day. She tried hard to hide her concern, but he noticed and as he walked her back to her rooms after the party, he broached the subject.

'You shouldn't take what Patric says to heart. You know he always looks on the dark side.'

Fiona glanced at him. 'He should keep his opinions about Robert's fate to himself. He should know he'll only upset people with talk about Robert's death – especially when the whole idea is pure speculation.'

Finnlay gave her a half-smile. 'Yes, I heard you telling him off. I was touched that you'd go so far to protect my feelings.'

He tucked his arm about her waist and turned her into the corridor leading to her rooms. When they reached the door, Fiona paused, glancing up and down the passage. They were alone.

'Finn, I understand you want to find Robert. I know he's your brother and you're worried about him. We all are.'

'But?'

'But what if he doesn't come back?' Fiona took a breath and continued before Finnlay could reply. 'I know I'm being very selfish about this – but what if he doesn't return? And if he does, what if he . . . if he won't . . .'

She couldn't finish. It was too hard to voice aloud. She'd worried about this for so many months now that it had become like a seething parasite inside her imagination, running around and around so fast it made her dizzy.

Finnlay put his arms around her and pulled her close. He kissed her gently on the forehead. Then he watched her gravely with those dark eyes, patiently waiting for her to go on.

'I know he's your brother, Finnlay, but do you really need his permission to marry?' Fiona said this so fast she almost lost her breath. She gulped in air and continued before she could lose her courage, 'You're a grown man. An adult. You've run Dunlorn alone for years. You've been a successful Seeker for years. You've established and developed our Combat School here almost entirely on your own. You studied hard to be able to teach skills you could never perform yourself because you believed we would need them – and you did so against the advice of people like Henry. I'm sorry, but I just don't understand why you need Robert's permission to marry.'

Finnlay gazed at her a long time before answering. Then he took her hands between his own. 'Robert is my brother, but he is also the Douglas, the head of my House. I know you tend to forget things like that now that I'm living here permanently, but nevertheless, they're still real to me. Unless something happens in the meantime, I am Robert's heir. I know he'll never marry again and he'll never have a son of his own to inherit . . .'

'How do you know that?'

'I just do, my love. The point is, that although I can't go back home at the moment, some day I may. Our children will inherit Dunlorn and all that goes with it. Yes, I admit, it's tradition that I have Robert's permission to marry – but I also want his blessing. I'm sorry if that means we'll have to wait, but he means too much to me to discard him merely because he's not conveniently around when I need him. His life doesn't revolve around my needs.'

Fiona dropped her eyes to their hands while her heart leaped into her throat. 'And what if . . . he says no?'

A rumble of laughter erupted from Finnlay. 'So that's what you're worried about! Why on earth would he say no? And even if he did – do you think I'd leave him alone until he consented? Do you really think I'd let him get away with ruining my future happiness? By the gods,' Finnlay gathered her up again in his arms, 'I would hound him to the ends of the earth – and he knows it. Don't worry, my love, we will be married and soon.'

He gave her no more opportunity to argue, kissing her long and deep before opening her door and ushering her inside. He blew her a goodnight kiss and disappeared down the passage, leaving Fiona praying that he was right.

*

The darkness reached out from the bed to the highest and furthest corners of his room. The only light he could see was imagined, his eyes keeping the memory of the candlit refectory and the oil lamps in the corridor outside. He was alone and it was blissfully quiet, but still he couldn't sleep.

Finnlay rolled from his side on to his back and tried to restructure in his mind the shape of the ceiling above without using his other senses to fill in the detail. He tried going over the combat exercises he would teach tomorrow, completing each one in his imagination with careful precision. He even attempted to plan the next year's worth of classes, but none of it made any difference. The moment he started to drift off to sleep, he was startled awake by the same rush of energy, as though he needed to be alert and ready to defend himself.

Could it be Carlan trying to reach him by some means, trying to get hold of him through his sleep?

No. Carlan had been looking not just for the Enemy but also for the Key. If there was any way he could have found Finnlay, he would have been here by now. Not only that, but he would have been making the attempt every night since Finnlay had escaped, so many months ago, rather than just over the last few weeks.

Then perhaps it was as Patric had suggested, some deeper worry about Robert.

Finnlay sighed and closed his eyes again, focusing this time not on the mystery of Robert's disappearance, but on the man himself. Strong, stubborn, sensitive, clever, demanding, uncompromising. So much in one person – and so much of it Finnlay missed. He breathed deeply, just as he would before going into a deep Seeking, and conjured up the face of his missing brother—

Finnlay?

Startled awake again! This time, he sat up, his heart pounding and his mouth suddenly dry.

Had he really heard something, or was his imagination really playing serious tricks on him?

Frantic now, he tried again to breathe deeply and settled himself back down, resting his head on the pillow. He closed his eyes and thought of Robert again.

Finnlay? Can you hear me?

By the gods!

Damn it, Finn, I know you can hear me! Just answer. I know you can do it. You have to be able to.

Answer? How? He didn't have the gift of mindspeech. How could he make any kind of reply.

By the gods, Finnlay, if you don't answer me I'll have your hide!

That voice . . . he could hear it clearer and clearer now . . . but it wasn't Robert, it was . . .

Jenn?

That's it, but push harder, Finn. I can keep the connection open from this end. Focus on me like you would with a Seeking. Concentrate. You just have to respond with a little more volume.

JENN?

Okay, perhaps not that much volume. Well done!

I can't believe I'm doing this! How did you manage it?

Practice. I've been trying for weeks to get through to you. I had to wait until you were almost asleep before you'd be receptive. Micah kept telling me off, saying it was too exhausting for me . . . but I knew I'd get through eventually.

I'm afraid to move in case I break something.

Oh, you can move now that I've got you. It was making the initial connection that was hard. Fun, isn't it?

Fun?

Now that you mention it, yes.

So how are things? I understand you and Fiona are to be congratulated.

Don't start, please. I don't ever want to hear you say . . .

I told you so? Okay, I won't. Listen Finn, I can't keep this up indefinitely. Despite what I told Micah, it is quite draining after a while. He watches me like a hawk now with . . . Anyway, I have some news you need to know. I only found out a few days ago.

What news? What was it she was hiding? Why did she keep starting to say something and then change the subject?

Wonderful news and terrible news. Bishop McCauly has been rescued. I don't know how or who did it – but he's finally out

369

of prison. I've no idea where he is. Selar's in a rage about it and Eachern has been charged with finding McCauly. Unfortunately there's nothing I can do to stop him.

But surely you must have some influence over him?

Only a little – and I have to use most of that to stop him from throwing Micah out. Besides, I'm back at Elita at the moment and Eachern is out roaming the countryside. But that's not the only news.

Why was Jenn back at Elita? Tell me.

Kenrick has been found. He'll be reunited with Selar in a couple of days . . .

Serin's breath!

I've heard no word about the Queen but I fear the worst.

And the Princess? Samah and Kandar?

Nothing. I dare not ask. I'm hoping to get some word to your mother soon as she may have heard from Duke Kavanagh what happened. Fortunately there's been no mention of where Kenrick was found, so I can only hope the whole thing is still secret.

Gingerly, Finnlay sat up with his back against the board. He reached out in the darkness and drew a candle closer, waving his hand to bring the flame to life. Then he clasped his hands before him and took a deep breath. *Are you all right?*

Me? Of course. Why shouldn't I be?

Well, I was just wondering why this should be such a drain on you. You're easily as powerful as Robert. I can't imagine why mindspeech – even over this distance – should make you tired. From what you've said about it before, it doesn't work like other powers. I believe you said it sidestepped your normal powers.

Silence.

Well?

It was uncanny; he could almost hear her thinking.

Jenn?

Her voice was subdued but he could still hear it clearly. *I'm quite well, Finn, I promise you. Do you doubt Micah's ability to look after me?*

I wouldn't dare – I know what he's like.

Then you mustn't doubt my . . .

You're pregnant! Finnlay bit his lip instantly and held his breath, waiting for her answer.

Yes. But please don't tell anyone just yet.

Why not? When is it due?

In about two weeks. Her voice was still subdued – even though he'd guessed the truth. *Unless* . . .

By the gods!

The baby is Robert's, isn't it?

Finnlay! How can you suggest such a thing? Suddenly the subdued voice was gone. Almost frantic now, Jenn continued, *I don't know* . . .

Then it is Robert's. Sweet Mineah! The Bonding! So it was all true. Does he know? Does anyone?

There was a silence which stretched so long Finnlay began to wonder if she'd deserted him. Then, *I believe Micah knows, though he's never said a word about it. Unlike some people, he's far too discreet to mention it to my face.*

Discreet! Jenn, what are you talking about? Don't you realize the prophecy has just taken its first step forward? Don't you understand what that means? If Robert was unable to withstand the Bonding then he'll . . .

By the gods, Finnlay Douglas – I don't give a damn about the prophecy! I'm talking about people's lives here. I must have your oath on this: You must never tell anyone.

Well, of course I wouldn't tell anyone outside the Enclave . . .

No one at all. Ever. There was a brief pause. *Especially not Robert.*

But he must know! You have no idea how he's longed for a child of his own. After Berenice died he'd convinced himself that he would never . . .

Finnlay. I want you to listen carefully. You must never tell Robert that this child is his. Firstly, you'd endanger the life of the child itself should Robert ever let on to Eachern. Secondly, you have no idea of the damage you would do to Robert. He'd never be able to forgive himself for leaving me here to marry Eachern. I must have your word on this, Finn. Please, don't make me threaten you.

But are you sure it is Robert's baby? I mean, this is not the time to be making guesses.

There was a long pause, which ended with, *I can sense its aura, Finn. There's something very powerful there, but also something very familiar. I kept hoping . . . but . . . I can't describe it. You'll just have to take my word for it.*

And you will tell Robert? One day?

I don't know. Perhaps. As it is, I doubt I'll ever get the chance.

The weight of understanding hit Finnlay. Now it all made sense. It hadn't been Selar that had driven Robert away, it had been Robert's failure to withstand the Bonding he'd tried so hard to deny. That's why he'd gone and that's why he wouldn't come back.

Subdued himself now, Finnlay replied, *You know he's in love with you, don't you?*

That's not the problem, Finn. It never has been. But how did you know?

The same way you knew how I felt about Fiona. I'm not all thick. I'm sorry, Jenn. I'm sorry it's worked out this way.

There's no point in being sorry about things we can't control. But you must promise never to repeat this to anyone.

Very well, I promise. I just hope you have the opportunity to tell my brother about his child one day.

I must go, Finnlay. I can sense Micah pacing up and down in front of me. If I don't cut the connection soon, he'll do it for me. I'll try calling you again tomorrow night after you've had a chance to pass on the news about Kenrick and McCauly to the council.

I suppose I won't be able to initiate contact?

I doubt you will for a while. This thing takes a bit of practice – it even took Robert a while. To be honest, I wasn't even sure I could speak to you in the first place. I think, though, that mindspeech has something to do with Bonding. That's why I can talk to Robert and why I could contact you in prison at Kilphedir. Doing it over this distance was the hard part. Take care, Finnlay – and remember your promise. I'll speak to you tomorrow night.

And with that she was gone.

McCauly free at last. Kenrick returned to his father, with no word of the others.

And Robert would be a father in about two weeks – and never know anything about it . . .

. . . and Finnlay would be an uncle. Margaret would be a grandmother! By the gods, if only he could tell them!

Wait a moment.

Finnlay strode across the bedroom and pulled open the door. With quick strides he reached the fireplace and tossed some logs into the pit. He raised his hand to spark the fire, but paused.

This child would be Robert's child – a Douglas, even if he never knew it.

But it would also be a Ross.

. . . and if it was a boy . . .

Sweet Mineah! If it was a boy . . . then . . .

He couldn't form the words, not even silently. It was too tenuous, too terrifyingly close to reality. There was still two weeks before the child would be born and anything could go wrong between now and then. Why curse it by confronting the possibilities now? Especially when . . .

What if Carlan knew about Jenn's condition? Would he see her as suddenly vulnerable? Was that why Jenn had gone back to Elita? She would be safer there than at Clonnet.

Hell!

Jenn was in danger and she knew it. But Finnlay could do nothing about it. There was only one person who could fight the Angel of Darkness.

Damn him! Why had Robert gone missing now, when he was so needed?

Of course, because of the Bonding. Robert must have been devastated with his failure. What was it he'd said? He refused to have anything to do with the prophecy because he knew what would happen. He knew how it would end.

And how did he know? Because the Key had told him, twenty years ago. But had it told him he would have a child? Probably not. Definitely not. No, Robert had said time and time again that what the Key had told him was dangerous. So what could be dangerous about the Bonding, and was the baby a part of that, and if that wasn't dangerous, then what was it Robert was hiding? Had he gone again because he now believed he was incapable not only of preventing some parts of the prophecy – but *all* of it? The dangerous part, too? But surely he was strong enough to withstand . . .

Finnlay's eyes widened and he stopped breathing completely.

No . . .

'By all that's holy, I can't be right!' Finnlay sank to the floor as though his legs had lost their will. 'Oh, Robert, I know what the Key told you. How could we have been so blind?'

But it had been so simple a thing to miss in all the fuss about the prophecy. All that time trying to work out why there would be a prophecy in the first place and where it had come from. All that going back and forth over silly things like the relationship between the House Marks and sorcery and whether the Key would ever tell them where the Calyx was and whether Carlan would destroy them all to lay his hands on something that had been promised him centuries ago—

And never once had they guessed what Robert was hiding.

Not a prophecy alone, no. Something infinitely more dangerous and terrifying.

And in trying to escape it, Robert had unwittingly left Jenn in danger from an adversary only he could face.

Finnlay straightened up, leaving his gaze on the fireplace. 'Robert, my dear brother, I think it's time you stopped running from your destiny.'

With that, Finnlay raised his hands, clapped them together and the fire burst into life. He turned to his writing desk with a wry smile. At least he now knew why he'd had so much trouble sleeping.

27

Jenn opened her eyes to find Micah leaning over her with a cup of strong, sweet brew in his hand. He was also wearing a frown.

'How do you feel?'

She took the cup and swallowed deeply. The hot liquid burned her throat and she would rather have had wine, but Micah wouldn't allow it. He'd once said that his mother had drunk neither wine nor ale while she was with child and had managed to successfully bring a huge brood of young Macleans into the world without losing one. Jenn had had no choice but to bow to his directive.

'I feel fine, Micah, really.'

He pulled up a stool opposite her, but his gaze was still full of concern. 'You were gone so long. I take it you got through? To Finnlay?'

'Yes. I told him about McCauly and Kenrick.' The rest he had managed to guess all on his own. What else had he managed to work out without her help? Would he at least have the sense to keep it to himself until he could speak to her? She would have to ask him about it tomorrow night.

Jenn handed Micah the cup and levered herself to her feet. Her body was becoming more cumbersome by the day. At least she'd made it to Elita without any trouble. And tomorrow Bella would arrive – and probably fuss around her even more than Micah. Was it perhaps time to try Sealing Bella? She was here to help with the birth. Perhaps it would be safer if she did Seal her – who knew what might happen when the child made its way into the world.

The view from her old bedroom window had not changed. There was still the beautiful lake before her, the hills beyond and the forest hiding the ruins of the old mill – the place where she'd last seen Robert.

'Micah,' she began carefully. 'Finnlay knows the truth. He guessed and I couldn't really stop him, nor could I deny it.'

It was best that she not look at Micah. It would make it that much easier for both of them. 'I must ask something of you. Something I have no right to ask. Especially after everything you've done for me. You stayed with me when you would much rather have gone after him. I know you wanted to.'

'He asked me to stay with you. I was happy to.'

'I know – but now I must ask you something.'

Micah moved to stand behind her, but still she would not face him. 'What is it?'

'Promise me you'll never tell Robert the truth.'

Micah made no response: not a sound. Slowly, Jenn turned away from the window until their eyes met. 'You of all people should understand why I ask this, Micah.'

'And you of all people should know why I would not want to give my word.'

His voice was harsh, a tone Jenn had never heard from him before.

She swallowed hard before continuing. She didn't want to go on, but she had no choice. 'Believe me, Micah, I do understand how you feel. Do you think I want you to do anything to hurt him? Do you think I want you to keep such a thing from him? Do you think *I* want to? I know you serve him, Micah, and I know I have no right to ask this of you, but I must.'

Micah stared at her a moment and then glanced away, every movement reeking disapproval. Eventually he replied, 'I learned a long time ago that to serve him also meant to serve you. I'd hoped neither of you would ever ask me to divide my loyalties.'

'And I'd still never do that to you. I know how you miss him. I don't ask this for my sake, Micah. I ask it for his. He must never know.'

'But why?'

'Because . . .' Jenn almost faltered at this, still unsure and yet equally convinced. 'I can't tell you that. At least, not yet. I have to be positive I'm right. I promise I'll tell you when I know.'

Micah slowly turned away to the fireplace where the logs

376

had been laid but not yet lit. 'And if I say no? Would you place the same kind of Seal on me that you put on Eachern? Would you force me to comply?'

Sudden tears sprang into her eyes at this, at Micah's anguish. These months had been so hard on him, knowing the real reason for Robert's absence. And yet he'd been so very strong, a constant comfort. True to the last. He didn't deserve this. Not from her.

'No, Micah,' Jenn moved forward and touched his sleeve. 'I'd never force you to do anything against your will. If you'd rather not promise, then I will leave you to use your own judgement should Robert ever come back.'

'Did you extract such a promise from Finnlay?'

'Yes. I had to. I knew that if I didn't, he would blurt it out at the first opportunity.'

'But you would leave me to make my own choice?'

'Micah,' Jenn pulled on his arm, making him turn and face her. 'I trust you as Robert trusted you.'

Micah closed his eyes and nodded slowly. 'Yes, I know. I'm sorry. I guess I just ... well, it doesn't matter. It's your decision, Jenn, not mine. But please, don't ever expect me to lie to him because I won't – and that's as much for your sake as his.' With that, Micah reached out and squeezed her shoulder. Then he left her alone in the cool of the evening with only her thoughts for company.

'And this latest business only makes the situation more unsettled. For almost a year, we've had roving bands of soldiers searching for sorcerers, the Queen and now for the errant Bishop McCauly. Selar's mismanagement is costing the country a fortune.'

'Father, please,' Bella began, glancing at Jenn before continuing. 'I beg you to exercise a little caution with what you say.'

Jacob gazed down the dining table at her and sniffed. 'What? Are you now going to tell me I have spies in my household? Hah! I would have been arrested years ago and you know it. Why the sudden caution? You're no less a critic of our sovereign than I.'

Jenn put down her knife. She wasn't really hungry anyway, and she wouldn't feel comfortable trying to contact Finnlay later while sitting with a full stomach.

'I think what Bella is trying to suggest, Father, is that you can't tell whether any of Eachern's guards might be wandering around, listening in.'

Jacob attacked his dinner with more gusto than usual. 'Hell, Maclean has them well under control. There're only six of them. Come to think of it, I still don't understand why Dunlorn's man is now serving you. I always thought the two of them were inseparable.'

'I told you before, Father,' Jenn murmured, sipping mulberry juice, 'I asked him and he agreed. I'm lucky to have him.' And would be lucky to keep him after last night. Micah had been unusually quiet all day, spending most of the afternoon with Shane in the stables. What those two had to talk about for so long puzzled Jenn. Still, at least Micah had returned with some of his old humour in his eyes.

'The point is,' Jacob continued, 'all these patrols achieve is to make the people nervous. Nobody knows who to trust any more. Everyone is afraid they'll be reported for some little trifle – and be hauled up for treason.'

'But surely that will make hiding the Bishop all the harder?' Bella rose and refilled Jacob's cup with the sweet white wine Jenn loved so much.

'Not a bit of it. McCauly was always trusted. That was Selar's problem. The longer McCauly stayed in prison, the more people knew he could be trusted. Now that he's free they have someone to rally around.'

'Do you think McCauly is the sort of man to make an armed stand against Selar?'

Jacob picked up his wine cup and rolled it between his palms. 'No, not armed. He's no soldier. He's a man of peace – and a very clever man at that. I know him quite well. He married your mother and I.'

Jenn exchanged a surprised glance with Bella. Together they chimed, 'Really?'

'Yes,' Jacob said with a smile. 'He was newly ordained at the time, and had just finished writing one of his famous theological books. In his younger years he was considered one of the finest minds in the Church – which is surprising, considering his background. After the conquest, he kept his activities contained, staying put in that monastery down in Cean Airde. He did write more books, but they weren't widely distributed outside the Church. I tell you one thing about Aiden McCauly, he's very tough. I was never worried about him falling apart in prison. I'm not surprised he survived long enough to be rescued.

'But,' Jacob took a mouthful of wine and continued, 'I find I care less about it these days with the imminent birth of my grandson.'

'Oh, Father,' Bella laughed, 'you don't know it will be a boy.'

'Of course it will be a boy!' Jacob smiled at Jenn. 'What else would my Jennifer have? And when he's born I intend to do the Presentation myself, whether Eachern is here or not. No matter where his father has come from, your child, Jennifer, will be a Ross, descended from a line of Kings and heir to these lands. Tiege Eachern's title and lands were only given to him as reward for his efforts during the conquest. Their price was the blood of a thousand Lusarans. My grandson will have the touch of Kings on his forehead before that of a murderer.'

Bella frowned. 'And what if it's a girl? Will you still take the Presentation yourself?'

'Of course!' Jacob laughed. 'I've not done so badly with my girls so far, have I?'

Jenn had to smile. Jacob was irrepressible, and so very excited about the coming event. She opened her mouth to ask another question, but a sudden wave of tiredness swept over her and she drew in a deep breath to cover a yawn. Bella was not so easily fooled. 'I think it's time you were in bed. Come, I'll take you up.'

Jenn kissed her father goodnight and allowed Bella to help her up the stairs to her room. Once inside, Bella dismissed Addie and took great joy in restoking the fire and pulling back the covers on the bed while Jenn changed. She mumbled all the while about how things were never arranged as they should be, but Jenn was far from complaining. Once in bed, however, Bella did not leave her alone but sat beside her with the candle on her lap.

Jenn watched her for a moment, then clasped her hands together. 'What is it?'

'I suppose I could ask you the same question.'

'What does that mean?'

Bella played with the bed cover. 'You're too quiet. Even Father has noticed it. You are feeling well, aren't you?'

Jenn closed her eyes and turned her head away. 'Why is it that everyone is so concerned about this baby? I'm healthier than it's possible to be! I just wish everyone would stop asking!'

'I wasn't asking about the baby, Jenn,' Bella murmured gently. 'I was asking about you.'

Oh, yes indeed. Bella wanted to know how she was dealing with being married to Eachern, how she felt about living away in Ayr, how she felt about . . .

'I'm fine, Bella, really. I'm just tired. I'll be all right tomorrow.'

There was no response, but eventually Bella rose to her feet and kissed Jenn on the forehead. 'I'll be close by if you need anything.'

For a long time after the door closed Jenn stayed where she was. Why hadn't she told Bella the truth? Why hadn't she taken the opportunity to Seal her? Bella had come to her, offering comfort – and Jenn had turned away.

What was wrong with her?

Cursing silently, Jenn sat up. She pulled a shawl over her shoulders and went to the dressing room door. She knocked on it once, then took a seat by the fireplace. After a moment, Micah came in.

'Have you put a warning on the door?'

'No. There's no point. Once I'm talking to Finnlay I won't sense anyone approaching anyway. That's why I need you here.'

Micah didn't sit immediately. Instead, he stood by her chair. He had something in his hand. 'This arrived while you were at supper with your father. I think you should read it before you try contacting Finnlay. It's from Dunlorn.'

Jenn looked up sharply at that and took the letter from him. Her hands trembled trying to open it. Eventually she handed it back to him. 'I can't read it. What does it say?'

Now Micah sat opposite her, but he didn't need to read from the letter. 'Lady Margaret has had word from Kavanagh at Flan-har. The raid which rescued the Prince also brought about the death of the Queen.'

Jenn's hand flew to her mouth. 'Sweet Mineah!'

'The Princess, Samah and Kandar are safe and unharmed. Kavanagh is already moving them out of the country on a ship to the southern continent. He believes they'll be safe there.'

Jenn bit her lip and took in great gulps of air to try and control the tears which threatened to flow. The brave Queen – dead. Her sacrifice for nothing. Now Selar would bring the Prince up in his own image, just as Rosalind had always feared. There would be no stopping the son from becoming the monster the father was.

'There's more. From Kavanagh's description, I would guess those responsible were Malachi.'

Jenn gaped at him. 'But how can ... Malachi? Then *he* must have had something to do with it! Carlan – but what can he be interested in? Why would he bother getting the Prince back? It doesn't make any sense.'

'And yet Kavanagh swears the only way anybody could have got past his guards was by sorcery. He knows nothing about it, of course, but I've met him and he's not a fanciful man.'

Micah broke off before he could say anything more – but his expression spoke for him. If only Robert were around ...

Jenn shut her eyes tight against the sudden pain in her chest. She couldn't afford to give into it yet. There was still work to be done.

Without waiting, Jenn sent her thoughts across the night in search of Finnlay.

Jenn? Is that you?

Yes, Finn. It's me. How did it go?

Fine . . . What's wrong? You don't sound well.

There's nothing wrong with me. I've just heard some news about the Queen. She's dead, Finn – and Kavanagh believes it was Malachi who took Kenrick. You'll have to get the council to send someone to investigate. I don't think this is something we can let slide. If Carlan was behind the Prince's return, then we need to know about it – and why.

I agree – but I'll have to send a message back. I've left the Enclave.

Jenn's heart almost stopped. *You've what? Finnlay, are you mad? Where are you? What are you doing?*

So many questions. I swear you haven't changed a bit since I met you. There was laughter in Finnlay's mental voice, as though he were deliberately trying to lighten her mood, but she resisted.

Finnlay – you aren't going to do anything silly, are you?

Like what? I'm just on a little wander. I had a good long think after we spoke last night and a few interesting things occurred to me. Before you ask, I had the foresight not to discuss them with anybody. I just felt it was time I stopped sitting in apathy and watching things happen around me.

What are you doing?

Looking for Robert.

Jenn couldn't respond for a moment. Eventually she managed, *Where are you now?*

I'm camped at the foot of the Goleth. It took the whole day to get down. Tomorrow I'm heading towards Dunlorn. I fancy a visit to my mother on the way. I want to introduce her to Fiona. It will be a short visit if I'm to find my brother before the month's out. After I've had a good look around, I might come and see you, if you're still at Elita. Tell Micah to keep an eye out for me.

Jenn couldn't say anything. In one short breath, everything had moved past her so fast she couldn't keep up. *Finnlay . . . please be careful.*

Of course – and I have Fiona along to keep me in line. Don't worry. With any luck, I'll be with you in time to see my nephew born. Was there anything else?

No. Just take care. I'll call you in a week at about the same time. As you get closer, you might try calling me back. I'll listen for you.

Goodnight, Jenn.

Goodnight, Finnlay.

She took a deep breath in the ensuing silence and opened her eyes slowly. Micah was watching her expectantly. For some reason, Jenn found it suddenly difficult to speak. She opened her mouth, but nothing came out – and tears began to flow down her cheeks, unbidden. Instantly, Micah was at her side, kneeling. He reached out and took her hand.

'What is it?'

'Finnlay's left the Enclave to go looking for Robert.' Jenn gulped in another breath. 'By the gods, I hope he succeeds!'

28

Thunder rolled across the sky, among clouds invisible in the night. Finnlay could hear rain on the other side of the forest, but so far the little shelter he'd built had remained untouched by the downpour. He didn't mind the rain – but he did mind the waiting. Fiona had been gone for hours now and although she wasn't exactly late, she would be soon.

Impatient, he got up once again and adjusted the cover over the huge pile of wood he'd collected during the day when he'd had nothing better to do. Then he peered among the dark trees, trying to see if she was out there moving towards him. He didn't dare Seek her. That was how Carlan had found him in the first place.

Carlan. Was Jenn right? Had he been responsible for returning Kenrick to Selar? The whole country was afire with the story – though it seemed Rosalind's fate was unknown. Of course, Selar would hardly go about announcing that he'd had his own wife murdered. Jenn's last call a few days ago had given him no further news and he'd forbidden her to talk long because she was now so close to her time.

'You never did have a very good sense of direction, Finnlay Douglas.'

Finnlay whirled around to find Fiona approaching from the other side of the forest, carrying bundles under her arms and drenched to the skin. 'But I could have sworn . . . Oh, it doesn't matter. Here give me those.'

He brought her under the shelter and dropped the bundles, turning quickly to build up the fire before she could get cold. He took her cloak from her and threw his own dry one over her shoulders.

'I don't see much point in me trying to get dry. The rain is heading this way and we'll both be drowned before the night's out.'

'No we won't,' Finnlay smiled, taking a seat by the fire. 'This shelter is very strong, you know.'

'Well, we'll see.' Fiona collected one of the bundles and unwrapped the cloth. She passed him a hard brown roll and a piece of flat cheese. 'I'm sorry there's not more. There's been a garrison stationed in the town for a few weeks and they absorb most of the available supplies.'

'A garrison? And you still stayed all day?'

'Calm down, Finnlay,' Fiona soothed, 'I was in no danger. Who's going to know me?'

'Well, did you find out anything?'

'Yes and no.' She paused to take a sip of the brew Finnlay handed her, then continued, 'The major topic of conversation is still Kenrick's miraculous return – but in the quieter moments, people are talking about McCauly.'

'And what are they saying?'

'Mostly that they're glad he's free. They expect things to change for the better now – though how they work that out is a mystery to me. There's one thing I heard, however, that I find quite disturbing. If it's true, then we could be in a lot of trouble.'

'What's that?'

'I heard it twice – and that was because I was hidden and eavesdropping. The whisper is that McCauly's release was somehow brought about by your brother.'

'By the gods!'

384

Fiona said, 'Yes, that's what I thought. Do you think it's possible?'

Finnlay sat back and shook his head. 'I don't know. It doesn't seem likely. I mean, Robert could have done something about McCauly a long time ago. He's always blamed himself for McCauly being arrested in the first place.'

'And there was always that rumour that Robert had helped Rosalind escape. These people think that Kenrick was returned because Robert was busy getting McCauly out of prison.'

Pursing his lips, Finnlay stared into the fire. 'I suppose there's always a chance that Robert might have done something – but I would have guessed in his current frame of mind it would be most unlikely.'

'Then you still think we'll find him?' Fiona was watching him carefully, and carefully, Finnlay replied.

'It might take a long time, but yes, I'm convinced he's still in Lusara. I think that's the penance he'll make himself pay.'

'Penance? For what?'

Finnlay smiled abruptly to cover the mistake. 'For whatever crime he feels he's committed. Now we're so close to Elita, I don't see much point in you trying to Seek him tonight. Have a rest instead and we'll start again after we've seen Jenn.'

Fiona folded her arms. 'I don't know how you expect me to find Robert. You're far stronger than me – and if he's shielding, I won't have a hope of locating him. Others have been trying this for months, Finn. Why do you think I'll have any more luck?'

With a smile, Finnlay shifted closer to her and put his arm around her shoulders. 'I just have a feeling about it, that's all.'

'Well, feeling or not, this is getting harder every day. There are just as many patrols to dodge now that McCauly's missing as there were with the Queen's disappearance. We can't keep this up for ever. One day somebody is going to recognize you and then what will you do? Hell, it's not even safe for Churchmen to travel any more.'

'What do you mean?' Finnlay stiffened.

'Oh, some priest has been arrested by the Guilde. I saw them taking him to the garrison as I was leaving town. An old man.'

'You saw him?' Finnlay sat upright. 'What did he look like?'

Fiona frowned at his sudden urgency. 'Short, almost completely bald. A round face, kindly, I suppose.'

Scrambling to his feet, Finnlay strode out of the shelter and stared into the forest as though he could see as far as the town. 'Hilderic.'

'Yes. How did you know his name?'

'Archdeacon Hilderic. You remember a few weeks ago Father John sent a courier to say that Hilderic had gone on a mad quest to Mayenne? The Guilde must have found out and arrested him for treason. Fiona, we must do something!'

Fiona grabbed his arm and pulled him around to face her. 'What can we do? You dare not show your face in public – even in disguise.'

He gazed at her a moment, his mind racing. Then he turned swiftly to the clearing and lifted the first saddle at hand. 'We'll leave the horses on the edge of the forest. I'll put a blanket on the pack horse. If anything goes wrong, head straight for Dunlorn. Don't stop for a moment. My mother will help you. Tell her to hide Hilderic. Deverin will know when it's safe to move him. Trust him. He trained Robert. He knows what he's doing. If things get too difficult, you may have to take Hilderic to the Enclave.'

'Finnlay, stop!' Fiona strode towards him and tore his hands away from the saddle. 'This is mad! How can you rescue this priest? You'll be captured yourself! I won't allow this.'

Finnlay dropped the saddle and took her hands in his. 'My love, I have no choice. Hilderic will die if we don't get him out now. The time for waiting is over. We can't afford to sit back any longer. We have to do something – and now. Hilderic will be easier to rescue here than if they take him to the dungeons of Marsay. You know that.'

Fiona's eyes grew flinty and hard. 'I can't stop you, can I?'

'No. But you can help. Stay with the horses and take care of Hilderic. If all goes well, we'll have breakfast together.'

'And if it doesn't?'

She was hiding her fear well, but not so well he couldn't see it. He leaned down and kissed her cheek gently. 'I survived my encounter with Carlan. I lead a charmed life. If we get separated, I'll go to Elita first, then see you back at the Enclave. Now, we'd better pack up.'

Nash leaned back in his chair, planted his elbows on the arms and steepled his fingers together. The tent was very well lit, but the four tall lamps in each corner also made the air thick with heat. The guards on either side of the door were already sweating and even DeMassey, standing at his side, wiped his hand across his brow to remove the moisture.

Nash felt no such discomfort. If he had, he would certainly have had better sense than to show it to the prisoner before him. The old priest was on his old knees, his hands bound in front of him. His face was fixed straight ahead, looking neither left nor right.

'You're a fool, Archdeacon,' Nash breathed. 'How could you, with so many years at court behind you, truly believe you could make your own private embassy to Tirone without anyone knowing about it? Eh? Did you really think you could just wander back home and have no one the wiser?'

Hilderic didn't answer. His jaw was firmly shut, the muscles of his cheeks taut against temptation.

'I could make you speak, Father, really I could – but is there any point? Would you tell me something I didn't already know? My spies at Tirone's court have already informed me of how you went to plead with our sovereign's brother to free the traitor McCauly. I was also told how you clumsily hinted at Selar's plans to invade Mayenne. I was even told how upset you were when Tirone turned you down.'

Nash leaned forward now, his eyes fixed on Hilderic's. 'Have you any idea how upset the King will be when he hears what you've done? When he hears what Tirone has done? Have you any idea how upset I am?'

'I care not for any Guildesman,' Hilderic spat.

Instantly Nash was out of his chair and standing on the ground before him. 'But I'm not just any Guildesman, priest. You will understand that all too well, soon. Just before I order your execution.' Nash gestured to the guards. 'Take him away. Tie him to his tent post at throat and foot. If he moves in the night, let him strangle himself.'

The guards came forward and dragged Hilderic to his feet. The old man did not struggle as they took him away. Nash turned to face DeMassey.

'You're not really going to let him die, are you? What will your precious King say?'

'I don't really care,' Nash said. 'I can't see Selar being too upset. He's always despised Hilderic – and now that the meddling fool has warned Tirone of the coming war, Selar will loathe him even more. By Broleoch's breath, how can we invade now that Tirone is moving troops to cover the border?'

DeMassey strolled forward and delicately removed the Guilde cloak from his shoulders. He draped it carefully over the back of the chair and straightened his richly embroidered jacket with hands gleaming with rings. 'There are ways around such things. It just means you'll have to wait a while longer. My men will deal with it.'

'You mean those that aren't already within the ranks of the Guilde? I'm surprised you have so many at your beck and call. Is there anyone left at home?'

DeMassey grinned. 'Plenty. As many as we need. So, what do you plan to do with the priest?'

'Well, dead or alive, he's already been useful. I'm glad my men had the sense to inform me the moment Hilderic was caught on the border. By now half the country will have heard about his arrest. Hilderic would hate it, but he could be instrumental in the return of McCauly – but I don't have time for any more of this tonight.'

'Oh? Have you a more pressing engagement?'

Nash glanced at the handsome young Malachi. The light of speculation was there in his eyes. Nash was almost sorry to disappoint him. 'The King is due here any minute. He's on his way back to Marsay. Having paraded his heir around the country, he's anxious to do the same at the capital.'

'Ah,' DeMassey smiled. 'I see. So you do have a more pressing engagement. It is to be tonight, then?'

'Yes. I won't get another chance for a while. While I'm with Selar, I want you to keep an eye on the boy. He's my key to controlling the father. Make sure nothing happens to him.'

'Of course,' DeMassey nodded. 'Anything you say, Governor.'

Finnlay kept to the shadows cast by torches scattered through the camp. There was no moon, favouring his intent. After the onslaught of rain an hour earlier, he was cold and wet and no longer entirely sure this was such a good idea.

Keeping to his hiding place, Finnlay scanned what little of the camp he could see without moving. He had his *ayarn* out and was ready to pull together a Mask if needed, but there were few people about. At this late hour and in this weather, just about everyone of the hundred or so Guilde soldiers were either out on patrol or in their beds, dry and warm. There would be no better opportunity for the rescue. But he would have to wait a little longer, until Hilderic's tent was completely quiet and empty of everyone but the ancient priest. Then all Finnlay had to do was slip into the tent, cut the bonds and slip out again with Hilderic in tow. It was only a hundred yards between the camp and the forest – he could carry the old man if he had to. And if there were any problems, he could send Hilderic on towards Fiona and stay here himself to Mask their escape.

Yes. No problem at all.

He settled back into the shadows and gripped his *ayarn* hard against the uncontrollable trembling.

Despite the evening's bad news, Nash had to smile. Selar was stretched out on the bed, his eyes closed and his wrist laid bare. Blood seeped from the shallow wound Nash had made and each drop drew the King closer to a complete and permanent Bonding. He would do anything Nash told him to do. After tonight, even if Osbert failed to discover the library's whereabouts, Nash would find a way to use Selar's authority. He'd pull the Guilde Hall down stone by stone if he had to.

Nash rested back on his heels and closed his eyes, trying to conserve his energy. This would almost drain him. But he had plenty of time to recover. He would rest here a while and then gather his men and make steady progress towards Marsay. He would give Selar a week of peace with his son before Nash returned to start work. Very generous, when he thought about it . . .

What . . . was that . . . ?

Familiar . . . and very close.

Nash's eyes snapped open. The Enemy! Here. In his camp. What the hell was he doing here? Nash had to move. He had to get out there and find him. But if he left Selar now—

No. It was done as much as it would ever be done. The Bonding would hold as long as Nash would need it.

Moving swiftly, Nash bound up Selar's wrist and quickly absorbed the blood on his ring. Then he stood and threw a cloak over his shoulders. He strode out of the tent and into almost total darkness. Only a few guards patrolled the area, saluting as they saw him.

Calling two men to follow him, Nash ran the length of the camp to the tent where Hilderic was being held. The guards outside were startled at his appearance, but he didn't stop. He tore the door open to find the tent as empty as he'd suspected.

But the Enemy was still close. He could feel it.

He dashed around the back of the tent to find a huge rip in the cloth, and footprints of two men in the mud. Calling out to the guards to follow him, Nash ran into the darkness. Douglas was not going to get away this time. He would be alone, with the old man slowing him down. This time, Nash would kill him.

Finnlay struggled desperately to get Hilderic to move faster, but hours of imprisonment had left the man's legs numb.

Then, before they were even halfway to the forest, Finnlay heard the shout. The escape had been discovered.

'Go on,' Finnlay hissed, 'as fast as you can. Fiona is straight ahead. She'll get you to safety.'

Hilderic grabbed his arm. 'But what about you?'

'Just go!' Finnlay almost pushed him, then turned back towards the camp. He had to get the guards to move away from where Fiona was hiding. He ran forward a little until he could just see the outline of figures moving towards him, then darted off to his right. Another shout from behind and he knew they were following him, not Hilderic.

Finnlay kept running, stumbling downhill on the thick grass. Behind the garrison he could see the lights of Calonburke. If he could get close enough, perhaps he could lose himself in the back streets.

With his lungs fit to burst, he scrambled into the shadows of the first building he came to. From the smell, it was a stable. He chanced a glance over his shoulder. Four – no, five men following him, that was all. At least for the moment. He didn't wait any longer. He kicked in the door of the stable and ran along the stalls until he found a huge, powerful stallion. He didn't have time for the niceties of a saddle. He just grabbed the horse's halter and pulled it out of the stall. He got as far as the door.

'At last, Enemy!' came a voice from the darkness. 'Like a fool, you've come right back to me – and this time, you won't get away.'

And then Finnlay could feel it. The same reeking stench of evil he'd learned to fear. Carlan.

Yes, he had been a fool, but he didn't have time for lengthy reflections now. He had to get away before the monster could get hold of him again. Without speaking, Finnlay let go of the horse and drew his sword.

'I doubt even you will be able to fight your way out of this, Finnlay Douglas. Go on,' Carlan urged his men, 'kill him.'

Finnlay could hardly see a thing in the darkness. There were just shapes and movement. He heard a rush of air and brought his sword up to block the blow. Twisting around before another could close in, Finnlay pushed the man back, then sliced across his waist. Another immediately filled his place, striking Finnlay before he could bring his sword to bear. Pain tore down his left shoulder and he stumbled forward.

'Now move in and kill him!'

Carlan's voice was enough on its own to make Finnlay move. He straightened up at the same time as he swung his sword diagonally across, striking both men at the same time. One fell to his knees, but the other pressed in closer, exchanging blows with Finnlay that made him shudder to his bones. He was cut again, a stab to his thigh. And again, a ringing stroke to his head, just above his eye. Blood poured, blinding him on that side. He struck out again, stumbling over his feet. The horse behind him reared up, screaming at the smell of blood. Finnlay took one more shot, cutting the sword from the soldier's hand. He roared in agony and fell back. But there was still another to replace him.

And behind him stood the Angel of Darkness.

Finnlay's breath was coming in gasps now, but every moment he fought bought that much more time for Fiona and Hilderic. If she did as she was told, they would be on their way towards Dunlorn now, far beyond the reach of this monster.

Steel clashed against steel as Finnlay struggled with the last of his strength to hold off the attacker. He was pushed back further and further, towards the horse. He could feel it stamping with fear. If he were not careful, the animal would finish the job these Guildesmen had begun. He danced out of the horse's path and felt his enemy's blade slice across his right shoulder. The agony was intense. He was finished. He had only one chance left.

Gathering all his fading strength, he took one mighty swing with his sword, making all his injuries scream out together. The soldier stumbled and fell and Finnlay swung again, cutting his throat. Without pausing, Finnlay turned to the horse and leaped on to its back. He kicked hard and the animal reared, springing forward into the street. It reared again – right in the face of Carlan.

The Angel bellowed and raised his hands to fend off the horse. One hoof clipped him as it came down, and then Finnlay was off riding through the town.

'Are you sure about this?' DeMassey demanded as Nash swept by him. 'I can't believe he'd be fool enough to come out of hiding to rescue a mere priest.'

Nash didn't wait to explain. He pulled his bloody shirt from his back and grabbed a fresh one from Lisson. His head hurt like hell and he was in no mood to be argued with. If it hadn't been for his Bonding Selar that night, he would have blasted Finnlay Douglas into tiny little pieces even his own mother wouldn't recognize.

'Look, I don't have time for this. I have to get after him. Go and recall the patrols. Keep the King's guard out of it. Tell them it's Guilde business only. I don't want them getting in the way. Most of my men here are Malachi anyway. Have them saddle up and be ready to move out by dawn. The Enemy will have only a few hours' start on us. In the meantime, I have to get some food into me so I can risk Seeking him, now, before he can get too far. Once I know in which direction he's heading, I'll be able to find him anywhere.'

Nash stopped in the middle of the tent, a fresh jacket in his hand. 'Well, don't just stand there. Go. Get them moving. You stay behind with the King. Follow him to Marsay and don't even dream of doing anything until I return.'

Finnlay rode blindly into the night. The horse, fired by fear and the smell of blood, galloped without his help. The pain was enormous, overwhelming. He could do nothing to stop the blood flowing from his wounds. His left eye was completely shut now and his right was filmed. Dazed and drifting more as each moment went by, Finnlay put all his concentration into steering the horse in one direction. If he could just get to some shelter, he would be fine.

And yet, all he could think of was that moment when the horse had reared at Carlan. Finnlay had finally seen the face of his tormentor. In one brief second, that face had been

393

dusted in light, turned in fury towards him. It was a face he would never forget: one he knew better than his own.

Robert's face. Just like the nightmares that had plagued him for weeks after his escape from Carlan.

He rode on, kicking the horse with the last of his strength when it would have stopped to rest, across fields and streams, until he came to a wood spread down the slope of a hill. It was familiar enough to give him hope, and hope gave him the energy he needed to go the last distance. Then he saw the lake and the castle beyond.

Blindly now, Finnlay urged the horse onwards, hardly able to stay on its back. He clutched at the mane, falling forward with every step.

Jenn? Jenn, by the gods, you must hear me!

Finnlay? Where are you?

And then he was there, by the garden wall. He brought his leg over the back of the panting horse and slid to the ground. How long he lay there he couldn't guess, but after a while, there were faces over him. One of them was Micah.

Nobody asked him questions. They merely lifted him and carried him inside. For a few minutes he drifted in and out of a blackness so deep he wanted to drown in it. Then he could see some light through his remaining good eye. A shape above him, that looked like the roof of Elita's hall. Then Jenn's face close to his.

'In the name of the gods, Finnlay, what happened?'

'Finnlay? What's this?' another voice called across the hall. A voice older and rasping. 'By all that's holy, Daughter, what's going on here?'

'Father . . .'

It was Jacob, and he didn't give Jenn a moment to explain. 'So it was all a lie, was it? He wasn't dead and you knew all along? All those stories about sorcery were true – don't try and deny it! Your life here has been one long lie and I've had enough.' Jacob paused only to draw breath, his voice dead of any warmth. 'Stay here until your child is born. Then you will leave. From this day forward you are no longer my daughter.'

'Father . . .'

But Jacob was gone and Jenn, her eyes full of tears, bent over Finnlay again. 'Finn, you must tell me what happened.'

Struggling with the last of his strength, Finnlay managed a whisper. 'It's the Angel of Darkness, Jenn. I'm sorry. You need to . . .'

But even as he tried to tell her, to warn her, darkness folded in around him and he sank into its depths.

29

Had the world always been this big?

How much of it had he travelled since they'd come for him? How long ago was it – four days, a week? Sleeping in snatches both day and night and riding at a gallop in between had robbed him of all sense of time. No – two years in prison had done that already. That and much more. It was dark now, but how late? Midnight? Near dawn?

His two companions rode beside him in silence. Now and then they would glance in his direction to make sure he was awake. Their faces were grim and determined, unknown to him. They were only his couriers. But he had known the men who'd rescued him. They'd not passed the job to someone else. Payne and McGlashen, heroes both – and the young priest who'd helped them. Even now he could conjure up the memory of terror as they had brought him out of his cell, the silence, the footsteps, the breathless escape – a seemingly impossible task, and yet, they'd survived. A miracle, surely – and every day since he'd prayed they'd not been discovered for their crime.

'Not far now, Bishop.' The man to his left raised his hand and pointed at the mountainside.

They were travelling along a cart track, steep in places and treacherous with ice. They were surrounded on all sides by bleak shadows, mountains glowing with layers of late spring snow, unyielding to the seasons.

'Where are we?'

'The north-eastern tip of the Goleth range. Ahead is the Abbey of Saint Germanus. Do you know it?'

'No. I mean, yes, but I've never been here before.'

The man nodded. 'Good. That's what my lord was hoping. We'll leave you there, in good hands, I'm told.'

As they reached the top of a rise, welcoming lights appeared in the darkness. His friends stopped before the open gate and waited until he'd dismounted. Then, with a wave of farewell, they turned, taking the horse with them. They didn't even wait for him to say thank you. Nevertheless, he sent a brief prayer after them.

'Bishop McCauly?'

He turned with a start. Before him stood a man his own age holding a single lamp. The man was alone. 'I'm Father Chester, Abbot of this house. Welcome. Please come inside where it's warm. There are no soldiers here; we were searched yesterday. I promise you, Your Grace, it is quite safe.'

For a moment, Aiden couldn't move. So many days on the run had dulled his senses. Was this monk true? Was this safety?

Chester reached out gently and, with a smile, took Aiden's arm. 'Please, come inside. You have friends here.'

'Father Abbot I . . .' Aiden took a breath and clasped his frozen hands together. 'Thank you. But I beg you, do not call me by my title.'

Chester smiled again. 'Of course, Father. Come.'

Brother Damien shifted his bundle from one arm to the other and resumed the path along the edge of the orchard. Only here was the hard ground to be seen, between the lanes of apple and peach. And only here was there any sign that spring had even arrived. On the slopes above the abbey, snow still lay on the ground between the rows of grape vines. If this frost didn't end soon, the harvest would be painfully small this year.

He waved a greeting to Hob, who tended the orchard, then proceeded to the edge of the kitchen garden. Lifting his cassock, he stepped over the low wall and nimbly trod his way between rows of crisp soil, recently turned in preparation for the spring planting. He should have walked around the perimeter to get to the cloister, but he preferred to feel the earth beneath his sandals rather than the hard stone of the path.

'Good morning, Martin,' he called cheerily, waving a hand even though he knew the man wouldn't look up.

'Good morning, Brother Damien.'

Martin wore no shirt as he dug the turf at his feet, even though it was still blisteringly cold. His exertions kept him warm.

Damien gained the cloister and kicked the mud from his sandals before turning to his left. He went to the end of the square and climbed the staircase in front of him. Abbot Chester's room was at the top of the stairs. The door was open. 'You sent for me, Father Abbot?'

'Come in.'

Damien set his bundle to rest on the Abbot's desk. 'I found those books you wanted. They were way down the back of the storage room, hidden under a pile of old tally sheets. I don't know what they were doing there.'

'And good morning to you, Brother,' the Abbot replied gently. He stood with his back to the window and favoured Damien with a benign smile.

Damien came up short and smacked a hand over his mouth. 'Forgive me, Father Abbot. I did not mean to be discourteous.'

'Of course not.' Chester turned back to the window. 'I saw you cut through the garden, Brother. Did young Martin tell you off?'

Damien almost laughed at the thought. Martin wouldn't even tell the snails off for eating his cabbage leaves. 'No, Father.'

The Abbot was silent for a moment, then he glanced around. 'Brother Ormond believes Martin is simple. What do you say? You seem to be the only one among our brethren who can manage to get a word out of him.'

'Martin says very little to me beyond a greeting.'

'Which is more than anyone else gets – even me. Brother

Ormond was speculating as to whether Martin might be a spy for the Guilde.'

Damien's jaw dropped. 'Way out here? You've often said you think the whole world has forgotten about us. Why would the Guilde bother to send a spy here?'

Chester laughed softly. 'I didn't say I believed it myself.' The Abbot left the window again and came around the table. 'Brother Damien, I am about to ask you for your oath of silence. I have a delicate and sensitive job for one of your talents.'

'Of course, Father,' Damien swallowed. 'What can I do?'

'Come with me.'

The Abbot led him through the cloister to the oldest section of the monastery. There he turned down a narrow dark corridor and up a single flight of stairs. He knocked at the door and opened it to reveal a small room with one window covered by a thick curtain.

The Abbot addressed a man sitting on the bed in the corner. His face and everything else about him was in shadow. 'This is Brother Damien. He'll look after you until you're settled.' The Abbot turned with a smile to Damien. 'When he's ready, show him our monastery, anything he cares to see.'

'Yes, Father.'

It was four days before Damien could get his charge outdoors. By then, most of the snow had melted into slush and walking around the grounds was extremely difficult. The strange priest was mostly quiet and contemplative, but still managed to ask a lot of questions, not just about their work at Saint Germanus, but about his fellow brothers, the lay workers and the few folk from the town in the valley who bothered to climb the mountain to visit.

After that first time, Damien took him out every day. His companion seemed to revel in the open air and frequently stopped to look up at the sky, no matter the weather. Every time they went back to the cloister, however, the stranger would stop by the vegetable garden and watch the work being performed. It seemed he was just as entranced by the process of growing food from tiny seeds as Damien was.

Two weeks after he'd arrived, the stranger stepped over the garden wall to watch Martin digging another row of hard turf. The gardener ignored him, as he ignored everyone.

Martin stopped to take a drink from the flask he always left at the end of his row, but before he could reach it, the priest was there before him. He pulled off the stopper and held the flask out to Martin. The gardener glanced down at the flask and moved his hand to take it. Then the stranger spoke.

'My name is Aiden McCauly.'

Damien's heart leaped into his throat and beat like the wings of a hummingbird. Martin said nothing; he just took the flask, drank from it and tossed it back on the ground. Then, still without a word, he turned and resumed his work.

The stranger stood there a while longer, watching Martin with a calm face, then stepped back over the wall to join Damien. He patted Damien's shoulder and steered him towards the cloister. 'So now you too know who I am. Don't worry, I'm sure your Abbot gave me into your care because he knew he could trust you.'

Damien didn't dare speak until they were back in the priest's room. The fugitive Bishop immediately busied himself writing out a list of books which he handed to Damien.

McCauly was not exceptionally tall. He wore no monastical tonsure, but instead, his hair grew to his shoulders, light brown and flecked with a little grey. His build was sparse – no surprise considering how long the man had spent in prison – but his face was gentle and smiled well. Deep grey eyes picked out much detail in what he saw, while his fine hands were generally kept clasped together.

All in all, he was entirely unlike the figure Damien had thought the Bishop would be. Not that he'd imagined he would ever meet McCauly.

Damien took the list and glanced at it without reading. 'Forgive me, Father, but may I ask you a question?'

'Of course.'

'Why ... why did you reveal your identity to the gardener?'

'Why not?'

'But surely you must know the danger.'

'I wanted to see what his reaction would be.'

'Why?'

McCauly brought his hands together under his robe. With the greatest calm he replied, 'I wanted to know if anybody outside the Church still remembered me. Would you wake me for Prime, Brother? It's been a long time since I performed the orders of the day.'

McCauly turned back to his table once more, then paused. 'Do the lay workers usually attend mass?'

'Most of them.'

'And those who do not?'

'Well, Martin doesn't. He never has. He won't even go into the chapel.'

'Why not?'

'I don't know. He never really says anything.'

With a smile, McCauly nodded. 'I'd be grateful for those books.'

Long after the last monk had filed out of the chapel, Aiden remained in his seat. He didn't feel like praying – though the gods knew he had enough to pray for – it was just the sheer luxury of being able to sit in the house of the gods. How long would it be before he could do so openly? Even now, after these few weeks of freedom, he still watched each new arrival at the Abbey, scanned new faces for those he might recognize. The sound of a slamming door still sent a rush of fear through him, and some of the older rooms in the Abbey had the same damp smell his cell had acquired. He avoided going anywhere near them.

Such a little piece of freedom – but how sweet! To converse with monks and priests again, to be able to wander for as long as he cared, to be able to read whatever he wished ... To eat food – real food – again with relish, no fear of poison. The touch of the sun upon his face on some days felt like a kiss from the gods themselves.

And this was a good house, Saint Germanus. The people were good, the Abbot was good. McGlashen had chosen well. Now, if only Aiden could rid himself of his bad dreams, he could be well content – at least, as content as he could be having no knowledge of the safety of his rescuers. Surely if something had happened to them, word would come . . .

'Am I disturbing you?' Abbot Chester approached from behind and took a seat beside Aiden.

'I was just admiring your chapel.'

Chester nodded. 'Are you settled in? Do you have everything you need? Is Brother Damien looking after you?'

Aiden smiled. 'Very well indeed, for one so young.'

'And you? Are you well?'

Glancing aside, Aiden raised his eyebrows. 'By that, if you mean, have I recovered from my years of prison, then I must warn you I am unlikely to give you a good answer. I survive – and better so, each day. Much of it is due to you, of course.'

'Damien tells me you spend much time in the vegetable garden watching Martin.'

'I'm interested in the way he works.'

'Oh? How?'

'Each swing of the hoe or thrust of the spade is performed with exactly the same effort. He bends his back to the work, spending each day the same as the last, as though his only thought was to achieve perfection in digging the garden. In a way, his gardening is similar to the life of a monk – but the man never attends mass. He plies his devotion in a different manner to us.'

Chester gave a short laugh. 'I never thought of it that way. You know Brother Ormond has suspicions Martin might be a spy for the Guilde?'

'You think so?'

'You told Martin your name. Was that wise?'

Aiden came to his feet. 'If Martin had something to tell the Guilde he would have gone running off to do so the moment I told him. Has he been outside the Abbey grounds?'

'No.'

'Then you have your answer.'

Chester joined him and together they walked down the aisle towards the door. There Chester paused, ready to go back to his office. 'I suspect your faith is stronger than mine, Father.'

'Faith?' Aiden murmured, glancing up to the patch of blue sky he could see through a doorway. 'Interesting you should put it like that. I must thank you for the loan of Brother Damien. However, I think it's time he went back to his own duties. Would you thank him for me and tell him he's done a fine job.'

'Of course, Father.'

Aiden rose and washed as he did every morning. He attended Prime, bade the Abbot good day, then sat in the refectory and ate a light breakfast. After that, he headed for the garden, for the first time alone. Not that Damien had been even remotely akin to a guard, but the sense of freedom was all that more acute for the young monk's absence.

The sun was out for the second day in a row and the only snow visible now was that on the peak high above the monastery. With any luck, the sun would stay around now and give those poor trees a chance to bud.

The garden was empty.

With a frown, Aiden glanced around, but Martin was nowhere to be seen. On impulse, he headed for the orchard. He walked the whole length without seeing a soul. When he stopped, however, the sound of an axe against wood drew him deep into the rows of trees. He came to the end and found what he'd been looking for.

'Good morning, Martin,' Aiden smiled at the gardener as he hacked away at a thick row of berry bushes overgrown from the last summer.

As usual, Martin ignored him, so he found a fallen log to sit upon where the sun could warm his feet.

'Be careful of those thorns, there,' McCauly said after a moment. 'Even dead and dry, they can give you quite a cut.'

No response. Not even a hair turned in his direction. This was going to be much harder than he'd thought. 'Still, it's a good idea to cut them back at this time of year. They can take over a whole garden if you let them. I used to help my father when I was a young boy. He enjoyed working the land, just like you do.'

Martin swung the axe in a perfect rhythm, pausing only to pull at the branches as he freed them. He made a pile to Aiden's left which grew with every stroke.

'Of course, at that age, I had no idea I would find a vocation in the Church. People have asked me – but to be honest, I don't really know when the idea first occurred to me. I instantly rejected it, of course, and I didn't tell my father about it. He would have disapproved. Instead, I ran away to the coast and found a berth on the first ship to hand. For the next three years I scrubbed decks, climbed the mast and mended sails of a merchant ship plying the trade along the west coast. Then one day, while ashore at Ankar, I saw a face in the market crowd and immediately fell in love. She was the most exquisite creature I'd ever seen and I pursued her with all the fervour I could muster. I even missed the ship when it left. I got a job with a blacksmith and for a year I pounded steel and iron, trying to build up muscle and a small fortune with which to entice my love into marriage.'

Aiden paused and folded his arms across his chest. 'But as time went by, I found myself less interested in marrying her than I was in simply loving her. I never did actually ask her. I took my money and went back home, but somewhere along the journey I must have made a decision, because when I finally saw my father the first thing I said to him was, "I want to be a priest."'

With a sigh, Aiden continued, 'My father didn't wait for any divine sign, of course. He locked me in a room upstairs for a month, determined to change my mind. At the end he came up, unlocked the door and told me to go ahead and be a priest. Funny how things work out so opposite to what you expect.'

Martin had finished chopping the larger branches and now, with a scythe, began on the sharp spines which jutted out from the tops of the bushes.

Aiden went on, 'You know, becoming a priest was much

harder than I'd thought possible. So many years of study, so many years of serving my order, my superior, and yet all the while, I felt that I was doing the right thing, that I'd been born in the Church and that I should die in it. I rose every morning expecting to hate the hour and the cold and the interminable daily prayers – but I didn't. I loved it. Every minute of it. Right up until the moment they made me Bishop and I was imprisoned for it.'

Martin swung the scythe once more, but this time, into a thick branch where it stuck. Then he turned and strode right up to Aiden. Leaning close, Martin met his gaze with his usual calm – only this time it was touched with something harder. Then he spoke, his voice as sharp and hard as the blade he'd wielded.

'Leave me alone.'

With that, he turned and walked off through the orchard, leaving Aiden sitting on his log.

At first, Aiden couldn't work out what had woken him, then the bell rang again, over and over, and he almost fell out of bed. He grabbed the first robe to hand, shoved his feet into his sandals and rushed out of his room. In the cloister, he was nearly knocked over by monks rushing past him. He ran after them, ignoring the cold.

He got only as far as the orchard path before he realized what was wrong. The black night was lit up by the orange glow of a fire. The storeroom!

With a gasp of horror, Aiden ran to where the hastily woken monks were busily throwing pails of water from the stream over the nearest flames. They worked in lines, surrounding the building, handing the buckets along to be thrown against the heat. Aiden joined the nearest line and began working.

'Take another down there!' the Abbot bellowed over the roar of the fire. The stone building was already groaning with the heat. The whole effort looked to be futile.

As Aiden handed another pail to his neighbour, he chanced a look at the ancient storeroom, in time to see Martin emerge from the gaping door, a pile of manuscripts under his arm. He ran forward, coughing and gasping for air and dropped the papers. Without waiting, he spun around and ran back inside the burning building.

'What is he doing?' Aiden cried. 'He'll get himself killed!'

Martin was gone a long time. Then he emerged again, dodging a falling beam to bring more manuscripts out. Again he dumped them on his pile, just like he had with the berry bushes. Again he ran back inside. Voices called out to him to stop, but he either didn't hear or he ignored them.

Aiden couldn't stand there any longer. He handed the next bucket along, then left the line. The flames now rose high into the sky, illuminating the whole Abbey like a private sun on a summer's day. The lines fell back, unable now to reach the fire with their water. The monks waited at a distance, prepared to attack any spark that might ignite the buildings close by.

Martin had not returned. The building groaned again and another beam fell. Then he appeared and Aiden breathed again. He dashed forward to the pile of manuscripts in time for Martin to drop his next load. Before the young man could turn back again, Aiden's hand shot out and caught hold of his.

'Don't go. You'll be burned alive.'

Martin moved to snatch his hand away, but Aiden was not going to let go. 'I told you to leave me alone!'

Aiden hissed in a breath and held on as though his life depended on it. 'Robert! Don't do it.'

For a moment there was a flicker of something in the young man's eyes and then, as though he were swatting a fly, he snatched his hand from Aiden's grasp and turned back towards the fire. Aiden took another step forward. 'If you're going to die in there I won't let you die alone.'

A huge beam crashed to the floor at that moment, showering them both with flying embers. The man didn't move a muscle. Aiden threw his hands up against the sparks, then peered through his fingers. Robert remained, his shirt singed and black with smoke. Aiden waited behind him and watched. They both stood there for a long time, as though frozen against the searing heat. Then, without even a glance in his direction, Robert turned and walked away from the fire, disappearing from sight within seconds.

Aiden watched him go until he was dragged back to safety by the Abbot. 'Thank the gods you stopped him. I can't believe he risked his life for the sake of a few books. What did you say to him?'

Suddenly drained, Aiden wiped a hand across his brow. 'I called him a fool. He'll probably never forgive me.'

The light of dawn brought home to the whole community the extent of the terrible damage. The entire storeroom was gutted, leaving behind only four stone walls and a stinking pile of smoking ash. Aiden wandered among the smouldering mess with Brother Damien at his side. From time to time the young monk would bend down and turn over something promising, only to find the item destroyed beyond recognition.

A team of lay workers had already started cleaning up, but Aiden was loath to leave the place so soon. He could see the devastation on the faces of the monks who had fought the fire, on Damien's face too. Almost the entire history of Saint Germanus had been kept in this building.

'Tell me, Damien,' Aiden began, stepping over a smouldering beam, 'when did Martin first come here?'

'Well, it must have been autumn last year. He was certainly here before the first snow fell.'

'Do you know where he came from?'

'No. I asked once, but he didn't answer.'

Aiden frowned and glanced at him. 'Weren't you curious?'

'It's not unusual for a man to come to a monastery with a past he'd rather forget.'

'And what is Martin is trying to forget?'

Damien shrugged. 'I couldn't begin to guess.' He paused after a moment and took his eyes from the mess at his feet. He glanced over his shoulder at the others. 'We have almost one hundred monks here, Father, but not one of them got a word out of him. He just worked every day, without his shirt in the freezing cold, determined to do his penance.'

Damien lifted the edge of his habit above the black soggy

dust. Carefully he led Aiden out of the burned ruin to the muddy forecourt. 'That's why most men become lay workers. Some are quite willing to talk about their sins. Others not. Either way, we don't refuse their desire to pay recompense for their past sins.'

Aiden drew in a deep breath. This young monk would one day make a fine priest. 'Thank you for your insight, Brother.'

As he turned to go, Damien added, 'Do you think you can help Martin, Father?'

'I don't think he'll let me.'

Aiden walked alone back to the cloister. He wasn't surprised to find Martin – or rather, Robert – absent from the garden. After last night, it wouldn't be surprising to find the young lord had left Saint Germanus altogether. If he had, then Aiden was entirely to blame – but then, what else could he have done? Let the young man kill himself?

There was no point in trying to hide from himself. He'd handled the whole matter badly. Too many months in a prison cell had blunted his senses. Too many nights spent locked up in that damp place, too much time wasted. He'd forgotten how to talk to people, how to listen.

On instinct, Aiden sought out the peace of the chapel. He prayed for patience and wisdom, the same as always. He sat there a long time, long enough for his joints to start aching. Then, no closer to an answer, he left and wandered back to his room. As he passed the garden, he saw a familiar figure bend to the soil to plant a seed. A surge of relief swept through Aiden – but this time, he didn't stop and watch. This time, Aiden left Robert alone.

He took in a short breath, shuffled his hands along the axe hilt and leaned back. He lifted the blade, then brought it down with a mighty swing. It bit deep into the wood and he eased it loose again. Once more, he took in a breath, moved his hands and leaned back. He swung the axe and propelled it downwards with exactly the same force as the last hit.

Swing and chop, swing and chop. Over and over, the same movements, the same breath, the same balance. He ignored the jar as the blade struck the timber, the sun on his back and the sweat running down his brow. He watched only the log and the angle of the blade.

He thought of nothing but the task in hand. Nothing but the pitch and fall of the axe, the location of the next cut. He thought of nothing at all, just as he'd practised.

His mind silent, he bent his head and worked. Gradually the pile of logs grew beside him, stacked neatly with his own calloused hands. He worked away at the wood until his muscles began to shake with every strike and his breathing became heavy. When finally his body was beyond exhaustion, he stopped. His eyes remained on the ground, fixed on the wood chips and splinters. Then, with a sigh, he tossed the axe to one side and headed towards his bed.

Aiden picked up the book and glanced around his little room. For all that it was pleasantly presented – and there were no guards on his door – just being within four stone walls could still make his flesh crawl. Even though there was nothing to stop him walking right out of the Abbey, he would never survive alone in a country determined to execute him.

He sighed and went outside where the sun was working between drifts of clouds to warm the mountainside. He stopped beside a short stone wall surrounding the ruined storeroom. The Abbot had decreed the walls were unsafe to rebuild upon and so they had to come down. For the last three days, workers had laboured to bring the building to its knees. Some worked high on scaffolding, chipping away at the mortar, while others worked below in pairs, hauling the huge square stones out of the way so they could be used to build a new storeroom.

As Aiden settled himself on the wall to read, he paused to watch the work for a moment. Robert worked alongside the others. He lifted one block after another with no help, carrying them more than twenty feet to the growing pile.

Should Aiden stay, or should he find another place to sit and read? Would Robert be disturbed by his presence and leave? Aiden hovered in indecision for several heartbeats until Robert glanced in his direction and continued working. Breathing easily again, Aiden cast his gaze back to his book.

After a while, a light breeze kicked up the pages. He heard the chapel bell ring midday, but he felt no need for food and kept on reading.

'You're a brave man.'

Aiden started at the voice and looked around until his eyes lighted on a pair of boots not six feet away. Slowly he looked up. Robert stood in front of him, wiping his hands on a piece of cloth. Swallowing, Aiden tried to think of a suitable response – one which wouldn't send the young man away again.

'It's unintentional.'

Robert's gaze didn't waver. He finished with the cloth and shoved it into the pocket of his trousers. Absently, Aiden noticed the other workers had left to eat and they were alone.

'How did you know?'

Aiden's gaze shot back to Robert. Know? What? That he'd meant to end his life in that fire?

'How did you know who I was?'

Aiden took a deep breath and clasped his hands together on the book. 'I knew your father. The resemblance was too striking to be a coincidence.'

'Only on the surface.'

What was that supposed to mean?

Robert didn't appear to require a response. He walked to the corner wall and sat down, neither facing nor actually turned away from Aiden. For a long time they sat in silence. Aiden couldn't think of anything to say now that the moment had arrived. He'd waited five weeks to be able to speak to this man and now that he was here, Aiden was dumbstruck.

This was stupid! 'It wasn't your fault, you know.'

Robert didn't even glance at him. His response was idle, bored almost. 'What?'

'My arrest. The moment they elected me, I had a feeling it would come. If not that day, then soon. The synod had no idea how close I came to declining the Primacy.'

Silence again. Robert gazed out across the ruined building

and beyond, towards his garden. He seemed disinclined to speak – but if so, why was he here? Why didn't he just go off and be on his own?

'You shouldn't have told me your name.'

Aiden glanced back and found Robert's eyes were on him. For the first time he noticed the colour, a deep forest green, hard and flinty. There was no gentleness in that gaze, no conciliation within the whole face. No compromise.

'It's my name and I'll tell who I like,' Aiden replied without thinking. 'Don't start trying to place boundaries on who I can and can't trust. Better men than you have tried and failed.'

'I'm sure they have.' Robert's gaze returned to the garden in the distance. 'But those you would trust could just as easily be those who would betray you. Your position here is not so secure that you can afford to be careless.'

'I place my trust where my instincts lead me.'

'Are they always right?'

Aiden paused before answering. 'Not always, no. But I must trust someone, some time. Life would be intolerable without trust.'

'Have you ever tried to live without it?'

'No. And I wouldn't want to. I let my instincts guide me, yes, and every now and then I am disappointed.'

'Betrayed?'

'Very well, betrayed. But for every man who would betray a trust there are a hundred who would not. Discovering those I trust and knowing them is worth the risk of betrayal. That's part of what makes life rich.'

Robert's eyebrows rose lazily at that, as though he might be amused at the thought. He came to his feet and glanced down at the book on Aiden's lap. 'You should look more to your safety than your riches in life, Bishop. You've listened to your instincts once too often. You've given your secret to a man you know nothing about. A man you have already misjudged by comparing him with his father. A man who can be trusted with nothing.'

30

It was no use. Aiden tossed and turned, but his mind was wide awake and showed no sign of slowing down. Moonlight filtered through the curtain; he could just make out the rough surface of the stone wall opposite, built two centuries ago and untouched since.

What did Robert mean, he couldn't be trusted? Was he trying to make Aiden believe that he would leave here and send word to Selar? What on earth could a man like that have to run away from?

Suddenly impatient, Aiden threw off his blankets and got out of bed. He paced up and down between the door and window. This was not the first time he'd been unable to sleep in a cell like this. But he was free now – or as free as he could be for the time being – and freedom was wonderful.

So why would Robert deliberately imprison himself?

Aiden sat again on the same wall, a book on his lap. This time when the midday bell rang he put his book aside and waited. At first, Robert ignored him, finished the job he was working on. Then, with a glance in Aiden's direction, he came across, but didn't sit down.

'Why did you call me a brave man?' Aiden began without preamble.

'Would you be happier if I'd called you a foolish man?'

'I didn't ask the question so you could make me happy. I want an answer.' Aiden tried to subdue his curt tone. He needed to be calm.

'You told me who you were without being sure I wouldn't pass the information on to someone else. You were either brave or foolish. Take your pick.'

'Oh? So you weren't referring to me stopping you going back into the fire?'

'No.' Again, that bland, bored response.

Aiden wanted to kick him. 'To bring about your own death is a sin.'

Robert shrugged and sat down. 'Another one.'

'And you have so many already?'

'Doesn't every man?'

'Some more than others. No man can live an entirely faultless life. No matter how strong a man is, there will always be moments when the flesh is weak.'

Robert turned his head slowly and locked his gaze on Aiden. For long seconds, Aiden couldn't move. Then the gaze shifted and he was free again. Before Robert could turn away again, Aiden said, 'The gods made us that way and we must live with it.'

'Ah,' Robert murmured. 'The gods. Of course.'

'You're not going to tell me you don't believe.'

'I don't see how the gods can be blamed for a man being weak.'

'They can't be blamed. If a man is weak it's his own fault – but even within weakness there's a strength.'

'Really?' Robert replied dryly.

Was Robert mocking him? 'With every weakness there's the opportunity for strength if a man's willing to take it. Weakness is there to be examined, understood and learned from. If I had a weakness for peaches but they made me ill, I'd learn not to eat too many, wouldn't I?'

'I don't know, would you?'

'I'd learn to be strong enough to deny myself the overindulgence. In that way, I would gain a new strength from my weakness.'

'So simple.' Robert should have smiled with that, but didn't. Instead, he stood, ready to go back to work. 'I have but one weakness, Bishop. I believed I was strong.'

The coming of the Sabbath meant there was no work done on the ruin for the day. Aiden knew not to look for Robert in the chapel and so found a quiet place under the apple trees and sat on a blanket. He really wanted to write some letters to his friends and family, to assure them he was healthy and free, but of course, it was impossible. He liked

412

the peace of the afternoon, the quiet of the orchard. It didn't last long.

'So how do you reconcile a man's weakness with a belief in the gods?'

Aiden turned around to find Robert approaching almost silently, like a cat. 'What?'

'Why would they create us as weak creatures in the first place? As sport?'

There was something different about Robert today. But what? He wore a rough linen shirt with a worn black jacket thrown over his shoulders. In his hands he held a stoneware flask and two cups.

'Brother Damien thought you might like to try some of the wine St Germanus is not even remotely famous for.' He sat on the ground and poured them each some of the liqour, which was pale pink and smelt vaguely of roses. 'You didn't answer my question.'

Aiden suddenly felt very nervous. There was a tone he'd not heard before, as though this time it was Robert who was baiting Aiden. 'Are you asking me why we were given free will?'

'Why? Is a man weak by his own will?'

'No.' Aiden frowned. He'd have to concentrate hard in order to get around this man. Robert had already come to his own conclusions. 'I'm saying a man is weak by nature. If he wants to give into weakness he will. But the will to choose is free. Just like good and evil.'

'So a man can choose whether to be good or evil?'

'Of course.'

'What if a man is evil by nature, but isn't strong enough to overcome it? Where does he go then? Into the arms of Broleoch?'

'Don't say that name, even in jest,' Aiden replied, with an edge of steel. 'I don't know what you've done, Robert, but you're not evil. You're a man of honour. If you'd not been, you would have let me follow you into the fire.'

'Honour? Me?' Robert looked up at this and for the first time, Aiden saw a breath of humour in the man's eyes.

Robert came to his feet and towered over Aiden. 'Now that's interesting. And how did you come to that conclusion?'

Aiden quickly stood to meet the challenge. 'Don't take that tone with me.' The moment the words were out, he regretted them. But it was too late.

'Oh, tone now, is it? I thought we were discussing how I was a man of honour.' Robert's tone was light, almost playful, but there was an unpleasant edge to it. 'You know nothing about it. You know nothing about me. You've heard people talk about me and you knew my father and you trust your instincts, but you know nothing at all. All you see is this shell which reminds you of a great man and you assume I must be the same. I'm not. I never was and, I assure you, I never will be.'

Aiden tried to swallow down his gall. Such arrogance in one so young! Such . . . 'Don't insult my intelligence, Robert,' Aiden snapped, his patience finally gone. 'I don't form my opinions purely on what other people have told me and I don't judge you alone by your father. I see him in you. I see him in your actions. I may not have been at court with you, but I saw the work you did from Selar's council. I saw you turn his hand from destroying this country time and time again. I saw you refuse to be drawn into breaking your oath to him. Few men of honour would be that strong.'

Robert took a step back and shook his head. 'A man of honour would not have sworn such an oath in the first place! A man of honour wouldn't have left his country to die alone. A man of honour would never have allowed his uncle to become embroiled in a futile rebellion and any man of honour would have avenged that uncle's death. No man of honour would have stood by and watched his country be torn apart by a man he once called a friend, nor stood there like a fool as that friend cast him down. A man of honour would not have left you to rot in prison or . . .' His voice trailed off, but his gaze once again held Aiden in his place. Robert stood there for a moment, then turned away. He reached a hand up to the nearest branch.

Aiden gave Robert a moment to calm down. Gently then, he moved forward a little. 'What did you do?'

Robert spun around, but the voice was once again self-mocking and harsh. 'I betrayed her. She trusted me. I swore I'd protect her. I thought I was strong, but I still betrayed her. And all because I was a man of honour and couldn't leave her in those last few days.'

When Aiden didn't reply immediately, Robert continued, 'You're shocked, aren't you, Bishop? Still think I'm a man of honour? You should have left me alone.'

'That's enough!' Aiden snapped. 'I've never met a man more capable of self-loathing. You made a mistake – you did something wrong. But the truth is that you did nothing! That's really why you're here. Things went wrong and now you're hiding instead of trying to do something about it. You've betrayed yourself, Robert Douglas. No one else. Has it never occurred to you that inaction might not have been your best course? No, you didn't dare act because you'd have to take a risk. You'd have to put your precious honour at risk. Instead you had to hide yourself away here and drown yourself in . . .'

'Self-pity? How original! I don't pity myself, Bishop, only those poor folk who know me.' The ghost of a smile crossed his face. 'It wouldn't have mattered to you what I'd done, would it? Your judgement would still be the same. Just like everyone else, you assume you know enough about me to make that judgement. Well, Bishop, what if I'd told you I was a thief?'

Robert spread his arms wide and took a step back. 'What if I'd told you I was a murderer?'

'That's . . .'

Robert leaned close to Aiden's face and murmured, 'What if I'd told you I was a sorcerer?'

Aiden's head snapped up at this, but before he could say a word, Robert began moving away.

'That got your attention, didn't it, Bishop? Well, there you go. It just goes to show you don't know everything.'

Damien should have been in bed, rather than sitting here in the chapel where the stone floor sucked the heat from his feet with an unquenchable thirst. In less than an hour, the bell for Matins would ring and he'd most likely yawn his way through the liturgy. But he couldn't leave. Not when the Bishop was still in such obvious distress.

Keeping his distance, Damien sat halfway down the chapel while the Bishop occupied the area before the altar. At times McCauly would fall to his knees. At others he would stand and stare up at the trium. Most of the time he just paced backwards and forwards.

He spoke, but the words were not addressed to Damien, nor did they even sound like a prayer – and none of them made any sense. But Damien couldn't sit there for ever. He got to his feet and moved down the aisle a little, not venturing too far.

'Forgive me, Father, but Matins will ring soon.'

McCauly looked up, stopped his pacing and frowned distractedly. 'What? Matins? Is it so late already?'

'It's past midnight, Father.'

'Midnight, you say?'

'Father, is there anything you need? Anything I can get you?'

McCauly shrugged. 'A confessor, perhaps?' He reached out for the arm of the nearest seat and sank into it. 'Am I in need of a confessor? What was it he said? "What if a man is evil by nature?"'

Damien stood by with his hands folded.

'What do you think, Brother? Do you think it's possible a man could be born evil? With no choice in the matter? Of course, it is possible, but it would show, wouldn't it? I mean, you would have seen some sign before now. A thief? A murderer? No. It's not possible there're two men inside the one soul. What do you say?' McCauly glanced up, waiting for an answer.

'I'm sorry, Father, but I've no idea what you're talking about,' Damien replied.

At this, McCauly smiled gently and came slowly to his feet. 'Nor should you. I'm sorry, Brother. I've kept you up very late. I wonder, though, if you could do me one last favour.'

'Anything, Father.'

'Could you show me where Martin's room is?'

'Now? Surely you should get some rest.'

'Yes, I will, but later. There's something I must do first. Will you show me?'

'Of course, but let me get you a cloak. It's raining outside and Martin's room is on the other side of the orchard, above the stable.'

'Then let's go quickly, before I change my mind.'

The footpath was deep in water, a slick of mud impossible to navigate. Damien kept trying to turn him back, but Aiden was adamant. He had to see Robert. Tonight. He couldn't leave this alone. Perhaps it was pride, perhaps not. Either way, he had no choice.

Damien led him past the orchard and over the tiny footbridge crossing the swollen stream. Engorged by hours of mountain rain, the stream was fast becoming a river.

'Careful there!' Damien called, reaching out to steady Aiden as he slid on the mud.

Aiden could hardly see where he was going. The rain pelted down on his hood, blinded his eyes. He stumbled again, his foot sliding knee-deep into the water. Damien grabbed his hand and pulled, but as Aiden reached for purchase on a soggy bush, the ground gave way. Damien slipped to his knees, the bush came away in Aiden's hand and he fell further into the torrent.

'Hold on!' Damien cried. 'Let me get a better hold!'

But the rain worked against them both. Already Aiden was losing feeling in his feet. His body sank deep into the mud, but his hand held on firmly.

Then there was a shadow in the darkness and another hand grabbed his arm. Damien shrank back as Robert took a good hold on Aiden and dragged him out of the water. Aiden shivered on the slimy bank, unable to move for a moment.

'Go get help, Brother,' Robert ordered Damien. As the monk scurried away, Robert reached down and hauled Aiden to his feet.

'What the hell do you think you're doing?' he bellowed. 'Are you trying to get yourself killed?'

Aiden struggled for release, but he was powerless in Robert's grasp. Even in the darkness he could see the rage in the man's eyes, feel it in the fierce grip. He was trapped. 'I had to talk to you . . .'

'Why? So you could give me some more of your self-righteous judgement?' Robert's face was close as the rain poured down on them both. 'Some priest! You're just like all the others – worse even.'

With a violent shove, he pushed Aiden back as though he would rid himself of a demon. Robert stood there a moment, oblivious to the rain, clenching his fists and gasping for breath. 'Why did you make me remember?'

As Robert disappeared into the darkness, Aiden backed away, stunned. Suddenly remembering the river, he stopped and turned, spied the bridge and made his way across. Damien and Chester were hurrying through the orchard towards him, but he waved their concern aside. 'I'm all right. Just cold and wet. I'll be fine.'

Like clucking hens they ushered him to his room, brought hot water and fresh clothes. As soon as he could, Aiden sent them away, assuring them again of his health.

Alone, he sat on his bed and pulled aside the curtain. The small window faced on to the cloister. It seemed the rain had done its work. The worst had gone and now there was just the occasional spray driven by an aggressive wind.

He had no choice. He had to go back. Before it was too late. He couldn't fix what he'd broken, but there must be a way to help the man. There had to be.

The stream was still running strongly, but Aiden had a lamp with him this time. He moved slowly, picking his way between the water and the trees.

He came to the bottom of the slope where the Abbey wall crossed the stream. Before him stood the stable, a wide building with a stairway going up the right wall. He reached the top and, taking his courage between his teeth, he put up a hand and knocked once. There was a movement from within and then suddenly the door was wrenched open.

Robert stood before him, his face chalk-white. Dark rings encircled eyes in shadow of more than mere night. Hollow and tortured, Robert looked like a man who'd walked straight out of a nightmare.

'By the gods,' Aiden breathed, 'what have I done?'

A mere flicker of recognition on Robert's face made Aiden flinch. Robert slowly stepped back, holding the door open. Aiden moved inside and, by the light of his lamp, studied the man before him, trying to see beyond those haunted eyes. Eventually he whispered, 'It wasn't self-pity that drove you here. You really are afraid.'

Robert said nothing and in the gloom, Aiden couldn't be sure the man was even looking at him. He tried to still the trembling in his hands, 'Robert, I . . .'

There was movement in Robert's face, fractional and indecisive. 'What do you want, Bishop?'

Aiden steadied himself. 'I came to apologize.'

The silence was long and absolute. Should he continue? By the gods, what was Robert thinking? Why didn't he speak?

Desperate, Aiden continued, 'I was wrong. I had no right to judge you. I was trying to find out . . . I mean, I needed – no, I wanted – to know why you were here. Put it down to pride, if you like, but I thought I could help you. I didn't mean to make it worse.'

There was a pause, then Robert raised his left hand until Aiden could see it. Suddenly a candle flickered into life. Aiden should have known he would do such a thing, but that didn't stay his shock. He swallowed loudly and glanced back to Robert. Slowly Robert's expression changed, lost some of the haunted whiteness. His eyes grew focused and clear and gradually he took on more of the aspect he showed to the world. The effect wasn't wholly successful and seemed to take a lot of effort. Nevertheless, it was an incredible display.

'Sit down.'

Aiden found a chair and sank into it. He glanced around the room. It was small, but bigger than his cell. There were

419

hooks on one wall, with an assortment of leather straps and tack hanging down. To his right, by the door, was a rough washstand and, beside that, a small chest. Apart from the bed, table and the chair that Aiden sat in, there was no other furniture in the room.

Robert turned to the window and perched on the wide lintel. He laced his fingers together, stared out the rain-washed window and began to speak. His voice was full of cool detachment; his story could have been about a stranger. This wasn't a bored disinterest, but rather a lack of any interest at all.

'You wouldn't let go. I warned you, but you kept coming back, sure you were right, sure you could prove me wrong. You were so determined to win. We're as bad as each other, Bishop.'

Aiden didn't move. Robert took a breath and continued.

'There's an ancient prophecy which you and your brethren know nothing about. I was told most of it twenty years ago and it's ruled my actions ever since. I've fought against it, tried to control it, strived to understand it. Resisted in every conceivable manner. But it won't leave me alone. Each day it lives inside me, growing with every failure to resist it. One day I'll lose and the prophecy will come true. Part of it's already happened.'

Aiden frowned. How could a man like Robert Douglas be a slave to something so ... No. That was the mistake he'd made before, assuming he knew this man. Robert was giving him a chance to understand – so Aiden should try listening. 'How does the prophecy end?'

Robert paused. 'Does it matter?'

Aiden waited.

With a shrug, Robert replied, 'In devastation.'

Aiden frowned. Even now there was something left out. 'Is that all?'

'What more can you want?'

'The truth. All of it.'

Robert turned his gaze on Aiden, unblinking and unmo-ved, as if he were still unsure whether he should reveal the truth. He was silent for a moment, then he replied, his voice a leaden whisper, crisp and precise, 'By your very means, that born unto your hands alone, you will be the instrument of ruin. In the act of salvation, you will become desolation itself, destroying that which you love most.'

For a long breathless moment, Aiden couldn't move, even think. Then he shook himself. 'Sweet Mineah! Are you certain of this prophecy? That it means you?'

'Yes.'

Aiden climbed abruptly to his feet, paced up and down a little. A curse? Like that? Carried around for twenty years?

But Robert said he knew it was true. It had already begun. And if so . . .

'You love her?'

'Yes.'

'You love your country? Your people? Your family and friends?' Aiden turned around. 'Then I was right about something. You are a man of honour.'

Robert shook his head. 'Meaningless. What honour I began with I've successively thrown away time and again. I have only this little left which keeps me here, out of harm's way.'

Aiden's gaze narrowed. 'You try so hard, don't you? And you're so very clever. You know what question I'm going to ask before I do. You've covered all this before. You know all the answers.'

Robert swung his legs down from the ledge. He walked past Aiden to the little chest and brought out a miniature brazier, a pot and some cups. With another wave of his hand, the brazier glowed with heat and he put the pot on to boil.

'But you do know what you're doing,' Aiden added in the silence. He shook his head and regained his seat. 'I was mad to think I could help you. Too proud, I admit. Hell, now I'm making confessions to you, a sorcerer! By the gods, my father would turn in his grave if he knew I was sitting here talking to you instead of condemning you from every tower in the country. I don't even know why I'm still here! Pride. That must be it!'

421

'Oh, you're not proud, Bishop,' Robert murmured without turning. 'Just misguided.'

'Well, that's a great comfort, coming from you, of all people!'

'You think I'm misguided?' Robert brought a cup of brew back for Aiden, then perched on the edge of his bed, his own cup between both hands.

Aiden took a swift burning mouthful. 'Yes. Not only that, I still think you're wrong. Can I ask you a question without getting my head bitten off?'

Something like amusement flashed across Robert's face. 'Go ahead.'

'What happened between you and Selar? Why did you leave Lusara?'

With a short sigh, Robert gazed into his brew. 'Selar wouldn't keep any kind of control over the Guilde. They were growing too powerful and he let them. There was a land dispute which Vaughn had stuck his claws into. The decision would have been grossly unjust. I decided to intervene and had the land assigned to me. I sold the land to the rightful owner on a feu for one copper coin. Vaughn always hated me, more so when I told him I was a sorcerer – not that he can ever tell anyone about it. He demanded that I destroy the feu. If I didn't, he'd see I was thrown off the council. I refused and he went to Selar.'

'I heard you had a terrible argument with the King.'

'I told Selar that if he threw me off the council for defying the Guilde, I'd leave Lusara and never return.'

'So you left.'

'Three years later, I found myself having waking dreams about home. My aide had travelled with me and he needed to go home. I suppose I didn't think too clearly about the whole thing because if I had I wouldn't have done more than put Micah ashore.'

'You couldn't stand being away.'

Robert shrugged. 'Perhaps.'

'This lady? She's not your wife?'

'And never will be.'

'What does she say about all this?'

Robert shot a glance at Aiden. 'Much the same as you – only not quite so rudely. She did say the whole thing was killing me.'

Aiden almost laughed at that – the irony was too cruel. 'Very well, I admit I understand your dilemma. But I have to ask you one thing.'

'One more thing, you mean.'

'Please, don't be pedantic with me, Robert. I haven't had too much sleep since we started talking and it's starting to wear on me.'

Then it happened. A smile – a *real* smile – lit Robert's face in a way that Aiden wouldn't have thought possible. It changed his whole appearance. Even the dark rings about his eyes almost vanished. Robert bowed his head in obedience. 'I am tame, Bishop. Pray continue.'

Aiden stared at him. This man would drive a saint's patience through hell and out the other side! How could he be so close to the edge one minute, then like this another? The self-control was frightening. 'All those things you said about your uncle and Selar and everything. They came about because of your inaction, right?'

'Correct.'

'And you choose inaction because you're afraid you won't be able to alter your destiny to destroy, correct?'

'Right.'

'What would happen then, if you chose action?'

Robert sighed and came abruptly to his feet. 'Well, it's been nice talking to you, Bishop.'

Aiden raised both hands and nearly spilled his brew all over his robe. 'Now wait just a minute. I'm serious.'

'So am I.'

'Don't play games. Just tell me. Pretend I'm dumb. What would happen?'

Robert dumped his cup on the table and threw his arms wide in an aggrieved appeal to heaven. 'Why is it that nobody ever takes me seriously? Why doesn't anybody ever believe me?'

'Probably because you're such an ass.'

To Aiden's eternal surprise, Robert burst out laughing,

falling to his knees in the middle of the floor. After a moment, he took a deep breath and glanced up at Aiden. 'Ah, Bishop, you're one of a kind! Let me explain to you exactly what would happen. I would go out the gates of the monastery and very soon I'd come across some example of legal injustice. Having chosen action, I would of course . . . act. Now, assuming I didn't get either caught or killed in the process, I'd instantly become an outlaw, losing everything I own and turning my mother out on to the street. Then, of course, the King – and the Guilde – would come after me with lots of soldiers with very sharp swords and I'd have to fight them. Only I wouldn't be alone because, after all this time, there're a lot of people in this country who would just love to get into a fight like that. So we'd have a civil war on our hands. But of course, it would get worse because I'm a sorcerer and I have many more powers at my command than my opponents would know about – causing all kinds of confusion in people like you when everyone found out. And then there's the problem of who would take the throne afterwards, because I certainly don't want it and I don't know anybody alive who has any kind of claim to it. But anyway, one day, as sure as the sun will rise in a few hours – I'd be faced with the situation where I'd no longer be able to win by stealth and arms alone. Now,' Robert continued, getting to his feet, 'I can't tell you when that day will come. For all I know, it might come tomorrow, perhaps next week. All I know is that it will come and, I promise you, you don't want to be around when it happens.'

'But you won't tell me what it is.'

'Never.' Robert shrugged and sat once more. 'So, any other suggestions?'

Aiden sighed and shook his head. 'You know, I was right about you. We're both in prison, only of a different kind. You have the power to act, but not the will. I have the will, but no power at all. You have no idea how much I would give to trade places with you.'

Robert frowned. 'You still don't believe me, do you?'

'Oh, I believe you. It's just that I don't believe there's no solution.'

'But there is a solution. If I don't act, only I die, Bishop. If I do act, then many will die. I would have thought the solution would agree with your priestly soul.'

'For pity's sake, Robert, will you please stop calling me Bishop! Call me Aiden if you must, or Father in public, but never again address me by a title that's been dead for me for almost two years.'

Quietly sober, Robert straightened up. 'And you were wrong about that, too. It was my fault you were arrested. I just didn't say anything before because I didn't want to argue and have us start out on the wrong foot.'

Aiden groaned and rolled his eyes at the ceiling – but he had to laugh. This last few weeks had drained him like a porridge bowl at the end of breakfast.

'I suppose that means you'll leave me alone now, as I requested.'

Glancing across the room, Aiden was relieved to note the gentle irony in the young man's eyes. 'No, sorry. I should have warned you. Sometimes I'm hard to shake off. Besides, that was no request. That was an order.'

'And I can see you always do as you're told.'

Aiden would have taken the bait, but Robert's face took on a strange quality and he held up his hand for silence. 'Somebody's coming towards the stable.'

The words were barely out before Aiden could hear feet running through the mud and up the stairs. Instantly Robert was at the door, pulling it open. It was Brother Damien, breathless and dripping with the rain.

'Forgive me, Father, but the Abbot has sent for you. He's just received some news. He's asked that you come at once.'

Robert immediately grabbed a jacket. 'I'll come with you.'

They hurried through the orchard, slipping on puddles of mud and raised tree roots. Breathless and drenched, they reached the cloister. Abbot Chester waited in his study.

The Abbot was still dressed in his sleeping robe, but had thrown a cloak over his shoulders. He moved to speak, but paused when he saw Robert. Aiden drew them all into the room and closed the door. 'It's fine, Chester. He knows who I am. What is it? What's wrong?'

Chester frowned deeply. 'The worst news. Prince Kenrick has been returned to his father and the Queen . . . the Queen is reported to have died in his rescue.'

'Sweet Mineah!' Aiden shut his eyes for a moment, then opened them again quickly to look at Robert. Of all the news they could have received now, this was perhaps the worst.

Robert stood beside him, pale as the dawn. The fragile humour had drained and his face was wooden, immobile.

'But that's not all, Father,' Chester moved closer to them, a small sheet of paper in his hand. 'One of our brothers, Archdeacon Hilderic, has been arrested on charges of treason. It appears he went to Tirone for help in your cause. Now the King has let it be known that unless you give yourself up to his justice, Hilderic will be executed.'

'No!' Aiden breathed, but the life had just gone from his body. He reached for the nearest chair and sank down, unable to absorb this new horror. First the poor Queen, and now Hilderic . . .

'Have you any idea where they're holding Hilderic?'

Aiden's gaze shot up to Robert. Chester scanned the paper again, then replied, 'They were taking him to Calonburke.'

'Near Payne's place,' Robert murmured to himself. Then he turned swiftly back to Aiden. 'What are you going to do?'

'You have to ask me that? I'm going, of course.'

'Yes, that's what I thought you'd say. Well, come. Don't sit there feeling sorry for yourself. I'll help you pack.' Robert leaned down and unceremoniously took Aiden's elbow, lifting him to his feet. Months of digging gardens and shifting great blocks of stone had hardened already tough muscles and Aiden was powerless to stop him.

'But you can't go, Father,' Chester protested. 'Hilderic went to save you.'

'Which is exactly why I must go.'

'But . . .'

'Don't try and stop me, Chester. I'm sorry. I have to do this. Thank you for the sanctuary you've given me. A few weeks of freedom were better than none at all.'

Aiden barely had time to wave a blessing before Robert almost dragged him out the door. Then they were hurrying along the cloister towards Aiden's room. Robert somehow made the door open before they'd reached the top of the stairs. He propelled Aiden inside and shut the door, waving a hand over it before turning to face him.

'Well, don't just stand there, get packing.'

'But ... I don't understand,' Aiden frowned, doing no such thing. 'If I didn't know you better, I'd say you wanted me to go.'

'Well, you do know me better, but I still want you to go. Come on, hurry. Unless I miss my guess, we don't have much time. We have to get to Calonburke before they decide to move Hilderic.'

Aiden stood there in shock as Robert swiftly turned about the room, picking up everything he saw and shoving it into the leather bag in the corner. 'Can you ride?'

'Of course. How do you think I got here?'

'But can you ride well?'

'I used to hunt.'

'Well, I hope that's enough.' Robert came to a halt and noticed that Aiden wasn't moving. 'What are you waiting for?'

'Robert – just stop and tell me what's going on. What do you mean, we have to get to Calonburke?'

Robert stared at him a moment, then closed his eyes and let out a loud sigh. He crossed the tiny room and pressed the bag to Aiden's chest. Carefully, as if talking to a child, he said, 'You don't really think for one second that Selar will let Hilderic go if you scurry back? He'll just execute both of you – probably at the same time. The only hope Hilderic has is if we mount a small rescue. That means you and me. It's a two-day ride to Calonburke from here if we're quick and that means we have to leave now. Right now.'

'Just wait,' Aiden clutched the bag and tried to assert a shred of authority. 'Are you, the great hero of inaction, about to go against your own creed?'

At this, Robert stood back, his urgency in abeyance for a moment, though it was written in every line of his body. 'I helped Rosalind get out of the country, Aiden. I sent her to what I believed was a safe place and now she's dead and the child she hoped to save is back with his father. I promise you, the safest place in the country for you right now is standing next to me.'

Aiden studied him for a moment longer. 'Are you sure about this?'

'This is all I know how to do.'

'And the prophecy?'

Robert's expression became painfully whimsical. 'Please don't be pedantic with me, Father. I've not had much sleep over the last year or so and it's starting to wear on me. Now pack up the rest of your things and I'll meet you at the stables.'

Robert threw the door open. 'And don't fall in the stream this time!'

31

They rode through what was left of the night, tearing down the mountain at such a speed Aiden was sure he would fall from his horse and break his neck. Robert didn't seem to either notice or care, however, and the moment they reached the gentler hills, he pressed his horse to even greater efforts. They travelled away from towns and villages, skirting farms along the way. Mostly they kept to the valleys, but every now and then, Robert would bring them to the crest of a hill and pause only long enough to get his bearings. His stamina was extraordinary – long before dusk, Aiden was ready to fall asleep in his saddle. Nevertheless, he said nothing and just held on. Eventually, with the horses winded and ready to drop, Robert called a halt in a small glade beside a clear stream.

'Go ahead, you can fall off now.' Robert leaped down from his horse and came over to Aiden. 'Do you require help to collapse, or can you manage on your own?'

'I know what this is,' Aiden murmured, reaching out to

take Robert's hand. 'This is penance for some great crime I've long forgotten.'

He groaned and swore as Robert helped him down, then, when his knees refused to lock, he sank to the damp grass and peered up at the darkening sky.

Robert gazed down at him with mild amusement. 'How long have you been a priest?'

'I entered orders when I was nineteen. I was ordained six years later.'

'And how old are you now?'

'Forty-eight and never likely to make forty-nine.'

'Oh yes, you will – but I suppose, having spent so much time in the cloister, you never learned anything important like how to gather firewood or boil up salted beef?'

'No,' Aiden snapped grumpily. His head ached, his back ached, his knees and feet and hands were numb. He was in no mood to go hiking for firewood. He'd rather freeze.

'No matter,' Robert set about making camp while Aiden watched. He even laid the fire close to where Aiden was sitting.

Once the food was cooking, Aiden's mood melted a bit. Though his body was worn out, his mind was still alert. The strangeness of the situation was still fresh and he reviewed the things Robert had told him while they'd walked the horses through the day.

'Very well,' he began carefully, 'I understand all this business with Sealing and Seeking, but why do you think these Malachi are responsible for the death of the Queen?'

Robert squatted down on the opposite side of the fire and stirred the pot he'd 'borrowed' from the kitchen of Saint Germanus. 'Of course, I don't know for certain they had anything to do with retrieving Kenrick – but they're about the only people who could have. If I'm right, then the person who gave the orders is already safely entrenched at court, with some considerable influence over the King and probably in league with a man I hope never to meet.'

'Why? Is he something to do with this prophecy?'

'I'm afraid so. He's . . . well, I don't know what he is and I don't really want to find out. I do know he was responsible for the death of a very dear friend, among countless others.'

Robert was very businesslike in his responses. Detached almost. And always beneath his tone was a hardness. He may have taken a step back from the edge, but he could still see the abyss below. He was so changeable, so unfathomable that Aiden was hard-pressed to keep up. Drawing his feet close to the fire, Aiden turned his most perceptive gaze on Robert. 'And this lady of yours . . .'

'She's not mine.'

'Is she in danger from all this? These Malachi? This man you hope never to meet?'

Robert's eyes darted from the cooking pot to meet Aiden's, revealing a vulnerability too easy to touch. His gaze narrowed. 'I doubt she is at the moment. He's known her since she was a child and he's never worried too much about her.'

'So she's not the real reason you've come out of your . . . retirement?'

Robert ladled food into two bowls and handed one to Aiden. 'Eat your supper.'

The food was awful, but it wouldn't have been polite to complain. Aiden finished as much as he could, then put his plate aside and drew his cloak about his shoulders. Already his eyes were beginning to close. But still he had questions to ask. 'What are we going to do when we get there?'

'Don't worry about that now,' Robert replied with a surprising gentleness. 'We can talk about it tomorrow. Get some sleep. We'll be up before dawn.'

'Aren't you going to rest?'

'No, I'll keep watch.'

'But you need to sleep, too.'

'I don't sleep any more, Aiden. Now close your eyes and shut up.'

Aiden raised his head a little and fixed Robert with a baleful glare – at least he hoped it was. 'Are you always like this?'

'No,' Robert replied offhandedly. 'Sometimes I'm pushy.

I've also been known to be arrogant, selfish, pigheaded and stubborn – but I don't want to brag. Now go to sleep.'

They made good time the next day, even though every step the horse took sent a wave of pain through Aiden's exhausted body. He hung on though, determined not to give away the level of his discomfort. This time they rested in the late afternoon, starting off again an hour after dusk. They rode on into the dark until they reached the crest of a tree-lined hill. Below were the lights of a small town, nestled in the pre-dawn glow. On the southern side were arranged the tents and pavilions of a Guilde garrison.

'I know you're exhausted, Aiden, but I'm afraid we can't stop. If Hilderic is still here we'll have to get him out tonight.'

'And go where? Who's going to hide two renegade priests?'

Robert shot him a wry smile. 'A renegade lord, that's who. I can hide both of you at Dunlorn for an indefinite amount of time. Then, when it's safe, I'll get you out of the country.'

'What if Hilderic has already been moved to Marsay?'

'Then we'll just have to go after him and pray I don't lose my temper. Come on. We'll need to change our horses before we do anything.'

They rode on ahead, but before they reached the first buildings, Robert had Aiden dismount and they led their horses into the town. There were a few taverns still open, but by the look of it, most folk had already long since retired for the night. The streets were almost empty, apart from the odd reveller making an unsteady way home. Robert walked beside Aiden with his hood drawn over his head and, as an afterthought, he directed Aiden to do the same. It would not do for either man to be recognized in this place.

'I haven't been here for a few years, but there used to be a courier stable on this side of town. If we smile nicely, we might be able to get the proprietor to open up early and exchange our horses. We'd better buy a spare at the same time.'

Aiden didn't say anything. The whole idea of this rescue harrowed him to the bone. He was a man of the cloth, not a soldier. He'd be of no use to anyone in an escape. What was Robert thinking of?

'Here we are.'

Robert brought them to a halt before the doors of a tall stable building on the edge of town. It was not closed as Robert had expected. Instead, there was a burning lamp hung from a post inside and a man raking up straw beneath it.

'Good evening, ostler,' Robert began.

The man looked up. 'Yes, squire? What can I do for you?'

'A change of horses. We still have a long journey ahead of us.'

'Of course.' He leaned his rake against the post and gave the two horses a quick going over. 'Reasonable animals. Will you be wanting them back?'

'We'll not be returning this way, I'm afraid.'

'Then you can take those two over there. The black and the grey. It'll cost you a piece of silver for the two.'

'That much?' Robert murmured.

'Aye, that much,' the ostler said. 'I've already had one horse stolen tonight. I have to cover my costs somehow.'

'Ah.' Robert tossed him the coin. Then, with a nod to Aiden, he began to unsaddle their exhausted animals. Robert led the two fresh horses out of the stall and saddled them while Aiden held the bridles. With his head bent to his work, Robert whispered, 'There's something not right here.'

'What do you mean?' Aiden glanced around nervously.

'Can't you smell it?'

'What?'

'Blood. But he said the horse was stolen – so it can't be the blood of the thief.' Robert didn't say any more, but waited until both horses were ready before approaching the ostler with an aspect of casual curiosity. 'Do you often have animals stolen?'

'It happens to everyone once in a while. Can't be helped. This time though, the thief will regret taking a horse of mine.'

'Why is that?'

'Because the Guilde is on his trail, that's why,' the ostler reported with a grin of immense satisfaction. 'He killed three of them in here and almost did away with another two – one of them a governor!'

'Really? He must have been some swordsman.'

The ostler glanced conspiratorially out of the doorway, then leaned in close to Robert. ''Tweren't no ordinary thief, squire. This was a sorcerer. The Guilde said it was the same one caught in Kilphedir last year. They went after him, though he did have a few hours' start on them. They say he was sore wounded. They also said the sorcerer rescued some priest they'd arrested, but the sorcerer won't get far.'

'Oh? And why is that?'

'Because the Guilde knows where he's going, that's why. I heard them myself. They couldn't stop talking about it. They left not twenty minutes ago, heading east.'

'East?'

'Aye, towards Earl Jacob's lands. Elita.'

'Thank you,' Robert nodded a farewell and took both horses in one hand and Aiden's elbow in the other. Without pausing, he drew Aiden out into the street and towards the edge of town.

'Walk slowly and don't look around.'

'What? Why?'

'Because that man will probably report my questions to the next Guildesman he sees. The moment we're clear of the town, mount your horse and follow me, no matter what. When the horses tire, don't stop, I'll sustain them long enough to get us there.'

'But ... I don't understand. Didn't that man just say somebody already rescued Hilderic?'

'Yes.' When Robert passed the last building he threw back his cloak hood. 'And the sorcerer he's talking about is my brother. Come on, we don't have much time. We have to get to Elita before the Guilde.'

We have to get to Elita ...

In the name of the gods, what was Finnlay doing out of the Enclave? Was he mad? And to mount a rescue of Hilderic in a camp full of Guilde soldiers?

How badly was he wounded? Had he got the old priest

away to safety? Yes, he must have. The ostler had said nothing about Hilderic being recaptured. At least that much had succeeded, but . . .

What, in Serin's name, had possessed him to head towards Elita? Why not Dunlorn? Did he think Jacob might afford him a hiding place? But Jacob believed Finnlay was dead. It didn't make any sense!

Robert urged his horse on through the growing dawn, keeping his head low and his body moving with the animal. A part of his mind kept touch with the Bishop riding behind him. Already exhausted and tested to the limit, Aiden rode as hard as Robert without really understanding why. Yes, he was a very brave man indeed. Especially when he was fairly certain the priest had not yet come to terms with Robert's involvement with sorcery. That would come later – when the full import hit him.

The land flew past in a blur of spring green and cloudy grey. He couldn't sense where the Guildesmen were and couldn't afford to stop and look. He just took the straightest, flattest course to Elita and tried to still the threat of panic if they should get there before him.

He rode on and on through the day and night, into the morning, fogged over with grey and threatening rain. He drew in the mist and wrapped it around him, comforted by its blanket cover, its anonymity. And then, on the edge of desperation, he reached the edge of the lake. The castle stood on the other side, a golden tower surrounded by grey. The Guilde was nowhere to be seen.

Robert didn't pause. With a shout of encouragement to Aiden, he rode on, pounding along the bank until he gained the castle gate. It was already open for him. Together with McCauly, they clattered into the courtyard. Instantly, Robert jumped down from his horse, calling out for Neil. He climbed the steps to the hall in three long strides, burst through the door – and came to a halt.

Neil was there and so was Micah. The two of them leaned over someone lying on the great table. They whirled around at his approach.

'My lord!' Micah cried, a smile as huge as the sun

spreading across his face. Robert gained his side as Aiden followed him into the hall. It was then that he realized the body on the table was . . . 'Finnlay?'

The wounds were terrible. His face was barely recognizable. A deep gash over one eye, half his face swollen and red. And more. A cut to his side, shallow but bleeding, and others to his shoulder and back. 'Finnlay? Can you hear me?'

'He won't wake up for a while, Robert. I gave him something to make him sleep while we treated his wounds.'

Robert froze at the voice from behind. His heart stopped, his mind came to a complete halt. Then slowly, irrevocably, he turned until he saw her.

She stood not ten feet away. Her hair was bound behind, but some had come loose and fell around her face. In her hands was a bowl of water and the apron covering her gown was speckled with blood. Finnlay's blood.

And she was having a child.

She watched him gravely as though her first controlled words to him were all she could manage.

A child.

His child?

The bowl began to shake in her hands, but still neither of them could move. Then suddenly, Aiden was there at her side, taking the bowl. He brought it back to the table.

. . . How could she still look so beautiful . . .

'Robert?' Aiden grunted. 'Do you forget why we're here?'

'By the gods!' Robert swore, coming back. 'Where's Jacob? He has to call out the guard. Neil, leave that for Aiden and go order the gates closed.'

'But why?' Jenn came closer. 'What's going on?'

'More than a hundred Guilde soldiers are coming this way. I'd say we have no more than an hour to prepare. They're coming to get Finnlay and when they get him, they'll execute him for sorcery.'

Micah flew about the castle like a madman, passing on messages, relaying orders – and he was only one of many. However, he'd been the only one present when Robert had spoken to Jacob. The old man had sat in stony silence as

Robert outlined the situation and admitted that he'd brought Aiden McCauly with him. For a few seconds, Micah was sure Jacob would turn them all out. After all, why should he risk everything for the sake of a sorcerer? Micah could almost see the thought crossing Jacob's mind – but if he could, so could Robert.

'If you want us to go, say so now, Jacob, while we still have time to get away. I don't know if Finnlay's fit to travel, but we will go if you want.'

'What would be the point?' Jacob snapped. 'The Guilde would use any excuse to get within these walls – and they certainly wouldn't believe me if I told them you'd got away.'

Robert swallowed and glanced at Micah. 'If we can hold out long enough for some help to arrive, we can all get away to safety.'

Jacob shook his head, distracted. 'Your brother was an idiot for coming here in the first place, involving my daughter.'

'I agree, and if he lives through this, be assured I'll make him pay.'

Jacob frowned at this, turning his gaze squarely on Robert. 'You're one of them too, aren't you? A sorcerer?'

'Yes.'

For a long moment, the Earl said nothing. Then he turned his chair around and gazed out the window. 'I'm too old for this. Too old and tired. I wronged you, Robert. I wouldn't blame you if you'd brought this down on me in revenge. Jenn tried to warn me, but like a fool, I didn't listen. You see, it never occurred to me that a daughter I hardly knew could understand more of people than I did. When I didn't fight, she did in my place, shaming me.'

Robert moved and placed a hand on Jacob's shoulder. 'She's your daughter, Jacob.'

'Is she?' Jacob looked up, a bemused frown on his face. 'I think she's the daughter of this poor country of ours – and like a blind, tyrannical King, I have kept her enslaved by my ignorance and fear.'

He shook his head and something like a smile framed his

face. 'Go. Take command of my guard and make sure not one of those filthy Guilde pigs enters my castle!'

After that Robert ordered patrols to be doubled and lookouts posted on the towers of Elita. The people were obviously afraid, but Robert strode about the place with such authority and calm, gave his orders with such decisiveness that their terror was quelled for the time being. It would undoubtedly rise again the moment the Guilde soldiers were sighted outside the castle walls. Only when everything needed was in motion did Robert take Micah back upstairs to where Finnlay was laid out, tended by Bella and the renegade Bishop. Jenn was there, too, standing quietly beside the bed.

Robert didn't look at her. Instead, he came to the bedside and knelt down by Finnlay's head. After a moment, he murmured, 'Will he live?'

'He's . . . very weak,' Jenn replied softly, hovering beside McCauly.

'But will he live?'

'I don't know. All I can do is bind his wounds and hope the blood loss won't kill him. In a few hours the sleeping draught will wear off and the pain will hit him.'

'Let me know when and I'll do something for him.' Robert came to his feet with such barely contained force that even Micah took a step back. He turned to Jenn. 'Just keep him alive. I'll not have anyone else die because of me.'

With that, Robert turned for the door, pausing with his hand in the air, a finger pointed towards the Bishop. 'And not a word from you, either.'

McCauly raised his hands in innocence, but after Robert had gone, he threw a comforting smile towards Jenn. 'We had a slight disagreement – nothing to worry about.'

Robert strode along the curtain wall, checking the defences between every tower. Soldiers snapped to attention as he approached and responded to his questions crisply. Robert had to admit that Jacob had made sure his men were trained properly. There was nothing slovenly about either their weapons or their performance. How they would perform under fire was another matter.

When he finished his circuit, Robert returned to the top of the main keep and addressed the sergeant. 'Keagan, isn't it?'

'Aye, Your Grace. It's good to see you again.'

'Any sign yet?'

'No.'

Robert nodded and turned for the stairs. Micah was standing there, waiting for him. 'I knew you'd come back.'

Robert joined him by the wall, away from the lookouts. 'You must be a seer, then.' He paused and studied Micah for a moment, then he smiled. 'You know, my friend, I believe I missed you.'

Micah grinned broadly. 'Aye, I'm sure you did. Where were you?'

'Hiding.' Robert turned his gaze back to the hills in the distance.

Micah strode forward and glanced down into the court-yard. 'Do you really think we can get help before they overcome us?'

'No. I've sent word to Dunlorn already, but any force is seven days away, six at the least. I doubt we'll last three. I'm afraid we'll just have to win this one by stealth alone.'

There was a long pause before Micah spoke again. 'Are you really back now, or will you leave again?'

'Well, that depends on whether I get out of this alive.' Robert drew himself up straight. He couldn't bring himself to look at Micah. 'I didn't know . . .'

'She wanted to keep it a secret. In case somebody should see her as suddenly vulnerable. After what happened to Finnlay last year, I agreed with her.'

Yes. That's right. Carlan. Micah had told him all about it. It was a miracle Finnlay had survived. At least now they had a name for the Angel of Darkness. Now they were all named. The Angel, the Enemy and the Ally.

'And . . . how does Eachern treat her?'

'Well enough when he's around – which isn't often. She's worked out how to deal with him over most issues, such as coming here for the birth.'

Robert nodded. He couldn't ask – and especially not

Micah – and yet he . . . needed to know . . . the child. Could it be his child?

Could the gods be so cruel to her?

'Your Grace!' Keagan rushed across the keep platform and pointed west. 'There!'

Robert stepped forward to the edge of the stone wall and gazed ahead. There, in the distance, was the glint of steel flashing from a dulled sun. Yellow robes, brighter than the trees, other colours mixed in. A hundred men on horseback, heading towards Elita. No . . . more than a hundred. Twice that.

'They stopped to collect more men,' Robert turned swiftly and called out orders to Keagan.

'But that's not enough for a siege force.'

'They don't need to lay siege for long. If we don't surrender within a few hours, I'll bet we'll have King's forces down on us before the week's out. Damn, if only there was a tunnel like Dunlorn's! And why is Finnlay injured when I need him most?'

The force arrived at Elita and immediately surrounded the wall. Without haste, the soldiers took up their positions, prepared for both attack and defence. A single rider approached the gates, a white pennant flying above him. Robert moved to go down the stairs, but paused. There was something not right about all this. Something which tugged at the edges of his awareness with a strength that was almost painful.

'Serin's breath, no!'

'What is it?' Micah moved forward.

'That's not just Guilde down there. There're Malachi among them. A lot of Malachi. What the hell is going on?' Robert didn't wait any longer. He tore down the stairs and ran along the courtyard to receive the message as it was handed down from the top of the gate.

'Surrender the sorcerer, Finnlay Douglas, by dawn tomorrow.'

That was it. No more. No threats, no promises of retribution. A simple directive.

Given by Malachi.

Robert turned and entered the hall where Jacob was waiting for him. 'I think we can safely assume they're serious.'

Jacob took the note. 'Was there any doubt?'

'Well, at least they don't know McCauly's here as well, or we'd be in real trouble.'

'Define *real* trouble.' Aiden descended the stairs and joined them. 'Lady Jennifer's just asked me to warn you there're Malachi out there.'

'I know,' Robert nodded. 'Jacob, is there any secret passage out of this place? Something nobody knows about?'

'If there is, I never heard about it either. We do have a deep cellar, but we never use it because it's so damp.'

Robert glanced around at the others in the hall: Neil and Jacob's aide, Shane Adair. All of them were waiting for him to make a decision. They were all waiting for him to show them the way out of an impossible situation.

And what could he tell them? That he had no idea how to get out of this? That the moment he realized there were Malachi outside the walls, all his plans fell to dust?

'Neil, I want you to bring all the castle food supplies into the main keep – but be quiet about it. Bring the women and children in as well. I'm sure Bella will help. I want nobody but fighting men outside the keep.'

'Aye, my lord. And what about Eachern's men? Those who accompanied Her Grace?'

'Where are they now?'

'Micah had them locked in the guard room,' Neil replied with a grin. 'Out of harm's way, he said.'

'Well, we wouldn't want to endanger their lives by bringing them in here, would we? Leave them there with some water and bread. In the meantime, bring in enough water supplies to last a week. Then close off the well.'

As Neil rushed off about his tasks, Robert turned back to Jacob. 'I'm going to see my brother. Let me know if those thugs outside move a muscle.'

Jenn lit a single candle. She placed it on the table by the bed, then glanced outside to where the sun was beginning to set.

She heard the door open behind her, but she didn't turn to look. She knew who it was. She knew where he'd been, every movement he made. She could trace his steps about the castle without so much as closing her eyes. She was no Seeker, but she knew Robert had come to see Finnlay.

She heard his boots creak as he knelt by the bed on the opposite side to Jenn. He said nothing for a long time. Then there was more movement as he pulled up a stool and sat down. Now Jenn did chance a glance at him, but his attention was entirely on his brother. She could see Robert's face by the candlelight, his green eyes caught by the yellow glimmer. His hair was long, falling to his shoulders. It was brushed back from his forehead, revealing frown lines more than these few hours old. His face and hands were tanned and even from where she sat she could see new hard callouses over the old. He'd lost weight, too. There was now nothing spare on his frame, and yet he moved with the same lithe grace he always had.

If only she dared speak to him, but she could also see – and had seen the moment he arrived at Elita – the deep well of blackness which now almost consumed him. It had grown tenfold since she'd last seen him, beyond something that merely worried her into something that engendered terror. She couldn't warn him of it. She couldn't even breathe his name. All she could do was sit there and watch him.

'Does your Healer's sight tell you nothing more?' Robert murmured, his eyes not meeting hers. 'Can you tell how bad his wounds are? If he will live?'

'His wounds will not kill him. If we are to live, then so will he,' Jenn said softly.

'You sensed the Malachi outside?'

'Yes.'

'Can you sense anything else? Is he out there? Carlan? Is that presence you sensed at court beyond those walls, waiting for us to fail?'

'I . . .' Jenn began, but didn't want to go on. Robert didn't look up. Eventually she murmured, 'I'm unable to sense anything beyond this room.'

'Unable or unwilling? Don't you think we should know if he's out there?'

'I am physically unable to try,' Jenn bit her lip and tore her gaze from him. 'I must think of my child.'

'*Your* child?'

Jenn dared not move. She knew he was looking at her. She knew the question in his eyes. Could she lie to him – and would he believe her?

But Robert turned away without asking and Jenn began to breathe again.

'I think he's waking up. Finnlay? Can you hear me?'

Jenn got up from her seat and perched on the edge of the bed. Any kind of movement now was extremely uncomfortable.

'Robert?' Finnlay's speech was slurred as he emerged from his drugged sleep. 'Must be dreaming.'

'A nightmare, more like. How do you feel?'

Finnlay tried to open his eyes, but only one of them would obey him. Gradually he focused on Robert's face. 'Come to sit at my deathbed, Robert?'

For the first time since he'd arrived, Jenn saw Robert smile. 'I guess the flesh might be wounded, but the spirit is still as nasty as ever. What happened?'

'What happened? Didn't I tell Jenn . . .' Finnlay's voice trailed off as he turned and noticed her sitting by his left hand. She gave him a gentle smile, but said nothing. 'Must have passed out. How long have I been here?'

'Since dawn. You brought some friends with you, I see.' Robert shook his head. 'When will you learn to stay out of trouble?'

But Finnlay's flippant mood had gone. Instead, he reached out and grabbed Robert's hand. 'I've met him, Robert. The Angel of Darkness.'

'Yes, I've heard all about it.'

'But you don't understand. He's out there. He cornered me at Calonburke.'

Robert came to his feet. 'Do you know what he looks like?'

'No.'

Walking to the window, Robert said, 'But he thinks you're

442

the Enemy and he knows the Ally is in here. He must know. Therefore, he won't do anything too dangerous in case he hurts Jenn. Unless—'

Robert never finished the thought. At that moment, Micah knocked on the door and entered. 'Sorry, but Lord Jacob asked me to let you know. They want an answer. Now.'

'But they said we had until dawn tomorrow.'

'I know. Jacob is going out there to speak to the herald.'

'Very well, let's see what they want.' With that, the two of them left and Jenn turned back to Finnlay.

His gaze ran over her. 'And how is my nephew doing?'

'Please, Finnlay, this is bad enough as it is.'

'I know,' he caught her hand. 'I'm sorry. You're still determined not to tell him?'

'There's only one thing that would make me tell him and I don't even want to think about that possibility. How's the pain?'

'Growing, what else?'

Jenn moved across to the window and looked down at the courtyard below. Robert was there with Shane, pushing Jacob's chair across the cobbles. They stopped when they reached the portcullis. Shane took Jacob to the stone steps and, with another guard to help, they carried him up to the rampart where Jacob stood on his own feet, his weight supported by the men beside him and his own strong arms on the ledge in front. Robert moved close to the wooden gate and, in a gesture that was painfully familiar, he placed his hand upon the wood and listened.

Jenn couldn't hear what was called up to Jacob. She could only hear his response, loud and clear and full of blood-curdling determination.

'Your request is an abomination before the gods. Finnlay Douglas is no sorcerer and you have no right to arrest him. You are on my lands without invitation and I demand that you vacate immediately.'

There was a pause as Jacob listened to more words and then his voice rang out again. 'No. I will not hand him over to you. Now be gone!'

Jenn smiled as Jacob turned. Then suddenly he stiffened.

His weight fell back and the men at his side couldn't hold him. Without a rail behind him, Jacob fell to the cobblestones below with a thud. Only then could Jenn see the arrows protruding from his chest. Robert dashed forward as Jenn screamed.

32

Aiden held the door open as Robert brought Jacob in and laid him on the long table by the fire. Immediately, Aiden pushed his fingers against Jacob's throat, bent his head to listen for breathing, but there was nothing. Just the three arrows in his chest.

Men gathered around, silent and numbed. Then Jacob's oldest daughter pushed through until she could see her father. She came to a halt, silent in shock.

'Father!' Jennifer came down the stairs too quickly for one so heavy with child. But she didn't stumble. Robert would have moved, but Bella was there, reaching for her.

'They killed him,' Jenn whispered, her eyes filling with tears at the sight before her. 'He defied them and they killed him! Bella?'

The two sisters hugged each other close, Bella holding Jenn's head to her shoulder as they wept together. Aiden slowly reached out and traced the trium on Jacob's forehead, then turned to Robert. Their eyes met for a long time and for once, Aiden knew exactly what he was thinking. Then, just like before, Robert's gaze shifted slightly . . .

'Oh, hell!'

An instant later, Aiden heard a sound which sent a shiver through his soul. It was the sound of soldiers attacking the castle.

'Look after them,' Robert ordered and then, calling the other men gathered in the hall, he ran outside to take charge of the defence.

With his stomach clenched against his own fear, Aiden gave instructions to the servants to take care of Jacob's body. Remove the arrows, wash him and dress him in his finest clothes. Come what may, Jacob Ross, last male member of the ancient royal family, would be laid out with as much honour as they could manage.

Then, his heart heavy, Aiden put an arm around the two girls and gently ushered them towards the stairs, but, before they could reach the top, Jenn paused, a look of incomprehension on her face. She went to take another step, but suddenly doubled over with a cry of pain.

'Come, quickly, Father,' Bella urged. 'Help me get her to her bed.'

Half carrying her, they crept up the stairs one at a time. The corridor was easier to manage, but Jennifer was in too much pain to move fast. Every few steps she groaned again, shutting her eyes tight against the agony. Bella called out for help and a girl appeared, her plain face horrified. She rushed to them and together they got Jennifer into her room and on to the bed. Aiden stepped back, ready to leave, but Bella threw him a pleading glance.

'Please, keep an eye on Finnlay. Everyone else is busy on the walls. His room is just across the corridor.'

The night sky was lit by a ring of fire around the castle. The air was split with arrows and the cries of men on both sides of the walls. For a moment, chaos reigned.

But the illusion was transitory. As soon as Robert gained his viewpoint on top of the keep, a truer picture revealed itself. Soldiers ran along the curtain walls, fending off attempts to scale the defences. The real threat was the archers. They'd formed a phalanx along the lake side of the castle and from there, wave after wave of arrows rained down on the ramparts, clattering into the courtyard. None were high enough to reach the top of the keep. Elita's own archers fought back until Robert gave the order for them to save their bolts.

This wasn't a serious attack. Two hundred men could never bring a castle this well-defended to its feet. That is, two hundred *ordinary* men. No, with so many Malachi in their number, this first effort was nothing more than a test of resolve. Elita's soldiers had just lost their lord. How willing were they now to defy the Guilde when he was no longer around to protect them?

'Keagan?'

'Yes, my lord.'

'Have the men put out all their torches. They'll see better in the dark.'

'Aye, my lord.'

Robert joined Micah as he surveyed the circle of fire surrounding the castle. There was a bonfire every fifty feet, manned by at least three men in Guilde uniform. Already others were at the foot of the nearby forest, the sound of chopping wood reaching them above the rain of arrows.

'Micah?' Robert paused and glanced over his shoulder to make sure the other soldiers could not hear him. 'There may only be one way out of this.'

Micah turned slowly until he met Robert's gaze. 'Go on.'

'I'll need your help. If worst comes to worst, I'll need you to get the Bishop to safety. Take him to Dunlorn. Deverin can then get him over the border to Kavanagh.'

As though afraid of the question, Micah's response was stilted. 'And what are you going to do?'

'Try and hold out as long as possible. We might last until my men can get here, but if we can't – if it looks like the castle will fall – then I'll take Finnlay and give us both up at the same time.'

'What? But you can't . . . And what about Jenn and Bella?'

'They can say their father was bewitched by the sorcerers and disclaim any involvement. They might be under scrutiny for a while, but Jenn's husband will protect them both from too many problems. In the meantime, I stand a much greater chance of getting Finnlay to safety if we're away from the castle.'

'You're assuming they won't kill you both the moment you step outside the gate.'

'They won't kill me immediately,' Robert replied grimly. 'And Finnlay will offer them too great an advantage for a public execution of a real sorcerer. No, we'll be fairly safe at least for a few days – and a few days will be all I'll need.'

Micah shook his head slowly. 'You're wrong. Very wrong. You're just analysing this as though it were only the Guilde out there. But it isn't. Those are Malachi down there and they will kill any Salti they meet. You know that. What's more, Carlan is out there too – and he believes your brother is the Enemy. Do you seriously believe he'll let either of you live long enough to prove him wrong? In Serin's name, Robert, Finnlay has already escaped him twice.'

'Are you saying you won't help?'

'Are you giving me a choice?'

Reaching out a hand to Micah's shoulder, Robert replied gently, 'Micah, I've always given you a choice.'

With an uncharacteristic flare of anger, Micah twisted out of his grasp. 'That's not true and you know it! All these years I've followed you, served you as best I could, and now, when you need me the most, you want to shut me out again. No, Robert. You've done it once too often. I won't help you. I won't help you surrender to those murderers so they can kill you. If I'm the only one who can aid you to carry out this mad plan, then you'll just have to think of another way out because I won't stand by and let you die!'

Micah stood there, breathing rapidly after his outburst. Robert was in no doubt that he meant what he said.

Defiance. From the man Robert trusted the most.

He took a step back, ready to quell a rise from the demon . . . but there was nothing. No sign, no tremor – as though the demon had vanished all on its own. Just like when Jacob had died.

He felt nothing at all. In fact, he hadn't even felt anything when he'd heard about Rosalind. All he'd known was that he had to leave the monastery.

What was this?

'Micah, I . . .' Robert tried to speak, but he was suddenly breathless. The shouts of his men and the attackers around him faded into the distance. Even Micah seemed to move further away . . .

A sudden flash of light broke the sensation, snapping him

back. Without pausing, Robert whipped around in the direction of the flare to find one of the stable buildings on fire. Flaming arrows had hit the thatched roof and even now fire was eating away at it. Men scurried from all corners, throwing water ineffectually on the flames until someone, experienced, saw the futility and ordered the roof pulled down. As the straw came crashing to the ground, Robert saw again the fire at St Germanus, the enticing orange glow and the suffocating heat. It had been so easy to keep going back. To go back until . . .

He'd killed them all? Is that what his destiny was?

You will destroy that which you love most . . .

He was out there, the Angel of Darkness. And he knew the Enemy was within his sights and he wouldn't stop until Robert was dead.

'Find another way,' Micah intruded, coming close to whisper in his ear. 'There must be another way.'

Finnlay woke again and opened his eyes. For a moment, waves of the nightmare crashed against his awareness. The Angel of Darkness, his voice, his aura seething venom, the essence of corruption – but, as always, it was the face which haunted him. Why? Why would the Angel of Darkness appear in his dreams with Robert's face? They couldn't possibly look so much alike in reality or somebody would have noticed his brother's double roaming around the country.

Then it was something else, some deeper resonance of Carlan's power sifting in his mind, a more sinister meaning he would have to work out for himself. Either way, Finnlay would die rather than say anything to Robert about it. If it was only Finnlay's mind playing tricks, his brother didn't need to know.

Finnlay turned his attention to the room, thinking he was alone, but then he noticed an older man coming towards him, his grey eyes filled with concern.

'Who are you?'

'I'm Aiden McCauly.' The stranger stood before him, his hands clasped together.

'Don't be ridiculous.' Finnlay tried to sit up. A flash of pain struck his side and his head felt like it would fall off. In an odd way, he almost wished it would.

'Now that's being ridiculous,' the stranger murmured, making no move to help him.

Finnlay favoured the man with his most dire glare. 'Have you been spending time with my brother?'

'Why? Does it show?'

'No, not at all.' Finnlay tried again and this time McCauly moved forward to help him. With many grunts and bitten-back curses, Finnlay shifted himself up against the backboard of the bed. He took in a few swift breaths until the pain eased a little. He could see nothing from where he was, but he could certainly hear plenty. 'What's happening out there?'

'The Guilde are attacking the walls, but are in no danger of getting through. Robert is commanding the defence.'

There was a calm about the priest that caught Finnlay's attention. There was worry on the man's face, but no fear. 'And what about Jenn? And Bella?'

'Jennifer is . . .' McCauly appeared to choose his words. 'I believe her time has come. Her sister is with her across the hall.'

'Time?' Finnlay felt the blood rush from his face. 'Now?'

'I think the shock of her father's death may have—'

'Here, help me up.' Finnlay didn't wait for any more explanation. He had to see for himself. This was too import-ant. He struggled to get his legs over the edge of the bed, but he was too weak. His body just wouldn't obey, and the pain . . .

'What are you doing? You can't go anywhere!'

'Please, just help me.' Finnlay kept struggling, leaving the priest no choice. Slowly he stood up, his head spinning. By the gods, this was hard!

Leaning most of his weight on McCauly, Finnlay shuffled to the door. McCauly pulled it open and helped him into the room opposite.

Bella didn't glance up immediately, but Addie did. They alone tended Jenn. As Finnlay got closer to the bed, Bella hissed at him, 'What are you doing here?'

'How is she?' But Finnlay didn't need to ask. Jenn lay on the bed, her face white, her lips blue. Her breathing was so shallow as to be almost inaudible. Every minute or so, she would cry out with a sound wrenched from the pits of hell. 'Something's wrong, isn't it?'

Bella tried to get Jenn to swallow something, but she didn't respond. She just lay there with her eyes closed, shutting everything out.

Silently, Finnlay tried to reach her.

Jenn? Can you hear me?

Nothing.

Jenn?

. . . can't . . . must fight . . . can't fight . . .

'What's wrong with her?' Finnlay demanded, his knees beginning to tremble with the effort of standing. McCauly tried to get him to sit down, but he couldn't. Not yet.

'Hell, Finnlay, how should I know?' Bella snapped. 'She's in a lot of pain. Too much pain. The baby will never be born like this.'

'But can't you give her something?'

'I've tried, damn you! She won't swallow. Not even water. She's getting weaker and weaker. I'm afraid that she'll . . .' Bella bent again to her sister as another wave of pain made her cry out.

Finnlay drew on the last of his reserves and turned to McCauly. 'Help me to that seat, over there in the corner, out of the way.'

As soon as he was lowered into it, Finnlay suppressed a groan. 'Go and get my brother. I don't care what you have to do, what you have to say, but you must get him in here. Now.'

'But he won't leave the battle.'

'You said there was no danger. He won't need to be gone long. Please, just go.'

As McCauly backed away in obvious confusion, Finnlay turned his gaze across the room to where Jenn lay on the bed. *Jenn? Listen to me. Hold on. You'll be all right. Just hold on.*

. . . don't know . . . the pain . . . not right . . . he's out there . . .

Just hold on, Jenn. Don't worry. I'll help you.

Her mental voice was fading with each word and the claws in Finnlay's stomach had nothing to do with his own injuries. What was happening to her?

It was impossible to believe Carlan would want her dead now, not when he could have killed her at any time. No. He'd want her alive. So why would he deliberately interfere with this? *How* could he—?

—of course! He wanted to control her through the baby!

There were footsteps outside the door and then Robert was standing framed by the oak. His eyes merely flickered over the bed and then darted to Finnlay, thunderous with anger. 'What are you doing?'

Finnlay wanted to drag him over, but had no choice. 'Come here. I need to speak to you – and don't argue about having to be outside. The longer you argue, the longer it will take you to get back.'

Robert's eyes flashed, but he approached nonetheless. McCauly stayed by the door, wary, but not intruding.

Finnlay waited until Robert was close enough for them to speak without anyone else in the room hearing. With the sounds of battle coming through the window and Jenn's moans, Bella's murmurs of comfort, it was unlikely anything would be overheard. Nevertheless, Finnlay kept his voice low.

'She's in too much pain, Robert. She's fighting it. Carlan is interfering somehow. The longer she fights, the more danger she's in. Even Bella agrees there's something seriously wrong.'

Robert was unbending, his face like solid stone. 'Why tell me?'

'Because you have to help her.' Finnlay steeled himself against Robert's reaction. 'You have to ease her pain.'

For the first time in his life, Finnlay saw real raw fear in Robert's eyes. 'No!'

'You must. If you don't, the baby will die – and Jenn will die trying to save it.'

'And they'll die if I do!' Robert hissed. 'Do you think I

451

learned nothing from Berenice's fate? I killed her when she was having my child. They both died and all I did was try to ease her pain. I will not – *cannot* – endanger Jenn like that. I ... I can't, Finnlay, and that's all there is to it.'

'Well, I can't and you know it.' Finnlay reached out and caught Robert's sleeve, tried to impress in his voice as much urgency as he could. Robert *must* believe. 'Robert, Berenice died because your powers interfered with the child's own developing ability. Even so young. It was because it *was* your child that Berenice died.'

Robert's eyes widened and he shook his head, struggling. 'You don't understand, Finnlay ... I can't try this because there's a chance that ... that ...'

'Jenn's child might be yours?' Finnlay murmured, trying to put Robert out of his misery.

Robert froze.

'Please, Robert. You must try. If you do nothing, she'll die. Jenn will die. If you make the attempt, at least there's the chance she will live. If the child is Eachern's, Jenn will live. Surely that's important to you.'

'Important?' Slowly, painfully, he turned towards the bed. His fists were clenched so tight his knuckles were white. He moved around to the side opposite Bella and Finnlay could see his face again. As Robert knelt beside the bed and took Jenn's hand, his expression was nothing less than a man who was staring at his own damnation. Robert took a deep breath and held it.

And Finnlay sensed the power flow from Robert. A warm, gentle, tender comfort like mother's love and soft down. It was directed towards Jenn, but it was so strong that Finnlay's pain also began to fade.

In seconds, Jenn's breathing had slowed and each new intake was deeper, stronger, more determined. Gradually, her colour changed and lost the deathlike pallor. Most of all, her cries were silenced. After a few minutes, she opened her eyes and looked up at Robert.

Like shattering stone, he let go her hand and got to his feet. He took first one step back and then another. Then, without a word to anyone, Robert turned and strode out of the room, leaving an abrupt emptiness in his wake.

'Finnlay,' Bella began, 'I think you should go now.'

With a nod, Finnlay gestured his helper over and together they shuffled out of the room. With any luck they would all live long enough for him to pay for that lie.

In a hastily erected tent far beyond the walls of Elita, Nash opened his eyes and swore. 'Damn! The Enemy was not so seriously wounded after all.'

Lisson came across the tent with a cup of wine in his hand. He held it out to Nash. 'What happened?'

'I can't reach her. Something's blocked the path. I was so close and then – gone. Just like that.'

Nash took the wine and swallowed deeply. He came to his feet and slapped the cup on the table to his left.

'Then the baby won't die?'

'If it does, it'll be an accident. Still, it doesn't really matter. It's Eachern's child, not the Enemy's. Nevertheless, I have to get inside that castle. He may not be mortally wounded, but he's still weakened. I have to get to him before he can get his strength back.'

Nash walked to the door of the tent and pulled the flap aside. The castle stood before him, lit only by the perimeter fires. He had neither the men nor the time to mount a full-scale siege. Killing the Earl had done nothing to break the loyalty of his soldiers. The gate remained firmly shut, the Enemy safely inside. If Nash didn't resolve this soon he'd lose the opportunity. Reinforcements would come to aid Elita – and the King would send soldiers down to help Nash out, believing he needed it.

But he didn't. He didn't need any of them. He had all he required clothed in the garb of ordinary Guilde soldiers. So far they'd obeyed his every order, just as DeMassey had instructed. Now was the time for them to do more – and if they were clever about it, nobody would even know Nash had employed sorcery in the downfall of Elita.

The night was dark and cold. It was time.

*

Micah tried not to follow Robert about the castle, but he couldn't help it. At first, he'd even tried to keep some sort of distance between them, but it was impossible. For the first time in his life, Micah didn't trust Robert, didn't trust him enough to let him out of his sight.

Robert patrolled the walls, speaking to the men with all the charm he was so blessed with. The Guilde archers had ceased their bombardment and the night had become eerily quiet. Robert gave a word of encouragement here, a quip there. He paid attention to everything that was said to him, displayed his understanding of their fear – and he was out there, on the battlements along with them. He was in fine form, so fine that only the experienced eye could see the danger.

Robert was brittle, so brittle that Micah dared not say a word to him. He knew that his continued presence was probably adding to Robert's mood, but what else could he do?

They had almost completed the circuit when it began. Another volley of fire-arrows, wave after wave. The men on the wall took shelter, but it wasn't enough. One close by was hit and as Micah rushed to his aid he caught his first glimpse of the damage. Almost every building lining the courtyard was on fire. Within the space of a few heartbeats, straw and thatching and dry ancient timber caught alight, turning the darkness of night into a weird and terrible daylight. Then there was another noise. Low and vibrating beneath his feet.

'The gate!' Robert cried, already moving. 'The Malachi are going for the gate! Fall back. Everybody get inside the keep!'

Micah dodged running soldiers, nearly falling off the parapet. He tore after Robert, drawing his sword as he leaped down the stairs to the cobbles. Chaos reigned as men scrambled for safety within the keep, their way lit by the burning stables, the kitchens and storerooms. Huge beams fell around him, but he pushed his way forward until he could see Robert standing before the portcullis. Already a huge crack had appeared in the wall above, some unbelievable force pushing it inwards. Stone showered down while the ground trembled. Robert had his hands raised as though to ward off the heat of the fires, but he stood his ground.

'Get back!' Micah yelled.

'I can't hold it very long,' Robert called, strain showing in every word. 'Get everyone into the keep.'

Micah moved back a little until he could see the state of the withdrawal. Almost everyone was inside now, with only Neil and Shane waiting by the door. 'Come on!' Micah bellowed to Robert. 'Everyone's in!'

But Robert didn't move – and Micah didn't wait. He ran forward and grabbed Robert's arm. With every ounce of strength he had at his command, he dragged Robert back from the crumbling wall and across the courtyard. He didn't let go, he didn't let up. Together, the two of them made the door of the keep. Micah pushed him inside as Neil and Shane swung the doors shut and slid bolts and bars across. It would hold – but only for a few minutes.

Micah turned swiftly to find Robert had already made his way through the crowd gathered in the hall. He called out no orders, gave no instructions on what they were to do next. He headed straight for the stairs like a thunderstorm waiting to break.

Terrified, Micah tore after him.

Finnlay got up again the moment he heard Jenn scream. Over McCauly's protests, he made it to the door of his room and stumbled into the corridor. And then he heard something else. The mighty crash of stone, so close he almost jumped. The walls trembled around him and from the hall below he heard cries of terror. He glanced down the corridor as Robert appeared, heading for the stairs up to the roof.

'What's happening?' Finnlay called.

Robert was like a man in a dream, seeming incapable of speech. Just then, the door opposite opened and a face appeared. It was Addie.

'My lord,' she began, 'Lady Bella said to tell you. It's a boy. My lady has given birth to a boy. She's fine.' Addie smiled shakily. 'They're both fine.'

'A boy?' Finnlay murmured, for a moment forgetting everything else. 'Robert? Did you hear . . .'

Robert stiffened and straightened up. He turned on his heel and strode back along the corridor just as Micah turned the corner. Robert reached out almost in reflex and pushed Micah back against the wall. He left his hand on Micah's chest long enough to get his message across, then leaped up the staircase on his right. Micah didn't follow him.

Like a dark beast he climbed the stairs, one at a time. Each step he took brought him closer, higher, fuller. Every muscle, every sinew shrank and grew, taut against the pressure, straining against his flesh. His feet climbed without volition, spurred on by an ebony fire at his heels, smoking and smothering, drowning and defeating.

There was nothing in his mind. No sound, no light, no image to deflect his compulsion. It grew within him, untethered. It drove him to the top of the stairs and out into a darker blackness, out into the night.

Creatures around him shrank back, mere shadows of the raven sun flowing from his body. He stood there, hanging, drifting, until he was alone.

And alone he grew, filling his soul with a demon kept alive by prophecy and damnation, futility and impotence.

There was no seed of hope left, no hope at all. Alone, terribly alone, he looked to the sky – and straight into the eye of the abyss.

With a roar of defiance, the dam inside him burst and seething fury flooded his body, coursed through his veins and consumed his blood with a deadly poison. It filled his ears, nose, mouth and poured out through his eyes. A bubbling blackness, searing and seething, stinking with evil and centuries old.

An inferno of anger and hatred, a blazing corruption, the Enemy thrust his hands towards the black sky, clenched his fists—

—and spoke the Word.

eyes grew more accustomed to the darkness and he scanned the top of the keep, looking for something, someone. There was no movement, no life – but there in the far corner was a shadow, more substantial than the mere absence of light.

Aiden moved slowly towards it until he saw a familiar shape. He was sitting by the wall, his knees up, his arms around them and his head down. His hair fell around his face so Aiden couldn't even tell if he was alive.

Gently now, Aiden sank to his knees beside him. 'Robert? Robert, talk to me. Are you all right?'

For a long time, there was no movement. Then Aiden reached out to touch his arm and Robert slowly lifted his head.

'Robert?'

He moved, taking Aiden's hand and holding it before his gaze as though it were the last thing he expected to see. Then, cautiously, he turned his head until his eyes met Aiden's. Strangely, despite the black night, Aiden could see Robert's face clearly. The eyes widened and his mouth opened.

'Are . . . you . . .'

'What is it? Come, talk to me.'

Robert shook his head, disbelief in every movement. 'I . . . thought I'd . . . killed everyone. The demon . . . I couldn't stop it.'

Aiden took Robert's hands between his own. 'It's over, Robert. We're all safe. Your brother, Micah, everyone inside the keep. Even Jennifer.'

'Safe? Jenny?' Robert shook his head, bewildered. 'How can she be safe? I used it. The Word. How can she still be alive? How can anyone?'

'I don't know. Perhaps you were wrong. Perhaps the prophecy was wrong. But we are safe. Come. Let's go down and you can see for yourself. Finnlay and Micah are worried about you. Finnlay knew immediately what you'd done.'

'He did?' Robert glanced up again and slowly his gaze cleared a little. He started to get up, then paused, his hand gripping Aiden's arm like a vice. 'The Guilde. The Malachi.'

On his hands and knees, he scrambled to the wall and looked over.

'I don't know how you did it, but they've all gone. There's no movement out there at all. We'll have to wait until dawn to see what happened.' Gently, Aiden put a hand under his arm and ushered him to his feet. Robert rubbed his hands over his face, as though waking from a long sleep.

'Come,' Aiden repeated. 'Let's go down.'

It was the first rays of light touching Nash's face that drew him back to reality. Numbed and stiff, he opened his eyes and gazed at the pale sky above, a herald of fresh clouds, yellow and pink. A new day.

He had to move, but his body wouldn't respond. He could feel a weight on his legs, pressuring him down, forcing him to be still. There was pain, too, in his ankle, his hip, his back, and something that tasted like his own blood in his mouth.

In all his years he'd always been so quick and so absolute in his condemnation of the fools that lived and worked around him. Those people who had neither the wit nor the intelligence to see or understand what was going on right before their eyes. He'd cursed his father and grandfather for not having the will to pursue their destiny, for failing at the last when so much was at stake. He'd scorned the Malachi for their narrow vision and single-minded self-destruction.

And yet, all along, the biggest fool of all was Nash himself.

He'd constantly and consistently blinded himself to the truth. A truth that had been there all along for him to see. And then, as the moment had approached and he'd finally opened his eyes, as he'd felt the build-up of power and saw the man who strode to the top of the tower like a mighty storm about to break, it was too late for Nash to do more than throw up a hasty shield of protection.

Robert Douglas. He was the one Nash had searched for for so long. He was the one who should have been no more than a baby during the Troubles. He was the one who had grown to maturity and developed all the powers Nash had tried so hard to destroy.

And he knew the Word of Destruction.

The Enemy. Alive. More powerful than Nash had ever dreamed. More powerful than even prophecy had foretold.

The Key must have told him the Word. The Key would have recognized him. Yes, the Key.

Nash held his breath and once more tried to force his body to move. This time there was a tremor down his left side, a shadow of some former strength. He strained against the pain, pushing himself up on his elbows. There was something over his legs: a huge tree branch, torn from its home. Nash summoned what power he had left and tried to shift it. It didn't budge.

The Word of Destruction. The most powerful weapon ever conceived. Created, honed, perfected by his great-grandfather – used to almost kill him. And the damage went far beyond a simple branch. His special senses were gone, too: he was human, helpless for the first time in his life.

With a roar of rage, Nash twisted his body and clawed his hands into the ground, seeking any kind of purchase. Gradually, he began to move forward, his legs emerging from under the log, agonizing and bloody. Only when he was free did he look up to survey the damage.

Gone. It was all gone. There was no one left to help him. Even Lisson had vanished.

Despair threatened to overwhelm him, but he caught himself in time and began hauling his body towards the lake. His arms grew stronger as he worked, even though his legs were useless. He had to get away from this place. Had to get away before they looked outside and saw the movement. He could move in water easier than on land. If he could get to the other side of the lake, he could find help – some kind of help. *Any* kind of help.

He would escape. He would survive. He would find a donor with blood strong enough to rekindle his powers. A hundred donors, if necessary.

It would take time, but he would return.

As his body slid into the water, he cast a last look back at the castle. 'Ah, Enemy. I have you now.'

The icy water drew in around his body, numbing his

injuries and cooling his anger. Silent and alone, he swam away.

Jenn awoke to see a hazy dusk fill her room with a fine incandescent dust. Had it really got so late? She turned her head to see a familiar figure sitting on a chair close by her bed. In the dim light she frowned. 'Robert?'

'Sorry,' Finnlay replied, 'it's only me. How do you feel?'

'How do I feel? I feel just fine – but what are you doing out of bed? I . . .' Jenn pushed herself up on to her elbows, but her whole body protested the movement and she groaned. Then she noticed the tiny bundle at her side. She stopped abruptly and, with one finger, lifted the cloth covering her son's face. He was sleeping, his tiny hands screwed up by his chin. A fine down of raven hair framed a face now quite pink. She touched his fingers, his cheek in silent wonder. Was this her child?

Hello, my love.

'Have you chosen a name?' Finnlay asked softly.

Jenn nodded, but didn't speak it aloud. Not yet. She would do that later tonight, at his Presentation. As the coming event grew in her mind, so did the pain it brought back. Swiftly, so as not to disturb the baby, she turned away and looked at Finnlay.

His face was still a mess. The swollen eye was a mass of deep red and purple. He sat stiffly in his chair, as though afraid to move lest he pass out.

'You should be resting, Finn. You can't afford to keep getting up and moving around. If you start bleeding again, it'll probably kill you.'

'Oh, I'm too tough for that.' He lifted a hand and waved it in the air. 'I'm still in one piece despite the efforts of both the Angel of Darkness and the Enemy. I doubt even Broleoch himself could do away with me.'

'Oh, Finn!' Jenn had to smile. There had always been something irrepressible about him that no amount of hardship could break. 'Where's Bella? And Father McCauly?'

'Cleaning up, I think. I did hear something about finding food, but I confess I didn't pay too much attention. I will

462

warn you – your sister is not happy. But that's only to be expected.'

'Micah?'

'Is with Robert.'

Jenn glanced down and studied her hands. 'How is he?'

'Devastated. How would you expect him to be?'

She looked up sharply at that, but there was no reproach in his eyes. 'But – is he all right? I mean . . .'

'He's alive and breathing, if that's what you mean. He's surveying the damage of his efforts last night and looks on the surface to be quite his old self. I've always marvelled at that public face of his and how easily he seems to puts it on. There are, however, those of us not so easily fooled any more.' Finnlay sighed and laced his fingers together. 'I think, though, that he's past the worst. He can't quite believe he used the Word and didn't destroy us all. He's . . . in a lot of pain. McCauly has tried to help. He seems to understand what's going on in Robert's head better than any of us but . . .'

'What?'

Finnlay shook his head. 'I don't know. Robert needs you. I'm sorry, but it's true.'

'You . . . found a way to prove to him . . . that my son isn't . . .'

'Yes.'

'How?'

Finnlay lifted himself out of his chair and sat on the side of her bed. He took her hand. 'I used the only means I could. The irony is that that he thinks it proves your son is not his – it actually proves the opposite – but he won't question it again. He won't want to.'

Jenn gazed at him a moment. She knew he wouldn't say more. Instead she turned to the sleeping child.

'May I?'

'Of course.' She moved so Finnlay could see his nephew properly. Finnlay pulled aside the cloth wrapped around the boy until the left shoulder was revealed.

'He has no House Mark!'

'No.'

Finnlay looked up sharply at that. 'But that's impossible! Unless he's not Robert's son.'

'You've already proved he is.'

Finnlay opened his mouth – then shut it abruptly. Eventually he shook his head. 'This doesn't make any sense. You must see what he is.'

Jenn swallowed and kept her gaze steady. 'He's my son, Finnlay – and for the moment, that's all he is. Until his Presentation, he doesn't even have a presence to the gods. He's an infant, a child, nothing more. I won't have you or anyone else saying a word about this until he's old enough to understand for himself.'

Finnlay gave her a sharp glance, but nodded slowly. 'As you wish. But you know as well as I do that in the end, not talking about it won't change a thing. Besides, there'll be others who'll come to the same conclusion long before he reaches the age of understanding.'

'Yes, but as long as they believe he's Eachern's son he'll be safe.'

'Rather than the son of a hero and a sorcerer?' Finnlay got carefully to his feet. 'Or the son of two sorcerers? I won't argue, Jenn. I agree. I'll go now and let you get dressed. With any luck, Bella might have some food ready for us all.'

'By all that's holy,' Micah breathed, spreading his arms wide. 'It looks even worse from down here!'

He gazed across the remnants of what used to be the courtyard to where Robert stood, surrounded by piles of blackened timber, gravel and dust. Nothing, not a single building nor pile of stone, had survived intact. The ancient walls of Elita, having withstood three centuries of armed conflict, now lay in rubble at his feet. They could see clear across the lake to the forest on the other side. The line of trees marked the edge of the destruction. Scorched grass and flattened bushes filled the distance. Of the attacking soldiers, there was no sign at all. It was as though they had been blown out of existence by that terrible wind.

Only the keep had survived unscathed. It stood in the same place, rattled but unbroken. If only the same could be said for the people of Elita. Though they had lived to see the dawn of this awful day, one by one they had slipped away, terrified by the power unleashed to save them – and the man who had wielded it. Neil and his wife, Shane, Keagan and Addie were all that was left of this once-thriving castle. Tragic though it was, at least Jacob had not survived to see his beloved home destroyed so completely in such a manner.

'It's strange,' Robert said, 'but it's not as bad as I'd expected.'

'In the name of the gods, my lord,' Micah gasped, 'how could it be any worse?'

Robert looked at Micah. 'You were never one for sparing my feelings, were you?'

'And what good would that do?'

Robert gave a short laugh. 'Very little, I admit.' He wandered over to a pile of burned beams and touched the edge of his boot to the charcoal. 'I owe you an apology, Micah. I've put you through so much. Not just last night, but the last few years. You see, I always thought that because you wanted to stay with me it was all right. I convinced myself that that made it right.'

Micah said nothing as Robert turned around to face him.

'But your father said something to me.'

'You spoke to my father? About me?'

'He said that as an adult, you should've been able to see your error in serving me. He said you deliberately blinded yourself to the truth and that was unforgivable. Only you are not to blame, my friend. I am. I blinded you. I never let you see what was really going on. I deliberately let you close enough to care, but not close enough to understand just exactly what you were a part of.'

Oh really? With firm strides, Micah crossed the courtyard until he stood squarely in front of Robert. 'I made no error, my lord,' he said quite deliberately. 'Despite what you say, my opinion has not changed. I regret nothing – not the last few months, nor the last ten years. There was no error and, what's more, I'll only accept your apology on one condition.

that from this moment onwards, you cease to blame yourself.'

A quizzical frown creased Robert's brow. 'What is this, Micah? Have I gone away for a few months only to come back and find you've become your own man?'

'Take it as you will, my lord,' Micah remained stubborn. 'I know what I'm doing, even if you don't.'

That elicited another laugh from Robert and a smile that almost reached his eyes. 'I just can't seem to get rid of you, can I?'

'Though you keep trying.'

'Aye. Dare I say another failure on my part?'

'No.'

'Ah.' Robert nodded and glanced away. 'I thought not. Well, we've got a few horses left. Enough to get us all out of here. If my dear brother is fit enough, I think we should all leave tomorrow morning. It wouldn't do to stay around long enough for the King to hear about this. I'm sure word is already tearing across the country like wildfire.'

Micah said nothing for a moment, but Robert's silence was painfully eloquent. Micah swallowed. 'I can't go back home, can I? Not after all this. I can't even go back to Clonnet with Jenn.'

'If you tried, they'd take all their frustration and hatred of me out on you. If you were very lucky, they might only throw you in prison for the rest of your life. You'd be tortured and eventually executed. For all that you're Sealed, they'd never believe you didn't know I was a sorcerer – not after all these years.'

'But they believed you knew nothing about Finnlay.'

Robert shook his head. 'No, I convinced them Finnlay was dead and therefore couldn't be a sorcerer. This is different. You're too close to me. They'd kill you. I'm sorry.' With his voice low and uncompromising, he murmured, 'So what do you want to do next?'

For some reason, Micah's mouth went suddenly dry. He swallowed.

'Yes, I'm giving you a choice, my friend,' Robert added without blinking. 'What do you want to do?'

Micah stifled a laugh. 'What I want is for us both to go home to Dunlorn – but since that's impossible, I'll go with you.'

An involuntary smile flashed across Robert's face. 'But you don't know where I'm going.'

Micah grinned and turned back to the keep. 'Oh yes I do.'

34

'This is madness, Robert,' Finnlay blustered, waving his hands above the dining table. 'How can you think for one minute that Bella and Jenn can just go back to their normal lives after all this? There'll be an inquisition! They'll be asked every conceivable question and not one innocent answer will be believed.'

Robert reached for another slice of meat from the plate Bella held out to him. 'There's nothing so powerful in this world, Brother, than the picture of innocence.' Robert glanced down the table at each of them. At Neil, Shane, Keagan, Micah and Aiden McCauly. Finally his eyes lit on Bella. 'For reasons that have always eluded me, women have always been able to assume a dignified grace far beyond the skills of any man. With the right preparation both Bella and her sister will be able insist over again that they were merely hostages to you and I – even, if they care to do it – to Jacob's pride. It was no secret he despised the Guilde. Neil can be Sealed – if he'll consent. You'll have to go back to the mountains.' He took a sip of wine. 'We both know I cannot follow you.'

Finnlay stared at him and, not for the first time, marvelled at his brother's innate resilience. Despite everything he'd been through – despite having given into something that he'd fought against all his life – he was still sitting there, analysing their situation and plotting their escape. It was uncanny. 'And where will you go?'

'I don't know yet. I have to do something about that irritating priest—'

'Show some respect, Robert,' McCauly interrupted, 'or I'll start to think you don't like me.'

'—But I could just as easily leave him here to fend for himself,' Robert continued, deadpan.

Finnlay glanced down the table to see the others hide their smiles. They were happy that at least they had some joke to laugh about. Even though they'd stayed, there was an underlying nervousness of the sorcery they'd become a part of.

But Finnlay had to know what Robert would do. 'Will you come back to Lusara?'

'Please, Finn, don't ask me that question. Every time I say I won't come back I end up breaking my word.'

'I know, but this is important – for reasons completely unrelated to anything else.'

'Oh? What?'

Finnlay did his best to push his chair back and come to his feet; he had to lean most of his weight on the table, however. As formally as he could under the circumstances he said, 'I would like your permission . . . to marry.'

Robert's eyebrows shot up. 'I beg your pardon?'

'I would like your permission . . .'

'Yes, I heard that bit,' Robert got to his feet, a mischievous smile on his face. 'I just don't believe it. This is some kind of prank, isn't it? To cheer me up?'

'No, of course not . . .'

'Because I find it almost impossible to believe that somehow you have searched the length and breadth of this country to find the only poor, brainless girl who would be fool enough to accept a complete physical wreck like you.' Robert was almost laughing at Finnlay's stuttering discomfort.

'No, it's not like that, Robert . . .'

'No? Then tell me who she is and I'll happily make her aware of the mistake she's about to make.'

'Robert, please,' Finnlay held a hand up and tried to ignore the smiles and laughter wafting around the table. He knew his face was red, but he persisted, 'Don't you dare say anything to her. It took me a long time to convince her in the first place. I won't let you ruin it for me.'

'I know her?' Robert's laughter subsided and he watched Finnlay with hooded eyes.

'Fiona.'

For a moment, there was no reaction. Then a slow smile spread across Robert's face, lighting even the darkness in his eyes. 'Of course you have my permission, Brother, and I'm honoured you still wanted to ask. You'd better find a way to get Mother to the wedding. She'd never forgive you if she had to miss it . . . Hell!'

Robert's eyes widened, but Finnlay didn't need to ask. 'Mother! She'll be a direct target now. We have to warn her. Not only that, but Fiona is there, now, with Hilderic.'

'I'll go,' Shane said into the stunned silence. 'It would be better, my lord, if you make directly for your destination. I'll pass on the message and help in whatever way I can.'

'Thank you, Shane,' Robert murmured with a nod. 'And now I would like to drink a toast, to my brother and his future bride. May they have all the happiness together that . . . they deserve.'

'Are you sure about this?'

Jenn leaned over the bed and slipped her arms under the tiny bundle. She turned around and met Bella's gaze. 'Yes, I'm sure. He must be Presented to the gods properly or they won't know who he is. If I leave it any longer, the others will insist I do it their way and it'll be too late. I must go now while they're still at supper. Addie?'

'Yes, my lady?'

'Take him for a moment. Come with me to the chapel. I'll need you to keep him outside for a moment, but when I take him from you I want you to come back here. If anyone asks for me, tell them that I was tired and went to bed early.'

As Jenn opened the door to let Addie through, Bella moved and barred her way. 'How can you just go on with this after everything that's happened? What's happened to you? Don't you care about . . . about . . .'

With a glance at Addie, Jenn closed the door and turned to face Bella. Carefully, she clasped her hands together and took a deep breath. 'I'm a sorcerer too, Bella.'

Her sister took a single step back. 'But how can you be a sorcerer? There's never been anything in our family . . .'

'Nor in the Douglas House either, and yet we have both Finn and Robert.' Jenn had wanted to do this gently, but she didn't have time right now. 'I know how you must feel. I was . . .'

'How can you possibly know how I feel?' Bella snapped. 'Our home has been destroyed, our father killed and all because of sorcerery! You brought this down upon us, Sister. And now Robert is expecting us to just go home and pick up our lives! Is he mad? Are you?'

'Bella, please,' Jenn moved forward and took Bella's hand. She held on hard and forced Bella to meet her gaze. 'It will all work out, believe me. We can go back to our lives – but please give me time to tell you the truth. All of it. I do know how you feel. You're angry and hurt and afraid. But I promise I'll answer all your questions. Please, just be patient – if only for your nephew's sake.'

Bella pulled her hand away. 'That's cruel, using your own son to make me behave! You should be ashamed. Very well, I will wait – but I won't promise to change my mind. And yes, I will do it for your son, but not because you make me. Because he needs someone in his life who will not lie whenever it suits, nor use people to get whatever they want!' With that, Bella pushed her way past Jenn, pulled the door open and disappeared down the corridor.

Swallowing her pain, Jenn joined Addie and turned her mind to the task at hand. Bella would know the truth in time – and she would understand. But even so, it was no easy thing to hear her own sister accuse her of using people.

With everyone in the hall lingering over their meal, the castle was eerily empty. There were no lights glowing under doors, no fires to warm against the early summer night. Silently and gingerly, Jenn led Addie along the corridor to a

470

set of narrow stairs. Only one flight up and they could take another passage bypassing the hall – the only way she could get to the chapel without being seen. The door loomed ahead, open and dark inside. Jenn paused, keeping her emotions and her senses tightly controlled.

She glanced back at Addie, then slipped inside, closing the door behind her. She could have brought candles to life, but she didn't. Instead, she moved slowly forward in the filmy moonlight which fell like a ghost into the chapel. She stopped when she was still a few feet from the bier.

Jacob had been laid out properly, just as McCauly had ordered. His cold body lay still and lifeless, draped by a banner proudly displaying his coat of arms. The House of Ross.

'You didn't see,' Jenn began unsteadily, her voice and hands shaking together, 'you didn't see how well and bravely your men fought. You didn't see the loyalty of Neil and Shane, of Keagan and Addie. You would have been so proud of them. So proud, too, of the way Bella worked to calm the rest before they fled. She's taken care of us all since then, as she always took care of you and I.'

Jenn swallowed and took a step forward. She reached out and touched a finger to the banner. 'But I was proud of you, too. The way you defied the Guilde, the way your voice rang out. The way you accepted my work with the healers. The way you accepted you'd been wrong about Robert.'

She tried to go on, but her throat was tight, making it difficult to breathe. She swallowed again, determined to finish what she'd started. 'I was so proud, too, to be your daughter. I'm sorry I lied to you. I'm sorry I didn't just tell you the truth. I didn't mean to be a disappointment to you. I wanted so much for you to be proud of me. I didn't mean to hurt you. I didn't mean to hurt Bella. I know that doesn't make it right . . .'

Jenn paused, trying to get her thoughts straight. She would only ever have this one chance to say what she wanted. 'I just wish you could have waited until you saw your grandson. I know you would have loved him. I know you would have forgiven him his mother's sins. I just wish you could have seen him, just once – to know that the House of Ross will survive in him.'

No more words would come. Her heart was lead in her chest, her eyes suddenly blind with tears. She lifted her hands to her face, covered it against the pain.

And then there were arms around her, holding her tight. She didn't look up. She knew that touch. Robert didn't say anything. He just held her as she cried, silent against her anguish. His grip didn't loosen until her sobs gradually subsided and she lifted her face to look at him.

There was about him the appearance of a man who knew he was committing a crime. His deep green eyes gazed at her steadily and she realized that a single word from her could banish him from her life for ever.

But she didn't want him gone. Not for one day, one hour, one minute. She wanted him to stay with her, exactly like this.

She reached up a hand and gently touched the side of his face. He didn't move. She rose on her toes and brought his face down towards her. Hardly daring to breathe, she brushed her lips against his and felt him tremble. Then she kissed him again, long and deep, and his arms held her so tight she thought she would break.

She gazed into his eyes again, her tears gone. In the softest whisper she said, 'I just wanted you to know.'

'I can't ask you to come with me. You know that.'

'Yes – and you know I'd refuse.'

'Yes.'

He stared at her a moment longer, then gently released her, taking a step back.

'I didn't know you were in here,' she murmured.

'I gathered as much. I'm sorry I intruded. I came in here to do some thinking, away from prying eyes. Sometimes I get the feeling everyone is watching me.' Robert waved a hand at the altar candles and they glowed yellow and soft. 'I know why, of course, but sometimes . . .'

'Will you be all right?'

'Me?' His eyes fixed on her like two glowing beacons. 'Why should I not be?'

472

For a moment, Jenn couldn't work out why this question should worry her. But then she looked deeper and stopped in surprise. The well of darkness inside him, eating away at him: she couldn't see it any more! 'It's gone, hasn't it? The demon?'

'No. Just extinguished for a while.'

'It's no longer killing you.'

Robert looked vulnerable for a moment. For so long people had thought him immune to the many conflicts which faced him. None would have been able to guess the real damage they'd done, nor the consequences of his assumed invulnerability. Only now and then would the truth show, in a look, a glance, a self-deriding comment. The demon had been growing for twenty years, feeding off every evil Robert had ever encountered. For the moment, it was spent. How long would that last?

'What do you plan to do now that the world will know you're a sorcerer?'

Robert wandered up to the altar, touched the cloth beneath the candlesticks. 'I don't know. Believe it or not, I came in here to discuss that with your father.'

Jenn glanced once more at the shrouded figure before her. Strange that Robert should have come here, to see Jacob, a man who had for so many years believed him a traitor to his own people. She turned back to Robert to find he was studying the solitary stained-glass window above his head. 'What are you feeling?'

For a moment he didn't move. Then his head tilted to gaze at the moon through the window. 'For twenty years I've been running from a buried urge to use the Word of Destruction, believing I was strong enough to resist. But in the end, the demon won and although this keep and everyone inside survived, my failure still stands before me, a promise of the future.'

'But perhaps you didn't fail. Perhaps somehow you controlled the power . . . so that it wouldn't . . .'

He turned and faced her again, his hands behind his back. In his eyes was a strange light, almost of amusement. 'I had no control at all, Jenny. None. That's the way it works. I didn't even manage to kill the Angel of Darkness.'

'He escaped?'

'Finnlay sensed him after dawn. Just for a moment, before the man began shielding. I probably should have gone after him, but after last night?' Robert came back around the altar. He was silent for a second, then he frowned. 'I'm afraid to leave you.'

And Jenn was afraid for him to go – but what could she say? What could either of them say? Only pale words to give in place of comfort. 'I'll survive, Robert.'

She could see his hands reach for her again, but he stopped and took a step back, allowing himself merely to look at her. She could have stood there looking at him for ever, but a soft sound from beyond the door reminded her of the other reason she'd come in here secretly. Abruptly, her heart leaped into her throat. With a hand raised to Robert, she backed away and opened the door. Addie stood outside, her attention taken up by the baby in her arms. She saw Jenn and brought him over. Jenn took him with a smile.

'Go back to my room now, Addie. I won't be long.'

Jenn turned back into the chapel and closed the door behind her. She moved forward until Robert could see what she carried. With her voice trembling softly, she said, 'Will you meet my son?'

For a second she feared he would refuse, but then he came forward. He didn't look at the child in her arms; he looked at her. 'You're going to do the Presentation yourself?'

Again, Jenn felt tears threatening her resolve. This time she gained control. 'Father wanted to do it. I wanted him as well. I couldn't care less if Eachern were here or not.'

'A good thing he's not, then.'

'With no male relative available, all I can do is Present him myself, with my father's ghost as witness.'

'Jenny, I would be—' Robert paused, his face creased, '—I would be honoured if you would allow me to Present your son, on his father's – no, his grandfather's behalf. It is permitted, you know.'

Hardly daring to hope, Jenn nodded jerkily. 'Are you sure?'

'What is he to be named?'

'The name which has been carried down through my family since the first royal Ross.'

Robert smiled. 'Perfect. Come, let's do it before anyone finds out we're here.'

Her heart beating wildly, Jenn followed Robert to the foot of the altar. Then Robert turned to her and took the baby. She watched as he pulled back the blanket from around the baby's face.

'He looks like you. I'm glad.' Robert held the boy high in the air. Like a true Ross – and a true Douglas – he made no sound as his father began the Presentation. 'Blessed Mineah and Divine Serinleth, I call upon you to witness a new soul among your flock. This is your child and the child of my beloved Jenny. I Present you to her son, Andrew. I pray you keep him safe within your love, the love you hold for all our souls.' With that, Robert traced the trium upon the baby's brow and turned back to Jenn.

She couldn't help it. There were more tears in her eyes, but this time she couldn't tell Robert why. He handed Andrew back to her, then touched her face to wipe away the tears. 'He forgave you, Jenny. Jacob forgave you.'

'Oh, Robert . . .'

'Come,' he murmured softly, putting his arm around her shoulders. He kissed her forehead and turned towards the door. 'I'll take you back. You're exhausted and I don't think young Andrew likes this place much.'

As though proving him prophetic, Andrew began to squirm in Jenn's arms and before they were far along the corridor, he let out a huge wail which echoed through the empty castle. Jenn didn't try to quieten him. It would be a long time before he would have another chance to bellow in the house where he was born.

Aiden reached up to the light summer cloak thrown across his horse's back. Lady Bella had given it to him from her father's wardrobe. It didn't quite fit, but it would do for a cool, frosty morning like this.

He pulled the cloak around his shoulders and glanced behind at the others as they all readied themselves for their own journeys. The great walls of the castle stood in ruins behind them, warmed by a summer sun still shy in the sky. The few Elita retainers left were busy saddling horses, loading what goods they could carry. The injured Finnlay leaned on Shane's arm as Jennifer gave them some instructions.

'What are you staring at?'

Aiden looked over his shoulder to where Robert was adjusting the bridle on his horse. The ghostly look of the previous day had almost gone. In its place was a refreshing calm Aiden had never seen before. 'I was just thinking about what you said last night. About coming back to Lusara.'

'I didn't say anything about coming back.'

'That's what I mean.'

Robert straightened up and pointed a finger at Aiden's chest. 'Don't you start.'

Behind him, unseen, Micah was waiting by his own horse, an innocent expression warming the chilly morn.

'Have you told the others what you're going to do?' Aiden continued.

'How can I? I don't know myself yet.' Robert turned back to the horse, clearly unconcerned.

Aiden smiled. Robert did know – even if he wouldn't talk about it yet. As though sensing his thoughts, Robert shot him a wry glance. 'Well, you were the one who said my inaction hadn't produced any favourable results and that I should try something else. Let's face it – we'll both be surprised if it turns out you were right.'

'So what are you going to do?'

Robert left the horse and put his hand on Aiden's shoulder. 'Right now I'm going to say goodbye to my friends. Come.'

Most of the others were mounted up now, but Finnlay and Jennifer waited. Aiden approached Jenn with an easy smile. 'Take care, my child, in the coming weeks. I must admit, if I were a man who paid attention to signs and portents, I hardly think your son could have had a more profound entrance into the world.' He leaned forward, kissed her forehead and laid a hand on Andrew's head. 'I will pray for you both.'

'Thank you, Father. I wish you well.'

At that moment, Robert appeared at his side, his eyes on Jenn. Aiden would have moved back, but the touch of Robert's hand on his elbow made him pause.

'I won't be able to send word,' Robert began, not attempting to keep his voice low. 'Not for a long time. But you stick to your story. Blame me for everything.'

'But . . .'

'Jenny, I won't have you argue this,' Robert held up his hands. 'My reputation is gone – what there was of it. You sacrifice whatever you must in order to survive. Do you understand me?'

Jennifer met his gaze and pulled in her lower lip. Slowly she nodded, as if she didn't trust herself to speak.

With that, Robert began to turn for his horse but paused. He faced her once more, his shoulders squared. 'You just remember what I told you. At the old mill.' He took a breath. 'You remember that.'

Abruptly Robert was steering Aiden and Micah towards their horses. They mounted up. Robert raised a hand in farewell and turned his horse. Then they were galloping across the blackened field towards the forest. After a moment, Aiden looked at him. Robert was smiling.

'What's that for?'

Robert glanced aside and slowed his horse to enter the wood. 'I'm experiencing the strangest sensation. I've never felt anything like it before. It's odd.'

'Describe it to me.'

'I don't think I can.' Robert glanced at him again, then at Micah, the smile widening. 'But if I could, I think you could give it a name.'

The mood was impossible to miss. Aiden raised his eyebrows and willingly took the bait. 'And what name would I give this strange feeling you suddenly have?'

'I think,' Robert laughed, 'you'd call it freedom.'

*

477

ert rode into the shadows of the forest, Finnlay turned
 .in. Her eyes remained on the empty distance.

Finnlay looked at the others waiting, then murmured,
You didn't tell him, did you?'

'No.' Jenn replied.

'He wouldn't have gone, would he?'

'No.'

'And you don't think he'll come back.'

Jenn turned and faced Finnlay squarely, but said nothing.

'Come.' Finnlay limped towards her. 'Give me the baby
and let Shane help you to your horse. We've got to get
moving.'

'Do you know how to hold him?' Jenn asked.

'Of course! What do you take me for?' He reached out,
then added quickly, 'Don't answer that.'

With the briefest smile, Jenn laid Andrew in Finnlay's
arms, then turned to mount her horse. Finnlay stepped back
to allow her room and turned his gaze on the boy. He was
awake and looking up at Finnlay with eyes of the brightest
blue, matching the early morning sky. In truth, this was the
first time Finnlay had ever held a baby. It was certainly the
first time he'd held his nephew. But, child though Andrew
was, it was still impossible not to see the truth Jenn had
refused to speak of.

Andrew Ross Douglas, born Earl of Elita and one day
Duke of Eachern. This child was also the only true heir to
the throne of Lusara.